Green Ivy Publishing
1 Lincoln Centre
18W140 Butterfield Road
Suite 1500
Oakbrook Terrace IL 60181-4843
www.greenivybooks.com

ISBN: 978-1-944680-52-7

# You Don't Say
## *A Story about My Aunt Emma*

By
Moon Mullens

# Chapter 1

## The Cemetery

"**D**addy, Daddy, look at me!" shouted my son, Ben, as he hung from the bottom rail of the metal arch at the entrance to our family cemetery. He was attempting to hand-walk across it.

My daughter, Emily, his older sister, threw pine-cones at him as he made his way across the arch. They were laughing and enjoying themselves as they were caught up in the mystery of being at the family cemetery. A place they had never visited.

Their mother Jeannie warned them lovingly, "Y'all stop trying to outdo one another." She was afraid they may fall, and one of them would be hurt.

The family cemetery had been here 150 years. Originally, it was farmland, our family gave land for a church site, and later the church added a small cemetery. The parish built a one-room school, which later burned down and damaged the church.

Both the church and the school were abandoned and given back to our family. Our family continued to use the cemetery to bury our relatives and others from within the community. Many were buried here who died from a Scarlet Fever epidemic that swept through the area in the early eighteen hundreds.

Throughout the cemetery were many tall virgin pine trees. The trees were here when this region was first settled in the late seventeen hundreds, and they seemed to whisper whenever the wind blew. My grandfather, a saw miller, once said, "These trees were here when Columbus discovered America." He also remarked, "One tree had enough lumber in it to build three homes." They were tall and huge, and very majestic.

Many times when we came to visit the cemetery, the wind would seem to make the trees sing, giving it a mysterious aura. As a child, it actually was a little scary.

3

Our cemetery was enclosed with a new hurricane fence and a locked gate. It had become a popular place for lovers to come hide during their romantic encounters. Often they would leave behind their protection, which was the reason for the fence and the locked gate. However, today on this warm, beautiful spring morning, it was a shaded, peaceful place.

The cemetery was not far from my childhood home. You could say it was not a place my family looked forward to visiting. The arch Ben was playing on was the same arch I played on as a child. I especially loved to climb on those tall concrete pillars that held up its arch. The arch displayed the cemetery's name, and I too as a child would hand-walk across to the other side, which was about twelve feet away.

As children, we seldom came here, but when we did, we would hide behind the tombs and jump the gravestones, in an attempt to make the most of a place we loved and were afraid of at the same time.

As dangerous as hand walking the arch seemed to my mom and my wife, it was quite an accomplishment for any child. It was something we all loved to do, and now my children were enjoying it too. I was happy my children had an opportunity to do some of the fun things I did as a child.

My family and I came to help clean up and haul debris away that winters often leave behind in our cemetery. This was a family custom each spring for many years: one most southern families did in the early spring of each year.

Years earlier, the family cemetery had been neglected and was overgrown with Cherokee briars and small Tallow trees everywhere. You had to cut your way through to make room for a new gravesite;

our neglect is what caused our families to come each spring to help in its upkeep.

Just a few short years earlier, we reclaimed that beloved ground once again to make it a beautiful place to lay our loved ones to rest. A place we all could be proud to say, it honored our lost loved ones. This cemetery is an important part of our family.

While Jeannie was making sure our children could not injure themselves on the arch, I went over to the north fence line to rake leaves the winter winds had blown against it. I had raked about one third of the way down when I came upon the resting place of one of the most beloved members of our family, my Aunt Emma.

As I stood at the side of her resting place, memories of her in my childhood inundated my mind. There was a great deal of tragedy in her life; but the thing I remembered most was how she taught me to live life and how to enjoy it.

We did so many fun things together when I was a child that she seemed to be as much a kid as I was. This special lady had a major impact on what and who I had become. As the years fade away, I realized just how much I became what she had taught me to be and how much I admired her for it.

As I leaned on my rake, I remembered the very last thing Aunt Emma said to me. I said it out-loud as if she could hear me: "You can't take back a word said and you can't undo any action done by you. So, be careful in what you say or do because one day you may have to defend it." She would add, "Always be a man of integrity, and stand up for what is right."

I stood there shaking my head and laughed aloud as I said one of the many retorts Aunt Emma used to always say when she either realized something was really good or if something was not exactly right. "*You don't say!*" It was her favorite retort. I laughed again as I remembered how many times she said that to me. I always wanted to know the mystery that surrounded Aunt Emma's life and death. I had many questions that had gone unanswered.

I didn't notice, but Jeannie had come up behind me and heard me talking to Aunt Emma. Jeannie, who was standing directly behind me, put her arms around me and kissed me on my neck. She asked jokingly, "Just who are you talking to, honey?"

I was embarrassed she had caught me talking to the dead, but I answered her. "My favorite Aunt Emma, she was a wonderful woman."

"She sure must have been." Jeannie unexpectedly said.

Surprised by her remark, I asked her, "Why do you say that?"

Jeannie replied, "Well, I've been all over the cemetery and her headstone seems to be better kept than any here. Even the area around where she is laid to rest is cleaner. It is unusual to see fresh cut flowers in front of a headstone and she has some, along with several bouquets of artificial flowers."

I said, "If anyone deserves special remembrance, it would absolutely be my Aunt Emma!"

Jeannie asked, "Why was she so special to receive extra distinct treatment? Who is she to you?"

I swiftly answered her, "Oh . . . only the person who made it possible for me to get my college degree and in the process saved my life. But most importantly, she also is the reason I met such a wonderful woman as you."

Jeannie asked, "How in the world did she do all of that?"

I hesitantly answered her, "Well, it's a long story and I am not sure you would want to hear it all."

Jeannie lovingly said, "Honey, you know if it pertains to you, I am always interested in it, so please tell me."

I began enlightening her as to how. "I was in my senior year in college and about to graduate. The Vietnam War was still going hot and heavy, and my draft number was low: ten. My best buddy, Mike Booty, had a draft number that was even lower than mine, his was five. The lady who oversaw our local draft board recently told us there was no doubt when we graduated we would be drafted into the army."

Jeannie saw how serious I was, so she said, "Let's sit down over here." We sat down on the tomb of Aunt Emma's father, Thomas DeAngelo. I didn't think he would mind us doing that.

I continued telling her what happened. "We knew we would be drafted. We didn't want to be in the Army. If we were going into the service, we wanted to be in the best branch of the service, the Marines. We joined together in the buddy system. We were told by our recruiter, 'where one buddy went, the other one would always be with him.' He guaranteed it; as naïve as we were, we believed him.

"Each graduating senior in their last semester of college met with their advisor to ensure they had completed all the required courses. Much to my surprise, I was told the state had added a required course, and I had to take that course, offered only during summer semester, if I was to graduate.

"However, that was a major problem for me because Mike and I had already joined the Marines and were scheduled to leave for boot camp at the end of May right before summer term.

"I went to my recruiter with my problem, hoping he would help me get an extension so I could get my degree. I told him my recruiter, Louis McCracken from Ponca City, Oklahoma—I'll never forget his name—I needed an extension to graduate. He just laughed and said, 'No way would the Marine Corp give some poor dumb-ass country boy an extension.' He told me my ticket was already punched and my ass now belonged to the Marine Corp . . . period.

"When I told my parents what McCracken said, they were furious. My dad wanted to go whip his butt, but my mom held him back.

"I went to his Commanding Officer and explained my problem and how it was important to me and my family that I earn a degree. I reiterated that I would be the first in my family to ever receive a college degree. He suggested I go back and see if I could get the school or the state to substitute another course for it. I tried and the school tried too, but the state said they could not because it was a new law.

"It looked like I would have to wait to get my degree after my two years in the Marine Corps. Not being able to get a degree was a great disappointed for both me and my family. My parents made many sacrifices to send me to college, but it looked like it was not going to happen. Somehow my Aunt Emma got word of what was happening and she entered into the picture.

"She called me to find out exactly what had happened and what I needed done. After I explained the problem to her, she paused before answering me. I thought we had been disconnected, and then she said, 'You don't say! It is in the bag!'

"A couple of days later, McCracken's CO sent McCracken to my dorm room. The only thing McCracken said was, 'The CO wants to see you ASAP.' I went into the CO's office. He told McCracken to stay in the office with him and me. The CO came around from his desk and shut the door. The Commanding Officer told me that my extension had been granted and my new ship-out date would be one week after my graduation date from college.

"I was shocked by what the Commanding Officer told me, and I thanked him, but I was really stunned by what came next. The CO said, 'I think Staff Sergeant McCracken has something to say to you, Adams.' To my amazement, McCracken offered an apology to me. McCracken said, 'Adams, I was out of line to curse in front of you and to degrade you by calling you a poor dumb-ass country boy.' He told me, 'It would never happen again so please forgive me.'

"The CO told me unpleasantly after McCracken apologized to me, 'Boy, I don't know who the hell you talked to or who you are kin to, but you got some clout. You are dismissed. Get the hell out of my office.'

"I knew the CO had put me on his Black List as not one of his favorite people. However, I found out later, right before I shipped out, the reason I got the extension was because Aunt Emma had made a phone call to the Assistant Secretary of the Navy, Charles Winston, II. She and the Assistant Secretary of the Navy had met one another in WWII.

"It was he who approved the extension, and he personally contacted both the CO and Sergeant McCracken and chewed them out for not allowing the extension to happen. He told them it never should have gotten to him. Evidently, they had the power to approve the extension all along, but they were more interested in meeting their quota of recruits instead of helping this 'poor dumb-ass country boy' get his degree."

Jeannie asked, "Well, I don't see how that saved your life."

I told her, "That's the really difficult part for me to explain to you."

What I said baffled her. "What do you mean, it would be difficult to explain to me? Am I that difficult to talk to?"

I quickly said to her, "No, no. I didn't say that right. It didn't come out the right way!" I reiterated, "What I mean is it is difficult for me because of what happened to Mike."

Showing uncertainty, Jeannie asked, "What happened to him?"

With a very gloomy voice I said, "He got killed!"

Jeannie again asked, "How did that save your life?"

I dropped my head as I told her, "By Aunt Emma getting me the extension, it caused me to go into the Marines four months later than Mike. I would have been there with him when he died as sure as rice is white. We were in the buddy system. Where he went I would have gone, and vice versa. I would have been there with him when his whole squad was ambushed. Everyone in his squad was killed."

This stunned Jeannie and she could see I was upset. She did not know it, but Mike and I had been best friends all of Mike's life. We played sports together, we went to church together, and we were always in the same class in every grade. We would have done anything for each other. He was a good, loyal friend, and I felt guilty. I still do because of what happened to him. I felt I was not there for him when he needed me. I should have been there; maybe we could have saved each other.

Jeannie quickly shifted the conversation to a much lighter subject. "Will you please tell me how the extension caused us to meet?"

My spirits picked up as I said, "Wow! That day was the greatest day of my life!"

Teasingly, she said as she lovingly shook my shoulders and hugged me, "Oh yeah? Tell me about it, big boy."

Jeannie was only aware of some of the things that happened that day. I knew she wanted me to tell her all of it, but I always withheld some details to keep her interested in the story. I always played along with her and added a little more to the story each time I told it. It was a joy for me to see her face light up as I began to tell her what happened that day.

I decided to put a new spin on the situation and tie it into what Aunt Emma did to get the extension. It was true that our meeting would never have occurred without the extension because it happened during the semester I was supposed to be with Mike in the Marines.

I put on my serious face and began by saying, "If Aunt Emma hadn't gotten me the extension, I wouldn't have been hurrying down the staircase, accidentally knocking those books out of your arms. I was hurrying to catch the city bus to play a round of golf with my buddies."

I changed my serious face into a happy, smiling one and continued. "If Aunt Emma hadn't got the extension for me, I would have been in the Marines and not there to help pick up your books and look into your beautiful green eyes. When I first saw you, I immediately knew you were the one I was going to marry. It was love at first sight."

Jeannie laughed, looked at me with a mean scowl, and punched me in the arm. She said, "You hurt me that day when you bumped into me. I had a bruise for a week."

I changed my expression again to a sad face and said cynically, "Oh, I am so sorry." I continued, "If Aunt Emma hadn't got me that extension, I would not have been there to bump into you. Bumping into you made me forgot about the golf game, and seeing you caused me to decide to follow you to your next class."

Jeannie said to me with astonishment, "You followed me? I always knew you were a stalker. I should have had you arrested."

I quickly told her, "But you did arrest me, sweetie pie."

Jeannie said dejectedly, "That didn't happen!"

I told her, "Oh yes it did. You arrested my heart. I became your prisoner for life, locked into your heart forever."

What I said must have made Jeannie happy because she began hugging herself like she was hugging an imaginary person.

I continued: "If Aunt Emma hadn't gotten me the extension, I would never have come into your class that day and given your professor a note saying you had an emergency at home, and you were needed immediately, and you were to follow me."

Jeannie said, "I knew instantly that was a lie, but I played along with you because I did not want to be any more embarrassed than I already was. You were always a big liar."

I immediately told her, "That was no lie. There was an emergency. The emergency was that I loved you and wanted to marry you and take you home with me forever."

Jeannie said crossly, "Do you know what happened because of that fake note? I made a poor grade in that class! That day, my professor gave the class what was to be on the exam. I missed his summary, and I did not do well on the test. I got a C. It was all your fault."

I became serious again. "You don't say!" Then I delayed and said, "But Honey, ain't I worth more than a C when you should know by now you married an A? And this all happened because of the extension Aunt Emma acquired for me. It allowed me to get a college degree, to live, and to meet the woman God planned for me to marry."

Jeannie grabbed me and we hugged each other. Then I swung her around. I told her as we looked into each other's eyes. "You know something, everything that happened to us, was all because of what that woman did for me. I . . . no, we owe a lot to Aunt Emma. She was quite a woman, and I wish you could have known her."

While Jeannie and I were still in an embrace, we heard someone yelling to us, "Hey, you two cut all that out, we got too much work to do for that!"

I told Jeannie, "I only wish you could have known her, she was quite a special lady."

Jeannie told me, "I do want to know all about her. I can see how important she was to you. I want you to tell me all about her so I can discover what kind of person she was."

As soon as Jeannie said that, I turned to check on our children and saw a lady talking to them at the entrance of the cemetery. I immediately recognized her as Miss Mildred Law, one of my teachers in school. Her father and mother are buried here, and I assumed she had come to visit their gravesite.

I turned back to respond to Jeannie's request and told her, "I can do better than that, honey. Someone has just come into the cemetery who knew my Aunt Emma better than anyone, including me. They were best friends. I would bet money, if you asked her to tell you about Aunt Emma, she would be tickled to death to do it."

We both turned toward the entrance and waved to Miss Mildred Law as she was leaving our children and heading straight toward us. I hoped we would have the opportunity to hear her thoughts about Aunt Emma and their relationship. There were many unanswered questions rolling around in my head about why there was so much mystery and tragedy in her life.

# Chapter 2

## *Best Friend*

I had not seen Miss Mildred Law in years although I often thought about her. I had such great memories of her. I wondered if she had retired and how she was doing. She was walking slowly up the hill toward Aunt Emma's gravesite where we were. Miss Mildred Law looked much the same as she did when she taught me. She never seemed to age. I wondered if I should introduce her to Jeannie using her first name. I decided I had better continue referring to her as everyone else did...Miss Mildred Law.

Not only was Miss Mildred Law Aunt Emma's best friend; they were nurses in WWII together. Those two were always so happy whenever they were together. Thinking about them at Aunt Emma's house made me smile because I loved watching how they interacted with one another.

Miss Mildred Law's mother helped raise Aunt Emma after Aunt Emma's mother died during her birth. The Laws lived across the west pasture, only a few hundred yards from Aunt Emma.

Our parish schools housed grades one-through-twelve at one location. Everyone knew each other because we were such a small community. Miss Mildred Law was the seventh grade teacher at our local school, and I was blessed to be in her class.

Before entering into Miss Mildred Law's class, I had heard all kinds of terrible stories about how she treated her students. At first, I did not know if they were true because I had seen her joking around at Aunt Emma's house many times before. Hearing other students describe her just did not fit the portrayal I had of her. However, soon after being in her class for only a short time, I quickly surmised all the stories were probably true.

She was a very strict teacher. She always demanded your best effort, and if you did not give to her what she wanted, you would suffer the consequences of her wrath. She had taught just about everybody that was related to me. In fact, I honestly believed she had taught everyone in our community because everyone could tell stories about something that happened to them in her class.

She expected everyone to do what was right all the time, and she was the living example of it. She was a statuesque lady, very prim and proper. She dressed immaculately and had a pretty good figure for a teacher. Her hair was pulled back in a bun every day, and it was always in perfect place. Her makeup was exact. Her posture was excellent: shoulders back with her chest out and head up. And she insisted we be that way, too. When she ate, she used proper manners and chewed each fork-full of food at least forty times before swallowing it. She spoke perfect English, unless she got mad at you; then anything could come out of her mouth. When she was upset, she would cuss. It was her one non-conformist issue. You would never dream that habit belonged to her, but she cussed quite frequently. One time, we even caught her smoking: a shock to us all.

We all respected her and feared her at the same time. I was even scared of her today, years later as an adult. She had a mystical disposition about her, causing you to believe she knew everything about you. Even after you graduated high school, she still seemed to know everything about you. It is hard to explain, but that was how everyone felt about her. They loved and hated her at the same time.

She pushed education as a must for everyone. She preached to us that if you wanted to get ahead in life, you must get an education. To her, it was not a choice. In her class, if it looked as if we were losing interest in learning, she would tell us in a real sweet-like voice, "That's alright child, if you don't want to learn, there is always a need for grocery clerks or service station attendants." She could put you in your place in a second, and shame you into doing what you should have done in the first place. Nobody wanted to come under the wrath of *The Law* as everyone called her behind her back.

I laughed within myself as I thought about the time I was diagramming a sentence on the chalkboard in her class, and I had it all wrong. Miss Mildred Law went back over it with me so I could get it right. However, I did it incorrectly again, and she got mad at me. She told me she whipped all my little cousins' asses when they got stupid, and she would whip my ass too, even if I was Aunt Emma's favorite. I could not believe she said that out-loud at school.

She sent me to the football field to get a bamboo cane for a switch. I left to retrieve it and brought it to her, and she whipped me with it until it broke. I intentionally did not get a keen one, which was a mistake on my part. She told me I chose switches like I diagramed sentences: very poorly. She sent me back to get another switch and when I returned, she whipped me some more. Then after school, she called home, where I got another whipping.

Another time, she was coming down the stairs from the auditorium. Someone had left the boy's restroom door open at the bottom of the stairs. When she turned to look, she saw three boys trying to pee from across the room into the urinal. The urinal was twelve feet away from where they were standing. Someone saw her looking and hollered, "The Law! The Law!" They quickly closed the door, but it was too late.

Miss Mildred Law threw the door open and hollered into the restroom, "Ok, you boys. You better put those little peckers back into your pants because I'm coming in."

The three boys she saw in the peeing contest tried to hide. But if you did wrong, you could not hide from the eyes of "The Law." She grabbed two of the boys by their ears and told the third one to follow her to the office. I can still see them as she dragged them on their tip-toes climbing up the stairs, with the third boy following right behind her, looking like a whipped dog with his tail between its legs. She told them on the way up the stairs, "If you can pee that far, you need to join the fire department."

It was funny, but we did not laugh in front of her because Miss Mildred Law would have gotten us too. As soon as she disappeared, we all burst out in laughter. It was an unforgettable sight.

She did things that helped us in unusual and innovated ways. If teachers did some of the things the way Miss Mildred Law did now, they probably would be fired. I was a poor reader and I was not the only one in my class. Several of us read below our grade level.

Because we were poor readers, Miss Mildred Law would make us miss our twenty-minute morning recess to make us read. Not only was it embarrassing to be known as a poor reader, but most of us were not interested in reading. Miss Mildred Law had figured a way to make it more interesting to us, though.

She used as her strategy, a young man's greatest craving: the desire for women. She knew if a person practiced something enough, they would become good at it. For weeks, each morning we came in and she put us in the back of the room, sat us all in a row, and gave us sex novels to read. We did not know they were sex novels, but they did keep our interest. As we read the books, they sometimes caused us to adjust ourselves whenever the passage got really interesting. Believe it or not, our reading levels soared. It probably improved our love lives, too.

I can remember whenever she and Aunt Emma got together at Aunt Emma's house, they acted like two thirteen year old girls who were sharing all the secrets of life. They laughed, giggled, and whispered, both of them transformed into entirely different people, especially Miss Mildred Law.

You had to be careful what you said around Miss Mildred Law because she would tell it like it was. She acted like she knew all the secrets to life, and most of the time it seemed she did. There was very little that went on in our parish that Miss Mildred Law did not know the particulars about.

Miss Mildred Law finally made it to where we were standing in the cemetery, and she was out of breath and said, "Blake, I just met your lovely children. It looks like I might have been wrong about you."

Not completely surprised at anything she said to me, I answered not knowing what she meant: "How is that, Miss Mildred Law?"

She said to me, "I thought you would never make anything of yourself. However, after meeting your beautiful children, I see some of the things we tried to teach you rubbed off on them. You have reared them right. They are two well-mannered children. Emma would be proud of you."

I should have known by the time Miss Mildred Law reached Aunt Emma's grave that she had recalled everything about me and my family since I was born. I humbly told Miss Mildred Law, "Thank you for saying that, Miss Mildred Law. But I want you to know, you had a large part in making it happen, and I truly give you acclaim for that."

Miss Mildred Law ignored what I considered a compliment. Her thinking was always a step ahead of everyone, she looked down at Aunt Emma's headstone and sadly said, "You are just like the rest of us, aren't you? You miss Emma, too."

I responded sadly, "Yes ma'am, I do. She was a great lady. She taught me so many wonderful things. I was lucky to have her in my life, and I know you feel the same way about her, too."

Miss Mildred Law asked me curtly, "Boy, are you going to introduced me to this beautiful lady standing by you, or am I going to have to do it myself?"

Embarrassed for showing poor manners, I swiftly answered her, "Oh, I'm so sorry Miss Mildred Law, I don't know what came over me to forget introducing you to my wife. She is the real reason my two children have any manners at all."

Miss Mildred Law interjected, "Yes, I can see you haven't changed all that much, but I still don't know her name."

I apologized again and made a formal introduction. "Miss Mildred Law, this is my wonderful wife, Jeannie. She is the best thing to come into my life since Aunt Emma made all my summers so much fun."

Miss Mildred Law shook Jeannie's hand and told her jokingly, "It is a pleasure to meet you, honey child, and I know it has been a battle for you to keep Blake on the right path. It was a battle for both me and Emma, too. But I believe we did a pretty good job with him. His Aunt Emma was a wonderful woman that both he and I loved very much."

Jeannie offered her brief insight and told Miss Mildred Law, "From what I have heard about Miss Emma today from Blake, she must have meant a lot to many people. Blake tells me you knew her all her life, is that true?"

Miss Mildred Law proudly replied, "Honey, she was born the day after I was. That is the only time in my life that I was ever ahead of her. She was quite a lady. We did everything together from the time we could walk until right before she left. We shared secrets with one another . . . You know, I haven't been able to tell anybody anything private about myself since she left us. And sweetheart, I got lots of secrets I need to tell someone."

Jeannie and I laughed. Jeannie excitedly said to Miss Mildred Law, "We all need someone to share things with. I know I do. I would love you to share those personal things with me. And if it's possible, I would love to hear about Blake's Aunt Emma and you. If you could do that for me, I would love to hear about y'all. Then I can tell you things about Blake that will make him blush. Blake says you know everything about her because you and Miss Emma were best friends. Blake says that you are just the person I need to talk to."

Miss Mildred perked up. "Baby doll, I would love to tell you everything about us. You know, we were closer than sisters. We had a special bond. My mother spent so many hours at her home after Emma's mother passed away that I actually believed Emma was my sister.

"You did know Emma's mother died from giving birth to her, didn't you?" asked Miss Mildred Law.

Jeannie nodded her head as Miss Mildred Law kept talking. She never missed a beat. She was a historical fountain, filled with great wisdom and knowledge of many things in our community.

Miss Mildred Law said, "My mother told me as a child, she and I spent so much time over at Emma's house that I thought I had two houses."

We laughed at what she said and I could tell Miss Mildred Law and Jeannie had bonded into friends. Hearing Miss Mildred Law share her life was something I never dreamed could be possible, and here she was sharing her life's wisdom with my wife and me. It was too good to be true. They were talking as if they had known each other all their lives. I do not think they knew I was there anymore. I did not mind being ignored. I just wanted to listen.

I kept quiet and tried to absorb everything she said. It was like one of Aunt Emma's retorts coming true. Whenever someone talked too much, Aunt Emma would say, "You learn by listening, not by talking!"

Miss Mildred Law asked Jeannie, "Are you sure you want to hear about Emma from me? Most people want to run away when I begin telling them things?"

We laughed again. I never realized how funny Miss Mildred Law could be, but I knew what she said was true.

Jeannie, in sincerity told her why she wanted to know about Aunt Emma. "You may not understand this, but I feel the more I learn about Aunt Emma, the better I should be able to develop those same great qualities Blake tells me she had. Then I can nurture them. I can tell Blake loved and respected her. It makes me enviable of her. I'm not saying I want to be just like her, but I would like to have those fine qualities that Blake admired about her. You understand what I am saying Miss Mildred, don't you?"

Miss Mildred Law said, "Yes, honey, I do, and we all would be a whole lot better people, if we had some of Emma's fine qualities. But in just the short time, I have known you, and by talking to your children by the gate, I can tell that you, too, are a special lady with your own great qualities. You don't need to imitate anyone!"

Jeannie, a little embarrassed, humbly said, "Thank you, Miss Mildred Law. Do you mind if I just call you Miss Mildred instead of Miss Mildred Law?"

Jeannie asking that really stunned me. No one ever asked Miss Mildred Law if they could call her something other than Miss Mildred Law. I did not know the real story of why everyone called her by her full name. Someone told us there were three Mildred's teaching in the school at the same time when she first started teaching, and all the kids would get them mixed up. It infuriated Miss Mildred Law, and she made every child in school call each of the Mildreds by her full name. If you did not do it her way, and Miss Mildred Law heard you or heard about you doing it any other way than that, you faced the wrath of The Law.

Two of the three Mildred's were not married at the time. Even though Miss Mildred Law was married, she continued to use her maiden name, Law. Her married name was Mildred Law Shook.

Surprisingly, Miss Mildred Law said to Jeannie, "No, baby doll, I don't mind you calling me that at all. I always wanted to be called by my first name, but it just didn't work out that way. You just go ahead and call me Mildred. I would love for you to do that."

Now, my wife might be able to call her Mildred, but in no way would I ever take the chance of calling her by her first name. To me, and everyone who knew Miss Mildred Law, she was and always will be Miss Mildred Law. Here I am, a grown man in my thirties, and I am still afraid of my seventh grade teacher. Maybe calling her by her whole name is not as much out of fear as it is respect and showing honor to her. She is a lady to be respected, and I was always going to offer it to her.

Miss Mildred Law humbly addressed Jeannie: "Before I begin telling you about Emma and me, I would like to ask a favor. I don't want to be rude, but I see my brother at my parent's gravesite, and I promised him I would help him set up an arrangement for our parents. Could you two please excuse me for just a little while? I'll return and we can have a good, long visit."

Jeannie quickly responded to Miss Mildred Law's request, "Oh, it's me who should be apologizing to you for keeping you away from what you came for. Please, by all means, do what you need to do. We will be right here when you come back."

"I don't want you two to think I am dodging you, because I am not. I actually am looking forward to visiting with you, and I always enjoy talking about my best friend," Miss Mildred Law said happily.

Miss Mildred Law said, "I tell you what you can do, Blake, until I come back. Why don't you tell Jeannie about the time your cousins played a mean joke on you, and Emma taught you a lesson in life about the cream coming to the top? I think she will enjoy it as much as I did."

I was shocked to hear Miss Mildred Law speak about the joke. I could not believe she knew about it. Jeannie kindly told her, "I am sure that Blake would love to do that. I don't think he has ever told me that story. Miss Mildred, you just take all the time you need."

Miss Mildred Law left to go to her parents' graves, and Jeannie eagerly asked me, "What does Miss Mildred mean, 'the cream comes to the top,' and who are the cousins who played a joke on you?"

I did not know where to start, I began by simply telling Jeannie, and "Aunt Emma lived with her father, Mr. Tom, her sister, Olivia, and Olivia's two twin boys, Bernard and Leonard. In the summers, I stayed with them and we played together. One day, Mr. Tom took Aunt Emma and her sister grocery shopping and left Bernard and Leonard in charge of watching me. Before they left, we were told not to climb in the Trouble Tree."

Puzzled, Jeannie asked, "Why did she call it the Trouble Tree?"

Thinking about that large pecan tree caused me to laugh, as the memories of it flooded my mind. I delightedly told Jeannie, "So many things happened around that pecan tree. Every time someone climbed in that tree or did something around it, they always got into trouble, and it usually resulted in someone getting a good whipping. Aunt Emma always preached to us not to climb in that tree because all it brought was trouble."

Jeannie seriously questioned me, "Did you ever climb in that tree and get a whipping?"

Yes, I did climb in it, but I didn't get a whipping for that. I did, however, get whippings for other things. Miss Mildred Law is speaking about one particular time Bernard and Leonard got a serious whipping because of the joke they played on me.

Then I proudly added, "Bernard and Leonard were funny and fun to be around."

"What was so funny about them?" Jeannie asked.

I smiled as I told her, "I've never told anybody about the joke they played on me. The only ones who ever knew about it were the twins, Aunt Emma, Aunt Olivia, and my Mom and Dad. I never mentioned it to anyone else. I guess Aunt Emma told Miss Mildred Law I thought it was long forgotten."

Seeing my big smile, Jeannie asked, "Are you trying to keep something from me Blake?

I did not answer that loaded question. I just started telling the story, "As soon as they left to go shopping, it gave us our opportunity to climb in the Trouble Tree. It was a great tree to climb, and I had been longing to climb the tree with Bernard and Leonard. We assumed, since they were in town that we had enough time to climb it and not get caught, or at least we thought we did. When they left, we went straight to the Trouble Tree and climbed up into it.

"We walked out on a large limb that hung over the yard, Bernard and Leonard stopped to take a pee. Both of them pulled their pants down below their knees to see who could pee the highest."

Jeannie sarcastically asked, "Did you get into the contest with them, too?"

"You know I did. But as we were peeing, I notice they had hair around their private areas. Because I was an immature kid, I was very curious as to why they had hair there and I didn't. So, I asked them.

"Bernard, the more responsible one, started to tell me something . . . the truth, I guess, because he was the smartest twin. However, Leonard, who was a clown and a devil, interrupted Bernard's statement and quickly cut him off.

"Leonard told me, acting as if my not having any pubic hair was a shock to him, 'Oh, you sure don't have any hair down there, do you? You should have some hair by now. Probably the reason you don't have any hair around your talleywacker is that you haven't been fertilized yet.'

"By this time Bernard decided to go along with Leonard's little joke and said, 'Yes that is true, and it is probably why you don't have hair. You know what? You can have hair around your talleywacker by tomorrow if you fertilize it today.'

"I asked them not knowing what fertilize even meant, 'How do I fertilize it?'

"Leonard eagerly said, 'Let's climb down this tree and we will show you what you have to do to get some hair down there. It's all part of growing up, and I'm really surprised your father hasn't helped you to grow some hair down there. I guess he's been too busy to show you.'

"We pulled our pants up, climbed down the Trouble Tree, and went up under the fig tree where the chickens roosted. The chickens roosted mainly in the fig tree or sometimes under the house. It was cooler there, and they could find insects to eat. As chickens do, they left their droppings both under the house and under the fig tree.

"Leonard said to me earnestly as he was pointing to the chicken manure, 'Pull your pants down and put some of this fertilizer around your talleywacker. It is what will make the hair grow.'

"Even as a child I immediately realized what the fertilizer was: it was chicken manure. At first, I hesitated to put it on me because . . . if manure was what it took to grow hair, then I wasn't too sure I wanted to have hair down there or not. Deep down inside of me, I knew I shouldn't do it," I told Jeannie.

"However, Bernard said, 'Yes, by tomorrow morning you will have hair down there, just like us.'

"I said, believing him to be truthful, 'I did it'. I trusted Bernard a lot more than I did Leonard because Leonard was always getting whippings from Aunt Emma for lying or being bad."

Appalled by what I just told her, Jeannie asked, "You didn't do that, did you?" She laughed out-loud, putting her hands over her face as she saw me nodding my head, yes.

"Leonard appealed to my ego and told me, 'After you have rubbed the *chicken-shice*, around your talleywacker, you will be a man like us, tomorrow.'

I continued the story. "As I rubbed the mess all around my private area, they giggled, but whenever I looked up to see why they were giggling, they would stop snickering, and look real serious. They reassured me it was what I had to do to get hair down there. They said it would make me a man like them. After I finished smearing the fertilizer on me, they helped me pull up my underwear and pants, and told me to leave it there until tomorrow morning, and I would have hair there, just like them."

I said to Jeannie, "They even made me take an oath to promise I would not tell anyone about this, saying it was part of becoming a man and it was nobody else's business but us men.

"The promise went something like this: 'Cross your heart and hope to die and see the devil in the eye. And if I tell I'll go to hell.' So I promised. They probably knew Aunt Emma would find out, and I would tell her it was their idea, but perhaps if I make that promise, maybe I would keep our secret."

I sadly told Jeannie, "The rest of that afternoon I went around with that "chicken-shice" inside my underwear."

Jeannie was repulsed. She asked, "Did it burn you?"

I slowly answered her, "I really can't remember, but that evening when we ate supper around five o'clock, Aunt Emma kept asking, 'What's that smell?' She told us to check our feet to see if we had stepped in some chicken crap."

"Bernard and Leonard smiled a little, not wanting Aunt Emma to catch them. Evidently we did not check our feet well enough, because Aunt Emma still smelling it, made us stand in front of her so she could check our feet," I said.

I told Jeannie so she would understand, "Back then, children didn't wear shoes in the summer. Shoes were used only for school and church or special occasions."

"Aunt Emma checked Bernard first and he was declared clean. Then Leonard stood in front of her, and he was also declared clean. Then my turn came. She checked my feet and found none there, but she still smelled the stench. She turned me around probably realizing the smell was strongest on me. I guess she was checking to see if I had sat in some or either I messed in my pants," I said embarrassed.

I suddenly said, "It was then Aunt Emma realized the stench was not on us but it was in my pants. I remember being scared of getting caught. I wondered if I had done something wrong. I just wanted to be a man. I think Aunt Emma sensed I was scared, so not to frighten me anymore, she turned her attention away from me and toward the twins."

I laughed as I told Jeannie, "As I stood there she turned her stare at Bernard and Leonard. She seemed to look at them forever and not say a word. She made Bernard and Leonard come and stand up in front of her next to me, and still she was silent."

I watched Jeannie's reaction as I said, "Every once in a while Leonard and Bernard would crack a smile or giggle. But Aunt Emma found nothing funny about the situation. I guess she was waiting for one of them to tell her what had happened."

Jeannie asked, "Why didn't their mother, Olivia, ask the questions. Didn't she see what was going on? It seems like Aunt Emma was in charge and Olivia was unaware of what her children did."

I answered, "As a kid I thought the same thing, and always wondered why, too. My mom told me later that Aunt Olivia had a nervous breakdown, and she wasn't the same after that. I don't remember Aunt Olivia ever talking, and I can't ever remember her correcting her boys."

Jeannie gloomily replied, "Poor lady, it seems these boys were out of control. What did your Aunt Emma do?"

I quickly said, "Finally, after we stood there for what it seemed an eternity, Aunt Emma had figured right: the chicken manure was in my pants.

"She scornfully asked Bernard and Leonard, knowing she would never get a truthful answer. 'What did you two boys do to this precious little child?'

"Then she used one of her retorts and said with little emotion, 'This don't butter my biscuit, nor will it yours.'

"We all three stood there looking at Aunt Emma. No one said anything, but you could see both Leonard and Bernard knew they were in big trouble. Their whole demeanor changed. Aunt Emma never asked me what happened. She probably knew these two had made me promise not to say a word. She never put me on the spot. She was going to get her answer from them, one way or another," I said.

I told Jeannie, "Aunt Emma never asked who did it. She passed over finding that out . . . to why they did it. She knew Leonard and Bernard had done it. She just wanted to know why. She told them they were to stand there and not move until she called for them."

I told Jeannie, "She ushered me outside and helped take all my clothes off. The smell made both her and me turn our heads. The stench was bad enough, but I was more disappointed that I didn't have one hair around my talleywacker. Aunt Emma put me into the number five washtub. She never said another word to me or questioned me."

I exclaimed, "Next she called for Bernard to come outside. She told him to draw water from the well and to fill up the large, black cast iron pot they used to wash their clothes in and to boil the water in it so she could use it to wash me. Bernard put some wood around the pot, drew water from the well, poured it in, and started the fire."

I simply said, "She went back into the house with Leonard and Olivia. I guess Leonard was still standing at the table. Aunt Emma stayed in there with him and Aunt Olivia. I don't know what was said, but when she came back out to where Bernard and I were, she dejectedly told Bernard, 'Leonard says it was all your idea to put chicken mature into Blake's pants.'"

I told Jeannie, "Aunt Emma used the old psychological game of separate and conquer to find out the truth. She made Bernard believe Leonard had ratted on him and blamed everything on him. She knew Bernard would more likely tell her the truth than Leonard, and he did.

"Aunt Emma sternly asked Bernard, 'I only want to know one thing. Why did you two do that to him?'

"When Bernard told her the whole story, saying it was just a joke, I could tell it really hurt her. You could see what Bernard said had shocked Aunt Emma. She couldn't imagine someone related to her, could play such a cruel joke on an innocent child," I told Jeannie.

"Aunt Emma never showed that it hurt her, or that she was disappointed with the twins. But she was. She called Leonard to come out of the house and told him to help Bernard draw water and to keep bring warm water to wash me with. That was the only time I had a warm bath in that tub in all the summers I stayed with them. The only bad thing was Aunt Emma used a little bleach in the water to get the smell off of me, and she rubbed me so hard that I turned red all over," I said, sadly.

"It felt strange sitting in that warm tub, but what was stranger was neither Leonard nor Bernard said a word to each other and neither did Aunt Emma, that is, not until she was through bathing me. I was afraid to say anything, either. I was probably right to be afraid. Aunt Emma wrapped a towel around me and put me on the back porch. She told me to dry off and stay there until she came back," I said to Jeannie.

"She went back to where Leonard and Bernard were and told them to go to the side of the house by the fig tree to where the chickens roosted and where they had gotten the chicken manure for me.

"I saw Aunt Emma go over to the fence line to break a switch off a hedge bush. She walked back to where the twins were. I could hear her speaking to Leonard and Bernard. She never raised her voice or fussed at them. She spoke in a normal tone as she told them how disappointed she was with them. You could tell by the tone of her voice she was really saddened, she was almost to the point of tears," I said.

"In distress, Aunt Emma told them, 'Your mother and I left you two in charge of Blake to care for him and not to play a joke on him. That is what older and smarter kids do, care for younger kids, not take advantage of them. It is not fair to Blake what you two did. He is not able to understand it was a joke. He has no way to get even with you because he is so much younger than you two.'

"Aunt Emma unsympathetically told them, 'Because you two have not been obedient to me and your mother, you must be disciplined. Bernard, come stand here.'"

I said, "Aunt Emma whipped Bernard with the switch and in the process she told him he knew it was wrong, but he went along with it. She must have struck him seven or eight times until he cried.

"Aunt Emma called Leonard, 'It's your turn Leonard, come here. You need to stop being so mean to others, because one day it will get you into big trouble.'

"Then she whipped him, too. I wouldn't say she whipped him like she did Bernard, because Leonard refused to cry. What she did to Leonard was not a regular whipping. It was a *whopping*.

She struck him more times than Bernard; however, after twelve to fifteen lashes, the switch quickly overcame his resistance."

Jeannie rapidly stated, "They deserved to be whipped!"

"Aunt Emma said to them harshly, 'To be fair to Blake, I am going to take his place and return the joke. Take off your clothes and smear some chicken manure on your private areas and get under the house with the rest of the chickens. I'm doing this to you because you picked on someone who can't defend himself. Now, let's see if you like the same joke being played on you.'

"Leonard asked her, 'You really want us to get under the house naked!'

"Aunt Emma shook the switch at them and said, 'No, right now get under there with your underwear on, or get some more of this.'"

I told Jeannie, "Leonard knew she meant business, and he crawled under the house with Bernard.

"It was almost dark when she sent them under the house and Aunt Emma told them she would call them when she wanted them to come out. They stayed there to nine o'clock that night. After that incident, those two boys treated me with a whole lot more respect," I gladly said.

Jeannie burst out in laughter and said, "It serves them right because they took advantage of you, an innocent child. You were innocent, weren't you?"

I laughed and said, "Kind of. Maybe in this case." Both of us laughed even more.

# Chapter 3

## *Life's Lessons and Memories*

J eannie asked, "How did whipping the twins have anything to do with the cream coming to the top?"

Before I could explain, our laughter had caused our children to run up the hill to Aunt Emma's gravesite and ask what we were laughing so much about.

Jeannie quickly replied to them, "We were laughing about your father having a joke played on him by his cousins, and him almost getting a whipping because of it from his Aunt Emma."

Emily was having a difficult time imagining I could ever be whipped, so she asked her mother, "What did Daddy do that was so bad he had to be whipped?"

Ben, to make the situation funny, added, "He probably needed it! That is what Daddy tells me before he whips me." We all laughed at Ben's joke. He understood well what a whipping was for.

I said to them all in a very commanding way, "No way would Aunt Emma ever put the switch on me. I was a good child. In fact, I was her favorite nephew."

As Emily was looking around, she read Aunt Emma's name on her headstone and asked, "Is this the Aunt Emma you are talking about? Have I ever met her before?"

Jeannie answered modestly, "No darling, neither you nor your brother have ever met her. She passed away before both of you were born."

Emily noticing Aunt Emma was buried away from the rest of the headstones asked, "Why is Aunt Emma over here? She's by herself and not close to the rest of the people."

I gave her the answer I was told as a child, "Aunt Emma is there because the people of this community felt Aunt Emma belonged to them, too. They wanted her to be in an area where they had access to her, and where they could also care for her."

Emily announced something else interesting about Aunt Emma, which Jeannie had already noticed: "It definitely looks like someone really cares for her. Look at all the flowers and the area around her grave. She has more flowers than anyone else in the whole cemetery. They must have really loved her a lot."

I thought to myself after Emily made that statement, if only they could have known her, they would understand what most people knew about her. So I expressed my desire to them: "I wish all of you could have known her. You would have seen what a good person she was and how she lived the principles she believed. I learned a lot from her and from her family."

Ben, still contemplating me getting a whipping, asked, "Was she a mean person?"

Jeannie answered Ben modestly, "From what your father has told me, she was a wonderful person. Your Dad spent a lot of time with her and her sister, Olivia, and her two twin boys when he was youngster. However, it was a long time ago, I think when he was about the same age as you Ben."

The DeAngelo family had taught me a lot, especially Aunt Emma. Aunt Olivia's two boys taught me many things, too. Some of the things they taught me got me into the trouble.

I told my children, "The twins names were Bernard and Leonard DeAngelo."

Emily immediately stopped me and excitedly said, "Here is Leonard's grave, Daddy. He is buried over here by his mother, Olivia. Wow! Neither one of them lived very long. They died at an early age."

Ben, paying no attention to what Emily had said, broke into her statement: "Daddy, what kind of things did your Aunt Emma teach you?"

I quickly said to them, "The most important thing she taught me are the three things I have tried to teach you two…and that is how to live life right."

Emily with such an intrusive mind always wanting to know the reason for everything asked, "What three things did she teach you Daddy that you have taught us?"

My thoughts slipped into the past, to the day she sat me down at the table. It seemed like it was only yesterday. She said she was going to tell me a secret that few people learn in life. She said if people would learn to live life using these three principles, they would not only be successful in life, but they would always be happy. If I learned this secret and lived by it every day, I would become the person God wanted me to be.

"Aunt Emma said number one is to always do what is right. Number two is treat people fairly, don't trick or cheat them. And number three is to give to others only your best. That is what makes you a man. That is what God wants us to do," I proudly said.

Ben quickly blurted out, "I remember you telling us that daddy. You tell us that all the time. Your Aunt Emma taught that to you, too? Is that where you got it from?"

I wanted to explain to my kids how Aunt Emma lived by those three principles. She treated people with dignity, never trying to be unfair to them, and tried her best to do right. I told them, "If she said those three things to me one time, she said it to me a thousand times. She wanted me to know and live those principles each day, and not just live them when it was convenient for me to do so."

Emily, not wanting to agree with Ben, said, "Yeah Daddy, you tell us that all the time, especially when we do wrong. We know all about that, Daddy. You don't have to keep reminding us. Can you tell us about the joke the twins played on you?"

Wanting to express what kind of person Aunt Emma was, I quietly shortened the incident for them. "I was a young boy, just about Ben's age, when the twins played a mean joke on me."

Emily, wanting to know all the details of the incident, asked, "What did they do to you Daddy? Was it funny?"

I said to them, not wanting to divulge too much information—I didn't want to embarrass both Jeannie and myself—"Let's just say they did something that caused me to stink. Right after they caused me to stink, Aunt Emma cleaned me up, and she righted the wrong done to me."

I thought to myself, today a lot of people would think what she did was cruel and demeaning, but any time someone corrects a person, it actually is a show of love toward them. Aunt Emma knew giving a person a dose of their own medicine would make them understand that any ill treatment they intentionally do to others is wrong.

It was crystal clear to me that her method of correction worked. It allowed Bernard and Leonard to understand how mean and wrong what they did was. The under-the-house visit with the chickens allowed them to experience the consequences of their actions, and it was reinforced by the manure and the whipping for punishment. Experience and consequences are great teachers in life.

I delayed answering Emily's question to choose the best way to tell them about how Aunt Emma righted the wrong. I wanted to tell Jeannie and my children about the analogy Aunt Emma used: "The cream always come to the top."

My kids came from a different generation. They had no idea of what one could make from milk, or about milking a cow. I knew about those things because as a child we had to milk our cow to have milk to drink and to make cream or butter.

My mother taught me the money people made from cream during the Great Depression allowed many families to put food on their tables. That included our family and many others in our parish.

I told Jeannie and the children how Aunt Emma made cream. "Aunt Emma pulled a bottle of fresh, cooled milk from inside her churn. Cooled milk separates, with the cream in the milk coming to the top of the bottle, leaving the thinner milk underneath. She poured the cream into another glass and asked me if I saw the difference between the two milks.

"I said, 'Yes ma'am, the stuff on top is thicker. The thicker milk is cream?'

"Aunt Emma patted me on the back and told me, 'That's right son, it's cream. But there's something more important about it. The cream is more valuable to people because it's the best that milk has to offer. Cream coming to the top is something magical God does to milk. God brings the best up out of that milk to give us something better. It is the same with people. When people bring trouble onto a person, if they cool off before reacting, then the best in them will come to the top.'

"Aunt Emma picked me up and sat me up on the countertop. She looked straight into my eyes and said, 'When people treat you wrong or try to fool you like what the boys did to you today, you need to act like the milk. Wait too cool off before you make a decision, then the cooling off will allow your best response to come out. Just like the cream is more valuable than the milk, your cooled decision will make you more valuable to yourself and to others.'"

That lesson taught me to thank God for this beautiful lady who cared enough for me to teach me how to live life right, and make it more enjoyable.

Ben impatiently stated, "Cream doesn't sound like much fun, Daddy. What fun things did your Aunt Emma teach you?"

That question hit me like a snowball in the back of the head. The memories of the many new things I learned through that family flooded my mind. I knew I did not have much time, as Miss Mildred Law would be coming back soon. So I offered an abbreviated version of the many things I learned from the DeAngelo family.

I hurriedly said, "Well, Ben she taught me how to shoot a rifle." I knew Ben loved to shoot his pellet rifle, and that would grab his attention.

Hearing Aunt Emma could shoot a rifle surprised Ben. He said, "A girl taught you how to shoot?"

I was quick to add how well Aunt Emma could shoot and told Ben, "She never missed what she shot at. But, she never shot something just to kill it. She needed a reason to shoot."

I continued, "She taught me as a ten year old how to bridle and ride a horse, how to milk a cow, how to build a tree house, and she challenged me to climb every tree I could.

"She read bible stories to me about David and Goliath, Daniel in the lion's den, Samson and his great strength, and told me stories about Jesus. She would tell us God gives us everything, and whatever we do or say, we should understand God is standing right next to us, so we need to be careful and not hurt God's feelings by saying or doing something wrong."

As I listed what Aunt Emma had taught me, I had not realized that she must have really loved me for her to spend so much time when I was not even her child. I could never understand why such a loving person as Aunt Emma did not have any kids. She would have been a great mother. She gave so much love to everyone.

I knew I had to get away from concentrating on Aunt Emma because I could feel tears begin to well in my eyes. Thinking of our times together as a child made me realize how much I loved and missed her.

I told Ben, "I learned a lot of fun things from those two boys, too."

Emily's mind kicked into gear as she listened intently to what I was saying, and she asked, doubting, "How can an older kid teach a younger kid fun things to do?" Wasn't there a big age difference between y'all?"

I realized that as the times have changed, kids now have many things to entertain them as compared to back in the fifties and early sixties. I tried to explain. "Kids in our time had to invent ways to have fun. Believe it or not, we did a pretty good job of doing it. We didn't have the things kids have now to entertain themselves. We didn't have television with its cartoons or westerns to watch. We didn't have toys unless we made them."

Emily's mind began going into deep thought mode again and she announced, "It must have been real boring back then."

To be honest, I did remember the summers felt a lot longer than they do now, and Christmas seemed like it would never get here. Time seemed to drag on, as it does not do today. Even as much as I hated to go to school, I secretly looked forward to going, at least I did in the beginning of the school year.

I said to Emily and Ben, "At times it was boring, but when we did fun things, they were always great adventures."

"Like what Daddy?" Emily asked, skeptically.

"Well," I said. "Bernard taught me how to rope calves and how to ride a bucking horse, at least he did until he broke his arm. Aunt Emma was upset with him because they did not have enough money to pay for the hospital visit. She had to sell all her jellies and preserves she had put up to pay his hospital bill. The bill also took all her extra cream money she had saved."

I continued: "We went swimming every Thursday, and we would play King on the Mountain on the river bank. Bernard was the best at it because he was so much stronger than everybody else. Sometimes we brought watermelons and had watermelon fights, and we set lines out at night to catch catfish or go 'grabbing.'"

Emily quickly asked, "What's grabbing?"

I wasn't going to tell her because it was dangerous. You tie a giant hook on your left hand and a rope around your waist or foot. Then you dive under the muddy water into either a hollow log or a cave to grab or hook a large catfish.

When you hook him, it pulls you further into the log or cave. You depend on your buddies to pull you and the fish out quickly. If the fight lasts over a minute, you could drown. So I told her, "It was just another way to catch a big fish."

Emily seemed satisfied with the answer, and I moved on.

Then I said, "Bernard was a better student than his brother, Leonard, and at night he would let me read his collection of funny books."

Both Emily and Ben said at the same time, "What's a funny book?" My kids had TV and they had no use for comic books.

Bernard had a collection that went years back. He had inherited them from an older cousin, and he guarded them like they were gold. I did not know if he held onto them or not, but if he did, it would be worth a small fortune now.

One day, I found out why Bernard guarded his comic books in that cardboard box so carefully. I was at the house with only Aunt Emma and Aunt Olivia. The boys were at football practice. I went into Bernard's room where he kept them underneath his bed and began looking at them. Hidden underneath all the comic books was a Playboy Magazine. I looked at it and saw the fold down nude picture of a pretty girl. I knew I had better not let Aunt Emma catch me looking at it or she would whip me, so I quickly put it back.

Ben asked me, "What did you learn from the other brother?"

"His name was Leonard, and he was quite an athlete. He taught me how to throw a football and how to pole vault. He was a star at quarterback in high school and a state champion in the pole vault."

I told them, "Leonard could make and shoot a sling shot better than anybody. He could shoot birds sitting on the electric lines or break bottles off a fence post on almost every shot."

As soon as I said that, I looked at Jeannie and noticed three treasured friends walking toward us who I had not seen in years. I told my children, "Here comes some friends I haven't seen in a long, long time. I want to visit with them, so you two go play or help Mr. Stevenson to allow me and your mother time to talk to them."

Our children went running off to another area in the cemetery to look for more adventure. Walking up to where Jeannie and I were three of my favorite people: Miss Sis, her daughter Mabel, and her brother, Howard Brown. Howard and Mabel were helping their mother, Miss Sis walk up the hill to where we were. I assumed they

47

have come to visit her husband's gravesite because the black cemetery is on the other side of the north fence.

As they walked up the hill to where we were, I noticed two things about them. First, they looked a little older, and the second thing I noticed about them was that they were smiling ear-to-ear. I hoped they were as glad to see me, as I was to see them.

# Chapter 4

## *Olivia's Surprise*

As I walked down the hill to greet them, I saw how frail Miss Sis had become. I remembered when I was a child how many times she used to call me Master Blake. I did not like her to call me "master," but I was told not to complain about it to her. It was not that she saw me as her master, but it was the way she was taught to speak to show respect. She humbly showed that type of respect to everyone; well, except for the people she did not respect, or to Olivia. I didn't understand why she showed such little respect for Olivia.

Miss Sis's daughter, Mabel, was a couple of years younger than Aunt Olivia and a couple of years older than Aunt Emma. Mabel and Miss Sis helped around Aunt Emma's house with the chores. Miss Sis felt obligated to help; she called it payback for Mr. Tom's kindness. Mr. Tom paid them some money for their help, but it was so little.

Before I was born, the parents of Aunt Olivia and Aunt Emma allowed Miss Sis and her husband, Mr. Israel to live on their place without paying any rent, and still do. They were considered sharecroppers, and just like everyone else who lived out in the countryside, they were very poor and struggled to make a living. All the country folks believed only the rich lived in town because they were the only ones who had the modern conveniences that country folks did not have.

Mabel had turned into a lovely lady. However, she never married. She had gone to college and had become a teacher and a counselor. She was a well-respected person in both the white and black communities. From what my mother told me, Mabel had offered to teach at the black college but she turned them down to help care for her mother after her father died. I never knew Miss Sis's husband, but they say he was a good, hardworking man.

My mother said a few years after Aunt Emma got back from the war, she gave the tenant house and fifteen acres of land to Miss Sis for ten dollars. Aunt Emma gave Miss Sis the house and property to show how much she loved and appreciated all the things Miss Sis had done for her and her family throughout her lifetime.

Howard, her son, was the same age as Bernard and Leonard. He wanted to go to college, but he could not bring himself to leave his mother by herself. When Aunt Olivia had her breakdown, Aunt Emma moved Miss Sis into the house to help her care for Olivia and the boys, which allowed Howard and Mabel to be able to go to college. Aunt Emma paid their way to go to college. It was unheard of in that time, for a white person to pay for a black person's college education. Howard and Emma did not want to take the money, but Miss Sis told them to take it as a love gift. Howard and Mabel felt comfortable enough to know their mother was in good hands with Aunt Emma.

Howard was a good athlete in college, even though he never played any sports in high school. After graduating he had become a coach at a neighboring high school in Mississippi. He was physically well built. I recalled that as a kid he used to wrestle both Bernard and Leonard at the same time and when he got them in an unbreakable hold he would make them say, "Captain Boss," the signal that meant they had given up! I don't know where he got it from, but Bernard and Leonard would wrestle me and make me say it, too.

As Jeannie walked close behind me, we continued to move toward Miss Sis, Mabel, and Howard. After a few steps Mabel and Howard stopped to allow Miss Sis to rest. She struggled with the walk over the thick St. Augustine grass in the cemetery, and she had become winded and needed to rest. I was taught to call her Miss Sis, but both Aunt Olivia and Aunt Emma called her Aunt Sis. I was not allowed to call her "Aunt Sis," but I felt exactly the same way they did about her. She was just like a favorite aunt to me too. Howard and Mabel called their mother, "Madea," it was a cultural term of endearment to show love and respect to their mother. Most black children in our area called their mothers "Madea" back then, and we still hear it used occasionally today.

As soon as I stood in front of Miss Sis, she held her arms out to me. I grabbed her, hugged her, and picked her up off the ground in great joy of seeing her again. It was good to see her once again with her two children.

Emma and I were Miss Sis's favorite people; we had a special bond. Miss Sis always preached to us to do what was right. Once a week, my mom would pick her up and bring her to our house to do what Miss Sis called, "her special jobs." Miss Sis came on Wednesdays, she would watch my brother and me, and in between keeping us from fighting one another, she would clean our house.

Sometimes when Miss Sis came, she would bring Mabel or Howard and we would play hide and seek, cowboy and Indians, or home run derby inside the dog yard. But she was mainly there to keep my brother and me straight. Whenever we misbehaved or did something wrong, she would discipline us with a switch, and then deliver a sermon about doing right instead of wrong.

Her sermonettes always ended with her hugging me and telling me one day I was going to be someone special and very important. She really knew how to make you feel loved, which made you want to do right, just for her.

After putting her back down on the ground and making sure she could stand on her own without falling, I lovingly told her, "You don't know how much I hoped you would come to the cemetery today. I guess you came to visit your Mr. Israel, didn't you?"

She replied to me in her old black dialect, "No's siree, Master Blake, you is wrong's as usual. I's came's just especially to see's you and then visit's Israel and my sweet girl Emma."

I eagerly told Miss Sis, "Just seeing you has made my day. I have someone here I want you to meet." I looked around for Jeannie as she was standing close behind me, hiding, embarrassed from all my outlandish antics. Hugging black people in public back then in the South would be considered a no-no.

I reached for Jeannie and pulled her in front of me. I said to her, "Come here woman, so I can introduce you to a very, very special person and her children."

Miss Sis interrupted me by saying sharply, "Boy, ain't you's got no manners, I's taught you's better than t'at."

Being slightly embarrassed, I apologized to Miss Sis, "Oh, I am so sorry Miss Sis, I got so excited seeing you and Mabel and Howard, and I just got carried away."

I happily said, "Miss Sis, this is my wonderful, wonderful wife, Jeannie. She is just like you: sweet, smart, and beautiful."

Then I pointed to my children who were still playing around the arch. "And those two wild Indians over there are our two children."

Miss Sis said to me, "Lordy Mercy boy, you's is done's well. Miss Jeannie is really beautiful. And I's know's when I's first laid eyes on t'em two chap's over there, they had's to be y'arn. They's is beautiful, too."

I introduced Jeannie to both Mabel and Howard. We all shook hands and hugged each other and I knew it must have made a spectacle, especially for 1973. But I did not care. It was so good to see them again because we had shared a lot of good times and some troubles together as I grew up.

After we had told one another what we had been doing with our lives in the last few years, Miss Sis asked me, "What's is you's Master Blake and Miss Jeannie been's talking so seriously about's over here at my's sweet girl, Emma's resting place?"

It shocked me how fast Miss Sis's manner changed from sheer joy to being so serious. But I recalled how she always was straight to the point with her questions. So I quickly replied, "I was telling Jeannie about how delightful Aunt Emma was to be around and about all the good times we had with her."

Miss Sis mumbled under her breath, "Yea's, some's of it's was good, but most's was bad, and all t'at came from t'at evil sister of hers. She brought's all of it on's to her and's everybody 'rounds her too. T'at is why my sweet girl Emma is laying there's right now."

I didn't really know what to say. It shocked me to hear her be so critical. There were some things I did not understand about what happened in Aunt Emma's family, and I truly wanted to know what happened. I did not discourage Miss Sis from talking, and I sensed neither would Mabel or Howard stop her, either. I knew both Mabel and Howard did not care too much for Aunt Olivia because she had been mean to both of them and their mother.

For years, I wanted to know the whole story, but I was too young to fully understand what had happened. I knew the three of them knew how it went down and why things happened the way they did. I let our conversion roll and said to her, "Yes, Miss Sis, you are right, as always."

Miss Sis continued talking, "You's cannot tell's my sweet girl Emma's story without's telling Olivia's story too's and w'at t'at girl did. My sweet girl Emma was a happy child, a happy girl. And then t'at's evil sister changed everything for her's. And I's believe's she did it's all to hurt's her. And she hurt's everyone else 'rounds her too. She killed's her Papa, just might's as well's have shoot's him in de' head."

By this time, both Mabel and Howard had tried to contain her, but she had said too much already. She sharply told her two children, "You hush's now and leave's me alone. I's been wantin' to tell's him t'is for years, cause I's know's how much he loved my sweet girl Emma, just like's we's all does."

I did not tell them out-loud, but I really did want to know the complete story. I had thought about what happened in that family often and inside of myself, I was yearning to know. To not cause Miss Sis to stop with her story, I responded to them politely by saying, "Go ahead and let Miss Sis tell me what she wants to."

Inside of me, I was glad someone was going to tell me. I wanted to know and she wanted to tell me that my opportunity had come.

Miss Sis started her story: "To know's why my sweet, girl Emma had's her whole life's taken from her, you's need's to know's what all Olivia did's to cause t'at's to happen.

"When's my sweet girl Emma was only eleven and's Olivia was fifteen, and I's want's to tell you t'at's Olivia was some pretty girl. All the boys came's 'round's and we's had's to run's 'em off with a stick. But there's was t'is Peddler that's came's by the house once a month. And he's had t'is boy, his son, about twent-one, I t'ink's he was, he was much older than's her. Well's, he's and Olivia would sneak's in the barn and play's in the hay, but what's they's were doing whatin' playing. Mabel see's them in there's. She tell's me what's they' 'tis doing.

"Olivia's Papa keep's telling her to stay's away from t'at boy, but she's not listen to her Papa. She tell's her Papa t'at she want's to go with him to marry's him. Her Papa tell's her, no way t'at could happen, t'at's she's too young's to marry. So one month's, she leave's with t'at boy, and it 'bout's to kill her Papa, her leavein' him with's out his permission. But t'at's not bother her. She t'inks she is too pretty and too big's to listen to her Papa. She t'inks she is old enough to do's what's she want's.

"For month's my sweet girl Emma want's to know's where her pretty sister is. No's one's tell's her, they don't's know's either. No's one know's for sure. So one's December night, 'de police drives up to 'de house and's they bring's Olivia home. 'De police only say's t'at she got off 'de bus with no way's home. They pick's her up and bring's her to her house.

"She tell's her Papa she not got's married, and t'at's was good. But what's she got's was pregnant. This is 'nother knife in her Papa's heart's, but she'd no's care. Three month's after she come's home she babie's two boys. She has twins. I's call's them 'double's trouble.' They's don't even look's 'de same's, but they's brothers. Olivia won'ts names 'de boys; so's her Papa name's them's for her. 'De older boy, he names Bernard and 'de younger one's he name's is Leonard. No's one know's why he's name's them two boys these names, but I know's."

Miss Sis continued, "This is when's all 'de bad things begin's. T'at evil girl bring's to everyone's nothing but's trouble and sadness. She's steals away my sweet girl Emma's happiness and she's kill's her Papa's heart. At one time's, Olivia was 'uh sweet's girl. Doe's anything for y'a, but's her beauty was a curse to her and everyone's 'rounds her. It's makes her think's whatever she does is good and right. But's it what'in, it was selfish and's evil."

Miss Sis added, "She even ruins t'em two boys 'cause of what's happens to her. She's so selfish. She cares 'bout no's one's, but's herself."

Miss Sis seemed not to be able to stop talking about Olivia's life. It was as if Miss Sis were trying to get something off her heart by telling us how she saw things. Miss Sis continued talking, "That's Olivia, she's 'de reason t'at her boy, Leonard is not's here today. She's not teach t'at boy nothing right. He's was just like's her in lots of ways."

Miss Sis looked around as if she did not realize where she was and said, "You's knows Master Blake, I's got low blood, don'ts you know's t'at?"

I told her, "Yes Miss Sis, I had heard that about you, and I know talking about this is probably not helping that problem at all, is it?"

Miss Sis looked me straight in the eye and told me, "You's right, but I's knows you's want's to know's and so's I's tells you. I's got's lots more to tell's, but I say's one more thang and I's must leave's. All those things t'hat happen's with my sweet girl Emma and her sister Olivia is something that's shouldn't happen's to no's one's family in a lifetime. It's bee's too much. But's you's know's it ain't nothing t'at happen to's them t'at can compare to what's happened at t'at funeral. It's all came's out at t'at funeral. T'ats was something else."

Miss Sis looked down at the ground for a minute or two like she was in a trance. Then she said, "But's I's better get's over to where's my Israel's is resting and visit's with him a short bit, and then's maybe I's come's back here to see's you. You's still a good boy, ain't you's?"

I offered to take her over to the black part of the cemetery but she defensively told me, "No, no Master Blake, I's get's Mabel to take's me. She like's to visit's too, but's I's be back in a while, so don't's you's leave's."

"Okay Miss Sis. It will give me time to talk to Howard about what kind of football season they had this year."

Mabel and Miss Sis left to where the gate was between the black and the white portion of the cemetery, and they went into that section. As I watched them move toward that part of the cemetery, I wondered what Jeannie thought about what Miss Sis had said about Emma and her family. Miss Sis was not very kind in her remarks about Aunt Olivia. Jeannie probably wished she had not come here with me to help clean up because all she had been hearing was my family's troubles.

I asked Howard how everything was going for him. He told me everything at school was great and they had had a successful season that year but were knocked out of the playoffs in the first round. Jeannie just listened. She really did not have anything to add to our conversation. So she dismissed herself to check on our children.

When she left, Howard began telling me about his mother, Miss Sis. He regretfully said, "Ever since Aunt Emma had passed, Madea had become bitter toward Miss Olivia. She blames her for Miss Emma leaving and her early death. Madea insists Olivia kept Miss Emma from having the happy life she felt she deserved. She also blames Miss Olivia for what happened to Leonard."

I told Howard, "I understand what you are saying, and I understand how Miss Sis feels toward Aunt Emma. Your mother thought the sun rose and set on Aunt Emma. I did too, and so did many other people."

Howard agreed and said, "That is true, those two were good for each other. Both Madea and Emma saw life much in the same way. Miss Emma seemed to please my Mother in everything she did. My mother always wanted everybody to act right and treat each other right; Miss Emma wanted that, too. But to her, it seemed Miss Olivia and Leonard just couldn't do what was right. And their selfish choices seemed to creep into what others did."

59

My mind began to roam as I thought about the times we used to get together and play football over at the Dupre's house right before the Gillett Friday Night Fights. On Friday nights, the Dupre's would invite Olivia and her two boys over to watch the fights on their TV. The Dupre's were the only family in our neighborhood who had a TV. I was lucky that I lived next door to them and came over most evenings to watch TV.

The Dupre's had a daughter named Linda Kaye. Boy oh boy, was she a beauty queen. She was beautiful in every way. She had long black hair, cold steel blue eyes, and she was built very nicely. She was so nice to me. She was a baton-twirling champion and was the featured twirler in the high school band.

Olivia's boys usually came early so we could play football. Most of the time they brought Howard to make the sides even. Usually, it was me and Bernard against Leonard and Howard. Occasionally, Mr. Dupre would come and play and he would bring Linda Kaye too. When she played, we had to play touch. We had to be very careful not to touch her in the wrong places.

Howard would never touch her. He would try to scare her out of bounds. Bernard treated her like a lady. Leonard, though, took every opportunity to touch her anywhere he liked, even in her private areas, with her Dad there watching.

Mr. Dupre admired Leonard's athletic ability because he was a good athlete. He was fast, could pitch a baseball, throw a football, pole vault, and shoot a basketball. I assumed Mr. Dupre invited them over because he always wanted a son who would be an athlete, so he sort of adopted Bernard and Leonard as his boys.

Thinking about those times caused me to ask Howard, "Do you remember all the times we played football on those Friday afternoons at the Dupre's house, and all the fun we had playing in their hayloft?"

Howard quickly replied, "Oh yeah, we did have fun. But I didn't like being around Leonard. I actually hated being on Leonard's team, too. You couldn't trust him in anything."

I asked him, "I didn't know you felt that way. Why was that?"

Howard cautiously told me, "Oh, I got plenty of reason to feel that way. One day Leonard and I came to your house with Madea to help her. You probably don't remember, but your mom wanted us to clean out a Chimney Sweep nest. She told us the day before she would borrow a long bamboo cane Mr. Dupre had so we could break the nest up and push the twigs down into the fireplace to be hauled off. She said the cane would be at your house, behind the work shed; waiting for us."

Howard continued, "When I went to get the cane, I couldn't find it. I looked around for it but it couldn't be found. Leonard said she probably forgot to get it, but he knew where it was. It was in the front crib in the Dupre's big barn. He made a big deal about telling me he was not going to get it."

Howard said meekly, "Nobody wanted to argue with Leonard, you could never win an argument with him because he was too hard-headed to reason with. I volunteered to go get it. I went across the pasture and climbed the wooden fence in front of the barn to go into the barn to get the cane."

Howard swiftly said, "Well as soon as I got half way inside the pen, to almost where the cedar tree was, all of a sudden this Brahma bull came from under the barn and started snorting and pawing the ground at me. Even though it was a calf, that thing weighed about a thousand pounds and I knew if I ran, he would run me down and gore me. So, I stayed behind the tree. My hiding was not good enough for that bull: he wanted me. He chased me around and around that tree and tried his best to gore me."

Howard said, "I got tired, trying to stay away from him, but I kept stumbling over the roots knowing if I fell, he would kill me. I was so tired that I even considered giving up."

Howard's spirit lifted. He said, "Thank God David Tate came to check on Mr. Dupre's quarter horse. His mare was expecting a colt, and David saw me running from the bull, trying to keep him from goring me. David got mad at the bull. He jumped in the pen with the bull and started hollering and waving his arms to get the bull's attention off of me and onto him.

"David told me quietly, as not to upset the bull, 'When the bull turns to face him, run to the fence and jump over it.' He kept yelling at the bull and when the bull turned and faced David, I ran and climbed over that fence as fast as I could."

I asked Howard, "Did David run too?"

Howard said, "No he did something very bizarre. When the bull saw me running, he ran toward me, but I had already climbed the fence and was hollering at him and throwing rocks at him so David could get out."

Again, I asked, "Did David get out?"

Howard said, "No, he stayed in the pen with the bull! The bull circled back after chasing me and charged at David. But David didn't run. He charged back at the bull! I thought he was going to be killed. When the bull got close enough, David jumped up and kicked that bull with his boot heel right between the eyes. The bull fell straight to the ground and just laid there."

I told Howard, "Oh, you are making all that up."

Howard, thinking I did not believe him, answered, "That was no lie, it happened just like that and it could have been worse. I told David he'd saved my life, but he shrugged my thanks off. He said I could have done it too, because the bull was young and tired. But I knew the bull was not as tired as I was. I was glad David showed up when he did."

After saying that, Howard shared other information he felt I needed to understand why he felt the way he did toward Leonard. "David told me, he had brought the cane over to your mother's house yesterday. He said he told both Bernard and Leonard the day before not to come to the big barn because there was a wild young bull in the pen, and it could seriously hurt them."

I paused before I said anything. "It sounds to me like Leonard tried to set you up to get you hurt."

Howard said in agreement with me, "Yes, he lied to me about the cane so I would get in the pen with that wild animal and get hurt. When I got back to your mother's house, I found the cane stuck up against the back of a tree. Leonard had hid it. He didn't even have the guts to stick around after I came back, he lied and told Madea he had to be somewhere, and he left. I guess it was best he did leave because after what David told me, I wanted to beat the daylights out of him, and would have if he'd stayed."

Howard told me, "That's not all. Leonard was always trying to hurt me when we played football. He would throw the ball hard to me. He was trying to break my fingers. He thought it was funny, but I didn't. That boy was as mean as his mama was to me. Both of them would call me "nigger" whenever no one else was around. You know Miss Emma would never allow that to happen."

I told Howard, "I don't remember all that. I just thought you couldn't catch very well."

We both laughed and he said, "Well, you were too young to know what was really going on."

I quickly told him, "Oh no! I wasn't too young to know how much y'all like to sit up there in the hayloft and look at Linda Kaye as she twirled her baton, and how Y'all talked about her."

Howard quickly said to me in a very serious tone, "You might remember we looked at her, but only Leonard and Bernard talked about her. I never did, not me, never. But what you didn't understand was what Leonard talked about doing to Linda Kaye and what it eventually led to."

I didn't know where Howard was going with his last statement, but he now had my full attention, so I asked him: "What are you talking about?"

Howard said, "Do you remember what they told you happened to Leonard that caused him to be killed?"

I said yes, hesitantly. "Pretty much so, I guess. He got killed in a car wreck because he ran off the side of the road."

Howard said, "That was just part of the story they wanted us to know. There was a lot more to the story that they didn't want us to know. I honestly believe part of it came from those sexual things he talked about doing with Linda Kaye. It led to those things he did to that girl."

I still didn't understand what Howard was trying to tell me and I questioned him, "What girl? My Mom said he was killed in a car wreck. There was no mention of any girl with him that I remember. It was just him."

Howard said, "The car wreck was just one part of what happened before the wreck. He was running from the law for something he did which caused him to lose control and be killed."

I asked Howard, "What did Leonard do to cause him to be killed in that wreck?"

Howard did not hesitate to answer my question. He told me, "He sexually attacked the McKenzie girl and he was running from the police."

What Howard said was a complete shock to me because I knew nothing about it. I asked Howard, "Who told you that? I never heard of this before, are you sure his death happened because he was running from the law because of some attack he made on a girl?"

Howard replied to me, "Bernard told me about it. He found out about it a couple of months after the wreck from the sheriff's daughter. They told him the same thing they told you and me, but they didn't tell us all of it. They tried to protect everybody who was involved in that incident: the girl, her family, your family, and the community. You know how it was back then. I don't even think Miss Olivia or Bernard knew the whole story."

I thought about what he said a moment and asked Howard, "I wonder who's idea it was to cover it up?"

Howard quickly answered my question and said, "From what Bernard heard, it was Miss Emma. Somehow she convinced the police, the girl's family, the coroner, and the DA it would be best to have everyone believe that Leonard died in a crash and not ever mention the girl."

Howard said, "Miss Emma reasoned since Leonard, who was the guilty party, had already been judged and punished by God. By not saying anything about the attack, it would be best for the girl's reputation. It would help her to overcome the shock and embarrassment of what had happened to her and allow it to fade more easily from her memory. Miss Emma said no one needed to know what happened. She convinced everyone that all it would do was ruin a lot of lives unnecessarily."

Still in shock of what I was hearing, I said, "All this is so unbelievable. It must have worked because as best as I can remember, Jamie McKenzie never seemed to me to be any different after Leonard's death."

Howard replied, "Well, you know how everyone respected Miss Emma and what she had to say. It seemed she always knew what would be best. It was like she had a crystal ball and could see into the future, even at that early age."

I reacted to Howard's response, "Yeah, you're right, Howard. She was wise beyond her years. She always seemed to know the best way to right a wrong."

Howard responded by saying, "Yeah, it is such a shame Miss Emma did not have a crystal ball to see what was going to happen to her and David in the future. I never did get to thank David for saving my life."

I really was not exactly sure what Howard was talking about and I assumed it was about David leaving, so I said to him cautiously, "Yes, it is a shame he is not here for you to tell him; I am sure a lot of people miss him."

Howard said to me, "A lot of people liked David, but I will never forget what happened at that funeral, people still talk about it. It was like nothing I ever saw before."

I was unsure of what Howard meant, so I did not respond to his statement. I just kept quiet.

Howard looked back toward where Miss Mildred Law had gone to visit her parent's gravesite, and he told me teasingly, "Well,

well look who's coming. You are about to have company. It's Miss Mildred Law coming toward us with your wife."

Howard hurriedly said, "I think I will go check on Madea and help Mabel with her because I know for sure Miss Mildred Law is going to fuss at me and say I need to take my career more seriously and prepare my students to get ready for college. I know she's right, but I just don't want to hear it again."

Howard started to leave, but stopped to say to me, "I want to tell you this before I go. You have been a good friend to Mabel and me, and I appreciate that. Madea . . . she thinks of you as her own. To her, there is no one in the world as good as you. And you are a good man, and your family has been good to my family. You take care of yourself, and if I don't see you again, I wish you well."

# Chapter 5

## *The Way It Was*

When Jeannie and Miss Mildred Law arrived, Miss Mildred Law directed me, "Blake, get that lawn chair over there so I can sit down. I have been standing up too long, and I need to rest my feet."

Whenever Miss Mildred Law asked you to do something, you didn't make her wait. You immediately did it. I readily said her, "Yes ma'am, I will be right back with it."

I had brought four aluminum folding chairs and set them against a tall head stone in case someone needed to sit and rest. Some of our older generation looked down on sitting or standing on headstones. I hurriedly went to get them and set all four of them up. Jeannie was pleased when I helped Miss Mildred Law first and then her.

Miss Mildred Law quickly stated, "I want to say this before I begin telling y'all anything about Emma and myself. I want you and Blake to know what my and Emma's life motto is, 'To live life like you are making a statement.' We both tried to do that with our lives. Emma did it without any question, and I am still working on it."

One thing I learned from being in Miss Mildred Law's class was the less you talked, the more she would talk on the subject. Miss Mildred Law loved to talk . . . believe me she did. There was nothing worse than to hear someone in her class ask her an annoying question. She would go off on them. Her tirade usually lasted the rest of the class time. I did not want that to happen today because of the short time I knew we would spend with her.

I let Jeannie and Miss Mildred Law do all the talking. And I didn't want to bring any of her wrath onto me either.

The main reason I would be quiet was I wanted to hear Miss Mildred Law's memories of her and Aunt Emma. I knew they would be great, because both of those two ladies were grand ladies.

Jeannie swiftly started the conversation by asking her, "Tell me what you did as children. The reason I'm asking is so I can compare it to what we did as children."

Miss Mildred Law replied, "Oh honey, I really doubt your childhood was anything like ours. You got to remember we were in a depression back then. There was rationing and such tightness with everything, and everyone had so very little. But you know as kids, we never realized we were poor. We thought it was how life was for everyone. Our parents never made it seem any other way. I guess it was their way of making us believe we had everything . . . and we thought we did."

Miss Mildred Law continued, "As kids, we were really blessed to live where we did. We lived away from town and in the country, and we had friends close to our age who lived nearby. We were not just friends, but best friends. In fact, there were four of us, and we were close and still are. It was me and Emma, and the two Whitmore girls. One was a year older than us, and her name was Sophie. Her younger sister was named Mary Lou, a year younger than Emma and me. We got together every chance we could."

I hoped that by asking her about her past we were not stirring up bad memories as to cause her any pain. She continued telling us, "We played the regular things kids did back then with dolls, climbed trees, put puzzles together, played dress up, had slumber parties at each other's house. We even played school, where I was the teacher. They didn't like that too much, but I loved being in charge. Emma loved playing the doctor and nursing on all of us. Almost everything we did was outside. No way would any of our mothers let us play in the house and mess it up."

Jeannie asked, "What about Aunt Emma's sister, Olivia? Did she play with y'all too?

Miss Mildred Law abruptly answered, "Oh no Sweetie, Olivia thought she was too pretty, or too good, to associate herself with us 'little brats,' as she called us. Besides, she was four years older than us."

Miss Mildred deliberated before she continued, "Yes, I remember the time we put on a play, or as Sophie called it, 'a Production.' We put it on for the whole neighborhood to come and watch."

Miss Mildred Law laughed as she recalled the events of that play. "Yes, I can laugh now, but I couldn't back then. It was a disaster, and I still believe to this day that Olivia caused it to be one, too. She sabotaged it, and we four girls got the blame for it."

Jeannie, wondering why they got blame for a calamity caused by someone else, asked, "What do you mean you got the blame? Wasn't it a play that you four girls put on?

Miss Mildred Law said reluctantly, "Yes, honey it was. But what happened during that play was not part of it. What happened was none of our doing. However, it got us into big trouble."

Surprised, Jeannie asked, "What happened?"

Miss Mildred Law told us, "We four girls worked hard for a month building a set for a Robin Hood play in Mr. Tom's barn. We built and painted a castle set and moved bales of hay to create a stage. We cut tree branches and hauled them to the barn to represent the forest. It was a lot of hard work for twelve-year-old girls. I was the Sheriff and Emma was the lady Marian. Sophie was Robin Hood, and Mary Lou was Little John. We even built benches for the audience to sit on. Of course, Mr. Tom helped us.

"Our final scene was to be Robin Hood's band in the forest robbing the sheriff for his tax money to give to the poor. At the end of the play, Sophie was to shoot a magical arrow into the sky to make it sprinkle rain so the Sheriff would not be able to follow our trail. We had twelve buckets with water hung on the beams above us to make it sprinkle as our climaxing act. Sophie was to shoot the arrow. Mary Lou was to pull a hidden rope to make the buckets sprinkle through screen wire over us. However, someone had moved the buckets, and when Mary Lou pulled the rope it rained just fine, but it rained only on our audience instead of us. And it was not a sprinkling rain through the screen wire. It drenched them," said Miss Mildred Law.

I couldn't help myself as I laughed, and neither could Jeannie. Miss Mildred looked at us and dejectedly said, "Yeah, it's funny, but it wasn't to my father, or to the Whitmore's parents, nor to the twenty people there who had dressed up in their Sunday best. It soaked most of them. Our parents were so embarrassed, everyone thought we intentionally soaked them as a practical joke."

Jeannie and I were still laughing at the story and I saw Miss Mildred crack a smile, too. She began to laugh. "Yes, I can laugh now, but it wasn't funny then. I still believe Olivia moved those buckets to make us look bad, and it worked. We all got whippings and other punishments."

Miss Mildred Law continued, "I also remember the first day we turned teen-agers. It was at our thirteenth birthday party. Emma and I always had our birthday parties together on the same day. My mother did that for us since Emma did not have a mother to do give her one. Anyway, that was the day Emma ended our childhood days."

Jeannie, perplexed, asked, "How can anyone end someone's childhood? How did she do that, Miss Mildred?"

Miss Mildred Law continued. "Suddenly, on our thirteenth birthday, Emma fell in love. Our play days were over and Emma moved us into becoming young ladies before our time."

I never thought thirteen-year-old girls could be in love or become young ladies that soon; it stunned me. Then, for my Aunt Emma to be in love with anybody, especially at that young of an age, astonished me. Hearing that didn't seem to bother Jeannie, who acted as if it was supposed to happen at that age. But she still questioned Miss Mildred Law about it, saying, "I'm sure it was just a teenage crush, right?"

Miss Mildred Law turned her attention away from us, looked straight at Aunt Emma's grave stone, and made this declaration: "Oh, if only it would have been that way, she might still be here today."

Then she said, suddenly, "No, she really and truly fell in love with a boy. It was on our thirteenth birthday. There was no such term to her as teenage crush. She was in love for real and Emma thought it was for forever."

Miss Mildred Law said to me and Jeannie in a serious tone, "She looked at that boy the entire time he was at the party. I couldn't get her attention away from him until after we ate some cake and I angrily asked her, 'What is wrong with you?'

"She never looked at me as she turned all her attention back toward the boy and told me with her love sick eyes, 'Nothing Mildred, nothing at all. I am going to be fine for the rest of my life.'"

Miss Mildred Law kept surprising us with even more astonishing statements about Aunt Emma as she told us, "Emma looked at that boy the same way every day after our thirteenth birthday. It only stopped years later when she left. All through her teen years and even after she graduated, she noticed no one in all the world of the male gender, except David. She told me the next day after our birthday party that he was going to be her husband. She meant it, too... It could have happened... No, it should have happened."

Jeannie gloomily observed Miss Mildred Law. "You make it sound like she just abandoned you and forgot all about being friends with you girls."

Miss Mildred adds, "No, no, Darling! I didn't mean it to come out that way. We were always great friends. It was only when he came around. Neither I nor anyone else was in the picture for Emma, not until he disappeared. I was friends with him, too, and he was a nice boy. Emma did everything she could to put them together, and it was difficult to separate them once they were together."

Jeannie asked Miss Mildred Law, "Who was he? Did Blake know him?

Miss Mildred Law answered, "Yes, Blake does, it was David Tate. Blake, you met him at the funeral, didn't you? If you didn't, I am quite sure he made an impression on you from what happened at the funeral. That was quite a show he put on. One nobody will ever forget, wasn't it?"

I answered, "Yes ma'am, I did see him at the funeral, and what happened was quite unusual."

I had no idea Aunt Emma and David Tate were ever close, especially not as a romantic couple as kids. All I had ever heard about him was that he had left and come back to the funeral. It was the only time I remember ever seeing him. He made quite an impression on me and everybody else there, too. It was a complete shock to me, those two liking each other, and I knew Jeannie had no idea who Miss Mildred Law was talking about. I hadn't known him well enough to describe him to her.

Miss Mildred Law realized Jeannie needed a better understanding of who David was and told her, "I will tell you more about David later, after I tell you a little more of our teen years. I can proudly say this about our community and our school system: we received a good education and we still offer one today. The teachers and administration are dedicated to make that happen. When we went out into the world, it became quite evident how good our teachers had prepared us for life."

Miss Mildred Law did not sugar-coat anything that happened back when she, Emma, Sophie, and Mary Lou were youngsters. She told things like they were. As she continued her story about their school days, she said, "Emma's romance was not like the romances of today, where anything goes. Today it's free love, dope smoking, and hippies doing anything and everything they want to. They only do that to prove to their parents they are liberated from them. Hell, when they run out of money, who do they come crawling back too? Their parents. And they call themselves liberated. The only ones who believe they are liberated are themselves, they are just deceiving themselves.

"Baby doll, let me tell you how it was. As teens, we had daily chores to do. We did them in the morning, and more in the afternoon. Our fathers usually had a job or worked all day on the farm. Our mothers stayed home to tend to the kids and the house. They worked six days a week and when Sundays came it was a day of rest for the family to spend quality time together or at church. If a teen could find a job or some way to make some money, it would go to the family and not for them to spend on themselves. We were in tough times back then. Dang it, we were in a depression and we all felt it," said Miss Mildred Law.

"There was supposed to be no pre-marital sex back then either, just marriage. Girls seldom could date, and if they did, it wasn't until they turned sixteen or older. Then you had to be home early. Parents actually met the young man, and he had better have good manners and bring their daughter home at the agreed upon time. She had better look as good as she did when she left the house, or the young man would never be allowed to date the young lady again."

Miss Mildred Law said candidly, "Yes . . . don't misunderstand me, there were girls who didn't follow the norm and got pregnant. Usually they were whisked away to relatives or to an unwed mother home in another state for a year. Girls who smoked or had pre-marital sex got a bad reputation; they were called 'easy.' Other teens and their neighbors would snub them because they didn't want people to think they were like them.

"Kids didn't have cars back then either. If they went on a date, usually one of their fathers would drive them to where they were going, and come back to pick them up to bring them straight home. There was no place for hanky-panky. There wasn't any living together back then either. It was not like we see today. You know how it is. Our society has no morals, and it is truly a shame."

Miss Mildred Law smiled and said shrewdly to us, "I know you are thinking we did nothing and it was so boring back then. That is what you are thinking, isn't it? I can tell."

Jeannie didn't really know how to answer her, but she said very diplomatically, "I am sure that y'all found many wonderful things to do and had all kinds of fun."

Miss Mildred Law coolly replied, "Anything we did out of the ordinary was great. All four of us girls entertained one other so much that we didn't have time to be bored."

Jeannie asked, "What kinds of things did y'all do?"

Miss Mildred began telling Jeannie about all the things they did as youths. "I am sure you will think the things we did were strange as compared by today's standards. One reason why is because kids have cars today. All we had were horses. They were our vehicle to go places. We would ride to town and go visit our friends on them. We used them to take us to the river to swim, and we even had dates on them. Those horses gave us the freedom to explore our world away from home."

Miss Mildred Law eagerly said, "Occasionally we would be invited to go to Baton Rouge or New Orleans, of course not on horseback, but in a car. Oh, how we loved to go shopping in Baton Rouge on 3rd Street. That was a big thing. It was like we were going to New York City. We didn't go to the city much because no one had any money. We only went when one of our mothers needed something special, like a dress or a pair of shoes. Then they would take all four of us girls with them for a day in the city.

"We thought we were big stuff going to the city to shop. Sometimes we were treated to the soda fountain at the TG&Y. We considered that neat. We were so silly, flirting with the soda jerk behind the counter, trying to impress him and make him think we were older than we looked. Those trips usually only happened when Sophie's mother took us. Her dad had a good paying job at a plant, and they could afford a little luxury now and then," said Miss Mildred Law.

"In high school we attended as many sporting events as we could. The sporting events back then all happened during the daytime and not at night. There was no lighting on the football field and we did not even have a gymnasium. It gave us an opportunity to meet and become friends with other kids from other towns," said Miss Mildred Law.

"Going to church was a major part of our social activities too. Almost every kid came to church on Sunday because they had a lot of activities there. We had dinner on the ground, revivals, sing fests, hay-rides, and wiener roasts. They all were fun, and gave us the opportunity to find out who we were and what we could do," said Miss Mildred Law.

Miss Mildred Law turned her head in the direction of another area in the cemetery, and held her eyes there for about twenty seconds and said to us, "I remember one time, we were all around sixteen then, when we were at a revival at church when Sophie told us this fantastic, unbelievable story. I am still not sure I believe all of it was true. It was on a Saturday night revival meeting at our church. They usually lasted four to five hours. She'd left the main sanctuary to help watch the small children in the Nursery. The little kids were not old enough to understand the preaching, so we would sit with them."

Miss Mildred Law continued, "On the way to the Nursery, a young man, eighteen or nineteen, a stranger, came into the hall as Sophie was on her way to the Nursery and stopped her. Sophie said he introduced himself as Grady, and he told her he had been watching her because she was the most beautiful and graceful young lady in the church."

Miss Mildred Law wanted to make this view clear to us about Sophie's beauty, saying, "Now Sophie was cute, but she was a mile away from being beautiful. She did have a good figure and was well developed in those areas that boys liked. She looked older than she was. But in no way was she as beautiful as she made out he said she was. She was no Olivia or Emma."

Miss Mildred Law said, "I still doubt her story, but Sophie said this boy, Grady, convinced her to go on a date so he would be able to enter a dance contest. He wanted her to leave church and go with him to the dance. He promised he would have her back before the revival service was over. He promised her it was all innocent and they would have a good time with no strings attached.

"She told us, at first she was not sure she could trust him, but somehow she felt in her heart she could. Then she mentions the most interesting fact. He was good looking and that one fact made Sophie say, 'What the hell, I may never get another chance like this again in my whole life.' So she agreed to go with him," said Miss Mildred Law, apprehensively.

Jeannie interrupted: "Why in the world would she ever agree to go. I would be scared to death he was luring me into something that would later cause me to be in serious trouble."

Miss Mildred Law paused a moment, and you could see her mind drift. She mumbled to us, "You want to know something? She was right in saying she might never get the chance to do it again. We didn't realize it then, but she was right. You have to understand how we young girls thought back then. We spent a lot of time together talking about romance, having boyfriends, and how it would be to have them kiss us and do other things with us. Usually it was the only excitement we could generate, as all our romances had only been in our imaginations."

Miss Mildred Law looked at me as if she was not sure she needed to say this, but she allowed her thoughts to become words, "Some of the things we thought about doing with boys were not very ladylike. We discussed them among ourselves because we didn't have a clue as to what went on. Back then, no adult or older young person told girls anything about kissing, hugging, or having any physical touching with the opposite sex, let alone telling you about sex. A mother might tell her daughter about that . . . maybe the night before her wedding, if she told her anything at all.

"The only sex education we got came from the books we read or from listening to the girls who were easy. We couldn't be sure they knew either, from all we knew, they could be lying to us. Romance always was a great mystery, so all we could do was fantasize about it among ourselves," said Miss Mildred Law.

"If we talked or day-dreamed about those types of things, we were told by our preacher that we would end up in hell. Hell, we were just four dumb girls looking for any romance," said Miss Mildred Law.

Miss Mildred Law continued telling about Sophie's date, "Sophie said when they got outside his to car, she found it was a beat up old jalopy, with no top. To make matters worse, there was another couple in the front seat. They were making out in the church's parking lot. Sophie called it 'submarine watching.' Later, I found out that was a code name used by kids meaning they were ducking down like a submarine so no one would see them making out.

"Sophie said when she first saw the other couple, she had second thoughts and wanted to go back, thinking it might not be such a good idea to go with him. When they reached the car, she told the boy she needed to go back," said Miss Mildred Law.

"That was when the girl in the front seat heard what Sophie told Grady. The girl in the front seat told him sneeringly, 'Grady, I knew you couldn't get someone to come with you. Now we can't get in the contest because we don't have two couples. You are such a loser . . . as always.'

"Later on in the night, Sophie found out the boy had a date with another girl and the girl's father would not let her go with him because of the bad reputation of the girl in the front seat. The girl was known as an 'easy girl,' and the other girl's dad knew it and had refused to let her go with him," said Miss Mildred Law.

"Sophie recognized how degraded this girl had made both boys feel. It rubbed Sophie the wrong way. The girl in the front seat was making fun of them and treating them like failures. Sophie said she went into her acting mode, directing her hostility toward the girl in the front seat, "Oh no, you misunderstood me, honey. I meant, I need to go back to get my purse because I left it inside on the church's pew."

Miss Mildred Law said, "When she said that, it stunned them all, and Sophie continued her act by grabbing the boy's arm and pulling him toward her and she gave Grady a peck on the cheek and said, "I'll be right back. Y'all wait for me now.

"Sophie told us the way the girl was making fun of Grady had made her mad. She didn't know the whole story yet but she felt sorry for him, and the girl's shaming actions had made her change her mind and go with them," Miss Mildred Law told us.

"By this time Grady realized what Sophie was doing, and he began to play along with her. 'Oh, you don't need to go back to get your purse, you can pick it up when we come back. I got all the money we will need.'"

Miss Mildred Law continued, "Sophie said she was happy Grady said that because she didn't bring a purse to church anyway. Sophie turned to Grady, smiled, and said, 'Okay then! We're off.' They climbed into the back seat and sat real close to each other as they left the church's parking lot."

Miss Mildred Law smiled as she recounted as Sophie told them what happened later and she said, "As they drove to town where the dance was, she and Grady never said a word to each other. They just looked into each other's eyes and let their eyes do all the talking. Sophie said she felt as if she had known Grady all his life, and she unexpectedly felt comfortable and safe with him. She told us Grady had held her hand and squeezed it gently as they continue to look at each other during the entire ride to the dance.

"When they arrived at the dance, she found they had to have two couples to enter the dance competition. Sophie assumed that was why Grady came into the church to find a date. They wanted to be in the competition and needed two couples," said Miss Mildred Law.

"Sophie said they chose to sit at a table near the door in the corner away from the bandstand. She said the girls sat against the wall while the boys stood in the middle so they could watch the dancers. Grady did not want to be too close to the music or they would not have been able to hear one another when they talked," said Miss Mildred Law.

"Sophie said Grady was a complete gentleman the entire night. He bought her drinks, soft drinks, of course, and they talked about who they knew as mutual acquaintances. They only knew two or three mutual people because Grady was three years older than Sophie, and he was from another town," continued Miss Mildred Law.

As Miss Mildred Law spoke about Sophie's date, she seemed to treasure it all. It was amazing to me how she vividly recalled what was said, "Grady thanked Sophie for the act she put on at the church. He said her ingenious silliness was delightfully funny. He told Sophie the girl in the front seat was his sister, and she always was putting him down in front of others. He apologized to Sophie for her behavior, then he laughed and told Sophie the way she defended him really put his sister in her place."

Miss Mildred Law said, "Sophie said Grady was a good dancer, even though she was not very good with the popular dances. Grady was patient with her and showed her the right steps so she could enjoy dancing with him."

Miss Mildred Law stood up to stretch her legs. "When we were young, the only time any of us girls danced was when our parents were not around, then we would turn the radio on and dance. If they ever caught us dancing, it was considered such a deadly sin. The kids were told it would sent them straight to hell. We didn't know any dance moves. The only dance moves we saw was when we went to the movies."

Jeannie asked, "Were they in the dance contest?"

Miss Mildred Law said, "No baby doll, Grady did pay the money to enter it, but they did not compete. He had asked her if she wanted to compete, but Sophie said she would embarrass him and she did not want that to happen. Grady did not place Sophie in an embarrassing position, and decided not to participate. However, the couple they rode with did participate."

Miss Mildred Law's disposition changed to disappointment as she told Jeannie, "Sophie got upset because all the unattached girls kept coming up to Grady, asking him to dance. Grady refused every one of them, and after a while, he became aggravated at them. He asked Sophie if she wanted to go outside for some air. Sophie agreed and they went outside.

"Sophie said Grady wanted to know everything about her. What she liked to do, what her favorite color was, who her favorite actress was, and all about her family. It seemed Grady was genuinely interested in everything about her. Grady never made any advances toward her in any way. He was the perfect gentleman, which I believed frustrated Sophie.

"They went back inside and danced a few more dances. The time slipped away, and Grady told Sophie it was time to take her back. The other boy and his sister were still in the contest, but Grady and Sophie left the dance and headed back to the church.

"Grady brought Sophie to the side of the church, they parked close to where they came out together. Grady held hands as he walked her to the door. When they arrived at the door, out pops Sophie's younger sister, Mary Lou," said Miss Mildred Law.

"Mary Lou was shocked to see Sophie with a boy. Wondering who he was, she said, 'Where have you been, Sophie? I needed your help with these kids. I couldn't come to find you because I had no one else to watch them?'" Miss Mildred Law said.

"If Mary Lou had not seen Grady with her at the church holding hands, I would not have ever believed any of Sophie's story.

"Sophie told Mary Lou to go back in and that she would come to take over shortly. Mary Lou left Sophie and Grady alone. Grady told Sophie he had a great time, and he had appreciated her trusting him and helping him out. He told Sophie she was a special young lady who deserved someone nice in her life. He hoped she would find him real soon," said Miss Mildred Law.

"Sophie was flattered and told him, it was a special time for her, like a dream come true for her. 'I had so much fun being with you, and you too are special,'" said Miss Mildred Law.

"Sophie said Grady leaned forward, put his arms around her, and kissed her goodbye. As he turned and walked back to the car, she waited to see if he would turn to look at her, one last time. He didn't and disappeared into the darkness," said Miss Mildred Law.

Jeannie asked, "Did they ever get together again?"

Jeannie could tell her question oddly seemed to upset Miss Mildred Law. "No, honey-child. But we girls saw Grady a few years later after the war. He had not married, and I am not sure that even today he is married."

Miss Mildred Law continued, "Word spread throughout the young people in the church that Sophie had met a boy. No one knew she left the service. They all supposed this boy was at the service. After the service, we four girls met in the parking lot and Sophie would not tell us anything. She said we would meet at noon the next day at Emma's barn. Then she would tell us everything that happened."

Miss Mildred Law said, "The next day couldn't come quick enough for us. I got up at the crack of dawn, and it was my day to sleep late. On Saturday, my dad would let me sleep to 7:00 a.m., but that morning I was up so early that my parents knew something was going on. They never questioned me, but when they saw I was doing my Saturday chores without being told, they knew I had other plans for the day. I'm sure it was the same for the other girls, too.

"We all arrived at the barn before noon and Sophie came fashionably later than us because she had the information we wanted to know. We knew it was going to be colorful because Sophie couldn't wipe the smile she had off of her face as she walked up. None of us had had our first kiss or even been in a romantic situation. We had talked about it, and we wondered who would be first. We all believed it would be Emma because she was prettier than the rest of us, but it did not happen that way," beamed Miss Mildred Law. "Sophie was more modest about being the first to be kissed. If it were to be me, I would have rubbed it in."

Miss Mildred Law laughed heartily after saying that. It was unusual to see her laugh that way, because she was always so serious. It reminded me of the times I had seen her and Aunt Emma acting like teenagers. I think Jeannie reminded Miss Mildred Law a lot of Aunt Emma, and it made her feel at ease. Seeing how Miss Mildred

Law opened her life up to us and listening to her insights made me understand how people thought life was to be lived at the time I grew up. It made me appreciate them much more than I already did.

Miss Mildred Law added, "Sophie summed it up for us, telling us it was like a dream, she could not believe she had gone with him to the dance, but she was glad she had. And we all were glad for her, too.

"We asked Sophie so many questions, but the main thing we all wanted to know was whether he was a good kisser. Sophie couldn't honestly tell us because she had nothing to compare it to. She had never kissed a boy before. It was a great achievement for all of us because it gave us hope that maybe one day, we too might share in a romantic experience," said Miss Mildred Law.

"I remember exactly what Emma said at the end of our meeting in the barn loft after our excitement subsided and we were about to leave. Emma shared a retort about Sophie's first kiss, 'Blessings fall into the laps of the good,'" said Miss Mildred Law.

Miss Mildred Law paused before she said, "It seems like it happened yesterday. Emma's retorts seem to capture the moment. Sometimes she was funny, and sometimes she was serious. This time she used one of her retorts because she was happy for Sophie. We all were, and we were also a little envious, too."

# Chapter 6

## *Romance and Adventure*

"Oh, Jeannie I am so sorry I got away from telling you about Emma and all us girls. My memories of Sophie flooded my mind. It made me realize how much I miss that girl. She was always so much fun to be around," stated Miss Mildred Law.

Jeannie said, "There is no need to apologize to me Miss Mildred. You tell me whatever you like. It's all so amazing to me to hear about your lives."

Miss Mildred Law said to Jeannie, "No, no. I want to now tell you about Emma and David. They were quite the couple. Emma tried to put them together at every opportunity. Emma's father, Mr. Tom, thought she could do much better in choosing a boyfriend than David. He wanted her to stay away from him.

"David was not from our area. He was a city boy. His mother and father and two sisters were killed in an automobile accident when he was ten. He was a foster child and no one wanted to adopt him. It was not because he was a bad child, because he was really a good boy. But people wanted to adopt a child who was very young. David was older than what they were looking for, and they chose someone younger over him," said Miss Mildred Law.

"People who select a child from a foster home do not consider the effect it has on the other children, and who they may hurt in the process. Passing over a child from a foster home is a traumatic experience, especially if they are passed over time and time again. It becomes devastating to those not chosen," added Miss Mildred Law.

"David was fortunate. There was an elderly couple Mr. and Mrs. Hodges, in our community whose children were grown and gone. They took David in, even though he was fourteen. The foster home used the Hodges as temporary foster parents whenever they were overcrowded. When David entered their lives, the Hodges immediately fell in love with him. They had planned to adopt him, However, when Mr. Hodges suddenly died, the state would not let Mrs. Hodges adopt David without a living husband. Damn stupid government. They don't do anything right," said Miss Mildred Law, angrily.

"However, the lady who was in charge of the home had some common sense. She told Mrs. Hodges she would take care of the situation, and she left David with her. She knew they needed each other. And in David's mind, she was his real mom. After Mr. Hodges died, David worked the farm like an adult to help with the bills," said Miss Mildred Law.

"The first time we saw David was at my and Emma's thirteenth birthday party. We didn't know who he was or who had invited him. He came with Mrs. Hodges when she brought presents for us. She asked if David could stay to meet some of the children. My mother thought it was a wonderful idea," said Miss Mildred Law.

"When Emma first saw David, her world stopped. She instantly fell in love with him. David didn't detect how Emma felt toward him, but Emma lost no time letting him know. She made it crystal clear to everyone that David was hers.

"David didn't know how to deal with Emma's affections, but later he succumbed to them. From the hardship he had gone through, he needed someone to hold onto, someone who loved him. And believe you me, Emma loved that boy," said Miss Mildred Law.

"David didn't play any team sports in school, which was a shame because he was an excellent athlete. He didn't have the time. He had to take Mr. Hodges' place at home. However, he was allowed to participate on the boxing team. He was stocky, well built, and strong. When he hit his opponent, they went down. The coach let him practice during study-hall or at PE. David was good at boxing. He could whip any boy at school, which might have been the main reason the boys didn't come around Emma very much," said Miss Mildred Law, jokingly.

"Emma loved sports, she was the fastest girl in her class and the class in front of her. There were only two boys who could outrun her. One of them was David. I often thought she let David win, so he wouldn't be embarrassed that a girl had beaten him. Emma was always the first person chosen in any sport, even before the boys. She played sports as well as any boy in school," bragged Miss Mildred Law.

Miss Mildred Law stopped talking and looked hard at me. She said, "You know Blake, I never could figure out how someone so damn pretty could be that good in sports . . . and be a girl. It didn't seem fair to me."

Miss Mildred Law said, hesitantly, "Sports make me think about smoking. We girls decided we wanted to try smoking cigarettes one day. We planned exactly how we were to pull it off without our parents finding out, but we were mainly failures in doing it. Our first attempt was in Emma's barn loft where we stupidly tried to roll our own cigarettes. We couldn't get them to stick together, I guess our spit wasn't sticky enough. We finally gave up because we thought we might end up burning our lips. So our first attempt was a burst.

"In our second attempt, we got a little smarter. We stole two pre-rolled cigarettes and hid them in the barn. Our intentions were to cut them in half, giving each one of us a half to smoke. The next Saturday we met, but no one brought matches. Emma went to get some and hurriedly came back and passed out matches as each girl sat on a bale of hay with a half-cigarette in her mouth. We looked at each other and burst into laughter, the tears from our laughter got our cigarettes wet and they wouldn't light. We started blowing our hot breathe on them to dry them out, when we thought we had them dry enough, we became very serious." Miss Mildred Law laughed.

"We again placed the cigarettes in our mouth and were about to light them when Emma's father came into the barn and called out for her," said Miss Mildred Law.

"'Emma, can you hear me? Olivia needs some help with the boys. We need you down right now. Do you hear me?' said Mr. Tom.

"As soon as Emma's father called out, we all panicked and threw our cigarettes and matches in the bucket of water and quickly hid the bucket," said Miss Mildred Law.

"Emma called down to her father, 'Okay Papa, I'm coming down right now.' We didn't give up hope in learning how to smoke, but our second attempt was another dismal failure," said Miss Mildred Law. "Mary Lou stole a whole pack of Camels from her father during the week and we were ready for the next Saturday. This time, we got a bucket of water in case of fire, and a new box of matches and climbed up into the loft. We had determined we would not fail this time," said Miss Mildred Law.

"We settled in our places in the loft and wasted no time in lighting up. There was some snickering, but the snickering ended when I was the first to light up, take a puff, and blow out smoke. Sophie lit up next, then Emma. When we all watched Mary Lou light up and take a big drag off her cigarette, she began to cough continuously and we all burst into laughter," said Miss Mildred Law, smiling.

"The laughter made us all breathe in the cigarette smoke and it caused us all to cough. We couldn't stop coughing so we took the cigarettes out of our lips and tried to hold them the way the movie star Betty Davis did, trying hard to look real sophisticated," replied Miss Mildred Law.

"Then Sophie said we were doing it wrong. She heard we were supposed to swallow the smoke and make it come out of our nose. We tried to and it made Mary Lou so dizzy that she began to throw up. About the same time Mary Lou got sick, we heard Emma's father come into the barn," said Miss Mildred Law.

"He yells out to us, 'What are you girls up there doing?'"

"We heard him climbing up the ladder to the loft. We panicked and threw the cigarettes into the bucket. All the cigarettes made it into the bucket except Mary Lou's, it fell on some loose hay and began to smoke. We started stomping the hay to put the smoke out before it caught on fire."

"By the time we put the fire out, Mr. Tom was standing in the loft with us and had figured out what was going on. Mr. Tom placed his hands on his hips and told us to go home and tell our parents what we had done so it wouldn't be so bad on us. We thought Mr. Tom was stupid saying that. Who in their right mind would tell their parents they were smoking cigarettes? But you know, he was right. If we had waited for him to tell on us, our punishment would have been much worse.

"Even though when we came to church Sunday, we had problems sitting down. Sophie, Mary Lou, and I had received whippings and were not allowed to go anywhere. Emma got the worst of the punishment: her father had made her smoke each of the remaining cigarettes in the pack. She was sick all weekend."

Miss Mildred Law happily told us, "I guess you could say we were successful in our third attempt to smoke. Yes, we were successful in smoking our first cigarette, but were failures in smoking our first cigarette and getting away with it.

"Emma summed up our smoking adventure with a retort, 'God must love stupid people, because he made so many of us.'" said Miss Mildred Law.

Miss Mildred Law said, "That experience, taught us to never smoke again. However, I was not completely cured. I took up that nasty habit, but that experience did have an impact on how much I do smoke."

Miss Mildred Law told us, "I meant to tell you this earlier, Emma had another person in love with her, but Emma never took him seriously!"

Jeannie quickly asked her, "Who was that, Miss Mildred?"

Miss Mildred Law laughed and said, "His name was Frank."

We both asked in unison, "Who is Frank?"

Again Miss Mildred Law laughed when she said, "Frank is my younger brother who is still unmarried. He is five years younger than me, and he'd always been in love with Emma. He swore from an early age that he was going to marry Emma. When Frank was twelve, he heard Emma and David had plans to marry. He went to Emma and proposed. She didn't respond, so he went to David and threatened his life if he married Emma. Emma had some magical spell over Frank. He proposed to her three different times. Emma never gave him an answer. She felt it might crush his ego."

Jeannie asked, "Was he serious?"

"We don't really know, but after the war, he proposed to her again. He was eighteen, then. Emma did not give him an answer then either. But the last time, I think she knew he was serious. Still, she did not want to hurt his feelings, and gave him no response."

Miss Mildred Law said, "Since I told you about Sophie's first kiss, I ought to tell you about the other three girls first kisses too.

"Mary Lou was next to be kissed, and it happened at a birthday party when they were playing spin the bottle. She told us she spun the bottle trying to land it on her boyfriend, but it landed on her boyfriend's best friend. Mary Lou and the boy went into the closet and he kissed her.

"When they came out, her boyfriend asked his friend if he'd kissed her. He told him he sure had and it was really good. Then her boyfriend punches his best friend in the nose, making him bleed everywhere. They couldn't stop the bleeding and ended up taking him to the hospital. It was a devil of a way to break up a party."

Jeannie said, "That's funny, Miss Mildred! So who was next to be kissed, you or Emma?"

Miss Mildred Law said, "You would think it would be Emma because she had David. I never had a boyfriend in high school, but I did kiss a boy who I didn't know that well. He stood up for my honor, so I kissed him."

"How did that happen, Miss Mildred?" Jeannie asked.

"Well, Emma, Sophie, and I were at the Malt Shoppe. We were waiting for Sophie's dad to bring us home from a football game. We were flirting with this nice guy from the town our team had just played, and he flirted back. We walked toward the door to see if Sophie's dad had arrived, and a guy at the nice boy's table who was drunk grabbed my wrist and offered to take me for a ride. Before I could say anything to him, the nice boy we were talking to told the drunk to take his hand off of my wrist," said Miss Mildred Law.

Miss Mildred Law said, "The drunk boy told the nice boy to tend to his own business. So, the nice boy told him again, more firmly, to take his hand off of me because she is not that kind of girl. The drunk laughed and said, 'all girls are that kind.' The nice boy punched him and he dropped to the floor, out cold.

"The nice boy walked out with us and apologized for the drunk's behavior. Both the drunk and the nice boy were from the same town and knew one another. Emma and Sophie were amazed that he had hit him. I was, too, but I tried to make it seem like it was just an everyday thing. Since he had stood up for me, I felt I needed to do more than just say thank you, so I kissed him. He went back into the Malt Shoppe and helped revive the drunk boy," said Miss Mildred Law.

"Emma and Sophie were shocked that I kissed the boy. They didn't know it, but I was, too. They teased me for a month, calling him my Knight in Shining Armor," said Miss Mildred Law.

I listened to everything Miss Mildred Law was telling us. I could still not believe she was telling us her personal experiences, but I was thankful that she felt comfortable enough to share them with us. I had always seen her as a person who kept things to herself, and she had. Our conversation with Miss Mildred Law had given me a new perception about who she was.

Jeannie happily asked Miss Mildred Law, "When did Emma get her first kiss?"

Delighted, Miss Mildred Law said, "It happened not very long after the incident in the Malt Shoppe, and I am sure you have figured out who it was with. No doubt, it was with David. But David was a hard nut to crack. Emma told us many times they'd had the opportunity to kiss, but David was too shy even to try. David would not allow Emma to kiss him even on the cheek. It frustrated her because she longed to be held and kissed by David.

"Emma tried to set up her first kiss with help from David's best friend, Jimmy Ray, and his girlfriend. Jimmy Ray was all for it. He had told David many times before he should show Emma he cared for her by kissing her. Jimmy Ray's girlfriend was two years older than Jimmy Ray, and from what we'd heard, she was one of those "easy girls." She had been around the block a few times and probably with Jimmy Ray, too, if you know what I mean. But she loved the plan Emma had formulated and was ready to make their first kiss happen," said Miss Mildred Law.

Miss Mildred Law said, "The plan was the four of them would go horseback riding down to the river. On the way, however, they were to play a game of flipping the coin to see who would get to kiss his girlfriend. Emma told me the game cost her a brand new silver dollar because Jimmy Ray said it was his price to be in on the plan."

Miss Mildred Law added, "He was such a butt-hole, God rest his soul."

"David knew they were up to something because it had been a peaceful ride. Usually, Jimmy Ray would act like he was Roy Rogers riding a wild stallion down the mountain," said Miss Mildred Law.

"When they got to the river, Jimmy Ray said excitedly, 'Let's play a fun game.' David didn't realize the game was meant to coax him into kissing Emma. Jimmy Ray started by telling everybody he had just earned himself a new silver dollar for doing a good deed, and he felt like being kissed. He excitedly said, 'Let's play a kissing game!' Jimmy Ray laid out the rules for the kissing game," said Miss Mildred Law.

"He was going to flip the coin and if it landed on heads he and his girl would kiss, but if it landed on tails then Emma and David would kiss. Emma said David tried to back out of the game but Jimmy Ray and his girlfriend kept shaming him into playing. They told him he needed to grow up, be a man, and show his love to his woman. Emma encouraged him to play the game, but David gave no indication that he would play," said Miss Mildred Law simply.

"The plan was to not let David see what side the coin had landed on and make it where Jimmy Ray and his girl would make the first five or six kisses, hoping it would encourage David to kiss Emma. On the first five tosses, Jimmy Ray said he won, and he kissed his girlfriend. When Jimmy Ray said he won the fourth toss, Emma complained the game was rigged. Jimmy Ray retaliated by saying no way would he ever cheat his best friend, David. Then on the fifth toss Jimmy Ray said he won again. Emma said she needed to check the coin to see if it was a two-headed coin because no way could they win that many straight tosses. Emma did all the complaining in hopes David would join with her. But he did not say a word," said Miss Mildred Law.

"Then on the sixth toss, Jimmy said, 'You won, David! Kiss your girl.'

"Emma told me her heart was beating a thousand miles per hour in hopes David would kiss her. All the attention had now turned to David. He smiled at them, but he would not kiss Emma," said Miss Mildred Law.

Miss Mildred Law said, "Jimmy Ray flipped the coin again, telling everyone he had won and told David to look at how easy it was to kiss a girl. So Jimmy Ray kissed his girlfriend and flipped the coin again and declared that David had won again."

Miss Mildred Law said, "David did not move. He made no attempt to kiss Emma. This time Jimmy Ray's girl friend told David that she couldn't believe he would not kiss her. When she singled David out, it upset him and he turned his head away to show his disapproval to what she had said."

Miss Mildred Law said, "Jimmy Ray, not to be outdone by David's shyness, approached it another way: Jimmy Ray wanted David to see how important Emma had been in his life. 'Who taught you how to ride horses and swim?'

"David replied, 'Emma did.'

"Jimmy Ray asked David, 'Who taught you how to shoot a rifle and to fish?'

"David said, 'Emma.'

"Jimmy Ray asked David, 'Who looks after you like a mama and loves you more than she does herself?'

"David regretfully answered, 'Everybody knows it's Emma.'

"Jimmy Ray said, 'If I had someone taught me all those things and then looked out after me like Emma does you, I would think you ought to want to thank her by at least giving her at a peck on her cheek . . . don't you, David?'

"David turned back and looked at Emma, who was about in tears, and said, 'Yeah . . . I guess so!'

"Jimmy Ray said, 'Then at least kiss her on her cheek, please do that before she bursts into flames.'

"Emma leaned over toward David, offering her left cheek to David, so he could kiss her, which he did. Both Jimmy Ray and his girlfriend clapped and shouted with joy. Emma said their shouting was so sudden that it scared the horses off, but they all ignored rounding up the horses because they wanted David to kiss Emma again," said Miss Mildred Law.

Miss Mildred Law smiled and said, "Jimmy Ray told me Emma beamed with such happiness, and so did David. But it wasn't what he wanted from David. Jimmy Ray said he wasn't going to stop until David kissed her on her lips.

"Jimmy Ray flipped the coin again and said he won, so he kissed his girlfriend. Jimmy Ray flipped the coin again and told David, 'You win, so kiss Emma on her cheek.'

"This time, David did not hesitate to kiss Emma. Emma leaned toward him to let him kiss her on the cheek, but when he got about an inch away from her cheek, she turned her head toward David, grabbed his head and ears, and pulled him to kiss her on her lips. At first, David tried to pull away, but Jimmy Ray said Emma had held his head in a death-grip and would not let him go until David relaxed and kissed her tenderly," said Miss Mildred Law.

"Jimmy Ray said the game continued a few more rounds with David and Emma's kisses growing longer with each win. Emma smiled, so big that it could have shut out the sunlight. Jimmy Ray said he knew when that happened it was time to quit the game because David did not need any more encouragement. He was doing fine on his own."

Miss Mildred Law said, "When Jimmy Ray told us the story about the joy Emma and David shared with their first kiss, we were thrilled for them. Seeing Emma and David after their first kiss was one of the few times I remember Emma being that happy. She didn't know it, but soon her life would turn in another direction. I hate to say this, but shame on God for allowing Emma to suffer those terrible heartaches. She deserved much better than what she received."

I never saw the heartaches Miss Mildred Law was speaking of in Aunt Emma's life. To me she always seemed happy and on top of any situation. But I realized I was seeing things through the eyes of a child. Neither Jeannie nor I had any idea what Miss Mildred Law was talking about. I hoped she would make it clear to us.

Miss Mildred Law said, "It took Emma five years to get David to kiss her, he was a senior. It's hard to believe those two could be with each other that long and never have kissed. David was a senior and Emma was a sophomore, that year. Back then, they only had three years in high school. In David's senior year, he and Emma started making plans for their marriage."

"I didn't know if I've told you this, but Emma and David were each other's only boy and girl friend. They never went with anyone else. Everyone felt one day they would marry because they were the perfect match. Others tried to get them to date them, but they were wasting their time. Emma had eyes only for David, and David felt exactly the same way," said Miss Mildred Law.

Miss Mildred continued talking about David and Emma's relationship, "The two of them were a match; they never fought. They agreed on everything. They should have gotten married, but it didn't work out that way. Too many troubles came their way and changed everything from the way it was supposed to be. Emma made a comment about how things had gone off-track one day. She always had a way of saying things that gave us the right prospective. She told me, 'I used to have a handle on life, but it broke.'

"Whenever Emma's troubles would begin to overcome her, she would go walking," said Miss Mildred Law, "usually late at night." She would walk over to my house and tap on the window to get me to go walking with her. We would talk about her problems and my problems and we never seem to come up with a solution. We would end up at our special place on top of the lean-to on the back of the barn. We would lie down on the tin roof and just look at the sky. Emma used to say when she looked at the bigness of the sky that it made all of her troubles seem so small. Looking at the heavens comforted her in some way, at least until the next day came with the same troubles as before."

# Chapter 7

## Plans and Decisions

"**D**avid and Emma were making marriage plans during David's last year in high school. David grew to love the farm-life. Emma and David's dream was to marry and own a farm, and they actually found a farm. They even went to the bank to see if they could afford to buy it," said Miss Mildred Law.

"Old man Jake McCoy had a run-down sixty-acre farm he had tried to sell for years, but no one wanted it. People either wouldn't buy it because they didn't have the money, or they felt the farm and land was too far in disrepair. The house was a shack, the barn was rotten, and both leaked. The fences were all down, and the soil had been misused and was eroding.

"But to David and Emma, it was their dream come true. Their plan was for David to work and save his money while Emma finished school. Then, after she finished, the two of them would work another two years to build up enough money to make a substantial down-payment on the McCoy farm, and then they could get married. They felt the farm would still be available for them in three years. It had been for sale for years with no one interested in buying it. That would have timed their marriage in the summer of 1942.

"After graduation, David took a job at the local feed mill. He bought an old truck. He worked days at the mill and in the afternoons, he took care of the Hodges' farm. At first, their plan went well, David saved every penny he earned. On Saturday nights, when I came to visit Emma to listen to the Grand Ole Opera with them, she and David would be at the kitchen table making plans for their farm. They were excited planning about how it was going to be. It was an exciting time for them, and I was happy for them, too," said Miss Mildred Law.

Miss Mildred Law said to us, "You know, the Bible tells us the best made plans of man don't always work out. That is exactly what happened to their plans. David had worked a little over a year, then unexpectedly, Mrs. Hodges died that first summer. Her death caused David to be left with no home. The Hodges older children inherited the land and the house, but they lived and worked in Texas. They had no interest in owning it and understood how difficult it would be to own property and a house while living in another state, so they looked for a buyer."

Miss Mildred Law said, "They first offered to sell it to David, but he didn't have the money to buy it, nor did he want it. With only twenty acres, it wasn't large enough to farm. It didn't fit into David and Emma's plans, so the Hodges' children put it up for sale and the bank bought it.

"So now, David is out in the cold, so to speak. Emma wanted David to stay with them, but Mr. Tom was against that. There was not enough room for him to live in the house with Mr. Tom, Emma, Olivia, and her two kids. There was only two bedrooms," said Miss Mildred Law.

"Thank God for the kindness of Jimmy Ray's parents. They told David he could stay with them until he married. David didn't like the idea because he knew Jimmy Ray's parents fought a lot. Jimmy Ray's father was a heavy drinker, a known trouble-maker, and he had no job. However, David did not have much choice. He reluctantly agreed to move in with them. This seemed to keep David and Emma's plans on track," said Miss Mildred Law.

"This arrangement worked well until Jimmy Ray's father told David he ate too much and had become a burden on his family. Jimmy Ray's father told David, he should pay him rent each week for room and board. David had already been giving Jimmy Ray's mother extra money to help out, but they never told Jimmy Ray's father. They knew he would take the extra money and use it to drink.

Jimmy Ray's mother never asked David for money, but David offered her money because of the kindness they had shown him.

"David never told Jimmy Ray he was paying his father rent separate from what David was giving to Jimmy Ray's mother. David knew it would cause greater problems for everyone, even though the extra expense was taking a toll on his efforts to save," said Miss Mildred Law.

"Then, to make matters worse, Emma's father got sick with pneumonia and needed to be hospitalized. Emma had taken a part-time job at the hospital to help add to their savings. But Mr. Tom's sickness had drained those savings. Her father's sickness created such a major financial burden that Emma eventually had to use all of her earnings to pay his medical bills. Olivia did not help. She said she couldn't work because she had to care for her two boys. Actually, Aunt Sis and Mabel did all the caring for the twins. Olivia did nothing to help anyone in any way."

As Miss Mildred Law was speaking, I glimpsed at the Brown's leaving the cemetery and I could see Miss Sis was being led back to Howard's vehicle. However, Mabel was walking over toward where we were sitting. I assumed she was coming to speak to Miss Mildred Law because they were good friends. I hoped as Mabel walked toward us, her presence would not hinder Miss Mildred Law from sharing her memories with us about her and Aunt Emma.

To safeguard Miss Mildred Law resuming to tell us about their lives, I made it a point to take control of the conversation when Mabel arrived. I knew Jeannie did not want the story to end; neither did I.

As soon as Mabel got within talking distance of us, I invited her to sit with us and enjoy listening to Miss Mildred Law as she told us about Aunt Emma and David's marriage plans. Much to my surprise, Mabel accepted my invitation, even though her mother and brother were leaving. She came and sat with us. I hadn't realized it then, but she and Miss Mildred Law had visited one another earlier. That helped make the transition smoother, and as an added bonus, Mabel became an additional source of information.

Miss Mildred Law continued telling us about Aunt Emma and she involved Mabel into our conversation as she said, "I think, Mabel was there at Emma's house when David and Emma's marriage plans started going sour. In fact, both Aunt Sis and Mabel were there when Mr. Tom got out of the hospital."

Miss Mildred Law said, "That attack Mr. Tom had with pneumonia almost killed him. He never was completely able to get back on his feet to where he could help around the farm. Emma had just started working full-time at the hospital. She worked there all day, and after work she took care of the farm. Olivia never lifted a hand to help do anything, not even cook supper or bathe her children."

Mabel quickly added, "Yeah, that pneumonia took Mr. Tom for a loop, we thought he might not make it, but God intervened and he got better. You are also right about Emma, she did all she could to keep the farm going with absolutely no help from her lazy sister."

It was obvious from Mabel's tone that that she held ill feelings toward Olivia. Mabel said, "Olivia only thought of herself . . . and maybe occasionally about her boys. Instead of the older sister caring for everyone in the household, like an older sister would when their mother died, it was Emma, the younger daughter, who ended up caring for Olivia and her boys too. Thoughts of helping the family or sharing the load never entered Olivia's mind."

Mabel passionately added, "Yes ma'am Miss Mildred Law, I was there when Emma and David's plans began to fall apart. It was really sad to see them struggle to try to keep their plans from failing. One Saturday afternoon, David came over, and Emma and David were lying on the floor piecing together how their savings were progressing, trying to save enough to get that farm where they could get married."

With a lower voice Mabel said, "Emma added the figures together, and it didn't add up like they'd planned. In fact, their savings hadn't progressed at all, they had regressed. It was like a lightning bolt hit David. He jumped up from lying on the floor and made the statement that went through Emma's heart like a dagger. He looked down at Emma and told her with absolutely no emotion. You know, the same way someone tells a person that their mother just died? 'We're never going to have enough money for us to do what we want. There is no way we can buy that farm or get married!'"

Mabel continued, "Before David could explain what he meant, Emma sprung off the floor and ran outside crying. Those words from David were too much for her heart to take. David followed her outside to the front porch, and they sat on the steps as she continued to cry uncontrollably. Yes, that was a really sad scene."

You could see tears in Mabel eyes as she continued: "My heart broke for her, too. It was like someone had taken it out of my chest and stomped on it. David's statement seemed to please Olivia, though. I could almost swear I saw her silently applaud when David said that. That girl was jealous of her sister, and it delighted her to see Emma losing her dream."

Mabel continued talking. "It was an hour or so before Emma came back into the house, David left to go the Jimmy Ray's house. Neither David nor Emma was very happy when he left. I don't know what Emma and David talked about, but I could hear her sobbing late into the night as she laid in her bed."

Mabel said, "I believe Emma cried because she too saw the handwriting on the wall. It would have been tough on anyone. Just look at what had happened to them in that short frame of time. Mr. and Mrs. Hodges died, David lost a mother and father. Then he lost his home, he was forced to move in with Jimmy Ray's parents. Then he began paying double rent and board, preventing him from saving any money. Then on Emma's side, Mr. Tom got sick, and it took all of Emma's savings to pay his bills. Together, they were not making enough money to save and carry out any of the plans they had. It was heart wrenching seeing their hopes and dreams being choked out week after week. We all saw them losing faith in owning a farm and getting married."

Miss Mildred Law added, "David must have told that to Emma the same weekend I came home from college. Emma came to my window after midnight and asked me to go walking with her. As usual, we ended up on the roof of her barn talking about the situation.

"When she told me what David said, I didn't know what to tell her to do. I was afraid I might say the wrong thing and make matters worse, I knew how much she wanted to get married and help David fulfill his dream of owning a farm."

Mabel was surprised at hearing how Emma snuck out at night. "Is that where Emma would sneak off to? I know she thought no one knew when she left, but Mr. Tom and I would get up after we heard her leave those nights and talk about what we believed was her reason to sneak out. He believed she must have something on her mind, and I believed she just wanted to go somewhere so she could think. We decided not to discuss it with her because we knew she wasn't sneaking out to do anything wrong. That would be completely out of character for her."

Mabel chuckled. "So that's where she would always go. She came over to your house to get you . . . uh huh. I wished Mr. Tom was alive so I could tell him we were both right."

Miss Mildred Law said, "We climbed on that roof a lot. I thought y'all knew she left, but that particular night we discussed how quickly their plans just seemed to evaporate. I will never forget her concern for David. Even with her dreams falling apart too, she was more alarmed about how David would react to not being able to do what they had planned. Emma said to me so sadly, 'What is happening to David is like swallowing a mouth full of broken glass.'"

Miss Mildred Law said, "I remember every time I came home from college, I would visit Emma. It became depressing going there. There was so little joy in that house, David would come over, and he didn't smile or laugh like he used to, and Emma was just as bad. She didn't share those intimate thoughts with me as we did in high school. I can't remember them doing any planning anymore. At least, I didn't see them do it."

Mabel added: "Miss Mildred Law, you don't know the half of it. The only one who found any joy at that house was Olivia. She was tickled to death their plans were messed up. She didn't want anyone to be happy, and that included her two boys. She seemed to enjoy stirring them up to make them fight one another, too."

Mabel continued telling us about the unhappiness in Emma's house, "Olivia would say things about David to hurt Emma's feelings. She would tell Emma that David was no good and would never amount to anything and if they were to get married, it wouldn't last because he would never be able to support her or a family, and he surely could never own a farm.

"She would try to coax Mr. Tom to say something negative about their plans, so it seemed that he agreed with Olivia. But Mr.

Tom was too smart to be drawn into her trap, he would leave the room. She tried to get me and Madea to agree with her, but Madea would put her in her place. She would tell Olivia she had better stop trying to ruin Emma's life, get busy, and find herself a life and a husband . . . if that was possible for her to do," said Mabel, harshly.

Miss Mildred Law added to what Mabel was saying, "Yes, Aunt Sis always told things the way they were. I knew Olivia didn't like her, even though Aunt Sis treated her like a queen. She took care of her boys like they were her own. I hate to say it, but Olivia didn't care what anyone did for her or her children."

Miss Mildred Law said, "You know Mabel, your mother is a wonderful person. She has always been there for all our families. Whenever we had a problem, she always offered her help and still does. I know Emma looked at her like she was her mother, and she was. I hope God continues to bless her."

Mabel humbly replied, "Thank you so much Miss Mildred Law for those kind words. I know Madea loves you just like you are as one of her own children, too."

Miss Mildred Law anxiously asked Mabel, "Wasn't Aunt Sis there with us the night we got word the Japs bombed Pearl Harbor?"

Mabel answered her, "Yes she was, if you're thinking about when David came in with his new plan."

Miss Mildred Law said, "Yes, honey. That is exactly what I am referring to. I was on break for Christmas. I'd come over to Emma's and we were listening to Jack Benny on the radio. David burst into Emma's house and gave us his good news."

Mabel quickly interjected her thoughts and told her, "I think it was good news only to David. None of us thought it was good news, especially not Emma."

Miss Mildred Law smirked as she agreed and said, "Yes, you are right about that. It definitely was not good news for Emma. In fact, it was a major shock to all of us. How he let Jimmy Ray talk him into that, I will never understand."

I knew what Miss Mildred Law was referring to. David had joined the service. I was not sure if Jeannie understood what they meant because they had not yet said what he did, and I did not want her to seem ignorant so I asked, "What was the news?"

Both Miss Mildred Law and Mabel turned to me and said in unison, "David and Jimmy Ray joined the Marines."

Jeannie asked in disbelief, "Why would he do that? That is not good news, especially with a war coming. That just made it harder for Emma and David to get married."

Miss Mildred Law said, "That's exactly right honey, but to David, it seemed to be the only way they could ever have a farm or get married. He tried to explain it to us, but no matter what he said, it didn't sound logical. He was mixed up in his thinking and caught up in the moment in a wave of patriotism. I guess President Roosevelt's stirring speech helped him make that decision."

Mabel said, "David was some excited. He began to tell Emma he would be able to save all his money because the Marines would pay him and give him room and board. And when he came home, they could get married and buy the farm. He never took into consideration that he could be killed or never come back at all."

Miss Mildred Law said, "What a dumb-ass decision that was on his part. He gave no consideration for Emma or what could happen to him. Once we got David settled down, he began to tell us how it all came about."

Mabel said, "David told them, after he and Jimmy Ray had heard the President speak, they knew they had to go fight for our country. Jimmy Ray said he knew they were both unhappy with their jobs and the direction their lives were going. Jimmy Ray convinced David they were in the same boat . . . going nowhere. Jimmy Ray said joining the military would give them a new start with a better future than what they had then."

"He convinced David that he needed to join too. Jimmy Ray believed it would be the perfect answer for them both. Jimmy Ray's logic was that if they joined the best branch, the Marines, they wouldn't have to worry about being killed. The Marines would train them the best how to survive during the war. Then they could go over there and beat those low-down sneaky Japs who murdered our boys and win the war and come home. He told David they had better hurry because the war would be over in a year or two. They needed to join up before the war was over. And when they get home, they would have some money in their pockets and would be able to make a new start," said Miss Mildred Law.

Mabel let Miss Mildred Law finish her statement and added, "Do you remember, Miss Mildred Law, how we had to hold Emma up? When David told her that he and Jimmy Ray would be leaving in three days to go to basic training in San Diego, she fainted."

Miss Mildred Law answered, "Yes honey child, I did. It was the only time I saw Mr. Tom stand up to David and tell him he needed to leave the house. Mr. Tom reiterated what he meant by telling him, 'And-I-mean-leave-right-now.'

"It shocked David that Emma's father asked him to leave. David's good news upset Mr. Tom, too. He realized what David had just told Emma was going to devastate her. It would break her heart again and Mr. Tom did not want David to continue to talk to her that night because it would be more than she could handle," said Miss Mildred Law.

Mable said, "Yeah, after he told him to leave, Mr. Tom stood between David and Emma, backed David out of the screen door, and told him he could come back tomorrow morning to see Emma. David did not argue. He said, 'yes, sir' and left."

Miss Mildred Law said, "You know, I really didn't want to remember that night. Emma cried like a baby the rest of the night, and she wouldn't listen or talk to anyone. I spent the night with her, and it wasn't until early in the morning that we were able to get her to settle down. She was so heartbroken. Not only had her marriage plans been fouled, but now her only love was going off to war and he may never come back. That stupid jack-ass, David, never thought about how the ones who loved him felt with his dumb decision."

Miss Mildred Law said, despondently, "We all cried that night, Emma, me. You too Mabel, and even Mr. Tom. What David did upset him as much as it did anyone. I saw him shaking in his chair because he was so mad at David. He would have shot David if David had stayed any longer at his house. It crushed him to see his baby girl so heartbroken again. He knew she deserved better than what life had handed her."

Mabel said, "David came to Emma's house early the next morning, I heard him knock on the door very lightly. Madea answered the door and snappily told him he would have to wait until everyone got up. I couldn't hear everything Madea told him, and she fussed at him and gave him an earful of her opinion."

Miss Mildred Law said, "Honey, he was such a dumb-ass about the whole situation. He had no idea joining the Marines would cause such an uproar. He thought we would be proud he wanted to serve his country. In a sense he was right, because we were proud he wanted to serve his country; but his timing was bad . . . real bad."

Mabel said, "I remember how David's attitude changed after Madea told him he broke Emma's heart and upset everybody else. She said Mr. Tom was so angry with him that he was shaking. She told David, his decision upset the whole household and had caused everyone to cry all night. I think David realized after Madea explained how his decision caused such an uproar that maybe he better handle the situation with a little more tack than he used last night."

Mabel continued: "David waited on the porch until Madea got all of us up and fixed breakfast. Emma wanted to go out there to be with him before breakfast, but Miss Mildred Law would not let her."

"That is damn right I would not let her go to him," said Miss Mildred Law, angrily.

"What that boy did to Emma was a crying shame. He ought to have been horse whipped. He deserved to sit out there and wait. If it had been me, I would have made him wait until the cows came home. But that was not the way Emma saw it. She still loved that boy and would never hurt him, no matter what stupid thing he did," said Miss Mildred Law.

Mabel said, "Once breakfast was ready, Mr. Tom went out to tell David he could come into the house and eat breakfast with them. I heard David try to apologize to Mr. Tom, but Mr. Tom interrupted him. He told David he was sorry he had to ask him to leave. Mr. Tom told him he was proud of him for wanting to serve and protect our country. It was a very honorable thing. David managed to apologize to Mr. Tom for causing such a dilemma. He told him he never intended to hurt anyone. I am not too sure Mr. Tom wanted to hear it, but David told him anyway."

Miss Mildred Law said, "At the breakfast table, David apologized to everyone about the way he acted the night before. He said he was excited. But the reason he was excited was not about joining the Marines or going to war. His excitement was because he felt he had found a way he and Emma could get married. He said he was not concerned about buying a farm any longer. That was not important anymore. That now, the most important thing to him was to marry Emma . . . if Mr. Tom would agree. Mr. Tom nodded his head in approval and smiled. So David got down on his knee and formally asked Emma to marry him."

Mabel said, "Yeah, that boy handled that really well. He had us all crying again, but this time it was for joy. We all knew David meant well because we knew he loved Emma and never intended to hurt her."

Miss Mildred Law was quick to respond, "It was the craziest thing I ever saw. But it was so sweet. We were glad to be there and be a part of it. Emma stood up and pulled David up, off his knee and said, 'Yes, I most definitely will marry you.' They kissed and hugged, and we all clapped our approval. Even Olivia and her boys were happy for them. It was amazing how quick we went from sadness to great joy."

Mabel said thankfully, "Yes we were happy for them, but the conversation quickly turned from marriage to how much time David had before he would have to leave. It was only three days before he and Jimmy Ray would catch the train and head west on Friday at midnight.

"David stayed at Emma's house almost the entire time before he left for boot camp. The only time he left Emma's side was to go to Jimmy Ray's house to sleep. Early each morning, David would be back at Emma's house. Whenever I passed them in those few days, they never noticed me or anyone else. I overheard them making plans about where the wedding would be and who would be the Maid of Honor; of course, it was Miss Mildred Law. David shocked everyone when he announced he wanted Mr. Tom to be his Best Man.

"I am not positive they ever asked Mr. Tom. But I am sure he would have considered it a great honor."

Miss Mildred Law added, "After David left, I asked Emma a couple of very personal questions. I wasn't sure she would answer me, but I asked her anyway."

Mabel looked at Miss Mildred Law and said very sarcastically, as if it were a shock to her that Miss Mildred Law would ask a personal question, "Miss Mildred Law, I can't imagine that you, of all people, would ask anyone a personal question. That does not sound like you at all."

Mabel scowled and then a smile broke across her face, and she burst into laughter. We all snickered at first, and soon we joined Mabel with our laughter. Miss Mildred Law knew how demanding she was. It did not bother her. She felt at ease about who she was.

Jeannie spoke up and asked Miss Mildred Law, "What kind of personal questions did you ask Aunt Emma, Miss Mildred?"

Miss Mildred Law said, "I asked her two questions about her and David. I guess the first question was not as personal as the second, but I wanted to know. I asked Emma if they had talked about getting married before David left.

"Emma asked David if he wanted to get married before he went off. She told him she would, if he wanted her too.

"I asked Emma, 'What did David say?'

"Emma told me, 'David insisted we wait until he gets back because he wanted everything to be perfect when we married. He said if we married now, it would be too hurried, and he did not want that. He wanted me to have all the things that every bride should have in a wedding to make it a cherished memory.'"

Miss Mildred Law continued, "If they married now and he was not able to come back for some reason, it would place her in an awkward position to be a widow before she was twenty-five. Again, David said that would not be best for her."

Mabel, impatient to hear the second question, asked Miss Mildred Law, "What was your second question to her?"

Miss Mildred Law paused as she looked at me and then leaned toward the two ladies. She said, "I asked Emma if they were going to make love before he left."

Mabel immediately whispered back to her and said, "Well, what did she say?"

Miss Mildred Law said, "I thought the question might shock Emma, but she never batted an eye as she answered me. Emma said they had talked about it, but David decided they could wait for that, too. It would be wrong to do that before marriage, even if he was going to war. David said she might get pregnant, and with him away, it would be another hardship on her."

Miss Mildred Law surprisingly said, "After she gave her answer, she asked me if I thought they should have sex before he left. I was shocked that Emma would ask me that question, especially about her and David."

Miss Mildred Law paused to give us an opportunity to ask her the question we all wanted to know, which was: 'What was your answer to Aunt Emma?' But no one asked anything.

Miss Mildred Law said, "I know all of you want to know my answer. I avoided answering it because none of us had had any experience to be able to give an intelligent answer. We hadn't been told anything about it, so I said nothing and Emma never asked me again. I guess my not answering her was answer enough for her to give me her favorite retort: *'You don't say!'*"

# Chapter 8

## *Righting Wrongs*

"Friday came speedily, it was David and Jimmy Ray's last day before they would leave to go to San Diego. Emma and David had spent their time with one another, but six o'clock came quickly. New Orleans was only 120 miles away, but back then, people allowed extra time for travel, just in case they broke down or had a flat. The roads in the forties were not as good as they are now. If you were smart, you left early," Miss Mildred Law said.

"Jimmy Ray's parents volunteered to drive them to the train station in New Orleans. Around six o'clock, Jimmy Ray and his parents came to pick up David at Emma's. About twenty people were there to say goodbye to David and Jimmy Ray. It was a sad scene, but we all made as if we were happy they were leaving to serve our country. I know it sounds unpatriotic saying we pretended we were happy, but it was difficult to let them go. Somehow, we managed our way through it. We gave them a brown paper bag filled with goodies and waved our little America flags as they drove off. We wondered if they would ever return and prayed they would come back alive and in one piece," said Miss Mildred Law, sadly.

Mabel told us, "There was no teary-eyed scene at the farewell. David and Emma hugged and kissed one another and said goodbye without any great emotional scene. I guess it was the best way to do it. However, the tears and sadness did come and lasted through that night and many nights after. Emma wrote David every day after she got the permanent address. David wrote her too, but he must not have had much time to write because Emma wrote three letters to his one."

Mabel said, "Each time Emma received a letter from David, she read it to us. Of course, she held back the more personal parts written just for her. You could tell when she got to those parts, she would pause to read it silently and then skip to the next part. It frustrated Olivia when she did that. She wanted to know everything David wrote."

Mabel laughed as she told us, "One time Emma caught Olivia going through her letters from David. It was one of the few times that Emma lost her composure. She put the fear of God into Olivia. Many of the things David wrote seemed funny to us. I don't mean the Marines did funny stuff, no, it wasn't that. But the way David described it made it funny. We enjoyed David's letters, it was nice for Emma to share David's thoughts with us. I imagine Emma read them to us so we would not be asking individually what David had to say."

Miss Mildred Law said, "After Emma read David's letters, she would date and number them and store them in her hope chest. I remember one time we were all sitting on the front steps as Emma was reading a letter from David. She was half-way through it when Mr. Dan Turner came over to her house looking for help with a problem he had with Mr. Otto Hester."

Mabel quickly commented, "Yeah, that old buzzard Hester had a big problem: he couldn't keep his hands to himself. If he was anywhere around, you made sure you didn't get trapped in a room with him. He was a pervert."

Miss Mildred Law told us about Mr. Turner's visit, "Mr. Dan Turner was a white man who lived and worked on Mr. Otto's land as a share cropper. He and his wife had six kids, ranging in age from three to sixteen. It was common for poor people back then to live and farm on a landowner's place and share the profits from their crops with the landowner. Usually it was halved. But some gracious landowners would charge one third or even less."

Miss Mildred Law explained to us, "Mr. Otto had several sharecroppers on his place. All of them were black except one white family, the Turner's. Mr. Otto quit farming because he was unsuccessful at it. He was unsuccessful because he was too lazy to work. He decided it was much easier to allow poor people to farm his land as sharecroppers and let them make his living. They did all the work, took all the chances, and all he did was think of ways to rob them of their profits."

Mabel proudly told us, "My mother and father were sharecroppers on Mr. Tom's place. He didn't charge them anything. Mr. Tom believed his ownership of the land was temporary because the land belonged to God. He believed that whoever worked the land, even if someone else owned it, what they produced belonged to God and the person who worked it. If any profit came from their labor, the split would be between them and the Lord, and not the landowner."

Miss Mildred Law continued, "Mr. Dan stood there and waited for Emma to finish reading David's letter. When Emma saw him, she immediately stopped reading and asked Mr. Dan how he was doing.

"Mr. Dan said, 'Well, Miss Emma, I ain't doing so well right now because I got me a problem.'

"He paused and looked down and told her, 'It's a big problem too, and I think I need your help.'

"You could tell Mr. Dan did not want tell everyone his business, so Emma told him to walk around the side of the house where they could talk privately. Emma made me go with her," said Miss Mildred Law.

"Emma asked, 'What is your problem Mr. Dan?'"

Miss Mildred Law said, "I didn't know until later what Mr. Dan had told her. Mr. Dan said Mr. Otto Hester was trying to take his daughter from him.

"Mr. Dan had sent his daughter over to Mr. Otto's house to give him the payment on his share of the profits from Mr. Dan's corn crop. She was to tell Mr. Otto her father would pay him the rest of the money he owed him from last year when the cotton crop came in," said Miss Mildred Law.

"Mr. Dan said the reason he sent his daughter to pay Mr. Otto instead of going himself was that every time he went to Mr. Otto, he would berate him, causing him to lose his temper. That allowed Mr. Otto to threaten to run him off his property. It was a set-up so he could take advantage of Mr. Dan. Mr. Otto would force him to do extra work, and never pay him for his time.

"As soon as Mr. Dan's daughter gave Mr. Otto his half of the money for the corn crop, Mr. Otto pulled her to him and took all kinds of liberties with her. Mr. Otto told the girl he might just keep her with him, at least until her father could pay him. And if he didn't leave his daughter with him, he would run the Turner's off his land. She broke away from his clutches and came running home, crying. Her blouse was torn and she was terrified. She told her father what Mr. Otto had said and done.

"When Mr. Dan learned what had happened, he threatened to shoot Mr. Otto for what he did to his daughter. His wife encouraged him to cool down and told him that he needed to come talk with Emma," said Miss Mildred Law.

"Mr. Dan said to Emma, 'You know Miss Emma, that ain't right. Mr. Otto has no right to touch my daughter or to force me to send my daughter over to him.' Mr. Dan was in great distress. 'That was not the agreement we made. He knows that I will pay him,

I have always paid him what I owed him. He is forcing me to do something that is wrong, and I don't want to do it. Either I pay him all the money or I have to give him my daughter until I can pay him. Or I get off the land. I ain't got the money, Miss Emma.'

"Mr. Dan blamed himself, 'It's my fault because I should have never sent her over to his house. I should have gone myself.'

"Mr. Dan made it clear to Emma that Mr. Otto was not kidding. Mr. Dan knew if did not come up with the money or send his daughter to him, as demanded, Mr. Otto would kick them out of their house and run him off his property. It would cause him to lose his entire cotton crop to Mr. Otto," said Miss Mildred Law.

"Mr. Dan told Emma, 'I don't mind losing the cotton crop, but me, my wife, and our six kids don't have nowhere else to go.' He said, 'I came to you because I heard that you had helped another one of Mr. Otto's sharecroppers, Clarence Miller.'"

Miss Mildred Law said, "That incident happened when Mr. Otto kept more than the agreed upon amount of money. Mr. Otto had told Clarence Miller, a black sharecropper, that he could get more money for his crop if he let him take it to market instead of him.

"Mr. Otto did receive more for the crop, but Mr. Otto told Clarence Miller he hadn't. Mr. Otto gave Mr. Clarence a smaller portion of the profits, and he kept the extra profit for himself," said Miss Mildred Law.

"Mr. Otto was bragging to everyone at the feed mill how he made a lot of money by out-smarting Mr. Clarence. Emma found out what he did because David worked at the feed mill. He told Emma he overheard what Mr. Otto had said. David checked the books and found out how much money Mr. Otto had received for the corn crop, but he didn't know how much he had given to Mr. Clarence," said Miss Mildred Law.

"Emma being Emma, had to verify it and right the wrong, if one was done. She and I asked Mr. Clarence what his agreed percentage with Mr. Otto was. It was half. She asked Mr. Clarence how much money Mr. Otto gave him. It was two hundred fifty dollars, the same amount he got the year before. Emma checked the amount Mr. Otto was given and knew he should have given Mr. Clarence much more because it was under the agreed half. Emma didn't say anything to Mr. Clarence about the money. She asked him to come with her to Mr. Otto's house.

"What Mr. Clarence did not know was that Emma and I had an ace up our sleeve to play against Mr. Otto. A month earlier, Emma and I had ridden our horses over to the preacher's house to practice a song special for Easter," said Miss Mildred Law.

"We knocked on the preacher's door but no one answered. We walked to the barn to see if the preacher was there. When we opened the barn door there was Mr. Otto and the preacher's wife lying in the hay on a blanket, naked as new-born jaybirds doing the hanky-panky in front of God, the horses, the hens, and us!"

Mabel and Jeannie burst out in laughter. I was a little hesitant to laugh unless Miss Mildred Law did. She was too involved in telling us the story to laugh, but she smiled, and so did I. Miss Mildred Law said lightheartedly, "We didn't say anything to anyone. We didn't know who to tell anyway. I don't know if the preacher ever found out how unfaithful his wife was, but a year later she left, unexpectedly."

Miss Mildred Law said, "When Emma, Mr. Clarence and I got out of David's truck at Mr. Otto's house, Mr. Otto seemed happy to see us. He was always pleased to see women come to his house."

Mabel said, "Yeah, he probably thought that y'all had come so he could touch you, too."

Miss Mildred Law said, "Emma wasted no time with small talk with Mr. Otto. We knew not to get too friendly with him. He would take it the wrong way. She told him straightforward he owed Mr. Clarence some more money for his crop.

"Mr. Otto told her, 'What business is that of yours, girlie? That is between two grown men and not some child to worry about.'

"That rubbed Emma the wrong way. Emma told him, 'I've always been taught it is everybody's business to make sure things are done right. The Bible says it is our responsibility as Christians to do that for our brothers and sisters in Christ.

"Mr. Otto knew it concerned the amount of money he kept from Mr. Clarence. He resented telling Emma, 'Missy, that sounds about like the right thing to do, but how does that concern me?'

"Emma immediately told him, 'Oh Mr. Otto, I think you know exactly what I am talking about. I don't know if you heard or not, but there is a rumor going around that the preacher is all upset because his wife told the sheriff she was attacked in her barn by some maniac. The wife also told him there are two witnesses who could identify her attacker.'

"Emma paused a second, and told him, 'Mr. Otto, it would surely be a shame if those two unknown witnesses came forward and backed up the preacher's wife's story.'

"Mr. Otto knew we had seen what he and the preacher's wife were doing. Emma said to him, 'I bet the sheriff would like to hear their story about what when on. I know those two civic-minded citizens could positively identify him and back up the ladies' story .

*. . if they had to*. Or unless the attacker repented and did something right to make up for the wrong he did to someone else.'

"Emma told him, 'The law says whenever a man makes an agreement with another man, and he miscalculates his figures on accident or on purpose, that it is considered a crime. He could be arrested and prosecuted for it, especially if he has been going around bragging about doing it, and others could testify they heard him say he did it. Then, there are the books with records verifying what he has done.'

"Emma continued our ploy on Mr. Otto. 'We just elected a new DA. I am sure he could make a name for himself if he prosecutes people who commit crimes like those. I'm sure he could find plenty of hard evidence to prove his guilt if he was guided in the right direction. Evidence of two eyewitnesses, evidence written in the books, plus witnesses hearing him bragging about what he did. It would be pretty much an open-and-shut case.'

"Mr. Otto got the message, and his whole attitude changed."

Miss Mildred Law said, "You think what happened in the barn was funny. It doesn't compare to what Emma did to that man next. Mr. Otto pulled out his wallet and gave Mr. Clarence the rest of his money. He told Mr. Clarence he had been meaning to come over and give the money to him, but he had been down in his back. We knew he was lying." Miss Mildred Law laughed out-loud and said, "You can't imagine what Emma did next.

"She began telling Mr. Clarence how Mr. Otto had been telling her how he had been meaning to give him an additional hundred dollars to help fix that leaky roof on their house. Emma made a big production about her being so proud of Mr. Otto, because of the way he was taking care of his tenants.

132

"While Mr. Otto was giving Mr. Clarence the extra money, he told Emma, 'I sure hoped that was all I told you, before I go completely broke.'

"Emma had a retort for him: 'Well Mr. Otto, you know what the Bible says about money, don't you?'

"Mr. Otto said to Emma, 'No Missy, I don't, but I got a feeling that you are going to tell me anyway.'

"Emma looked him straight in the eye. 'A fool and his money are quickly separated.'"

Miss Mildred Law said, "We left thinking we had put Mr. Otto in his place where he wouldn't be harming anyone for a long while, but we were wrong. The man was rotten to the core, full of all kind of evil. Just look at what he was doing to Mr. Dan, as proof positive. Now we would be heading back to Mr. Otto to right a second wrong, and I had no idea what Emma would do next.

"We understood Mr. Otto was within his rights to demand the money he was owed because they'd made an agreement, and he had the right to put them off the land because it was his land. However, his plan for Mr. Dan's daughter was wrong. We knew the underlying motive of Mr. Otto was to take Mr. Dan's cotton crop. He didn't want the money, he wanted the girl and the cotton crop. Mr. Otto had ran off his wife and all of his kids because of the way he treated them. They didn't want to be around him," said Miss Mildred Law.

"Emma knew she would need a little extra firepower to help solve Mr. Dan's problem. The debt Mr. Dan owed created a more difficult set of circumstances to overcome. It would be difficult to con Mr. Dan a second time like they had done first with Mr. Clarence, but she knew something had to be done to stop his stealing before someone got shot," said Miss Mildred Law.

"Emma had a plan, but it was going to take a little timing to make Mr. Otto extend the debt and forget about Mr. Dan's daughter. I honestly believe Emma looked forward to doing battle with Mr. Otto again," said Miss Mildred Law.

"Emma told Mr. Dan, 'Go home and don't send your daughter to him. And don't you go anywhere near him until I come to get you tomorrow morning. Tomorrow, you are going to hear some things you won't understand. I don't want you to say anything, just let Mildred and me and whoever we have there do all the talking. Do you understand? Mr. Dan answered yes.'

"Emma put David's letter away and told me to get into David's truck. As she was driving she told me her entire plan, but first they were going to ask the preacher to come help in the morning to speak to Mr. Otto.

"When we arrived at the preacher's house, Emma told me, 'Mildred, be sure to smile really big at the preacher's wife. We want to make her fear that we are going to tell what she did. We need to make her feel very uncomfortable to be around us, so she will excuse herself. We want her to do that in front of her husband. That is an important piece of our plan so we don't have to tell the preacher what his wife did.'

"We smiled at her, not allowing her husband to see us do this. She excused herself, saying she had a serious headache. As soon as she left, Emma intentionally made a big deal about how sorry she was that his wife did not feel well, and how ill she looked. I reinforced Emma's sadness in his wife's sudden illness, and we did it again right before we left," said Miss Mildred Law.

"We explained to the preacher what Mr. Otto had in mind with the debt, the threat of kicking them out of their home, stealing their crop, and especially having the young girl move in with him.

He said he would be there with us the next morning at 9:00 a.m. The preacher said what Mr. Otto was planning was completely immoral and would make God hide His eyes," said Miss Mildred Law.

"Our next stop was with a deputy-sheriff who was good friends with us, and Jimmy Ray's cousin. We knew he had an unhappy history with Mr. Otto. As a child, he'd lived in one of his share-cropper houses. He remembered how hard Mr. Otto made everything on his family and how his father struggled to make ends meet because of Mr. Otto's underhanded demands. He couldn't prove it, but he suspected Mr. Otto was abusing his wife and children back then, and couldn't do anything about it," said Miss Mildred Law.

"We had to tell the deputy the entire story, from the barn episode with the preacher's wife, to how Mr. Otto stole money from Mr. Clarence, to his manipulation of Mr. Dan's family, and to the scam we ran on Mr. Otto. He loved the plan and was with us all the way. He agreed Mr. Otto needed to be stopped. Emma, again reiterated how important our timing had to be in order to make Mr. Otto believe he was close to being arrested and how Emma and I were his only hope of not being caught. The deputy said he would play his role exactly as Emma had laid it out for him. We were now ready to go," Miss Mildred Law laughingly said.

"The next morning, Emma and Mr. Dan arrived at Mr. Otto's house at the same time the preacher drove up. The preacher humbly asked Mr. Otto what the problem was with him waiting on the cotton crop to come in so Mr. Dan could pay the rest of the debt he owed. Mr. Otto never said a word to the preacher. That changed when the preacher mentioned he knew about the request Mr. Otto had made for Mr. Dan's daughter to move in with him until the debt was paid," said Miss Mildred Law.

"Mr. Otto indignantly told the preacher, 'That ain't none of your damn business, preacher. That is between me and Dan. I don't hear him complaining none.'

"Mr. Otto said to Emma, 'Missy, I know this is all you're doing. There you go messing in my business again. Don't you know how to tend to your own business?'

"The preacher said, 'Mr. Otto, what you are planning to do is wrong. It is immoral and against the law. That girl you want to live with you is only sixteen years old.'

"Mr. Otto quickly modified the preacher's statement: 'All I want her to do is to help tend my house and cook for me. She would be helping pay off some of the debt that Dan owes me, that's all. Ain't nothing wrong with that. I ain't going to hurt the girl. She is just a baby.'

"The preacher told Mr. Otto, 'That may be true, but that is not what she or her family want. She is just an innocent child and you are putting her in the middle of this. The Christian thing to do would be to forget about the girl and wait until Dan can pay you back. As a Christian, you shouldn't be threatening him with putting him off your land. He still has a crop in the field. If you put him off, you would be stealing his crop.'

"Mr. Otto said, 'Preacher, what I do with my own land is not any of your business or anybody else's, and that includes you too, missy.'

"The deputy and I were waiting around the curve and saw Emma's signal to take off her straw hat. Emma said to Mr. Otto as she took off her hat, 'So what you are telling us, Mr. Otto, is that you are not going to wait for the cotton crop to come in unless Mr. Dan sends his daughter to you or pays you off. Is that right?'

"Mr. Otto answered Emma overconfidently: 'That is about how I see it, missy.'

"Then Emma told him, "Well, I guess you got to do what you got to do, and I guess I got to do what I got to do. I don't think it is going to be too enjoyable for one of us.'

"As Emma was telling this to Mr. Otto, the patrol car came up his driveway. Mr. Otto stared at it intensely as it came to a halt about twenty yards away from his front porch. The deputy and I got out and walked toward the porch where everyone was," said Miss Mildred Law.

"The deputy came up to everyone and spoke to the preacher. 'Mildred told me your wife wasn't doing too well last night, preacher. How is she today?'

"The preacher answered back, 'She is still hurting, but Lord willing, she will get better.'

"Both Emma and I quickly butted into the preacher's statement because we didn't want him to say anything further. He was talking about a headache, but we wanted Mr. Otto to think it was about the attack, so I said promptly, 'Oh, I am so glad to hear that, she looked so bad last night.'

"The deputy answered back quickly and said, 'We are still looking for the suspect. Mildred said she saw someone running in the woods around here.'

"Emma backed up his statement by saying, 'Yes, we did see a man run into the woods as though he was trying to hide.'

"The deputy said, 'Well I thought maybe Mr. Otto might have seen something. Did you see anything Mr. Otto?'

"Mr. Otto swallowed real hard and answered the deputy gruffly, 'No, I ain't seen nobody in these woods.'

"The deputy replied back, 'Yeah, I figured that. I just wish we could find those two witnesses. They are supposed to know who he is. We are going to find them soon, I got a good lead on who they are.'

"Emma hurriedly said, 'Yeah, I hope you do find them, and real soon too, because whoever he is, he deserves to be put under the jail. Maybe they will have a change of heart because of the wrong he did and turn himself in.'

"Before the preacher could ask any question as to what they were talking about, the deputy told us, 'Well I got to go. I got a report that someone extorted some money from their share-cropper and I'm going to investigate that now. People will do anything for money nowadays. It ain't like it used to be, where people looked out for each other.'

"The deputy asked me, 'Are you going to ride back home with Emma, Mildred? I hope so. That way, I can go to the mill now.'

"I answered the deputy, 'Yeah, I'll ride back with Emma. I hope you catch the guy. We will talk to you later today, be careful.'

"Emma and I both watched Mr. Otto the whole time. We could tell he was worried. It was great to see him squirm. The deputy played his part perfectly. Later on, we took the deputy out to the Malt Shoppe for a meal, and we all had a big laugh," said Miss Mildred Law, joyfully.

"The preacher made another appeal to Mr. Otto, but he did not say a word. Emma told him, 'Well Mr. Otto, I still remember that you are going to do what you have to do, and now we are going to do the right thing.'"

Miss Mildred Law said, "I backed Emma up by saying the same thing. Yes, we definitely would do what we needed to do.

"Mr. Otto understood our meaning, and surprisingly, he said to the preacher, 'You know preacher, Dan is a hard worker. I think I am going to give him a little bit longer to pay off his debt. But he better have my money when the cotton crop comes in, or I'm going to put him off my land.'

"Mr. Otto looked hard at me and Emma and said, 'I believe if certain people keep their mouth shut about certain things, then things will come out right for everyone. What do you think about that, missy?'

"Emma replied to Mr. Otto with another retort: 'I will try being nicer, if you try being smarter.'

"It was important for Mr. Otto to say he agreed to allow Mr. Dan to pay him off after the cotton crop came in because we now had the preacher as a witness. Even Mr. Otto would keep his word, once he made a deal in front of the preacher," said Miss Mildred Law.

Miss Mildred Law said, "It was always surprising how Emma could make people do the right thing, even when they wanted to do wrong. She had a unique way. A lot of people called it a gift, and I guess it definitely was that. She was the same way during the war. I just wish you could have seen her in action."

# Chapter 9

## *David's War*

M abel said to us, "David's letters to Emma told us about what he was learning. You could hear a shift in the way he wrote. He went from being surprised about how things were done in the military, to being amazed he could be a successful part of it."

Jeannie asked Mabel, "Do you mean David was shaping up to be a Marine?"

Miss Mildred Law confirmed this. "Yes, I saw it too, Mabel. His first letters were typical of a new recruit. Everything was new and exciting because he was learning a new way of life. By the end of his boot camp, his letters had become much more serious. You could read between the lines. He was anxious to put what he had learned into action."

Mabel added to Miss Mildred Law's statement saying, "Emma saw it too, and it frightened her. We were afraid to discuss with Emma what we believed was happening to David, but we saw the change. Emma didn't read the last letters he wrote her before shipping out because she was afraid for him. She believed he may not come home. We saw her read his letters and pull them close to her heart like she was afraid of losing him."

Mabel continued, "I caught her several times late at night going back to her hope chest to get a letter to read. Then I would hear her cry. I wanted to go to her, but you know how Emma was. No matter how tough things would be, she would never let anyone believe it was getting the best of her. She didn't want anyone to see she was hurting because her hurt might hurt them."

"Yes, she was like that, tough as a nail on the outside, but you knew it was eating her up on the inside," added Miss Mildred Law.

Mabel asked, "Miss Mildred Law, do you remember how vague David's last letter was to her? She shared that one with us, it was like he was trying to tell her something, but he couldn't get it out. He told Emma he had been placed in a special unit and was directed not to write home after that letter. That really worried her."

Miss Mildred Law said, "Yes, I remember how difficult it was to understand his last letter. It was strange, especially the part about being ordered not to write home. But when Jimmy Ray came home after boot camp on a ten-day leave, he explained why David wrote that."

"On his visit, he told us David had excelled at boot camp. The drill instructors really liked him. He was an excellent shot and was the best hand-to-hand fighter they had. They had selected him to be part of a special recon unit," Miss Mildred Law said.

"We had no idea what recon meant. Jimmy Ray explained what David would be doing. He was in a special unit to be sent behind enemy lines to gather information and to coordinate the local resistance before the invasion came. Everything they did was in secret. No one would know where they were going, and that was why he couldn't write home. Jimmy Ray said something I wish he would not have said: the mission David was going on was very dangerous. Jimmy Ray told Emma that David told him to tell her not to worry, he would be fine," said Miss Mildred Law.

Mabel said, "We discovered that David had been shipped to Pearl Harbor for special training. He spent four weeks preparing for a mission as part of a coordinated effort to invade the Solomon Islands. It was the first island the Marines would invade to begin taking back the Pacific Arena. He was part of a twelve-man team dropped off from a submarine at night in a raft near the northern shore of Malaita Island. It was part of the Solomon Islands the Japanese held. His team had two missions to accomplish.

"David said the team was divided into two six-man squads. One squad was to meet with the resistance and be taken to the exact locations of their big gun batteries. They needed that information so when the invasion came they would know how and exactly where to knock them out. Then because the Americans had broken the Japanese code, they learned a certain Jap general would be there. The mission for the second squad was to capture that general and remove him."

Listening to Mabel tell about David's mission amazed me. I wondered how in the world she knew this in such great detail. I didn't want to interrupt her to ask how she knew because it was so interesting. However, I couldn't help myself. I stopped Mabel and asked her, "Mabel, how do you know all this?"

Mabel answered me, "That's right Blake, you didn't know David came home early. He told all of us what happened to him in that terrible war. He captivated us as we listened to him tell us what happened. I think talking about it helped him release some of the horror he still held inside.

"David told us that when the two missions were accomplished, the two squads were to meet at a rendezvous point seven days later exactly where they had come ashore. From there, they were to signal the submarine that they were ready to be picked up.

"David said he was with the squad who located the gun batteries. His squad was at the rendezvous point a day early. Both squads were successful in their mission. However, the second squad who had taken the general was being chased as they headed back toward the rendezvous point. The general must have been very important to the Japs because they wanted him back. The squad had tried to lose the search teams several times but had been unable to do so. David's CO was with that squad. He determined they would hide in the jungle, then cross the stream at dusk. It would be the only chance for all of them to catch the sub together.

"But the Japs were not going to let that happen. They knew if they didn't flush them out of the jungle before night, they would lose them. They set up an ambush on the other side of the stream, waiting on horseback with rifles and swords.

"David told us that about an hour before nightfall, the Japs lobbed mortars close behind where the squad was. They dropped them to flush them out from their hiding place. They wanted them to go into the river. They didn't want to the drop mortars too close because they might accidently kill the general. However, all of them were hit with shrapnel and it did its job of forcing David's squad out of their hiding place.

"David said the CO took his squad and the general downstream, trying to flank the Japs. The Japs figured the mortar fire would cause any reinforcements they might have to come to their aid from upstream. The Japs were right, because when David's squad heard the mortar fire they went to help them. The Japs were waiting in the jungle to ambush them. When the Japs saw David's squad meet up with the other squad, the Jap commander sprung the trap."

Mabel said David told them that the Japs had captured all twelve of them without firing one shot. "He said they stood in the stream holding their rifles overhead to surrender. But that did not stop those butchering Japs. Two Japs on horseback charged them with swords and murdered four of their men before the general ordered them to stop.

"David told us that the Jap commander lined up all of them on the bank and took all of their dog-tags. They figured he did that to turn them into the Red Cross as proof that they were killed. It was a part of their propaganda to scare Americans and to bring honor to the Japanese people. He ordered them to turn around but not face the Japanese soldiers because the Americans were considered beneath them. They were going to kill them all. The general stopped them again, he wanted to know who the leader was of the second squad.

"The general grabbed their CO from the line and pulled him over next to the Jap commander. The general surprisingly spoke to our CO in broken English, asking him, 'Who led the other squad?'

"The CO would not answer him. The General took a pistol from the Jap commander and shot one of the CO's squad members in the head, instantly killing him."

Mabel said David cried the entire time he told this part: "The general asked the CO two more times who the leader of the other squad was, and each time he asked, the CO refused to say anything. The general shot two more members of the CO's squad after each refusal to answer his question.

"David said the general told his squad that if one of them told him who the leader of their squad was, he would let all of them live. None of the four would say a word. The general took a sword from the commander and ordered them to kneel on their hands and knees. They knew he intended to cut their heads off if they didn't tell, but still no one said a word."

Mabel said David cried as he told them what happened next. "The general asked them once more who their squad leader was. No one said anything again. The general raised the sword and cut off the head of the man nearest him.

"David stopped crying and told us he knew he was next in line, so he tried to stand up to fight, but two Jap soldiers kicked him to the ground and put him back on his knees. When the Jap grabbed his shirt, a map with the locations of their gun placements fell out on the ground. The general stopped his questioning and told the Japanese commander something in Japanese. The commander grabbed David and put him next to his CO, believing that he was the other squad leader.

"The general had a smirk on his face because he believed he had found the other leader. He thought it was David, but it wasn't. The other squad leader was killed by the two Japs on horses. The Jap general was pleased at what he did. Now, he was ready to torture both of them for information."

Mabel said, "The general thought, since David had papers, he was the leader. He lived because of some papers in his shirt. Then he cut off the other two men's heads."

Mabel said, "David explained that the Jap commander had gathered all of the dead bodies of their team. He took the dead men and cut off their heads. He took all of the heads and placed them on sticks in front of the hutch that they put them into. David said they looked at those heads for two days. He said he could still see them."

Mabel said, "David wailed like a baby. What happened had shattered him.

"David said that for two days they were given no food or water. The CO and him were beaten with canes to gain information, but neither one of them said a word. The Jap general laughed at them and told them that when they got to the main camp they would wish they had talked to him instead of what they were about to face.

"They took their boots off and tied them up with the laces. The Japs marched them barefooted two more days until they met up with a larger group of prisoners. Most of them were British and Australian military. Any prisoner who was discovered to be a resistance fighter was instantly shot. The Japs hated them and made examples of them every chance they got.

"David said that the Japs shot and bayoneted anyone who could not make the march. David helped one British soldier who was about to be shot because he was too weak to continue the march. The Japs would not allow you to talk to them, but David signaled to the Jap soldier that he would carry him. Much to David's amazement, the Jap allowed him to do it. That was the only act of compassion he saw from the Japs in the six months he spent with them.

"David told us that the Japs marched them for another day and many of the soldiers were killed along the way. When they got to the POW camp, the Japs beat the prisoners into submission to make them conform to their camp rules. If any prisoner raised a hand against a Jap, he was immediately shot. No prisoner was allowed to look any Jap directly in his eyes. Prisoners must bow and look at the ground, or they would be knocked to the ground with a rifle butt. Any infraction of their rules could result in them being crucified up-side down or tortured as an example to the rest of the prisoners, or they would punish everybody. David said they loved doing that.

"The Japs used all of them as guinea pigs for their Japanese doctors. They chose certain people and gave them injections that gave them diseases. They did that just to see if they could cure them. Most who were given the injections died.

"David told us about the food," said Mabel. "The food was scarce, it consisted of rice and spit peas or rice and vegetable stew. They never got any meat or fish of any kind. The rice was raw or maybe steamed, but it was always laced with maggots or rat droppings. They gave them no eating utensils, no plates, cups, or forks. Food was dipped either in your hands or on green leaves, if a man could find one.

"David told us about their sleeping conditions and work. They had shacks to sleep in, with no bed or bed coverings. Some shacks had no floors, so boards were torn out of the ones that had floors and given to others so they did not have to sleep on the ground. If a person had three boards to sleep on, they were blessed. The main thing for every prisoner was to keep well. Almost every person who became ill, died. The Japs gave them one of two jobs. Either dig ditches or repair bridges.

"David talked about his escape," said Mabel. "One day, the Japs decided to move some of the prisoners to another location. David was in the selected group. They were told they were moving to a mine somewhere near the coast in the mountains. Every prisoner who was selected to leave thought he was being moved to be killed. This time, they didn't have to march. They took them in trucks.

"David said that on the way to the new location they were attacked by mortars and automatic weapons in an ambush. It was the resistance fighters and they did not care who they killed as long as they got some Japs.

"David said the prisoners and the Japs bailed out of the trucks to either get under them or in the ditches. He was on the way to get in a ditch when a mortar landed near him and the concussion threw him into the air severely injuring him. His back and butt area received shrapnel wounds and the concussion knocked him unconscious. His wounds had made him unable to walk. He was bleeding and could not see in one eye. He also couldn't hear a thing.

"After any attack, the Japs would first round up the prisoners who could continue their journey and shoot the injured. The Japs saw how badly injured David was, and knowing he could not walk, shot him. Thank God, the Jap was a bad shot. He shot David in the neck, but the bullet only grazed him.

"When the Japs moved on, the resistance fighters would move in to see what ammunition or equipment they could scavenge. They would also look to see if anyone was still alive. Usually, if they found

150

anyone alive they would be too far gone, so they would mercy-kill them. They were about to bayonet David. It took all his energy to lift his hand in the air, but he managed to. He was signaling them not to kill him and said as best as he could: 'American, American.'

"They bandaged David up, packed him on a litter to their camp. There they medically treated him the best they could and contacted the American military, saying he was alive and desperately needed medical attention. Arrangements were made to put David in a fishing boat to be picked up by submarine in three days. He couldn't show it, but he was glad to get out of that jungle.

"The sub picked up David and took him to a military hospital in Darwin, Australia. From there, he was shipped to Pearl Harbor, next Walter Reed, and then home to Louisiana."

Jeannie quickly said to us, "Thank God, he got home alive. Is this when David and Emma get married?" she inquired.

Miss Mildred Law said to Jeannie, "Baby doll, do you remember when Mabel told you about what the Japs did with their dog tags when they were first captured? The Japs took David's and the other Marine's dog tags to give to the Red Cross."

Jeannie, looking puzzled, said, "Yes ma'am, Miss Mildred, I do remember. What does that have to do with anything?"

Miss Mildred Law told Jeannie and me, "Well, the Japs gave the dog tags to the Red Cross and told them all of the men who wore those dog tags were dead. So, the Red Cross had informed the Defense Department of their deaths. The Defense Department sent telegraphs to those men's home informing them their son or husband were KIA, (Killed in Action). That letter came to Emma. Emma believed David was dead."

Jeannie, still confused, said, "I still don't understand. If David came home, it still should have been a happy time for Emma. David is alive and back at home! They could get married now, right?"

Miss Mildred Law said to Jeannie, "No, honey. They couldn't . . . because Emma was not at home. When she thought David was gone forever, she joined the Navy Nurse Corps, and when he came home, she was gone overseas."

# Chapter 10

## The Girls' War

Miss Mildred Law realized Jeannie and I did not know the timeline of how things happened to Emma and David. Miss Mildred Law began putting things into a chronological order so Jeannie and I could have a better understanding about how things transpired.

Miss Mildred Law told us, "David was captured on his first mission sometime in May of '42. Emma received word that David was KIA in June of that year. Emma enlisted in the Navy Nurse Corps the next month, in July, and was shipped out overseas in September. Her ship was sunk the same month. David escaped from the Japs the next month in October of '42. Word of him being alive did not come home until November. David came to Mr. Tom's in January '43."

Miss Mildred Law explained to Jeannie, "You see honey, when the telegram came from the War Department saying David was KIA, Emma was crushed. She wouldn't talk to anyone, except God. And she was mad at God too, for letting David get killed."

Mabel said to Jeannie, sadly, "Emma locked everybody out of her life for a while. It was her way of mourning for her lost. She was dejected because the love of her life was gone. She thought he was gone forever. When she started talking to us again, she denied David was dead. She kept telling everyone that maybe he was hiding in the jungle somewhere, maybe even hurt, just waiting for someone to rescue him. After her anger of God passed, then she got mad at the Japs."

Miss Mildred Law said firmly, "That was when she decided to do her part to get even with the Japs. She was angry at them. She wanted to get her gun and go after them, but she knew no one would let her do that. That was when she decided to join the Navy Nurse Corps."

Mabel contentedly said, "Yeah, I remember that day. You, Sophie, and Mary Lou came over to the house to be with Emma. I know y'all came over there to console her. But Emma's attitude changed completely the moment she made her decision to fight the Japs. Instead of being grief-stricken, she was charged up and ready to go against them."

"She sure was! Wasn't she, Mabel? We couldn't believe the change," said Miss Mildred Law excitedly. "It was a shock to all of us. It was like she became a different person with a mission. She had not told Mr. Tom her decision yet. She was waiting to tell us girls, first."

Mabel said to us, "Emma said she wanted y'all to be there when the Navy Nurse Corps recruiter came to talk to her and Mr. Tom. After you girls left, she told Mr. Tom and Olivia what she was going to do. Mr. Tom wasn't very delighted with her decision, but he said he understood and supported her it. Olivia was mad at Emma because she thought Emma was only trying to draw the attention to herself."

Miss Mildred Law said, "We were there when the recruiter came that evening. She explained how long the training would last, how we would be in San Diego and Hawaii to be trained, and told us possible places we could be stationed. She assured Mr. Tom that Emma would be safe at all times. The service Emma would be providing to her country was very important."

Mabel said, "The woman recruiter was really good. She was so good that I wanted to join, too. The recruiter would have made a good used car salesman or a preacher."

We all laughed at what Mabel said. But my thoughts turned to how it was in the '40s. Even if Mabel wanted to serve back then, she couldn't because she was black. Our country has gotten much better in our treatment of other races, but we still have a long way to go.

Miss Mildred Law said to us, "Yes, the recruiter pitch was good. In fact, she was so good she had convinced everybody in the house that joining was the right thing to do for every young person. She said everyone should be in some service to our country. Both Sophie and I decided we wanted to join up, too. The recruiter promised that all three of us could be together the entire time, and that one fact was what made us decide to join."

Mabel smiled and said, "When Emma saw you two girls wanted to join and go with her, she was ecstatic. She was beaming with joy the same way she did when she was around David. I hadn't seen her that happy in a long time. Emma needed y'all."

Miss Mildred Law said lightheartedly, "We were happy that we would be going with her too. It was exciting for us. We would get to see the world, help people, serve our country, and we thought we would be safe. We had just one more little problem to overcome to make it happen: to convince our parents."

Jeannie asked, "How did that go over with them?"

Miss Mildred Law said, "At first, not too well. But when the recruiter came to my house and talked to both of our parents, they agreed it seemed safe. They felt we would be helping in the war effort, and it would be good for us, too."

Miss Mildred Law said, "So off we went to San Diego to the Naval Training Station on the Pacific Ocean. Oh . . . how I remember the way I felt when I first saw the Pacific Ocean. It was indescribable. We thought the Mississippi River was something, but compared to the ocean, it was little. I never thought I would end up hating the ocean after I saw it, but I did."

Miss Mildred Law said, "We spent six weeks in San Diego being indoctrinated to Navy rules and regulations. It was nothing like in the letters David wrote to Emma. They taught us discipline, first aid, and the Navy code of ethics. The Nursing Corps was different from what we thought. Not only was it instructive, it was very fascinating. We learned a lot in a short period of time.

"We shipped out to Pearl Harbor for more training. What a beautiful place Hawaii was. Even though the Japs tried to blow it to hell, we got to visit some magnificent sites. We received our training of how to care for the wounded and sick there. It was intensive. We learned how to care for many types of wounds. They drilled into us how important it was to keep an injured man's morale up. They taught us if one lost hope, most would usually die. I never forgot that," said Miss Mildred Law.

Mabel quizzed Miss Mildred Law, with her knowing the answer to her question, "Didn't you get married in Hawaii? Why don't you tell Jeannie and Blake about that?"

Miss Mildred Law looked at Mabel as if she had punched her. She sarcastically answered, "You know very well I got married. But we are telling them about Emma . . . and not me!"

Mabel replied back to Miss Mildred Law, "You and Emma were like two peas in a pod. If you knew one, you knew the other. Y'all were just alike. So, go ahead and tell them. I'm sure they would love to hear the story, just like I would."

Jeannie pleaded with Miss Mildred Law, "Oh, please Miss Mildred, I would love to hear about your marriage. Please tell us."

Miss Mildred Law said in a contemptuous voice, "Okay, okay I will, but it will be very brief. While at Pearl, I met this young, injured boy from North Dakota when we were doing our intern practice on a ward in the hospital. He wasn't injured in the sense he

158

had been shot. He was the platoon leader of his company and he had "jungle rot." It was a crippling foot fungus that many soldiers got because their feet were always wet. His feet had become so bad that his Commanding Officer made him come to Pearl to be treated."

Jeannie excitingly asked Miss Mildred Law, "What was his name? Was he handsome? Tell us about him."

Miss Mildred Law paused a second and thought about her man and said, "His name was Jerry Shook. He was from Carlson, North Dakota. He was not the most handsome man in the world, but he was built like Hercules. He had beautiful blue eyes and was so polite and caring. I can truly say this about that boy, I loved that boy from the first time I laid my eyes on him, and I know he felt the same way about me."

Miss Mildred Law continued. "I spent every available minute with him. I became his private nurse. In fact, I got into trouble with the supervising nurse. She complained that I was not allowing him to get his proper rest."

We laughed and could see how happy it made her to talk about him. Jeannie instantly asked, "When did y'all get married?"

Miss Mildred Law said, "Jerry and I found out the doctors were going to release him in a week and then give him a seven-day leave to recuperate. After that time, he would be shipped back to where he was. I had no idea where it was, and he wouldn't tell me. You know, "Loose Lips, Sinks Ships.

"I was still in intern training with three weeks left before I would be shipped out too And he would be gone in two weeks. We had only known each other for two weeks. We didn't want to part and take the chance of never seeing each other again. We both realized the moment we met that we were made for each other. So, Jerry proposed to me there in the hospital. We got a priest to marry

159

us the next day while Jerry was still in his bed. The doctors did not want to release him early because he was not completely healed. They said he needed to have another week of complete bed rest."

Miss Mildred Law laughed as she said, "Somebody must have convinced the doctor it was exactly what I had in mind for him. I am sure Emma arranged it. She always could get those doctors to do what she wanted. She was so damn pretty, and they all just melted when she asked them anything. So they released Jerry early, and it gave us a few extra days to be together."

Miss Mildred Law stated, "However, there was another problem. There was a shortage of nurses at the hospital. I still had to work my shifts because I needed the training to be certified. The Navy had just sent out a large number of nurses to different hospitals around the Pacific, and it caused a shortage there at Pearl.

"Emma went to our Supervising Nurse, and she volunteered to cover all my shifts so Jerry and I could go on a honeymoon. At first, the Supervising Nurse said it would be impossible because of the way the shift was set up. Emma convinced her if she placed her on a different shift from me, then she could cover both shifts without any problems. Emma said when Jerry was shipped back, I could do double shifts to make up for the training I had missed," said Miss Mildred Law.

"So everything was set up for us to marry and go on a honeymoon however there was still one more very important problem. Neither Jerry nor I had any money to go a honeymoon. No problem, Sophie went around to all the wards and collected money from doctors, nurses, and anyone willing to contribute to this *good cause*," as she called it," exclaimed Miss Mildred Law.

"She came back with more than enough money and we were off on our honeymoon. We found a place right on the beach. It was a shack, but it was everything we needed. We spent a great ten days together. During that time, we made plans for what we were going to do after the war. We were so happy with one another and couldn't wait for the war to end so we could be with each other forever," pined Miss Mildred Law.

"Jerry shipped out, and in a week we nurses shipped out too. Once on board, we were told we were headed to Australia to set up hospitals there. It was all in preparation for the Island Hopping Campaign the military had made to take back the Pacific territories from the Japs.

"Emma and Sophie were so pleased for me. They wanted to know everything, and I wouldn't tell them anything. You know, things between a husband and his wife are private," declared Miss Mildred Law.

Her voice changed to a sadder tone. "Then a terrible thing happened. We were in the Coral Sea, thinking we had traveled far enough out of the reach of the Japs. Then one of their submarines torpedoed our ship, and we sank."

Miss Mildred Law said, "I can still see those sailors hustling to make sure they got all us nurses on those life boats. Many of those boys lost their lives saving us. We were hit early in the morning and had to stay in the water until the next day. The Japs sent two destroyers to pick up the survivors. They pulled those they wanted out of the water and shot the rest. They showed no mercy to those helpless men who had struggled so long to stay alive. They just mowed them down like they didn't matter."

Miss Mildred Law told us, "The Japs brought us to a POW camp on Tarawa. The nurses were in pretty good shape because we were in life boats. We made an effort to treat the injured, but the Japs wouldn't allow us nurses to do that. They separated the men from the women. They beat many of the men, even shot some who resisted them. The ones who were killed probably were better off dead as compared to what lay ahead for them."

Miss Mildred Law said, "They lined us nurses against the fence so they could search us. They put their nasty hands all over us. Every once in a while one of the guards would drag a nurse into a guard shack. They raped them and brought them back to the fence and laughed and bragged to the other guards."

Miss Mildred Law said, "One guard kept looking intently at Emma. We all noticed him staring at her. Finally, he grabbed her to take her to the guard shack, but Sophie jumped out of the line to draw their attention away from Emma and she starts ballet dancing and singing. All the guards stared at her, I assume thinking she had gone crazy. They began laughing at her and making fun of her, and then for no reason at all, one of them shot her. I tried to go to her but a guard stopped me by throwing me against the barbed-wire fence. As I struggled to become untangled from the fence, Sophie's life slipped away. I had to watch her die as we listened to her gurgle blood from her lungs, struggling to hold onto life. I only wish I'd had a gun. I would have killed that piece of trash who shot her and all the rest of them for laughing."

Miss Mildred Law continued . . . "Sophie's distraction did stop the guard from taking Emma into the guard shack. The gunshot caught the attention of an officer and he came to see what was going on. He ordered the guard to place Emma back into the line. He chewed the guard out and sent him away. He directed his instructions to the other guards and began fussing at them, I assume it was about the way we were being treated."

Feeling remorse, Miss Mildred Law said, "Emma could never forgive herself because Sophie had given her life to save her from being raped. We were not given an opportunity to treat Sophie or even mourn for her because there was another disturbance in another part of the camp. We could hear people yelling and then automatic gun-fire broke out. The guards quickly took us out of the fenced area into a building outside of the gates. I could see through a window there were many bodies lying on the ground."

Miss Mildred Law said, "The same Jap officer that fussed at the guards came into the building and told us in perfect English to take a seat on the floor. He apologized for what had taken place outside and told us he would be moving us tomorrow morning to another location."

Miss Mildred Law said, "Emma raised her hand to ask a question. The officer allowed her to speak. Emma asked meekly if she could go check on her friend who was just shot to see if she can help her?

"The Jap officer coldly replied to Emma, 'There is no use, she is dead. I'm sorry.'"

Miss Mildred Law continued, "We spent the night in the shack, all forty-three of us nurses. The next morning, the Jap officer came with his men to transfer us to the docks and loaded us on a transport ship. They were also moving other POWs and military supplies. They confined us to a section away from the men and the same Jap officer came in and told us we were going with him to the Philippines to be part of a hospital there. He told us we would be treated with respect if we cooperated with him. We were also told we would be used to help civilians and POWs there. He told us this, hoping it would motivate us to feel we would be doing something we were trained for."

Miss Mildred Law complained, "I don't know how many days we were inside the ship, but it seemed like it was an eternity. When we docked, we were transported in trucks to a new camp in Los

Barnos. The Japs had taken a fifty- to sixty-acre area and put barbed-wire around it. They were also building a thirty-bed hospital there.

"They had already built a dormitory. At first, we had plenty room, even though all we owned was the clothes on our backs. We were welcomed there by another Japanese officer, who we later found out was a UCLA graduate. Later, he was a blessing because he allowed the nurses to make life tolerable. We were allowed to exercise, grow vegetable gardens, do chores, play American music over the PA system, hold dances, play baseball, even allowed us to go in and out the compound as long as no one tried to escape. We had food, but it was not plentiful so we didn't starve. We even had some meat, fish, eggs, and of course rice," confirmed Miss Mildred Law.

Miss Mildred Law also said, "The Jap commander admired Emma. He used Emma to keep the others nurses motivated and in check. He told them if they cooperated with him, they would continue to have as much freedom as they needed. Emma was not the high-ranking nurse, but she was the one he used to speak for the nurses. He recognized she had a way to get people to do things they asked. We learned later following their rules was best for us."

Miss Mildred Law said, "At the hospital we did treat some civilians, but we mostly treated sick and injured Jap soldiers. Occasionally they would bring in an American or British officer for us to treat. The Japs never wanted any Ally officer to die. Officers knew too much valuable information to be killed, or to let die."

Miss Mildred told us, "Emma always worked the night-shift so she could be free for most of the day. One night, the Japs brought in this American officer. His name was Charles Winston. He was from Virginia and his family was wealthy. He had been shot in his knee and it would not heal. He had been running a high fever, and the Japs thought he was going to die. They brought him to this camp because the care where we were was better than anywhere else."

Miss Mildred Law's spirits lifted as she told us, "Believe this or not, Emma fell in love with him. When he first got there, he was near death. The doctors treated him the best they could and told Emma and the other nurses his fever was so high that he probably would not make it through the night. Emma decided to do all she could to bring his fever down. She sent the orderlies to bring in buckets of cool water from a spring nearby. Its water was much cooler than the hospital's supply. She put the officer in a bathtub and had them change the water every thirty minutes to help bring his fever down. As they did that, she swabbed him with alcohol on his head, wrist, and the back of his neck."

Miss Mildred Law continued to explain what Emma did to help Charles Winston, "She also put compression bandages around his knee and rotated it every fifteen minutes to give him a fresh supply of blood. She stayed with him all day and all night, and all the next day and night. His fever finally came down, but he kept going in and out of consciousness. Emma stayed with him the entire time. She slept on a gurney next to him."

Miss Mildred Law said, "When that officer came to, Emma was there. The other nurses said he looked at Emma and smiled. The officer told Emma he thought he had died because every time he came to, he kept seeing this beautiful angel, and the angel kept telling him he was going to live. Now he was awake, he realized the face he saw was no angel. It was Emma."

Miss Mildred Law said, "The evening Charles snapped out of the fever, we came in late to check on him. Charles was sitting up in his bed, eating some hot soup. When he saw Emma, he jumped and spilled the soup on himself. The soup burned him. Emma laughed at him and told him, 'Here sir, give me the spoon and let me help you. I think I can do better than you.' They both laughed.

"As Emma was feeding him the soup, the officer told her, 'Nurse. The doctors tell me I owe you my life. That you single-handedly brought my fever down and kept the infection from coming into my knee. I personally want to thank you for saving my leg and my life.'"

Miss Mildred Law said with a smile, "I guess Emma couldn't resist using one of her retorts on him. She told the officer, 'Don't take life too seriously, no one gets out alive.' Then she said, 'You are very welcome, I was saving you for me.'

"The officer didn't understand her last remark. 'I know we all want to get out of this war alive. But why would you say, 'you are saving me for you?'

"Emma told him jokingly, 'Because I want to run all my evil experiments on you to see if you are really alive.'"

Miss Mildred Law said, "He stayed in the hospital for about two weeks before they took him away. Emma spent every waking minute with Lieutenant Charles Winston. There was no doubt she was smitten by him. He was really good-looking, and together they made a nice looking couple."

Miss Mildred Law said, "It wasn't long after he left, in early '44, that life at the Los Banos camp really changed. An imperial Japanese officer took over. His name was Konashen, and we jokingly imagined his name meant 'idiot.' He really made all of our lives miserable. He tried to starve us to death, especially the nurses. He hated Emma because she had more control of the camp than he did. Even the Jap soldiers respected Emma more than they did him. The Japs knew the Americans had landed in the Philippines, but we didn't know."

Miss Mildred Law said, "The Japs ran the civilians from their homes and forced them to come to the POW camps. We were

166

flooded with so many sick civilians that we couldn't help anybody. Our morale fell, we had no food, we had to move into cramped quarters, the Japs would not allow us to leave the camp, and they limited where we could go inside the camp. Everybody was miserable.

"One day in January of '45, the Japs told us they were leaving us to run the camp ourselves. They left, and as soon as they did, we ran an American flag up the flag pole and sang the national anthem. It was the sweetest sound I had heard in years. Our freedom lasted one week, and the Japs came back," said Miss Mildred Law.

"The reason the Japs left was because they had found out the General MacArthur had ordered the 11th Airborne to rescue everyone in Los Barnos. When they didn't come within a week, they figured it was just a rumor. They thought because we were so far behind enemy lines they would never try to rescue us, so they came back. But they were wrong.

"A few weeks later, planes flew over our camp and paratroopers dropped out of them. At the same time the paratroopers fell, amtracs with the Marines and guerillas attacked the guard barracks and the front gate killing most of the Japs. The fighting lasted about ten minutes." Miss Mildred Law said.

She told us, "Emma and I were at the hospital when an amtrac came rolling up to the front door and men came pouring out of it. I remember thinking I had never seen anyone look that good in years. The guys who came out of that thing were in such good physical shape. One officer asked me if I knew where the commander's office was. I knew they wanted to take him alive, so I made like I didn't know where it was, because if anyone wanted to see Konashen give up, it would be Emma. I told him this lady knew, pointing to Emma. I didn't want to deprive her of the opportunity of seeing him go down. Later on, Emma told me it was a glorious sight. Konashen cowered in a corner trying to kill himself and he couldn't even do that right."

Miss Mildred Law summarized the events of the rescue. "The Marines started yelling to the POWs and civilians to load into the amtracs. It was three thousand of us. Everyone was running in all directions except to the vehicles, so the Marines set the hospital on fire to get them moving in the right direction. The amtracs took the sick and crippled, and trucks came in to take the rest of us across the lines. It was a great day. We were being liberated. Within an hour we were across the front lines and under American protection."

Miss Mildred Law said, "Before we left the Pacific, Admiral Kinkaid gave us a dinner to honor us. It was a feast of the best food with steaks as the main dish. I don't think any nurse took more than a few bites. Our appetites were gone because we had lost over thirty percent of our body weight and our stomachs were too small."

Miss Mildred Law said, "When we reached the states, we were the star attraction. Everyone wanted to take pictures with us. We were given dinners, free shopping sprees, autograph sessions, and even medals. One great thing was that we got was our back pay and three months of leave to help us recuperate. We all suffered from some form of malnutrition, but it didn't take long for us all to recover. The best thing of all was that we got to be back in America—thank God for America."

Miss Mildred Law said, proudly, "When we were being processed out at San Diego, the War Department sent couriers to our homes to let our folks know we had been rescued, and we would be coming home soon. All the nurses would be brought to their front doors by special couriers."

Miss Mildred Law said, "We were looking forward to that great day, and I am sure our folks were, too. But for Sophie's parents, there would not be any great homecoming for them. At that time, we didn't know it would end up that way for Emma. Too. That day would hold great, mixed emotions for everyone. Even though her folks would be happy to see her alive and well, she would make a discovery. It would change her joy into . . . I don't even know what to call it. But what she was about to see had happened in her family wasn't anything happy, because the shock of it would kill all of her joy and bring her great sadness."

# Chapter 11

## *The Homecoming*

eannie and I were confused about what Miss Mildred Law had said. I knew Jeannie was wondering, just as I was, how Emma's coming home could be anything other than joyful. When she arrived, Emma would see her father, her sister, her sister's children, Aunt Sis, and Mabel and Howard who she hadn't seen in four years. Most important of all, she was going to find out that David had not been killed. It had to be a jubilant occasion for them all. There was no way the joy of seeing them could surprise her and make her sad.

Miss Mildred Law saw the confusion on our faces and said, "I know both of you are mixed-up. Bear with us and you will understand after you hear what went on while Emma was a POW."

Mabel told us, "If y'all would have seen Emma's reaction to what took place, you too might have thought she may have been happier back in the POW camp."

Jeannie told Mabel, doubtfully, "I don't understand how you can say something like that?"

Agreeing with Mabel, Miss Mildred Law said, "I wasn't there to see what happened when Emma arrived home; however, Emma did tell me she said she would have been happier staying in the POW camp. What she discovered had happened while she was away was too much for Emma to grasp."

Jeannie asked, "How? What happened? What did she discover that would be so awful?"

Miss Mildred Law said, "Jeannie, just be patient and we will tell you the whole story as to why Emma told me later on that she would have been happier back in the POW camp instead of coming home. But we must go back to when she came home and what all took place to cause her to say that."

Jeannie begged them, "Please, by all means, explain it to us!"

Mabel said, "We were sitting on the front porch when we saw the military car coming up the drive bringing Emma home. We had expected her that day because the sheriff informed us he had received a call telling him she would arrive that day. The courier drove Emma to the side of the house and opened the door for her. The twins ran up to the car and were jumping up a down with eagerness. It was like Christmas to them because our excitement of her return had spread to them. Mr. Tom hurried as fast as feeble legs would allow him. He was the first one to greet her. Emma hugged him and they held each other a long, long time. Mr. Tom wouldn't let go of Emma, for he was so glad she was home safe."

Mabel continued. "Of course, Madea was not going to let Emma just say how-do-you-do and move on. Madea grabbed her and hugged her so hard that we heard something in Emma's purse break. Neither Emma nor Madea checked to see what was broken, they were just happy to be able to touch one another. Emma had such a big smile on her face, I don't think she could have wiped it off if she'd tried. She was thrilled to be home. Emma kept mumbling, 'Thank you God! You got me home!'

"When Madea let her go, I hugged her, too, and told her we all were so glad she made it back safe," said Mabel.

"Emma told us, 'I thought about each one of you every day, and I prayed every day to see you. It's so good to be home. You just can't imagine how much. I can't believe I am here myself.'"

Mabel said, "The boys hugged Emma and when they let her go, Emma told them she had a surprise for them in her suitcase. The boys begged her to show them what it was, but Olivia, who was standing away from the welcome group, rudely told her boys to be quite. Emma reached for Olivia with both her hands and hugged and kissed her on her cheek.

"Emma told Olivia, 'Big sister, I really missed you. You are as beautiful as ever. I told everybody in my unit that I had the most beautiful sister in all of Louisiana. You and I have so much to catch up on. I want to know everything that has happened since I've been gone.' Emma kissed Olivia on her cheek again, but Olivia never offered any affection toward Emma."

Mabel gloomily said, "When Emma said she wanted to know everything that had happened, a hush fell over us. We didn't know what was going to happen next. We thought Olivia would do something vain, but she didn't. She didn't have to, because David came out of the house on his crutches to where we were. He stopped about ten feet from our group to look at Emma, with tears rolling down his cheeks, he began to sob."

Mabel said, "Emma didn't see him at first. She noticed everyone was looking away from her, and she turned to see what we were looking at. That is when she saw David.

"Emma squealed and cried in the same moment. She fell on her knees and said, 'My God, My God it's a miracle. You are alive! Oh, thank you God! I knew you would answer my prayers. He is alive. I knew it! Praise You God!'"

Mabel gladly said, "Emma jumped up and ran to David, knocking his crutches out from under his arms, and almost knocking him down. She hugged him, kissed him, and wept. David hugged and kissed her, too but then he intentionally avoided her kisses. We knew why, and it was killing him, especially after we found out what Olivia had done. Seeing those two together again caused us to cry, and it wasn't because of their joyous reunion. We cried because we knew what the situation would bring. Emma had no idea what was coming next. Her emotions were about to be ambushed, and she would go from great ecstasy to a greater agony."

Mabel said in as a despicable sounding voice as she could muster up, "Then that hussy, Olivia, walked over behind David, and put her arms around him while Emma still had her arms around him, she told Emma sneeringly . . . 'We're married!'"

Mabel said, "Emma let David go and turned to look at us, as if she were saying to us, 'How could you let that happen?' Emma was in panic. We couldn't help her. Our hearts went out to her, but we couldn't do anything to take the jolt away. We wanted to, but we felt as helpless as she did. Emma burst into tears and ran to the barn to hide her great unhappiness and disappointment."

Mabel said, "Those military couriers who brought Emma were in shock, too. They came to take pictures of this great happy reunion, of a POW nurse coming home to her family, and it hadn't quite turned out as anyone had expected. Mr. Tom realized the position the couriers were in. Anybody would be confused at what had just taken place. I knew what was coming and I was still mixed-up. Mr. Tom thanked them for bringing Emma home, and they left. I'm sure they talked about what they thought had happened, but they really had no idea what the true story was."

Astonished, Jeannie said, "My God, that can't be so! How in the world did that marriage happen?"

I didn't say anything. It had shocked me too. How could David leave the love of his life and marry Olivia? It didn't make sense, and I was very anxious to hear their explanation of how this marriage had come about.

Mabel confidently said, "When David came home he was in bad physical condition, and he needed a place to stay. When he left for the Marines, he had had no home and when he came back, he was in the same predicament. Mr. Tom allowed David to move in with him, Olivia, and the boys. Mr. Tom felt everyone in the community knew David would someday marry Emma. He felt David was part of his family, and having a younger man would be good for the boys. David needed help and Mr. Tom offered his home to him. It was the right thing to do. Mr. Tom realized there might be some foolish talk, but he had done nothing immoral or wrong."

Mabel told us, "Mr. Tom knew he could depend on Madea and me to help care for David. David's physical condition was serious. The concussion from the impact of the mortar had caused him almost to be an invalid. He could walk very little, and his hearing and vision on one side was nearly gone. Later, his vision improved, but his hearing was still poor. That mortar round had done a number on him. The only good thing that came from the injury was that it allowed him to come home.

"Mr. Tom was good medicine for David, as he helped him readjust to normal life. David had terrible nightmares when he came back. He had us up at night dodging bullets and bombs. Olivia was no help at all, she imagined she helped, but the only thing she did was . . . "

Mabel paused to say her next phrase. "Was to fall in love with him, if you can believe that."

Her statement shocked Jeannie. She asked, "How did that happen? David was Emma's fiancé. Did David fall out of love with Emma and in love with Olivia?"

Mabel answered, "No. Not really, but that didn't make any difference to Olivia. It was only important to her how she felt."

Mabel continued . . . "When David first came, Olivia wouldn't have anything to do with him, but as David improved, she began talking with him about different things. She realized how sweet and kind he was. He was everything she wanted to become but wasn't. I assume it was during those times she decided she wanted him, and she started taking steps to make it happen."

Jeannie asked, "Did she not have any concern for Emma at all? Didn't she understand she was stealing Emma's fiancé. Did she realize when Emma came home she and David would be married. Didn't she care how that would affect everyone?"

Mabel simply said, "I really don't know what was in her heart, but evidently she didn't care. At first, I didn't see her making a play for David, but later on it became all too obvious."

Mabel told us, "Soon after David came home, Miss Mildred Law's mother came over to tell us some shocking news. She read that the ship the girls was on had been sunk by a Japanese sub and there was no word of survivors. Mrs. Law said more details would be made available as information came in. This bad news horrified our families. We didn't know what to expect."

Mabel said, "Three weeks later, Mrs. Law came back with the news she had received another telegram telling her Mildred had been rescued and was a in a POW camp in the Philippines. She said there was no mention of anyone else, but she felt sure if Mildred had made it, Emma and Sophie probably had, too.

"Mr. Tom said to Mrs. Law, 'It is not good news to hear Mildred is a POW, but at least we know Mildred is alive.'"

Mabel sadly said, "The next day, Sophie's mother received a telegram telling her parents she had drowned when the ship sank. Mrs. Law came over to see if we had received a telegram about Emma and told us that tragic news. Mr. Tom told her he had not received any news, but he was going to Sophie's house to be with her parents at this sad time."

Miss Mildred Law started cussing, "Them damn lying Jap rats. They murdered that girl for no reason except they enjoyed doing it. They didn't even have enough guts to tell the truth. We didn't even get a chance to help her or even to say goodbye to her, and all we have of Sophie is a headstone. Her body isn't even here. It's still over there on that stinking island, somewhere."

Mabel hurriedly said, "Two days later, Olivia came from town, crying. She told us she'd read a telegram saying Emma had drowned, too. She was crying so hard that Mr. Tom couldn't make sense of what she was saying. Finally Olivia calmed down enough to tell us that after she read the telegram, she got so angry she burned it, and came home to tell us."

Jeannie saying lowly, "Well, we know that was a lie, don't we? Did she really get a telegram?"

Miss Mildred Law said, "We know one was sent, but we don't know how Olivia got it. We have hashed that over for many years without really knowing the answer. We concluded she probably received it the same day my mother received hers. Then she didn't tell anyone right away because she was waiting for a telegram on Sophie. When it came and it said Sophie was dead, it played right into her plans, which didn't include Emma. It gave her more time to get David for herself, especially after telling us that horrible lie."

Mabel angrily said, "Olivia made like Emma's death was the worst thing that ever had happened to her, playing it for all it was worth. She loved the attention everyone gave her. People came by the house telling her and Mr. Tom how sorry they were about losing Emma. They would have told David, too, but he had climbed into a hole within himself. He couldn't face anyone when he was told Emma was dead.

"Mr. Tom's health plummeted after he believed he had lost Emma. She was the love of his heart. Mr. Tom loved both his daughters, but one he was proud of and the other was just beautiful. That was exactly how he characterized them. Olivia gave him all the beauty his eye could behold, and Emma was his heart."

Mabel despondently said, "It crushed Madea. It took all the energy I had to keep her going. I pray to God that neither Howard nor I go before her. After seeing how hard she took Emma's death, I really believe she would just lay down where she was and die. But thank God, it looks as if she is going to outlast us all, and I hope she does."

Miss Mildred Law said, "She just might. How old is Miss Sis now Mabel?"

Mabel proudly answered, "She is eighty-six. She tells me all the time she has seen many things in her lifetime. She has gone from the horse and buggy era to spaceship travel. Madea still doesn't believe they landed on the moon. She says they are fooling us. That they filmed the moon landing somewhere in Hollywood, and it is not real."

Everyone laughed at what Mabel said; there are many old timers who don't believe there was a moon landing. There was little doubt Miss Sis had lived to see many good and great things, but she also has gone through many hard and harsh things, too. It is amazing to see how far man has come with his inventions, but the sad thing about man is that he still has the same evil desires one generation after the next. And I doubt it will ever change."

Mabel exclaimed, "As the grief of losing Emma faded, Olivia turned her attention to capturing David. David was still in a state of mourning, and Olivia made every effort to console him. That was when we notice Olivia enticing David. Madea said after Olivia had

180

her twins, she had lost all interest in men, but now for some reason, she was making a play for David. She started dressing up a little more than normal, and she would wear makeup. Because of the war, it was only used on special occasions. I guess, to Olivia, David had become her special occasion."

Mabel quickly said, "We also noticed they were spending much more time together, and staying up later talking to each other. We assumed they were only consoling each other to help each other make it past Emma's death."

Mabel said, "One evening, Olivia and David went for a walk. David walking without the use of crutches was new to him. However, he could travel a short distance without them. But that night, David came back to the house upset, he sat in the swing to compose himself. Mr. Tom saw how troubled he was, and went to David. He asked him what seemed to be the problem."

Mabel told us, "I was cleaning the bedroom, and they didn't know I could hear them. David told Mr. Tom dejectedly, 'It's nothing Mr. Tom. Olivia just said something that upset me, that's all.'

"Mr. Tom, mildly upset, told David, 'She knows better than to do that. I will go to talk with her and straighten her right out.'

"Mr. Tom started to get up and David quickly reached out to stop him. He said, 'No, Mr. Tom. Don't do that. It will only make matters worse.'

"Mr. Tom sat down, puzzled. 'Okay David, if you say so, I won't. Is there anything I can help you with? I can't imagine what Olivia could say to upset you so much.'

"David blurted out, 'She wants me to marry her . . . and to do it soon.'

"Mr. Tom was stunned by what David had said. He paused to gather his thoughts and very diplomatically said, 'That is a mighty big request, David, particularly at this time, and don't you think that will require much more thought?'

"David answered, 'It sure does, especially after the news about Emma, and I don't know how to answer her.'

"Mr. Tom knew David was seeking his help to give Olivia an answer. 'Son, I wouldn't know how to answer that request, either. You have a lot to consider, the timing for one thing and knowing if Olivia is the right one for you. I think you better think on it some more before you decide.'

"Mr. Tom got up and walked into the house. I saw Olivia come up the drive, and she came to the porch and sat with David," Mabel said to us.

"Olivia pressured David for an answer and condescendingly said, 'Now that you are over your little mad spat at me, what do you say about what I have asked you?'"

Mabel said, "David didn't say a word to her. He kept silent I guess because there were too many things going through his mind.

"Olivia slipped her arm around David's shoulders and kissed him on his ear and neck and told him, 'There is no reason for you to wait any longer because she's not coming back. She doesn't have anything that I don't have. I can make you very, very happy. Let's do it. You know you want to. Come on.'"

Mabel told us, "I'm going to say this. I don't want to, but it's true. Olivia was one physically beautiful woman. If she entered a beauty contest, she would win. If she placed her charms on Satan, himself and told him he had to do right, he would. I say that to let you two understand this is what David was up against. She was a very desirable, physically attractive, woman that any man would want, especially if she charmed them."

Mabel continued, "At first I was not sure if she was talking about marriage or something else. However, David quickly cleared that up for me when he told her, 'It's not that I wouldn't marry you. But what would people say if we married so close to after we have found out Emma was dead?'"

Mabel quickly said, "Did David ever say the wrong thing. Olivia became blistering mad and told David, 'Who do you want? A dead memory, or me! A memory can't do for you what I can. Just look how we have cared for you. Don't you appreciated what I have done for you?"

Mabel told us, "Olivia weaved her magic on him and painted David into the corner. She preyed on his emotions. She was telling him he should marry her because of what her family had done for him. She never mentioned anything about loving him or him loving her."

Mabel, upset, said, "David was squirming in the swing because Olivia was telling him he was not grateful for her family's help. It put him in a frustrating position. David looked at her and asked her, 'Do you think it would be right to Emma, because if you do, we will get married?'"

Mabel said, "Him asking her that would be like asking a kid in a candy store if he want anything. Of course, she said yes it was right. She lied to him, and told him it would be what Emma wanted for him to be part of their family."

Mabel told us, "I wanted to go out there and slap both of them: her, for forcing him into agreeing with her, and him, for being so stupid to fall for her charms. I knew it was wrong, and I knew in my heart, that he knew it too. But he went ahead and agreed to marry her anyway."

Mabel said, "I should have known she was lying about everything because of what she did next."

Jeannie asked her, "What did she do?"

Mabel said, "Most girls when they accept a proposal want to tell their family, but not Olivia. She kept it a secret until they married. The next day, she drove David across the state line into Mississippi, and they got married. In Mississippi, they will marry anyone at any age. They don't need a blood test or a three-day waiting period. They just marry. David and Olivia didn't even take a honeymoon. They came back, and Olivia called us together and made the announcement. That she and David are husband and wife."

Mabel said, unhappily, "Everyone in the room reacted in different ways. Her kids ran and hid, Leonard cried and Bernard picked up a comic book and started reading it. Madea and me shook our heads in disgust and left the room. I had already told Madea I thought they were about to get married, so it wasn't a total shock to us."

Mabel said, "Poor Mr. Tom. When Olivia told everyone the news, tears began to roll down his cheeks. I knew it reminded him that Emma was gone, and he would never see her again. I knew in my heart he was thinking it should be David and Emma instead of Olivia and David. Mr. Tom had warned David he had a lot to consider with marrying Olivia. Evidently, David didn't take the hint that it wasn't a good time for a marriage or she might not be the one for him."

Mabel disparagingly said, "From what I saw, the only one who seemed happy in the room after she announced they were married was Olivia. David did not seem too thrilled about the event."

# Chapter 12

## *The Marriage and the Lie Revealed*

"After Olivia married David, she was the happiest I had seen her in years. She had a man other women wanted. That was important to her, but even more important to her was she had the man Emma wanted," Mabel said.

Mabel continued, "Olivia treated David the way a wife should, at least she did at first. I'll just say she made him know he was a man and she was a woman. Some mornings they didn't come for breakfast, and other times they didn't get up to help get the boys off to school."

Mabel harshly stated, "Once she got a hold of David's military check . . . Olivia thought only of herself. She began treating David like an old Christmas toy. She set him aside, and his money gave her the freedom to buy what she wanted.

"When she cashed the first check, the honeymoon ended, and the house became a war zone between David and Olivia. They argued about her wasting money. She would buy things she didn't need, and then brag to Mr. Tom and David how much money she saved because it was on sale. She didn't use any common sense at all, and it didn't matter to her that we were still in a depression and had to ration everything.

"David's truck was always a source of an argument. Olivia would use the truck and bring it back with the gas on empty. She would go to use the truck again and blame David for it being empty. To our disbelief, he would apologize. What Olivia wanted was a car. She didn't care if they didn't have enough money to buy a car. She just thought that riding in a truck was beneath her," said Mabel.

Mabel continue to tell us about Olivia, "I would hear David grumble that Olivia never wanted to be close to him anymore. He wanted to know why they never talked like they did before they married. Olivia would hatefully answer back, saying he never did

187

anything for her, and then she added the only reason he married her was for her to take care of him. She would turn every one of David's complaints around on him. It was amazing to me that it didn't seem to bother David how Olivia treated him. He still supported her as his wife no matter how bad it became.

"You know what? I never heard her say to anybody—including Mr. Tom, her two kids, or David—that she loved them!"

Jeannie told Mabel, "The way their marriage was set up, it sounds to me like it never had a chance to be anything other than bad."

Mabel replied, "You don't understand, Jeannie. Olivia made the marriage go from bad to worse. She began doing mean and cruel things to David intentionally. The things she did to him could only come from a woman who hated her husband. She was trying to make him leave her.

"Things got worse. David and Olivia made their marriage a public spectacle. Olivia would intentionally put David down or try to embarrass him in front of everybody. I really felt sorry for David. He didn't have a chance and I guess that's why it all came out at the funeral. If you'd seen what happened there, you would understand," grumbled Mabel.

"However, the strange thing about Olivia was she didn't want David to leave her. David as her sugar-daddy, and she didn't want to lose him. She actually needed him emotionally, which made all of us wonder why she treated him so badly," protested Mabel.

Mabel laughed as she paused and said to us, "Sometimes Olivia would do stupid things, and as I think about them now, they were funny." She began to tell the story about David's shoes. "David and a friend had planned to go to a football game. Both teams were undefeated, and the game would decide who went to the state playoffs. David and his friend had been talking about this game for weeks in anticipation of being there.

"David had told his friend he would pick him up an hour before the game began, but Olivia didn't want him to go. She made like she was sick, and she wanted David to stay with her to take care of her. Her artificial illness caused a big argument, and Olivia tried to get Mr. Tom to side with her, but he wouldn't and he left the room.

"Olivia complained and coaxed the boys into crying, which made David mad. Olivia kept whining that David was wrong to leave his wife to go to a silly football game. She asked him if the football game was more important to him than she was. At first, David didn't say anything. Then he tried to reason with Olivia, telling her he had promised his friend he would pick him up, and he was late in keeping his promise.

"Olivia kept complaining about him leaving her when she was sick and asked him again what was more important. Finally, David told her that right now the game was more important. He told her he was going to change his shirt and leave to get his friend to go to the game.

"That infuriated Olivia. When David left to change his shirt, she got his good shoes and hid them where he couldn't find them. She knew he would never go out in public in his old brogans or barefooted. Back then, people only had two pair of shoes: one for work and one for going places. People would be shamed by others if they dressed up to go somewhere in their nice clothes and wore their work boots or went barefooted.

"David came back to put on his good shoes and he couldn't find them. He always kept them under his bed, but they were not there. He looked everywhere in the house but he could not locate

189

them. He assumed Olivia must have hid them, and he asked her where they were.

"You would think Olivia would lie to him and say she didn't know where they were, but she didn't do that. She told David she would not tell him where they were. David asked the boys where they were, but the boys were told by Olivia not to say a word. David looked for them again but was still unable to locate them. He became more frustrated and went to Mr. Tom to ask him if he could borrow his shoes.

"Mr. Tom's shoes were too small for David, and Olivia laughed at him thinking she has got him now. However, David walked out of the house, got into his truck and left without any shoes. David leaving with no shoes shocked Olivia. She didn't know what to say or do.

"I thought it was funny how David just walked out. Madea and I were proud of David. He had finally stood up to Olivia in some fashion.

"After the game, David returned with no shoes. Olivia was waiting for him out on the front porch to pour out her wrath out on him. She asked David, "I guess you went to the game with no shoes?" David didn't say a word to her. He just smiled at Olivia and went to get ready for bed. However, Olivia was going to have the last word. She followed him into the bedroom, and confronted David, asking if he'd actually gone to the game.

"David answered her, 'Yeah, I sure did.'

"Olivia didn't know how to react to what David said, so she asked David, 'You mean to tell me you went to the game barefooted? Do you realize how embarrassing it will be for me? People are going to say, Olivia's husband is so poor that he has no shoes. I can't believe you did that to me.' Olivia slammed the bedroom door as she went out to sleep with the twins in their bed.

"The next morning as Madea and I fixed breakfast for Mr. Tom and David, I overheard Mr. Tom ask David about the game. David told him our team lost in the last minute 20 to 19 because we fumbled on their four-yard line and didn't score.

"David and Mr. Tom finished eating and were drinking coffee when Mr. Tom asked David, 'Did you go to the game bare-footed? David laughed and said to Mr. Tom, 'Oh no, I couldn't do that. You saw how upset it would have made Olivia.'

"Mr. Tom said, 'I'm pretty sure I overheard Olivia say last night that you went to the game bare-footed.'

"David said, 'No, I didn't say I went barefooted, she did. Olivia just presumed I did, and I didn't let her think otherwise.'

"Mr. Tom asked David, 'Well son, what did you do for shoes?'

"David said, 'I borrowed shoes from my friend's dad and returned them last night after the game.'

"Mr. Tom broke into laughter. So did Madea and me. It was the only time I ever saw David get the upper hand on Olivia. He took so much mess off of that mean girl. He was so patient and forgiving to her. She didn't deserve his kindness, but that was how he always treated her.

"When Olivia found out what David did, she was furious at David, and she gave him the silent treatment. I think David kind of enjoyed it, at least he had a little peace and quiet for a while. But Olivia took it much further. She held a grudge against him for making her look foolish."

Mabel quietly said, "In the preceding months before Emma came home, the relationship between David and Olivia was uncertain. It was an emotional roller-coaster. Olivia continuously tried to turn everybody against David. Madea and I stayed as neutral as possible. Olivia encouraged Mr. Tom to side with her, However, Mr. Tom stood firmly behind David and secretly, Madea and I agreed with him, too. But Olivia saw through us like a tainted glass and treated us like we were polluted."

Mabel told us, "Olivia and David were sometimes like two ships passing in the night. They ignored one another even if they were in the same room. At the beginning of spring, David and Olivia had one big argument. I was ironing clothes, but it brought the whole house to see what was about to happen. We were always concerned that one of them would hit the other, so we always came into the room they were in. I don't remember what they were arguing over, but Olivia told David he never loved her, and she couldn't understand why he ever married her.

"It must have rubbed David the wrong way, because David forgot about being kind to Olivia and told her his real feelings," said Mabel.

"David, in a very calm, collected voice said, 'I'm ashamed to say this, but the only reason I married you was because I felt obligated to Mr. Tom. This family took care of me in my hour of need, and I appreciated that. But to be honest with you Olivia, you are right. I never loved you and I knew it before we got married.'

"David said, 'I tried to make myself believe we would grow to love each other with time.'

"Then, dejectedly, he said, 'But I see now, I was wrong.'"

Mabel hastily said, "When David said that to Olivia, it astonished her. I actually believed it wounded her. Olivia never responded to his statement, she left the room and went to the front porch to be by herself. Later, when Emma came home, Olivia finally revealed her true reason for marrying."

Mabel said, "David's thinking was not incorrect. It could have happened the way David said. They could have grown to love one another, but they never became one. Instead, they grew further apart because the marriage never had a chance to develop into love. David married from gratitude, and Olivia married for spite. The only thing that grew from their marriage was a lack of respect for each other, and lots of misery for the rest of us.

"Olivia's self-centered actions caused Madea to completely change her viewpoint toward her. Each Thursday, while the twins were at school, Mr. Tom, David, Madea, and I would make our weekly run to Baton Rouge. We would deliver the eggs we collected for the week to a cafe, a truck stop, the stockyard, and a grocery store near Baton Rouge. The money Mr. Tom made from that weekly sale was used to pay for feed for his animals. As a reward to us, and out of the goodness of his heart, he would treat us to a burger, fries, and a malt. We would take our meal to the roadside park and have a picnic. We always looked forward to Thursdays, it was a relaxing time for us.

"About fifteen minutes into our trip, Mr. Tom discovered he had left his account book on the dining table at the house. Mr. Tom allowed his customers credit, and that account book revealed how much each customer owed him. David, realizing how important the account book was, quickly turned the truck around, and we headed back home to get it.

"As we were coming up the drive, David saw a Logger-head turtle in the ditch, and he stopped to catch it. This turtle was large and David had cornered it. We were about 150 yards from the house, and Madea, not being involved in the chase, decided to walk to the house to get the book."

Mable said, "Madea came into the house through the backdoor and walked to the table in the hall to get Mr. Tom's book. As soon as she picked the book up, she heard some giggling. Madea went to investigate and discovered Olivia is in bed with one of David's friends."

Mabel told us politely, "It was an awkward situation for everyone. Most people who run into that type of situation would excuse themselves and leave. But that's not the way Madea operated.

"Madea looked at them and bitterly told the man, 'You's better get's yo' ass out t'at bed before I tells Mr. Tom and David. Or I's goes to's take the shotgun to's them, and they's goin' to blow's you's to hell.'

"Madea didn't wait for him to answer before she got the shotgun from the corner and swiftly said, 'Now's you's want's me to goes get's them?'"

Mabel laughingly said, "I couldn't help from laughing when Madea told me that, I could picture him popping out of that bed, and scrambling to get his pants on to get out the house."

Mabel continued telling us what Madea said to Olivia. She pretended to be Madea, but she didn't speak the black dialect, "'Girl, I can't believe you are at it again. You are a devil-woman. You know what you are doing is wrong, and it's going to cause you to be in hell . . . that's where you belong anyway. If your father knew, it would kill him. I know you don't think much of David, but no Marine would ever allow this to happen to his wife. Even if his wife doesn't love him, he would be justified to kill both of you. Which is exactly what you two deserve for this evil.'"

Mabel said, "Madea surprised me when she said that. You would think Olivia would be ashamed of her actions, or at least beg Madea not to tell her father or David. That would be what a normal person would do. But not Olivia. She was not typical. Madea said she acted proud of what she had done. She let the sheet fall away from around her and stood facing Madea completely naked.

"Olivia conceitedly told her, 'As you can see, I'm not a girl anymore. I'm a beautiful woman who needs a real man. If I can't get what I need here at home, I'll go shopping, and that is exactly what I'm doing. You can go tell them if you want to, I don't care. In fact . . . I want you to go tell them. It's about time I stop playacting anyway.'"

Mabel coolly said, "What Olivia said shocked Madea. She thought if she told, there might be a killing . . . or two. Then there was Mr. Tom. What Olivia did to him each day was bad enough, but . . . this atrocity would kill him. Then there were the twins to consider, too. If they found out, it would ruin them for life, if Olivia hadn't already done that."

Mabel said, "Madea didn't answer Olivia. She took the account book, went out the front door, and walked to where the truck was. She hadn't told a soul until she told me and Howard after Olivia's funeral. I always wondered why Madea never cried at Olivia funeral, but after she told us that story, I understood why. Olivia was one selfish, evil woman."

Mabel said, "Life around the DeAngelo's house after Olivia's encounter was more intense than normal. She would get angry and fly off the handle for no apparent reason. No one understood why she had become that way. We assumed it was because of past tensions between her and David, but it wasn't. Olivia thought Madea held the upper hand over her and was waiting for the right time to tell everyone what she had caught her doing.

"Madea's choice not to respond drove Olivia crazy. It turned out to be the best way to handle her. She didn't know what to expect, it confused her and kept her in check. The uncertainty of what was to come was worrying her. That is why Olivia was in such a bad mood," said Mabel.

Mabel shifted the conversation away from the marriage. "One afternoon a black car came up the drive. Mr. Tom, Madea, and I went to the front porch to see who was coming. David was at a friend's home helping work on his barn, and he had taken Olivia to town. It was a Defense Department courier who had come to deliver an official letter to Mr. Tom.

"The courier stopped in front and walked to the front porch where we were and modestly asked, 'Is this the residence of Tom DeAngelo, the father of Emma Estelle DeAngelo?'

"Mr. Tom said to the courier, 'Yes, I am Tom DeAngelo, I am Emma's father, why?'

"The courier kindly said, 'I have a letter here for you sir to read, and it will explain everything. You can read, can't you sir? If you can't, then I will read it for you.'

"Mr. Tom told the courier, 'Yes I can read.' Mr. Tom took the large brown envelope and opened it. After reading the letter, he looked at the courier who smiled back at him. Mr. Tom reread the letter and told the courier earnestly, 'Mister, this must be a mistake, this can't be possible.'"

Mabel said, "This confused the courier. He replied, 'I don't understand what you mean, Mr. DeAngelo. It's all right there, and what it says is very plain and easy to understand. There is no mistake on our part. May I ask what you are referring to?'

"Mr. Tom said, 'We got word our daughter Emma had drowned when the ship she was on sank.'

"The courier patiently listened to what Mr. Tom said and replied, 'According to the information I have sir, the Defense Department sent you a telegram informing you that your daughter Emma was rescued from that ship, and the Japanese sent her to a POW camp.'"

Mabel said, "Madea and I were stunned by what we had just heard. We were impatiently waiting to see if what we heard could possibly be true . . . Emma was alive.

"Mr. Tom snapped back at the courier, 'I never got any telegram telling me what you are saying. What are you talking about?'

"The courier told Mr. Tom, 'Well sir, I have right here in my briefcase a copy of the telegram, dated, signed, and received, telling you Emma Estelle DeAngelo was rescued by the Japanese Imperial Navy and sent to a POW camp in the Philippine Islands.'

"The courier pulled out the telegram and he said, 'It plainly says your daughter, Emma, was rescued and sent to a POW camp and it has the signature of the person who received it. The telegram is right here. This letter today is from the Defense Department telling you that your daughter will be coming home next month.'"

Mabel said, "Madea and I were holding onto each other, and I could feel Madea's legs get weak when the courier said Emma would be coming home. It was unbelievable. We both thought we were dreaming, praying it was true.

"Mr. Tom told the courier, 'Could I please see that telegram you said the Defense Department sent me earlier, sir.'"

Mabel said, "The courier handed Mr. Tom the telegram, and he read it and who signed for it. He didn't tell anyone anything about the telegram.

"Tears started coming down his cheeks and he began to cry. He dropped on his knees and cried out to God, 'Thank You God for Your mercy. You have saved my daughter. All glory goes to you, Father. I thought my daughter, Emma, was dead. But she is alive!'"

Mabel eagerly told us, "When we heard Mr. Tom say Emma was alive, we screamed as loud as we could. Our screams were so loud that the dogs started barking. We praised God for the great news. It was too wonderful to believe. If the United States Defense Department said it, then we believed it was the truth.

"Mr. Tom composed himself and he asks the courier, 'Sir, can I have this telegram and the receipt? I really need it.'

"The courier paused to think and then replied, 'Your request is a little unusual, I never had anyone ask to have one of our documents, but I don't see any reason why you can't have it. All I need is your signature right here sir, saying you received this letter. I want to tell you how happy I am to bring this good news to you. After you sign, if you could be kind enough to tell me how to get to the Law's house. I would appreciate it. I have good news for them, too. Their daughter, Mildred is coming home the same day. The Defense Department is providing transportation for all the nurses who were POWs. Each nurse will be personally delivered to their homes by two couriers.'"

Mabel joyfully told us, "The courier granted Mr. Tom's request. After Mr. Tom directed him to the Law's residence, the courier left. Madea and I just looked at each other and smiled, we broke out into laughter and grabbed each others' hands and danced in a circle. Mr. Tom grabbed our hands too and joined us. It was such a joyful time knowing that Emma was alive and coming home."

Dejectedly, Mabel said, "After our joy subsided, we became concerned how Emma would react when she came home to find her sister was married to her fiancé. I wasn't going to be the one to question Mr. Tom about it, but I knew he was thinking about it.

"Madea was not as diplomatic as I was, and she said to Mr. Tom, 'What's my Emma goin' to do now, Mr. Tom? T'ats goin' to be's real bad's for her and for Olivia and David too, ain't it?'

"Mr. Tom looked at Madea, and he told her, 'Sis . . . bad is not even the half of it. No one but God knows what is to take place when she learns what has happened, but I know in my heart, it is going to be worse than bad.'"

Mabel said, "Mr. Tom made us promise not to say anything to either David or Olivia about the courier coming. He told us he would tell them right after supper."

Mabel said, "We never realized there could be something worse to be exposed later from that telegram. Mr. Tom could keep things to himself better than a woman could. Women couldn't hold that kind of news in. It would burn a hole in them to get it out. I am sure it troubled Mr. Tom too, but he never let it show."

Mabel humbly said, "That evening while we were eating supper, Mrs. Law came to the house with her good news that Mildred was coming home, and with Emma the same day. Mrs. Law was so excited, you would have thought she was telling everybody about a new grandbaby being born. She invited us all to eat with them in celebration of the girls coming home on Sunday."

Mabel said, "When Mrs. Law told us the news, David wasn't sure he heard her correctly. He immediately asked, 'Who is coming with Mildred?'"

Mabel said, "Olivia heard clearly what Mrs. Law said, and she excused herself to her bedroom.

"Mrs. Law, unaware David had not heard the news, said to him before Mr. Tom could stop her, 'It must have been a real shock to you, David, to find out Emma was alive. It was great news for all of us, too. It is a shame that Sophie wasn't coming home with them.'

"David, still in shock of what he had just heard, asked in great astonishment, 'Emma is alive? Is that what you just said? Is that true? How do you know that?'

"David kept looking around puzzled, thinking she wouldn't say that unless it were true," cried Mabel.

"Looking for verification, he asked, 'Mr. Tom, is she really alive? How do you know that's true?'

"Mr. Tom calmly told David, 'Settle down, son. I was going to tell you and Olivia later tonight. However, Mrs. Law came to share her good news with us before I could, and I'm glad she did. Actually, she did a much better job of telling you than I could have.'"

Mabel said, "The realization of what David heard began to work on his emotions, and tears began to roll down his cheeks. Madea grabbed him and hugged him as he looked for Olivia. David didn't see her. She had left.

"Mrs. Law, seeing David looking for Olivia said, 'Oh Tom, I hope I didn't spoil any surprise you planned for them. I thought David already knew. I'm so sorry, I didn't know.'

"Mr. Tom was not delighted Mrs. Law had told them the news before him, but to be polite to Mrs. Law he kindly said, 'No, no you didn't mess up anything, Mrs. Law. You only brought us more good news knowing they both are safe and coming home to us. It's just too wonderful to believe. I pray to God, that by some miracle He will allow Sophie to come home to us, too.'"

Mabel told us, "As soon as Mrs. Law left, Mr. Tom quickly asked David to come with him to find Olivia. David was still overwhelmed with emotion as he followed Mr. Tom to the bedroom where Olivia was. They walked into the room and Mr. Tom closed the door."

Mabel humbly said, "I am ashamed to tell you this, but Madea and I sneaked down the hall to listen to what Mr. Tom was going to say. We thought Mr. Tom was going to fuss at Olivia for rudely leaving. We had no idea what we were about to hear.

"They found Olivia lying on her bed face down with her head buried in her pillow. She was whimpering and David reached for her to console her. She sat up and allowed David to hug her. Mr. Tom sat on a chair next to the bed and he told Olivia, 'Honey, I was going to tell you and David after supper that we had a visitor today from the Defense Department. He told us Emma is alive, and she is coming home. What do you think about Emma coming home, honey?'

"Olivia didn't respond. Mr. Tom restated the question differently: 'Olivia, are you happy about Emma coming home?'

"Olivia responded with no emotion: 'Yes Sir, Papa, I am happy she is alive and is coming home.'

"Mr. Tom told both of them calmly, 'You both know when Emma gets home it is going to present a problem, and we want to handle this the best way we can. We don't want the situation to be worse than it has to be for Emma.'

"Olivia inquired of Mr. Tom, 'Why does everything always have to be for Emma's sake? It is always about what is best for

Emma. I live here, too. I'm your daughter too.' Olivia began to cry and David comforted her again.

"Mr. Tom respectfully said to her, 'Yes, Olivia. I know you are my daughter. I also want you to know I love you as much as I love Emma. The happiness of both of you is very important to me. I don't want to see either one of you hurt. However, we are going to face a problem, and it needs a tender solution.'

"David appreciated what Mr. Tom was saying. He told Olivia, 'Don't cry. Emma is coming from a really bad situation back to her home. She is going to come here thinking I am dead, and she is going to see that I'm in fact alive and now married to her sister. That is going to be a big shock to her. What your Papa is telling you is we need to deal with it in a way that will make it easier for her and us too. You do understand how upsetting that will be, don't you?'

"Olivia answered David with disdain. 'Yeah, I understand. We don't want to hurt our precious little angel, Emma. She's all that matters. It's all about her.'"

Mabel austerely said, "When Olivia said that, I had to hold Madea back. I knew she wanted to go in there and give her a piece of her mind because Olivia was being impossible and selfish, as usual.

"Olivia's self-centeredness upset Mr. Tom, and he harshly asked Olivia, 'Don't you think you at least owe it to David . . . and to me, to be cooperative?'

"Olivia immediately became defensive to what Mr. Tom said. 'What do you mean by that statement? What do I owe you or David?'

"Mr. Tom unsympathetically said to Olivia, 'Well, because of what you did. You lied to us, saying Emma was dead, when you knew she was alive.'"

Mabel said, "When Madea heard Mr. Tom say that, she stopped pulling against me and listened more intently. She and I strained to hear what would be said next. We couldn't see David's reaction, but Mr. Tom's statement must have shocked and confused David, too, just like it did us. We were perplexed, wondering why Mr. Tom said that.

"Immediately, Olivia snapped back at her father and defensively said, 'What do you mean, I lied? I haven't lied about anything.'

"Mr. Tom pulled out the telegram the courier had given him and said to Olivia, 'I have the telegram right here that you signed for. You know, the one that came from the War Department that you told us you read and burned. You know, the one you said that Emma drowned when the ship sank. However, the telegram read she was rescued and sent to a POW camp. How could you be so cold-hearted and tell us that wicked lie, and make us endure that kind of grief and suffering?'"

Mabel smugly said, "There was such a hush in that bedroom. It was quite as death itself. But soon it filled with crying. They were not Olivia's cries, but it was Mr. Tom's. Later joined by David, after he read the original telegram. He saw it was signed received by Olivia. She had lied about what it really said. David must have understood Olivia did it to mislead him so that he would marry her."

Mabel told us, "Olivia never cried. She burst out of the bedroom, almost running over Madea and me. Fuming, she went outside, got into David's truck and left. We went into the room and saw Mr. Tom bent over in the chair crying, and David was still clutching the telegram, crying too. It was a sad, sad scene. We all had mixed feelings about Olivia's lie. We didn't know whether to be joyful knowing Emma was coming home or to be angry because of the grief Olivia had brought to us or to cry in anticipation of the sadness that was evident to happen when Emma came home."

Miss Mildred Law said, "What was really sad was the hurt Olivia had brought to those who loved her with her evil lie. Only a vile person would do what she did. With one lie, she left David in a broken state because he knew their marriage was born from a lie. Then she had stolen Emma's happiness and her dream of marriage to David. Even worse, she had taken her father's happiness. The lie actually destroyed his motivation to live.

"In fact, didn't Mr. Tom suffer a mild stroke soon after that event?" asked Miss Mildred Law.

Mabel glumly answered, "Yes, he did, the very next morning. Olivia returned later that night and went into Mr. Tom's room, fussed at him, and took the twins to her room.

"Olivia walked into her room and told David cruelly, 'Get out. Go sleep with Papa. Y'all seem to be in this thing together. I need my kids close to me tonight.'

"The next morning, David went into the kitchen to get his coffee, and the twins came running into the kitchen hollering that Papa looked real strange.

"We all went in to check on Mr. Tom and found he'd had a stroke sometime during the night and couldn't get up," said Mabel.

"David went to get the truck. He pulled it up to the front porch. We loaded Mr. Tom into the truck and set out for the hospital. It looked real serious to us, and we didn't know if we had time to make it before he died. Madea and I prayed all the way to the hospital. Miraculously, on the way to the hospital, Mr. Tom started coming out of the effects of the stroke. The doctor said he was fortunate in that he only had a mild stroke. He told us with a couple weeks of rest, he should be fine.

"I don't know if anyone ever discussed Olivia's lie with her again. Maybe they were afraid the lie might cause Mr. Tom to have a heart attack, no one wanted that to happen. Everyone realized where they stood because of Olivia's lie, and no one liked it. But they knew they could not change a thing about it."

Mabel continued, "Olivia's lie caused David to recognize he was trapped in a bad marriage that he couldn't end, with a woman he did not love. Olivia's lie caused Mr. Tom to mourn a child who was not dead, a lie that almost killed him when he found out his daughter was alive. What the whole family didn't envision was what other tragedies were about to enter into their lives, and most would be brought on because of Olivia or her lie."

Mabel told us, "That is why we told you earlier that she might have been better off back at that POW camp. Olivia's lie had put everyone in her family in a state of constant turmoil. The troubles that came with her lie just kept coming. No one seemed to be able to stop them. Emma was twenty-one, and in her short life, she had been through more calamities than a person who was eighty. Most people would just quit, but not Emma. Even though she had just discovered her fiancé was alive and her sister was married to him, she was determined to make things work for the best."

# Chapter 13

## *Sudden Change*

"Shorty after Emma arrived with the couriers that had brought her home, Olivia wasted no time revealing to Emma that she had married David," Mable said. "The sudden shock of that news caused Emma to run to the barn to be alone. Mr. Tom knew he couldn't walk to the barn to console her because of his recent stroke, and no way would he send either David or Olivia to get Emma. Mr. Tom sent Madea and me to the barn to bring Emma to the house. We had anticipated Emma would be upset, but we hoped we could come to some level of understanding where everyone could function within the family.

"When we got to the barn, we found Emma brushing down her horse. We stopped at the entrance of the barn to listen. She was talking to her horse. She was telling her horse, through her tears, how she had longed to come home and be happy, but it just didn't seem that God wanted her to have any happiness," said Mabel.

Mabel said, "When Madea heard Emma say that, it aggrieved Madea deeply and she wept. Her whimpering was loud enough for Emma to hear her. Emma turned around and saw Madea crying. Madea held her arms open for Emma to come to her, Emma ran to her open arms, and they hugged each other until their tears ran out.

"Finally Madea told Emma, 'It's alrights girl t'at you's cry, it be's good for yuh. You's goin' to haves a happy life. Yo life's just beginning. There's much happiness ahead fur you. Don'ts yuh talk t'at way girl. T'ats not you's.'"

Mabel said Madea continued telling Emma, "'Do's you's remember 'de time when you's was little and you's was tryin' to catch yo' horse. You's chased that horse 'round and 'round 'de pen, and you's couldn't catch him. Then you's got mad at 'de horse and blames the horse. Does you's remember what's I told's you's back then?'

"Emma shook her head yes and gratefully said, 'Yes ma'am I do. I can't walk into the horse's life and expect him to do what I want him to just like I can't walk into a person's life and expect them to bow down to my wishes. You told me, I would have to figure out a way to please both of us to get what I wanted. You said, happiness comes to all when they please one another. I remember.'

"Madea put both her hands on Emma's shoulders and looked directly into her eyes and said, 'Child, t'is be's one of thos' unhappy times. You's gots to makes 'de effort to please's the other to be's happy. I's knows this ain't easy to take, but's it's needed. You's takes what God gives you's, and's you's goes with it. He's pointin' you's in His direction t'at He's wants you's to go. And it be's the right direction too. For God don'ts makes no mistakes. No's siree.'

"Madea caught her breath and said, 'You's got's David back. You's thought's he was dead. You's be's happy for him, even thought's it's not like's it used to be's. God gives us yo' David back and He's given us you's back too. Ain't God good?'

"Emma said, 'You are right Aunt Sis. You are always right. You are so wise, and I am happy he is alive. I lost him years back when we got the word he was dead, but now God sent him back to us. I should be happy he is alive. I'm blessed to be back home, too. Life is good, even though our situation has changed, and he is married to Olivia instead of me. Their marriage doesn't mean I can't be happy for him and for me, too.'"

Mabel said, "We left the barn and went into the house where Mr. Tom, David, and Olivia were sitting at the table. They were waiting for us. We came in and Emma sat at the table.

"Madea asked Mr. Tom, 'Does you's wants us to sit's too, or do's you's wants us to serve 'de meal?'

"Mr. Tom looked at Madea like she's made some crazy remark, and asked her this rhetorical question: 'Aren't you and Mabel a part of this family too?'

"He waited for an answer, but Madea would never talk back to Mr. Tom. Mr. Tom answered for her, 'I think you are, so sit down. We will eat after we talk. We need to iron this situation out, so we all can have some peace.'"

Mabel said, "Emma couldn't take her eyes off of David. You could see she wanted to talk to him, but she didn't. Olivia kept looking at Emma and occasionally would look over to David to see if he was looking at Emma. I remember thinking what a mess Olivia had created."

Mabel told us, "Mr. Tom summarized the situation of what happened after Emma received word that David was KIA to the present time of her arriving home. This allowed Emma to understand what had taken place while she was gone.

"Mr. Tom said, 'We got great news, that David was alive and coming home, but we didn't know how badly injured he was. When he arrived home, he had no place to stay, so I allowed him to stay with us. Then word came to us that you and Sophie were drowned at sea, but Mildred had been rescued and sent to a POW camp.'

"Mr. Tom continued, 'That is when David and Olivia married. Later, we are astounded when we received word that you were rescued and alive, coming home to us. Basically that is where we are today.'"

Mabel earnestly said, "Everyone at the table knew Mr. Tom left out the part about Olivia lying about the telegram that said Emma was alive and a POW in the Philippines. I am sure we all wondered if it was right to tell her or wrong not to say anything. It was a question none of us wanted to answer. We knew Emma would eventually find out, but I'm sure we felt that for that day what Mr. Tom said was enough.

"Emma appeared to accept the story of how things emerged. The strange thing to me was that Emma never asked any questions," said Mabel, gently.

"Mr. Tom concluded our meeting by saying, 'In life, things don't always go like you plan. The situation we are facing today is one of those times. We need to accept what has happened, realize we can't change it, and move on with our lives. The Bible tells us that all things happen for a reason, and many times in this life we won't understand why."

Mabel said, "No one said anything, so I assumed that we silently agreed to accept what had happened as an act of God."

Mabel said, "We ate the meal, but Emma didn't eat very much. She made the excuse that her stomach had not yet adjusted to real food. The only discussion we had at the table was how the sleeping arrangements would be. Olivia made a suggestion to Mr. Tom for Emma to be placed in the mystery room. Her suggestion upset Mr. Tom, he reiterated strongly to all of us, that that room was not to be used for any reason. As far as we knew, no one except Mr. Tom had ever been in that room, and we had no idea what Mr. Tom used the room for. It was always locked and was always a mystery what was in the room."

Mabel plainly said, "They decided the sleeping arrangements would be Mr. Tom and Emma to sleep in one bedroom and in the other bedroom would be the twins in one bed and David and Olivia in the other bed. Somehow we made it through the first night without any more drama."

Mabel joyfully said, "The next day Miss Mildred Law came to Mr. Tom's house and everyone was thrilled to see her. We hugged and kissed her in such joy of her return, it amazed me how much weight Miss Mildred had lost. She was really thin. Emma and Miss Mildred decided the first thing they must do was to visit with Sophie's parents to tell them what had happened to her."

Miss Mildred Law said, "When we got to the Whitmore's house, they were pleased to see us. Mary Lou and Mrs. Whitmore could hardly take their hands off us. You could tell the loss of Sophie had really affected them. Mr. Whitmore greeted us when we got there, but he was unsociable. You could tell he was having a difficult time adjusting to the loss of his daughter. I'm sure our being there did not help because we reminded him of his loss.

"Emma humbly asked what the Defense Department said about Sophie's death," Miss Mildred Law said.

"Mrs. Whitmore told us, 'They sent us a telegram, telling us Sophie had drowned.'

"I angrily responded to Mrs. Whitmore's statement, telling her, 'That was a bold-faced lie. Those sorry Japs murdered her and lied to the Red Cross that she drowned,'" said Miss Mildred Law.

"Mr. Whitmore was astonished by what I said and he enquired, 'She didn't drown? She was murdered? I knew it had to be more to it than what we were told,'" continued Miss Mildred Law.

"Mr. Whitmore broke down into tears as Mrs. Whitmore told us, 'He took Sophie's death very hard and has not been the same after we got that telegram. He couldn't believe she died the way they said. I thought he was wrong, but now we know that he was right,'" said Miss Mildred Law.

Miss Mildred Law continued telling us, "Emma asked them if they would like to hear the full story of how it happened.

"The Whitmore's eagerly asked her to tell them," said Miss Mildred Law.

"Emma began telling the entire story, from all of us being rescued, to Sophie's murder, and our being moved. Emma painfully cried as she told Mr. and Mrs. Whitmore that Sophie's death was her fault, and she apologized to them for asking her to go and for placing her in such a dangerous position," said Miss Mildred Law.

Miss Mildred Law said, "Surprisingly, Mr. Whitmore wanted to know how Sophie had distracted them. I told him he would have been proud of Sophie. Her quick wit not only saved Emma, but it probably saved many more women from rape or death. Those sorry Japs were pigs. What she did was really brave of her. At first, the Japs were entertained by it, they laughed and imitated her, then some Jap bastard shot her for no reason. We tried to go to her but they stopped us from trying to help her. I am so sorry, Mr. Whitmore, that we were not allowed to help her.

"To our amazement, Mr. Whitmore laughed," said Miss Mildred Law.

"Mr. Whitmore exclaimed, with a smile on his face, 'I knew she had to go down fighting. She wouldn't just drown. She was too good of a swimmer, and a fighter.'

"Mr. Whitmore thanked us for telling us the truth of what happened. He also told us he didn't blame us for Sophie's death. He believed somehow it was part of God's plan for her, and he was proud of her and us too. Then he sadly told us . . . 'but you know something, I do still miss her so much,'" said Miss Mildred Law.

"It took some time for everyone there to regain composure. We loved Sophie, and missed her funny antics. I reminded the Whitmore's not to forget they were invited over to our house on Sunday after church. They did come, and we had a wonderful time sharing our experiences with everyone. Our visit to the Whitmore's helped them as it did both Emma and me. It allowed us to accept the fact that our best friend was gone forever. Probably the one who was helped most by our visit was Mr. Whitmore. Months later, his wife told us, Mr. Whitmore began to accept the fact that Sophie was gone, knowing of his acceptance helped us, too.

"On our way home, I asked Emma how things at home were going. I could tell Emma didn't know that Olivia had tricked David into marrying her. Emma sensed I knew more, and she asked what I meant. I explained to her that the courier who brought the news of us coming home seemed confused as to how Mr. Tom could get you being rescued so messed up. Smartly, my mother offered to clear it up for him if he could remember who signed receipt of the telegram sent to the DeAngelo's. He told my mother it was a relative and her name was Olivia DeAngelo," said Miss Mildred Law.

Miss Mildred Law said, "It didn't take my mother long to figure out why David and Olivia's marriage happened so fast. She figured Olivia must have lied to him and Mr. Tom because she wanted David for herself before Emma came home.

"Emma quickly asked me, 'Did my mother know if David knew she was alive before the marriage?'

"I told her I didn't think so, but I wasn't sure," said Miss Mildred Law.

"I didn't give Emma time for Olivia's lie to soak in before I asked her to help solve my problem. I told her I needed help in locating my husband. I had tried to find out what happened to him and where he was when we got to the states, but we were too busy. I didn't believe anyone really tried to help me as they said, but I knew Emma could help me. She had a gift for accomplishing the impossible. If anyone could help, I knew it was she," said Miss Mildred Law.

Miss Mildred Law said, "Emma told me she would help me locate Jerry. However, I recognized the news of Olivia tricking David was weighing heavy on her mind. I knew she would tackle that problem first before she would work to solve mine.

"Later I found she had written Charles Winston's father, to see if he would help find my husband, Jerry. Charles Winston, Jr., told her his father was a U.S. senator, and if she ever needed help with anything to get in touch with him. Charles Winston made her memorize his address, Emma knew he could help faster than having us try to trace him down. Emma gave him all the information I had on my husband. Emma knew as much about Jerry as I did."

Mabel said, "I remember the day y'all went over to visit the Whitmore's. I also remember that Emma didn't waste any time when she came home. She went straight to Olivia and asked her if they could talk in private. They went into Olivia's room and Emma asked her if she got the telegram that the Defense Department sent to Papa about her. But before Olivia could respond, Emma asked her why she had lied and told everyone she was dead.

"Emma asked Olivia, 'Did you lie to trick David into marrying you, or was he part of the lie?'

"Olivia happily told Emma, 'Yes, I told everyone you were dead, no one was sad about it either. No one cried. In fact, they were glad.'

"Olivia justified her lie, 'I figured you would probably die in that POW camp anyway, and I didn't have time to wait for that to happen. I wanted David, and I wanted to get married right then.'"

Mabel said, "At first Emma didn't say anything to her, but Olivia laughed, thinking it was funny and she said to Emma, taunting her, 'And David wanted to marry me too . . . it would not have made any difference if you were here at that time. David wanted me and not you.'

"Emma controlled her anger as she wanted Olivia to answer whether David knew or not. 'I can't believe you did that to me and David. You knew we planned to be married, you didn't even give us a chance to let it happen.'

"Olivia said, 'At the time, if you remember, sister dear, you thought he was dead. So, I figured that made him available. He was free to do what he wanted to do with whomever he wanted. He wanted to marry me and he did. He is mine now . . . and there is nothing you can do about it.'"

Mabel said, "After Olivia told Emma that she left Olivia in the bedroom. I went to Madea and told her what I had heard, and she went to Mr. Tom to tell him Emma had found out about the lie Olivia told us."

Mabel said, "Mr. Tom went outside to find Emma and see her by the big pecan tree. As Emma was staring out into the pasture, Mr. Tom called her to the front porch, and they sat in the swing to talk.

"Emma, with tears rolling down her cheeks, asked Mr. Tom, 'Papa, why didn't you tell me Olivia lied about me being alive. Olivia said I was dead when she knew I was alive. She did that to steal David away from me, didn't she? How could she do that to me, my own sister?'

"Mr. Tom pulled Emma close to him to console her and said, 'I didn't tell you about it because it wouldn't change anything. All it would do is create hard feelings . . . just like it is doing right now. Right now, you don't need any hard feelings. You need to feel loved and to be at peace. Those hard feelings would only poison you, and you know Olivia didn't care what you wanted.'

"Emma pulled back from her father and asked him, 'Papa, did David know I was alive?'

"Mr. Tom said to Emma, 'Baby, I really don't know, but I believe with all my heart he didn't know. If he did, he would never have married Olivia. That boy has such a kind heart, he would have waited for you until hell froze over if he knew you were alive. Even so, it doesn't change how it is now. They are married. All you can do now is move on, and I know that is not easy to do. But there is no other course for you to take. I am so sorry I didn't figure out what Olivia was up to before it happened. I should have checked into things more closely.'

"Mr. Tom continued, 'Darling, it was not your fault. It actually is my fault. I should have straightened Olivia out years ago, but I let her have her way in everything because she was so young when her mother died. I'm sorry, Emma, that this happened to you. You don't deserve this.'

"Emma told Mr. Tom, 'Papa, I am blessed to have you as my father. God gave me such a good and loving father, and He made you so wise.'"

Mabel gladly said, "Mr. Tom reached for Emma and they hugged each other. After Emma found out what Olivia had done, Mr. Tom knew it crushed her, and that hurt Mr. Tom. I truly believe it had a lot to do with his untimely death. Madea said it would have been more merciful if Olivia had taken a gun and shot Mr. Tom in the heart right then and there than to make him undergo all the heartbreak she caused him."

Mabel said, "The next morning at breakfast, David and Mr. Tom came early for coffee, and Emma joined them before Olivia got up. David did not know Emma had found out about the lie. Emma asked him, 'David, you have never lied to me before and I want you tell me the truth. Before you married Olivia, did you know I was alive and in a POW camp?'"

Mabel said, "David was surprised that Emma had found out. At first he looked at Mr. Tom, and then looked quickly back to Emma. He answered her, 'No Emma, I did not know. If I had known, I would have waited to marry you. I thought you were dead, we all thought you were dead. I'm sorry about what happened. Can you ever forgive me?'

"Emma earnestly told David, 'I don't blame you or anyone. I don't understand why it happened like it did, but I have to believe God allowed it to happen for a good reason. I only hope we live long enough on earth to know why. I am going to honor your marriage to Olivia and try to do everything I can to make you two happy.'

"David told Emma, 'I don't exactly know what to say about that, Emma. But I wouldn't expect anything less than that from you. We need you here, so please don't leave.'"

Mabel said, "David had been at the house long enough to know everything that happened in that house was known by everyone there, and I mean everyone. So David spoke even louder to be sure we in the kitchen heard him: 'Isn't that right, Miss Sis and you, too, Mabel?'

"We both answered him back: 'That is right. We need you Emma. Don't you go nowhere.'"

# Chapter 14

## *Farewell*

"We were sitting on the front porch enjoying the nice cool breeze that a cold front had just brought to us. It was Friday, and we were already discussing what we wanted for dinner after church on Sunday. We noticed a car hurrying up the lane creating a cloud of dust as it approached us. Immediately, we saw a red light on top of the car and knew right away it was the sheriff of our parish," said Mabel.

"He was far enough away for Mr. Tom to make a comment about our sheriff. 'He's always in a hurry to get where he is going, but when he gets there . . . he never does anything. Well, that's not altogether correct, he lets the rich get away with murder and he goes after the ones who can't help reelect him,'" said Mabel, laughing.

"We laughed as we watched the sheriff park on the grass near the front door. Our sheriff was so lazy, he didn't want to get out of the car and walk to tell us why he was there."

Mabel said, "He seemed aggravated, which is why I guessed he was so impolite. He ignored everybody, never acknowledging any of us. He rolled down the window and told Emma, 'Emma, you must be somebody real important. You got some US Senator wanting you to call him back, so get in the car and let's go make the call.'

"The sheriff said, 'He called my office to contact you and give you the information you wrote him about. I told him I would write it down and deliver it to you, but he wouldn't agree to that. He wants you to call him back . . . collect. I didn't tell him, but I should have told him I don't like being no delivery boy.'"

Mabel said, "Nobody responded to his protest, and then he asked, 'When are you people ever going to get a phone out here? I got better things to do than to be a delivery boy for some Senator I don't even know.'

"Emma told the sheriff, 'Let me get my purse, and I will be right back, Sheriff.'"

Mabel added, "Mr. Tom decided he was going to pick at the sheriff a little bit and told him, 'Emma can't go with you, sheriff . . . not right now!'

"The sheriff was puzzled and asked, 'Why not, Thomas? Is she sick or something? She just told me she would be right back.'

"Mr. Tom told the sheriff, 'Noooo . . . I don't think it will be real soon, Sheriff. You know how women are, she's got to go put on make-up and pick out a nice dress. She can't go talk to a US Senator and not be all gussied up. That wouldn't be right.'"

Mabel said, "We laughed, and I know the sheriff didn't appreciate being made fun of, especially in mixed company, being that some of us were black.

"The sheriff understood he was being made light of and said slowly to everyone, 'I ain't got no time for your BS, Thomas. Tell Emma to hurry up, I got to go.'

"Mr. Tom asked the sheriff, 'Are you going to bring Emma back home, or what?'

"The sheriff said, 'My job don't call for me to be no taxi. I just need to get her to my office where she can make the call. How she gets home . . . that ain't none of my business.'"

Mabel told us, "Emma was back on the front porch by the time the sheriff had finished saying that. She asked David, 'Would you go over to Mildred's house, pick her up, and bring her to the sheriff's office? And then you can bring us back. I would really appreciate you doing that for me. The call is really for Mildred, not for me. Thanks so much, David.'"

Miss Mildred Law said, "On our way to the sheriff's office, David tried to explain to me what was going on, but he didn't know any more than I knew. When I got to the sheriff's office I didn't know what to expect, Emma had already talked to the Senator and had written down all the information needed to help me find what had happened to my husband, Jerry Shook.

"When I walked up," Miss Mildred Law said, "Emma was on the phone. From the way she was speaking, I thought she was speaking to a friend. Her conversation didn't sound as if she were talking to a US Senator, or to someone giving her information for me."

Miss Mildred Law said, "When Emma saw me come through the sheriff's office door, she told them she needed to go. Later, she told us she was talking to the Senator's son, Charles Winston Jr., the same young man she had helped at the POW camp when he was injured. Charles had offered her a job in Washington. He told her all she needed to do was come up there, find him and he guaranteed he could get her a good job with the Secretary of the Navy."

Miss Mildred Law said, "Emma told me the Senator said Jerry Shook had been seriously injured at the Bougainville invasion. He was sent to Pearl and later to Walter Reed in Washington. Emma said the Senator didn't know anything about Jerry's injuries, only that they had released him and he had gone home. The Senator gave her his parent's address in Carlson, North Dakota.

"I looked at Emma and said, 'Well, at least we know he was alive when he came home, and we know where his home is, that's a great start. Did the Senator give you a phone number?'

"Emma quickly said, 'I asked the Senator if he had a telephone number, but he said he didn't have one. He told me he didn't know if they had phones out there yet. The Senator said people out there usually didn't have many modern conveniences and they probably didn't have a phone.

Miss Mildred Law said, "Emma asked, 'Do you think I need to go there with you?'

"David immediately spoke up and told me," said Miss Mildred Law, "'If I was injured and I had a wife, I sure would like for her to be there with me. I would imagine he is looking for you to come, he may still think you are in a POW camp. Who knows? The only way you going to find out is by going to where he is.'

"Emma joyfully said, 'Do you want me to go with you, Mildred? I think I can get away from the house and manage that,'" said Miss Mildred Law.

Miss Mildred Law mockingly imitated how and what she said about Emma's question: "'I'm a big girl now and I'm married. I don't think I need any help from you to find where my husband is,' and we all left the sheriff's office."

We all laughed at what Miss Mildred Law said as Jeannie turned to ask Miss Mildred Law, "Did you find him in North Dakota?"

Miss Mildred Law said, "Well . . . kind of. The information the Senator gave us was not complete. The address was right, but when I came to Jerry's parents' house, the situation was nothing like I had expected it to be.

"I had expected to see Jerry, but he had died. When I first got to their house, I didn't think they were going to let me in. They were very standoffish toward me, because I was a stranger. When they found out I was the girl their son had married, they treated me wonderfully. They were German immigrants who had moved to that

226

part of the country and settled near Carlson," said Miss Mildred Law.

Miss Mildred Law shivered as she said, "It was so cold there, and I know it must have been very difficult for anyone to make a living in that place. There were no trees anywhere, only a never-ending wind. After I convinced his parents who I was, they told me they knew Jerry had married. He had written telling them he had gotten married, but all he said in the letter was what my first name was and that I was from Louisiana. They couldn't read the letter because it was in English, and it took them a month before someone could get through the snow to read it to them. It was the last letter he wrote to them before he was injured."

I saw Miss Mildred Law take a handkerchief from her purse and wipe her eyes. I always believed she couldn't cry. She had always been so emotionally tough and unbreakable at whatever came her way, her tears surprised me. I knew I had witnessed a glimpse of her soft side, which came through her rough and hard exterior.

That dear woman had been through a lot of heartache too, just like Aunt Emma. When I saw her tears, my heart melted for her and I told her, "I am so sorry, Miss Mildred Law. It must have been very difficult to find out he was gone."

She must have still felt great sorrow about losing her husband because she never responded to my comment.

Miss Mildred Law quickly said, "Jerry's parents told me, the hospital in Washington had sent Jerry home, but he was so badly injured in an explosion that he could not see or hear. He had lost his right hand and his entire left arm. His mother said he just lay there each day wanting to die. And finally he did.

"They took me to his gravesite. I remember the ground where he was buried was so hard I hoped the frozen ground wouldn't crush him. His parents tried to get me to stay longer, but I couldn't handle it. They gave me several pictures of Jerry as a child before he joined the service. The pictures I had of us on our honeymoon were lost when our ship went down, and I didn't have anything to share with them," Miss Mildred Law said, sadly.

"I invited them to come visit me and my family in Louisiana. I knew they would never come, and I also knew I would never make a trip up there again, either," said Miss Mildred Law.

Jeannie walked over to Miss Mildred Law, hugged her, and told her, "I'm so sorry Miss Mildred. I'm sorry I made you bring those sad memories back up."

I thought to myself, as I watched Jeannie console Miss Mildred Law, how fortunate I was to have Jeannie and my two children in my life. It is truly a blessing from God to be able to watch my family grow in love toward each other. How blessed I was to see them each day. What happiness they have brought me. It did not seem fair, I have these wonderful people in my life, and Miss Mildred Law has no one. It made me realize that life is not fair.

Mabel saw the emotion building in Miss Mildred Law, and to avoid her becoming overemotional, she said, "I remembered what happened when you three got back from the sheriff's office. Olivia was waiting for Emma, and she was livid. She told Emma she wanted to talk to her, and she meant now. She and Emma went to the back of the house, but we all could hear what Olivia said. And I couldn't believe how harshly Olivia spoke to Emma.

"Olivia bitterly told Emma, 'How dare you tell my husband to do a favor for you without asking my permission? You have no right to ask him to do anything for you. He's not your errand boy. He belongs to me now!'

"Sternly, Emma answered, 'I'm sorry you feel that way, Olivia. The call from the Senator was very important to Mildred, and I didn't have time to get permission. In fact, I didn't know I needed to get your permission. I knew Mildred needed to be there, and I thought your husband was a grown man who could make up his own mind about what he could do without requesting your blessing.'

"Olivia said to Emma, 'You better be glad Mildred came back with you, or I really would have been upset.'

"Emma unpretentiously said to Olivia, 'Just what are you trying to say Olivia? Are you insinuating David and I are trying to do something behind your back . . . like you did to me? If you are, then you are dead wrong. I told both of you that I would honor your marriage, and I will. You have nothing to worry about from me. From what I have heard, it is David who has something to worry about . . . from you. You need to get your act together, and stop worrying about me. I am the least of your problems.'

"Olivia responded by saying, 'I don't know where you are getting your information, but I have an idea. You can't always believe everything you hear. What you are talking about has nothing to do with what I am telling you. You just better keep away from my husband or you will be sorry.'"

Mabel said, quietly, "Olivia didn't know I was listening from the kitchen. I could have been on the front porch and heard it all because their exchange got louder and louder with each passing word. I was proud Emma stood up to her. She needed to be talked to that way because Olivia had been allowed to do whatever she wanted for too long, and to whomever she wanted to do it, too."

Mabel said, "Olivia was making it difficult for everyone. When Emma came back, Olivia was no longer the queen of the house. Everyone had been bowing down to all of her wishes. We felt like we had to walk on eggshells around Olivia. Anything you said to her could cause her to lose her temper and explode."

Mabel said, "Let me tell you what else she did that really upset Emma. Leonard had gotten into trouble at school. He had been punching all the boys in the arm as hard as he could and laughing about it. He ran out of boys to hit because they all started avoiding him, so he started hitting the girls. His teacher sent notes home with Bernard to give to Olivia, who read them but never acted on any of them. She threw them away. Since the notes to his mother were not doing any good, the principal sent a note by Bernard to Mr. Tom."

Mabel told us, "Mr. Tom approached Olivia, asking her to help Leonard before they expelled him. Mr. Tom said they had already held him back a grade and now he was becoming a discipline problem."

Mabel said, "Emma discovered the reason Leonard was hitting the other kids. He couldn't do the work, which prevented him from playing sports. The kids would tease him and he would hit them in retribution."

Miss Mildred Law said, "Emma approached his teacher about what needed to be done. The teacher said that Leonard needed additional help that most kids got at home with their parents, but Leonard was not getting any help. The teacher said Leonard asked his mother, but she told him to go play and leave her alone.

"The teacher said she caught Leonard cheating. She didn't want to embarrass him, so she kept him in at recess to talk to him. She sent letters home but got no response from his mother. When the teacher asked Leonard why, he told her his mother didn't believe education was important. Emma asked the teacher to give Leonard another chance because she would give him the extra help he needed to catch up and be successful," said Miss Mildred Law.

"Emma had a heart-to-heart talk with Leonard, and she confirmed everything the teacher had said. Emma asked Leonard if he wanted to do better. Leonard said yes because he wanted to play sports. Emma told him she would help, but he would have to do his part so he could play sports. She told Leonard not to tell anyone, not even his mother. It had to be their little secret," said Mabel.

Mabel said, "I saw Emma pull Leonard up next to her. She kissed him on his forehead and told him she loved him. She told him she knew he was just as smart as anyone in his class, but he had to promise her he would work with her each day to catch up with the other kids so he could play sports."

Mabel said with a big smile on her face, "I wish you could have seen Leonard that day. He was as happy as I ever had seen him. Emma had given him hope. Along with that new-found hope, she offered him her love. He wasn't used to that."

Mabel contemplated as she told us, "As I think back to when Leonard and Bernard were kids, I don't think I ever saw Olivia hug or kiss either one of those boys. However, Emma made him feel loved that day, and it made him as happy as a kid in a toy store."

Miss Mildred Law said, "I remember Emma helping Leonard. I think he was about ten or eleven at the time. He had become a handful, because Olivia just let him run wild. Emma talked about how much his grades improved, and how happy he was because the other kids were not making fun of him."

Mabel happily told us, "Yeah, Leonard got his grades up so much and he was allowed to participate in the parish rally. In case you two didn't know, the parish rally was when the two schools in our parish competed against one another in track-and-field events. It was a big deal. They let school out and all the parents and grandparents came to watch their children compete."

Miss Mildred Law said, "I remember watching Olivia and Leonard set up a pole vault pit in the middle of their pasture. They put a fence around it to keep the cows out. We would watch those two from our kitchen window as Emma demonstrated to Leonard how to pole vault. It was hilarious to watch. She could actually do it. She vaulted over seven or eight feet, she was pretty good for a twenty-two-year-old woman. She must have done an excellent job teaching Leonard, because in high school he was the state champion in that event for two straight years."

Mabel said, "He did real well in the parish rally that year, too. He brought back four medals. He was first in the long jump, and they won all the relay teams he was on. He was a good athlete in everything he did.

"If Emma had been his mother, he would have never gone down the wrong path. There is a proverb somewhere in the Bible that says, 'If a child has his own way, he will make his mother ashamed.' That was particularly true in his case. Any normal mother would be ashamed of a bad child, but not Olivia. She just let him do anything he wanted and it made no difference to her.

"But the year Emma tutored him, he walked a straight line, did well in school, and was happy. It may have been the only year he made good grades," said Mabel.

Miss Mildred Law said, "I remember Emma telling me she had to tutor him in the barn. She had been secretly helping him. Did Olivia ever figure out the reason Leonard was doing so well in school?"

Mabel told her, "She accidently discovered Emma was helping Leonard. It was probably the main reason Emma decided to leave. One afternoon, while Leonard and Emma were in the barn studying, Olivia came into the barn and found them. She tore into Emma like a protective cat watching over her kittens with a hound dog there. Olivia told Emma she had no business butting into her family's life or messing in any of their business."

Miss Mildred Law spoke harshly about what Olivia had said: "Doesn't that sound just like her. Here is Emma giving her time and heart to Olivia's child, and Olivia doesn't even appreciate it. Emma was doing what Olivia should have be doing, and she couldn't even say thank you to her own sister."

Agreeing, Mabel said, "Their argument got so bad that Leonard came running into the house to get Mr. Tom because he thought his mother and Emma were about to fist fight.

"The two boys got to them first and by the time we got there, Olivia had accused Emma of trying to destroy her family by turning her boys against her," said Mabel.

"Olivia nastily told Leonard that he was never to go to Emma or have her help him with anything. If he needed help, he was to come to her, his mother. That was when Olivia told Emma she needed to leave this house because she was making everybody's life miserable. She told Emma they all were a lot happier when she wasn't there and they all thought she was dead.

"By the time Mr. Tom arrived, the damage had already been done. Olivia had worked her evil spell on Emma. Mentally beating her down, and making her feel unwanted by telling her she had no reason to stay here," said Mabel.

"Emma told Olivia, 'Maybe you are right, Olivia. Maybe I do need to leave. Every time I try to help someone, I always run into a roadblock, and that roadblock is usually created by you.'"

Mabel said, "Emma said she couldn't take Olivia anymore. She thought maybe everybody would be happier if she left. Emma told Olivia she was right. She had no real reason to stay there anymore.

"Olivia twisted the knife in Emma's heart again, telling her, 'Yeah, you need to leave,'" said Mabel.

Mabel said, "When Mr. Tom heard her say that, he yelled at Olivia, 'Girl, don't you say that! Emma, don't let Olivia run you off! I just got you back, and now you are talking about leaving. Please don't do that to me!'"

Mabel gladly said, "Mr. Tom verbally tore into Olivia like I'd never seen him do to anyone. Mr. Tom told Olivia, 'Shut your mouth up because everything that comes from it is poison and lies. You lied to me and you ran off and got pregnant. You lied to us and said Emma was dead. You lied to David and tricked him into marrying you. And now, you are telling your own sister the evil lie that we don't need her. Shut your mouth up and get to the house before I whip you in front of your own two boys.'"

Mabel told us how distressed Mr. Tom was after Olivia left. "'Emma, don't listen to a word Olivia has told you. She has treated you wrong all of her life, and it is never going to stop until one of you is dead. You know, it is all my fault, too. I don't want you to ever leave, I need you.'"

Mabel said, "Emma walked over to her Papa and hugged him to console him. Emma told her father, 'Papa, I am going to go to Washington and take the job that has been offered to me. I really believe it would be best for me to go, and it would take some of the pressure off you because Olivia and I can't live in the same house together. I see that now.'

"She told Mr. Tom, 'Papa, you know I love you and everyone in this house, but I'm going to go. Please, don't try to stop me. I have a few friends who I need to say goodbye to, and after I do that, come Monday, I'll be leaving.'"

Miss Mildred said to us, "Emma came the next day and got me to go with her to say her goodbyes. When we finished making the rounds, my little brother Frank came to Emma and proposed marriage to her again, his second time. He was deadly serious about marrying her and Emma knew it. Again, Emma handled Frank as diplomatically as she could, since it was his second proposal to her, she knew he meant it."

Miss Mildred Law said, "She didn't said yes or no to him. She told him she needed some time and space to help her find herself. Frank said he understood what she meant, and he would talk to her when she got back. He told her he had loved her ever since he was a little kid, and one day he knew they would be together as husband and wife."

# Chapter 15

*The Strange Illness*

"I had been home for a year-and-a-half, and I was close to getting my teaching degree," said Miss Mildred Law. "After Emma left, I found myself feeling alone and missing our camaraderie. I knew that only she could make that feeling leave.

"Olivia was once again managing the DeAngelo household, and had been doing pretty well, even though Madea said Olivia continued slipping back into her old ways. She was too involved with herself to see Mr. Tom's health was deteriorating. "Emma's leaving caused both Mr. Tom and Madea's morale to fall. Without Emma, there was so little for them to be happy about, and it got worse when Bernard came down with a strange illness."

Miss Mildred Law probed Mabel. "Was that the sickness which was such a mystery to everyone?"

"Yes, that was the one. None of the doctors could figure out what was wrong with him," said Mabel to Miss Mildred Law.

Jeannie, concerned, said, "I hope it was not too serious?"

Mabel said, "He would run a fever, he quit eating, he vomited a lot, he quit going to the bathroom, and it wouldn't go away. He was in constant pain, he couldn't sleep, and he kept asking us if he was dying because his pain had become intolerable. At times, his pain was so intense that it caused him to ask God to let him die.

"He suffered for nearly a week before Olivia finally decided she needed to take him to a doctor. Our local doctor couldn't figure out what his medical problem was and wanted Olivia to take him to the hospital in Baton Rouge," continued Mabel.

"The doctors in Baton Rouge couldn't figure out the cause of the illness either. They told Olivia and David that Bernard needed to go to an internal specialist in New Orleans. They brought Bernard there. One specialist said it was one thing, another said it was something else, and they wanted to do exploratory surgery," said Mabel.

Mabel said, "Olivia quickly told them, no way would she let them cut her boy up to hunt for something they had no idea what to look for. It was the first time Olivia ever did something for someone else that made sense."

Mabel told us with some reservation, "Olivia had been listening to some people in church tell her about a minister in Jackson, Mississippi, named Huey Scott. He was a faith healer. They assured her he could lay hands on Bernard and cure him. Olivia believed them and decided it was where she was going to take Bernard."

Mabel said, "Mr. Tom did not agree with her, and they argued about it. Mr. Tom said all that minister was going to do was take their money. We were split in the house over her decision. Mr. Tom and David were against it, and Sis and Olivia were for it, I wasn't sure which way to go."

Mabel told us, "They took Bernard to see the faith healer and it was exactly as Mr. Tom had said. The only thing they got was swindled. David said they took their money going in and coming out. The anointing with oil, the laying-on of hands, the prayer to God, and the advice that God works on a different time schedule than we do did nothing to take his pain away."

Sadly, Mabel said, "David said with the long ride home, it didn't take long for Bernard's pain to return. The next morning, Bernard had gotten much worse instead of better. The prayer towel they sold to Olivia did absolutely nothing to help stop Bernard's pain. His fever concerned them, but what scared them the most was that Bernard's color changed. It looked like he was choking.

"Mr. Tom told us that it looked like some of the soldiers who were gassed in WWI, right before they died. It really scared him and he became very angry with Olivia for trusting in a faith healer. Mr. Tom told her he was going to take Bernard to the gypsy lady to see if she could help him."

Mabel said, "Olivia angrily told her Papa, 'I don't believe in that witch and all her potions. She could kill my boy if we took him to her. All she ever helped was dogs, horses, and mules, not people.'"

Mabel said, "Mr. Tom fired back at Olivia: 'That is nonsense! She has helped many people around here when no one else could. I have seen it myself. We got to do something or we are going to lose Bernard.'

"Madea joined in agreement with Mr. Tom," said Mabel.

"Madea said, 'She be's cured many a folk of evil illnesses, just like's t'is one. I believe's t'at Madam Adrienne could help's Bernard too. If's we don't's do something soon, he is goin' to die . . . Child, put's yourself in yo's son's place. He wants help. He needs help. Let's yo Papa take's him to her, please Olivia. We don't want's Benard joining his mama in heaven. He is to's young to go's.'

"Madea told Olivia, without thinking of the impact it would have on her, 'I's bets you, if t'at be's Leonard, you' been already had took's him.'

"As soon as Madea said that, Olivia became furious at her," said Mabel.

"Olivia looked intently at Madea and said callously, 'I'll deal with you later, woman, and it ain't going to be anything nice.'

"David told Olivia, 'You got no time to be mad Olivia, you have to let him go or he is not going to make it. Please, Olivia, let us take him to her.'"

241

Mabel said sadly, "You would think after all those pleas directed toward her by her family she would give in to their requests. But she didn't. Not until Leonard begged her to let Papa take him.

"Leonard said caringly, 'Mama, I don't want to lose my only brother. Please, Mama, you got to let him go.'

"Olivia began crying as she said, 'Take him, but she had better not hurt him.' Olivia ran into her room and slammed the door.

"Mr. Tom nervously told David, 'Son, go get the truck and bring it to the front steps, and we will bring Bernard there.'

"David brought the truck around, and I packed Bernard to the truck and put him in the back, and stayed with him. Mr. Tom got inside the truck with David, and we sped down the road as fast as we could go. Thank God Madam Adrienne didn't live too far from us," said Mabel.

"She lived a mile off the main road, and only a three miles away from Mr. Tom's. You couldn't drive to it because there was no road to her house, only a path. She lived on the edge of a swamp. In fact, her back porch was a pier. She used a small hollowed out cypress log made into a small boat called a pirogue to find herbs and roots for her potions in the swamp."

Mabel said, "David carried Bernard and went ahead of us as I brought Mr. Tom up as fast as he could walk. David had laid Bernard on her front porch by the time we arrived. Madam Adrienne studied Bernard and after seeing the pain he was in, she went back inside to bring something to help ease Bernard's pain."

Mabel cautiously said, "Madam Adrienne was half-white and half-black, she was called a Mulatto. I had only seen her a few times. She hardly ever came out of the swamp. She wasn't a welcome person in our community because she was a gypsy. I never could tell how old she was. She wasn't young, and she wasn't old, either. She always dressed in a long, dark colored skirt with a bright colored blouse. She had a handkerchief as a head covering and had big earrings. She was actually an attractive lady, but she made it difficult for anyone to know because she avoided being seen."

Mabel continued, "Bernard was on the porch moaning in pain and Madam Adrienne gave Bernard some potion to drink. At first, Bernard refused to drink it probably because of all the things he had heard his mother say about Madam Adrienne. Mr. Tom insisted he drink it, so he did. Within just a minute or two, Bernard's pain ceased."

Mabel said, "When Bernard's pain subsided, he relaxed enough to where Madam Adrienne could ask him some questions. Madam Adrienne told him he needed to tell her the truth. In jest, she told him if he didn't tell her the truth, she would know, and it would cause an evil curse to come on him and his family, so he needed to be very honest with her.

"Madam Adrienne asked Bernard if he had been eating something large before his sickness came, or had if he been hit or kicked in his chest or stomach before the illness came on him."

Mabel told us, "Bernard hesitantly said that he and Leonard had gone to a friend's house and they had a raw potato eating-contest the day before the sickness came. Bernard saw how shocked we reacted to his first answer and he wasn't sure he wanted to answer the second question about being hit or kicked. However, Madam Adrienne reminded him again he needed to be honest or a curse would come upon him and his family. Bernard at first was reluctant to tell us, but he finally said after the eating contest, his friend had a wild pony and they tried to ride him. He said he had been bucked off the pony and the pony kicked him in the lower part of his stomach, right above his private area.

"Madam Adrienne went into her house and put together some concoction in a pot, brought it to a boil, and poured it into a bottle. Madam Adrienne told Mr. Tom and David, 'Take him home and give him this. One tablespoon in the morning and one in the night until his illness goes away,'" said Mabel.

Mabel said, "She also told them that the potion will cause him to have a violent reaction. She insisted there was no need to be afraid because it would straighten him out. Just be sure to give it to him and understand that after each dose he would react violently and then sleep the rest of the day. However, she did say to be sure to wake him up to give him the next dose.

"Mr. Tom humbly asked her, 'How will we know when he is cured?'

"Madam Adrienne said to Mr. Tom with a warm smile, 'Bernard will let you know. Don't worry.'"

Mabel said, "Mr. Tom thanked her and tried to give her some money, but she refused. However, David left a twenty dollar bill on her table.

"Once Mr. Tom and David got back to the truck, they decided not to take Bernard back to the house. They decided to take him to our house and let Madea take care of him. We all agreed it would be the best place to keep him until he got well," said Mabel.

Miss Mildred Law questioned Mabel: "What was the reason for not bringing him home, Mabel?"

Mabel answered, "They knew Olivia would not allow him to take the potion. They presumed if Bernard was going to have a violent reaction to it, it would panic Olivia and she would overreact. She overreacted anyway, but it was not from Bernard taking the potion. It was from them hiding him from her."

Mabel delightedly said, "Olivia was so mad you could have fried eggs on her when they came back without Bernard. Mr. Tom and David refused to tell her where Bernard was and told her she would have to trust them."

Mabel said, "Madea gave Bernard the potion that evening, and he did have a very violent reaction, just as Madam Adrienne had warned. His reaction was so frightening that Madea came to the house to get both Mr. Tom and David. When they saw how sick it made Bernard, they thought he was going to die. He continually vomited and it tore his stomach up to where he had absolutely nothing in him, and then he settled down and slept, exactly as Madam Adrienne said.

"The next morning, Madea gave him another dose and again he reacted violently. After the reaction passed he seemed better and went back to sleep. That went on for three days, until one morning, Bernard woke up and said he was hungry. Madea fixed him a good breakfast and he went back to sleep. Madea said she knew he was much better and on his way to getting well because he didn't have any more pain, and he was always hungry," said Mabel.

"That evening, when David came over to check on Bernard, he asked if he could come home. We knew then that he had turned the corner and was going to make it. We were very happy for Bernard," said Mabel, gladly.

"David brought Bernard home, and you would think his reunion with Olivia was a happy one, but Olivia made it into a battle zone. However, for Bernard and Leonard, it was a happy time. They were glad to be back together. The first thing Olivia asked Bernard was not 'How are you feeling?' But instead, 'Where did they hide you?'" said Mabel.

Mabel said modestly, "The next day, I went with Olivia. She took Bernard to a new doctor in another town to have him checked out. After hearing the story of Bernard's strange illness, the young doctor who was just out of med school, told Olivia it was probably a twisted bowel that had caused the illness. He said the other doctors probably never questioned Bernard like the gypsy lady had."

Mabel said, "The doctor told Olivia whatever the potion was, it did the job of straightening him out. It had dehydrated him to such a degree that it caused the intestine to shrink and twist back to normal. If she had not done what she did, Bernard might have died.

"The doctor praised Madam Adrienne, much to Olivia's disapproval, and asked if he could meet her so he could learn from her. Olivia thought what the young doctor said was a bunch of hogwash. She could care less about what Madam Adrienne did. The important thing to her was not Bernard getting back to normal, but now that he was back to normal, she was free to enact her revenge on Madea," said Mabel with disdain.

Jeannie had doubts about what Mabel said and asked, "Oh, I bet Olivia was glad it worked out fine, with Bernard getting back to his regular self and ridding himself of all the pain."

Mabel and Miss Mildred Law laughed, and Mabel said, "Most mothers would have been rejoicing that their child was saved from death and that someone had taken care of him like he was one of their own. But not Olivia, she was never appreciative for what others did for her.

"The thing Olivia was grateful about was that she had found out who hid her child from her," said Mabel. "When Bernard told her he was being cared for by Madea at her house, it put the icing on Olivia's cake. Olivia remembered what Madea had said to her earlier about her favoring Leonard over Bernard. It made her mad to be accused of favoritism to the point of allowing one child to die and one to live."

Mabel added some counseling wisdom. "Most of the time the truth hurts people much more than telling them a lie. What Madea said was true. However, Olivia didn't want anyone to think she was that vain."

Mabel said miserably, "To her, for Madea to take her child and hide him from her was an unforgivable act. Even when everyone told her it was her Papa's idea, Olivia ignored that fact. She was looking for a reason to justify hurting Madea, and now she felt she had one.

"The funny thing was, Madea was guilty of favoritism herself. She loved Emma much more than Olivia, and Olivia knew that. Of course, everybody felt that way, and Olivia couldn't do anything about it. However, she could do something . . . hurt Madea. Now that Emma had left, and Papa was too sick to go against Olivia's wishes, she could do as she wished," said Mabel.

"After Bernard's sickness, Mr. Tom's health took a turn for the worst. I watched him nights and in the mornings, Madea came to relieve me. The morning after the doctor checked Bernard out, Olivia had a surprise for her and me," said Mabel, seriously.

Mabel said, "Olivia and I were in the kitchen. As soon as Madea came through the back door of the kitchen, Olivia stopped her to tell her in front of me, 'I no longer need your services at my house.'

"Olivia told Madea in front of me so that I could hear her, 'I only plan to use Mabel in the evenings,'" said Mabel, sadly.

"Madea knew instantly that Olivia meant what she was saying, and she knew why.

"Madea told her, 'Girl, you's better gets t'at chip off's yurn shoulder, before's Mr. Tom get's on to you's.'"

Mabel said in a contemptuous way, "Olivia told her a lie and we both knew it, 'I talked this over with Papa last night and he is in full agreement with me. It is time for you to go. You better be careful what you say, I am still considering moving you out of the house you are staying in for free. After all, it is on my property.'"

Mabel said you could see the sadness on Madea's face as she asked Olivia, "'Why is you's wantin' to do's this to me?'"

"Olivia told Madea, 'You better be glad I am not having you arrested for kidnapping my child. I'll teach you of accusing me of favoritism. You were wrong for saying that.'"

Mabel said, "I tried to leave the kitchen and go talk to Mr. Tom but Olivia stopped me. She told me, 'That will be all today Mabel, you can take your mother home. I can handle it the rest of the day, I will see you at six this evening.'

"I tried to go out the back door, but I should have known Madea would not leave without imparting some of her wisdom to Olivia. Madea stopped me from going passed her too," said Mabel.

"Madea pointed her finger at Olivia and angrily told her, 'Girl, I should's have told's you t'is sooner, but's I didn't 'cause I knew's it only make's you's mad. I know's you's have had it hard, but most's of t'at is brought's on by yourself. You's runs off yo' sister with yo lies and now you's going to kill yo' Papa. I is not goin' to make's t'is a big deal, only 'cause of yo' Papa. I know's you's not goin' to believe's t'is, but's I still's loves you. You's still my child too. No's matter what's you's say, you's mine.'"

Mabel said, "Madea grabbed my arm and pulled me out the door and down the steps as fast as she could move. When I got where I could see her face, she had tears rolling down her cheeks. Olivia had accomplished her mission. She had hurt Madea deeply."

# Chapter 16

## *Papa*

"That evening when I came back to the house to care for Mr. Tom, David asked me, where Miss Sis was that day. Mr. Tom had been asking for her, and I needed her to mend a pair of pants for me," said Mabel.

"When David said Mr. Tom were looking for Madea, I immediately knew, as suspected, Olivia had lied to Madea and me," said Mabel, crossly.

"I told David that Olivia had dismissed her.

"David was puzzled by my answer and asked me, 'What do you mean she dismissed her?'

"I answered him coolly, 'Olivia let her go. She told Madea that she did not need her services any longer.'

"David was surprised to hear what I said and quizzed me. 'Does Mr. Tom know about this? He never said anything to me about her being let go. This is crazy!'

"I timidly said to David, 'Olivia told Madea and me that Mr. Tom had agreed to let Madea go. At least, that is what we were told.'

"I followed David to Mr. Tom's room, knowing he was going to ask if he knew Olivia had let Madea go. I knew Mr. Tom did not have anything to do with that contemptible decision. It was all Olivia's doing. She was trying to hurt Madea because she had embarrassed her when they took Bernard to Madam Adrienne," said Mabel.

"David and I gently slipped into his bedroom and David asked Mr. Tom if he knew Olivia had fired Miss Sis.

"Mr. Tom sprung up from his bed and barked out, 'What the hell are you talking about boy. You got to be out of your mind. Why in the world would Olivia do such a damn fool thing like that? She must have gone stone cold crazy. Go tell her I want to see her right now, and you tell her she better get her tail in here quick.'

"David left to retrieve Olivia. She came into his bedroom and asked him in an unusually soft, sweet voice, 'Yes, Papa? What can I do for you?'

"All four of us were standing around the bed and, regretfully, Mr. Tom told me and David he wanted to talk to Olivia alone and to close the door as we went out.

"I wanted to be there to see the look on her face when Mr. Tom questioned her. I know David wanted to be in there, too, because we both stood close to the door so we could hear what was being said.

"Mr. Tom began speaking calmly and asked her if she had fired Sis. Olivia told him she had let her go for a while to save money for the household. She continued to tell Mr. Tom, Aunt Sis was getting too old to do the things that were needed around the house, so she decided to give her a rest.

"Immediately after Olivia gave him that story, she told Mr. Tom, 'We didn't really need Aunt Sis anymore because Mabel and I are much younger and more able to do the heavy jobs around the house.'

"I could picture Mr. Tom patiently listening to Olivia knowing she was churning out more of her lies. We listened as Mr. Tom's calm voice changed into a much brasher tone as he told Olivia, 'What the hell do you mean she is too old to perform her duties? Hell, ain't nothing around here gets done unless Sis does it. I guess you think I'm too old, too. Maybe you ought to fire me!'

"Mr. Tom continued fussing at Olivia, 'Don't you know Sis is a member of our family? She was in our family way before you got here. Hell, you can't fire a member of our family.'

254

"Mr. Tom questioned Olivia's motive. 'And your reason for doing this is that you are saving money?'

"Mr. Tom paused before he said, 'Damn you, girl. I don't pay her nothing anyway. That woman raised you. She cooked and cleaned for you all your life, and you just up and decide to let her go, dismiss her for no real reason. Oh, yeah, I forgot, she hurt your feelings. If you want to dismiss somebody and save money, then get rid of me. I'm the one who is worthless. I'm the one who is costing this family money,' said Mr. Tom, earnestly.

"In the midst of the misery Olivia had created for Mr. Tom, he started violently coughing. I would have given a thousand bucks to have seen Olivia's face after he said those things to her, but his reprimand got even better after his coughing attack stopped.

"Mr. Tom harshly told her, 'You better have her back in this house tomorrow morning or someone else in this house is going to be let go. You had better tell her personally, you were sorry you did that to her and you tell her you were wrong. Do you understand me girl? You better understand'

"David and I were straining to hear what Olivia said back to her father. We could barely make out what Olivia told him, but we did hear her say delicately, 'Yes Papa, I will do everything you say.'

"I don't know when Olivia talked to Madea, but the next morning Madea came in to relieve me. She continued waiting on Mr. Tom and taking care of things as she always had. I noticed that Madea seemed to have a little extra pep in her.

"I asked Madea about Olivia's meeting with her, but she wouldn't tell me about their conversation. But knowing Olivia as I did, after she begrudgingly told Madea she was sorry, I would venture to say she probably told Madea she was forced by Papa to bring her back. I would also guess she told Madea when Papa passed away, that it was just a matter of time before she would fire her again.

"It was just a couple days after that little episode that we had to take Mr. Tom to the hospital because he was having difficulty breathing. We could tell his illness was developing into pneumonia," said Mabel.

Miss Mildred Law told us, "Yes, I remember. I came to the hospital to visit with him that weekend. My mother told me Mr. Tom wanted me to come see him. I was excited to be off from school because the mid semester exams had just finished and I looked forward to a rest. I had only one more semester to finish school. I had been offered a teaching job and was going to be able to teach here, in my home parish. It was where I always wanted to be.

"I came into Mr. Tom's hospital room and he had an oxygen tent over him. It was a little spooky to see an oxygen tent again because I remembered we only put them over severely critical patients during the war. From the way he looked and spoke to me, I believed Mr. Tom knew his days on earth were very short," said Miss Mildred Law, sadly.

"Mr. Tom was in a good mood when I came in, and we joked. He told me he would love to have a smoke. In jest, I told him I would sneak him one if he wanted me to," said Miss Mildred Law.

"Mr. Tom joked, telling me, 'Yeah, I bet you would get into trouble the same way you did when you were thirteen and I caught you in my hayloft smoking.' We laughed and it caused Mr. Tom to start coughing again," said Miss Mildred Law as she smiled.

"After the coughing attack ended, Mr. Tom's disposition became very serious and he told me Emma was very fortunate to have such a good friend as me. He said not many people would follow their friends into war as I had. He said he missed Emma so much, and I said I missed her, too. We grabbed hands and he clutched my hands tightly to his chest. It was as if he were trying to hold onto life itself through me. I could see the tears welling in his eyes as I did everything I could not to cry.

"I reassured him that Emma would be coming home soon. I told him that I just felt it would be true. I didn't want to tell Mr. Tom, but I had just gotten a letter from Emma saying she didn't think she would ever come home again. She said she didn't feel like she fit in anywhere anymore," Miss Mildred Law said, gloomily.

"Mr. Tom told me I was probably right, but it won't be to come home to stay. Then Mr. Tom paused before he told me, 'She will come home to say goodbye to me.'

"I had to turn my head away so that Mr. Tom couldn't see my tears. I knew he was probably right. My mother told me the doctors said his heart was barely beating," said Miss Mildred Law, tearfully.

"Mr. Tom must have realized why I turned away as he told me, 'You don't have to sugarcoat anything for me, I know my situation. My days are numbered. They are probably down to one hand now. I wish I could tell her one more time that I loved her.'"

Miss Mildred Law, near tears, said, "I could hardly contain myself as I told him, 'I wish you could, too.'

"Mr. Tom said regretfully, 'You know Mildred, I wish I could say that through my loins God produced two good children, but I can't honestly say that. Emma and Olivia are like night and day. I wish I could say it wasn't that way, but it is. I don't know what I did to make that happen, but they are different. May God forgive me.'

"Mr. Tom looked deeply into my eyes, reached for my hands again, and said, 'I know how strong-willed you are Mildred. I know how you and Emma are so much alike. Both of you want to make

257

sure things are done right. That is why I want you to do me a big favor. I know you can't help Olivia, she is too far gone, but I want you to look out after Bernard and Leonard and try to keep them on the right path after I'm gone. They respect you and are actually a little afraid of you, which is good. They need a strong presence in their lives, and I want you to be that presence. Emma is not here to do it, so it will be left to you. I hope you choose to watch over them because if you don't, they will destroy themselves.'"

Miss Mildred Law said, "I leaned over and kissed Mr. Tom on his forehead and told him I would be honored to do it for him. However, I told him I would have to wait a long time to do it because he was going to live a long, long time. Both he and I knew that was not true, but I felt it was the right thing to say at the time."

It was easy to see the great love and respect Mabel and Miss Mildred Law had for Mr. Tom. After listening to them talk about him that day, I knew Jeannie and I both had developed a similar love and respect for him, too. Even though we never met the man, we felt that same esteem for him that they had.

Mabel said, "The first day Mr. Tom was in the hospital was the same day David caught Olivia trying to cheat on him. I'm not sure if she accomplished her mission because I heard David stopped her before she could . . . I wish I knew, but everyone was so tight-lipped about it, I never found out."

Surprisingly, Miss Mildred Law told us, "Well, you are in luck . . . because I know what happened. David came to me that same day to ask me what I thought he should do about Olivia."

Mabel excitedly asked Miss Mildred Law, "Well, please tell me what happened. Did she get caught in the act or what? I was at the hospital with Mr. Tom. I think Madea knew what happened, but she wouldn't tell me what she knew. She won't even tell me now. She does that with everything."

"David came to visit me that day and he told me he thought he had caught Olivia trying to have a fling. I asked him what he meant. She was trying to have an affair? He realized he had not explained it well enough for me to understand, so David said, 'Wait a minute. Let me tell the story from the beginning and you will understand what happened,'" said Miss Mildred Law.

"David said, 'My friend and I volunteered to put in a door for a widow who goes to our church. When we tore out the old door, we realized we didn't bring a level. My house was closer, so my friend took me to Mr. Tom's place to get my level.'

"David said, 'When we got there, I thought it was strange Olivia and the truck were not there. On the way back, my friend noticed my truck was at Pete Miller's house. My friend said Olivia was probably looking for you, so we pulled into Pete's driveway. I knocked on his door to find out if Olivia was looking for me. Pete opens the door. He has no shirt on. I think, that's odd, especially if Olivia is there and he is not married. As I am talking to Pete, Olivia walks out of the kitchen with two shot glasses and a bottle of whiskey in her hands. It's a jolt for Olivia to see me there and shocking to me to find her in this suspicious situation.'

"David said determinedly, 'It didn't take a genius to put two and two together. Olivia wasn't there looking for me. I was the last person Olivia wanted to see at the door. I tried to go into the house to confront Olivia, but Pete put his arm across the door to stop me. Pete acted as if he was the fox who stole the hen from the rooster, and he was going to protect his prize. I tried to push pass Pete, and Pete resisted my efforts again. I punched Pete in the nose, which laid him out on the floor. I went on in and told Olivia she had better get

259

her tail back to the house where she belonged, and she better do it right now.'

"David said Olivia tried to explain why she was there, but David refused to listen. David knew she would lie to him," said Miss Mildred Law.

"That morning he'd told Olivia where he would be, so her being at Pete's house had nothing to do with her looking for him," said Miss Mildred Law.

"David and the friend left to finish the door job and instead of him going home after completing the job, his friend brought him to my house. He told me he didn't think Pete and Olivia did anything. He said they probably had planned to, but the reason they didn't was because he'd come in on them before anything could develop," Miss Mildred Law said.

"David asked me what I thought he should do. He said he was fed up with all of Olivia's mess. Living with her had been one calamity after another, and he was ready to get out of the marriage. He acknowledged she would never change," said Miss Mildred Law.

"David inquired if he should separate from her or just outright divorce her. After all, she had misled him into marrying her. He said he only married her out of gratitude, that their marriage was built on lies, and from those lies she had ruined his life and Emma's life too," said Miss Mildred Law.

"We discussed his situation. Should he stay or should he leave? We weighed the pros and cons of a separation as compared to a divorce. Back in that time, it was very unusual for a couple to separate or divorce. Divorce was frowned upon by everybody, and eventually continuing in marriage led to ruined lives. I told him I was sorry but I could not make that decision for him. It was his life to live," said Miss Mildred Law, knowing she never was in marriage long enough to really know.

Miss Mildred Law exclaimed, "I knew he had taken a lot of abuse from Olivia, and I understood exactly why he would want to get out of the marriage. The marriage was doomed from its beginning, and when Emma came back, it was over. David and Olivia only stayed together because it was what was expected of them, their marriage was an act to please other people."

Mabel said to us, "I don't know what happened back at the house, but Madea told me David and Olivia tore into each other like dog and cat. She said David got so angry at Olivia, that she became afraid for Olivia. She thought David was going to hit her. She had never seen David that upset before, but now he was very distraught. He couldn't take anymore arguing with Olivia, and he left in his truck and stayed gone all night. Madea did not give me any particulars of what they were arguing over, but I could imagine what was said to each other after catching her with Pete.

"I do know Olivia came to Mr. Tom's hospital room that night after their fight. She came crying to Mr. Tom to straighten everything out. Her visit had upset Mr. Tom so much that the hospital staff refused to let him have any visitors, particularly Olivia," said Mabel.

"That same night, as I sat with Mr. Tom at the hospital, he peacefully slipped away. I remembered his last breath. He let out a big sigh as the life in him just left. As I watched him pass, his face seemed to look as if death had given him release. I thought to myself that he really needed some peace from what was happening at his house. I know this sounds wrong, but I thanked God after he died because God had taken him out of the turmoil that Olivia had created in his life and our lives, too," said Mabel, sadly.

261

"I know people don't like to hear a person blame someone's death on another, and most of the time when they do that, it is out of line. But I still believe today Olivia's visit to Mr. Tom that night is what killed him. Mr. Tom was such a good man, so gentle and kind. Then to have to undergo all the chaos and tragedy Olivia brought into his life, it just didn't seem right. It is hard to believe he could have two daughters who were so different," Mabel said.

Miss Mildred Law said, "Yes, Mr. Tom was a fine man. He was the same way every day. He was always happy and had a smile on his face. He was even-tempered and very seldom got upset at anything, unless it was something Olivia did. I still miss all the funny things he said to us and how he loved to pick on us.

"Emma had given me a telephone number to call if there was an emergency at home. It was very difficult for me to call Emma to tell her that Mr. Tom had passed away," said Miss Mildred Law.

"She took it very hard, as I'd expected her to. She asked what the arrangements were for his funeral. I told her I didn't know. Emma told me to tell Olivia that she would pay for the funeral. She asked me to tell Olivia to embalm her father and not to hold the service until she arrived, just in case she had difficulty getting home," said Miss Mildred Law.

"It took Emma only a day to get here. Usually it would take two or three days. But Charles Wilson made arrangements and placed her on a military flight to Baton Rouge. I picked her up the next day at the airport, and we came to the funeral home," said Miss Mildred Law.

"In those days we didn't have a morgue to hold the body, the funeral home used Boudreau's Ice House. Most folks buried their people the day they died or the next day because they could not afford to embalm them," said Miss Mildred Law.

"To save money, people held the service at their home and moved the body to the cemetery from there. They held Mr. Tom's service at his home the day after Emma arrived. He would have wanted it there. He loved his home place," said Miss Mildred Law, sadly.

Mabel said, "It was beautiful on the day of the funeral, and many people came to pay their respects to Mr. Tom's family. The preacher did an excellent job. It was easy to eulogize his funeral because Mr. Tom was a good man. The preacher said some beautiful things about him, and it helped ease the pain of his loss. Madea took his death the hardest. She still has problems today talking about Mr. Tom."

Mabel said, "Madea sat in a chair beside the head of the casket the entire time of the wake and during the funeral itself. She never cried. That happened after it was all over. She felt she had to be strong for her family. Every time someone came to view Mr. Tom's body, she stood up to greet them and told them that the community had lost a good man. She consoled them when in reality she was the one who needed the consoling. Madea loved Mr. Tom like a brother. They had gone through a lot of trying times together, but now he was gone to be with his wife, Kate."

Miss Mildred Law said, "The only time Miss Sis left that coffin was when Emma showed up. Miss Sis walked to her, placed her arms around Emma, and told her she was sorry she had let Mr. Tom slip away from them. Miss Sis really believed Mr. Tom's death was her fault."

Mabel replied, "We had a hard time convincing her that God had chosen the time for Mr. Tom to leave this earth, that she had nothing to do with it one way or the other. Madea felt like it was her responsibility to keep everything going in the house, including the people. You know how she was. When she got something in her head, you couldn't make her let go of it. She is still that way today."

"Olivia didn't seem to be excessively sad over the loss of her father. She gladly accepted the condolences when friends came to console her, but she withheld any show of emotion," said Miss Mildred Law.

Mabel said, "Poor Emma. She was all torn up about her loss. She sat in a chair next to Madea and every time someone came to offer their condolences, all she could do was cry. She apologized to them for crying, telling them she couldn't help it. As people came by and greeted her, it would bring back so many great memories of them and her family. She told them her sadness was just too overwhelming, that only God could give her peace."

"Poor David . . . I know he felt left out. I don't think anyone in the family every came to him to console him. Olivia was so occupied with herself that she never thought about consoling David. I know Emma saw how David was. It was obvious he was broken-hearted, but she dared not go to him. Emma consoling David would have lit a fire under Olivia and probably caused an ugly scene. But David did look out of place. He looked like he wished he was somewhere else other than there in the house," said Miss Mildred Law.

Mabel said affirmatively, "Yes he took it hard. He and Mr. Tom were close. David had been with Mr. Tom for years. Mr. Tom was more of a father to him than anyone, and I know Mr. Tom felt like he was the son he never had.

"The boys were too young to understand about death. Their loss of Mr. Tom would not be realized until later when they understood that they would never see him again. It was sad to see them struggling with it later on. He was the only male figure Olivia would let discipline her children," said Mabel.

Miss Mildred Law said, "I lost my composure at the cemetery. It has been a long time now, and yet it seems like yesterday that Mr. Tom picked on us as kids for getting caught smoking in the barn. He was one of those men who seemed to know what was best to do in most situations."

Mabel said, "I was fine until I saw Howard sobbing at the cemetery. It caused me to lose my composure, too. Mr. Tom was like a father to me and Howard. He treated us like we were one of his kids. When he took us to the store, he gave us the same money he gave his own kids. He never treated us like we were second-rate people, not like a lot of folks did back then. I still miss him today."

Jeannie asked, "What happen to everybody after Mr. Tom died?"

Miss Mildred Law said, "Honey, it is funny that you ask that. Oh, everybody was headed back to where they were before Mr. Tom died, but a few strange things happened before that occurred."

Jeannie asked, "What do you mean 'strange things happened' Miss Mildred?"

Miss Mildred Law said, "Maybe I used the wrong phrase to describe what happened after the funeral. It was strange, or should I say shocking, for me to be told by my best friend that I would never see her again."

Jeannie asked, "Emma told you that? Was it the last time you ever saw her? Why would she say something like that?"

Mabel commented on Jeannie's question, "I'm sure we all planned to continue life as normal, but it didn't quite work out that way for Emma, or for any of us. I'm not sure I can put it into words. Olivia had such a negative sway on everybody's life. It not only made us distant to one another, she seemed to destroy any ambition or dreams we might have had.

"It was like what you saw at the funeral. We wanted to console each other, we needed to console each other, but because of Olivia and her attitude, we were afraid to. I guess I am trying to say, she caused us to lose all sensitivity," said Mabel, dejectedly.

"I don't understand what you are saying, Mabel," said Miss Mildred Law. "Olivia held that kind of influence on everyone, but there were still two in that house who had future plans which did not involve Olivia. They saw exactly what you were talking about, and that was why Emma told me what had happened between her and David after the funeral."

"What happened Miss Mildred? We want to know," asked Jeannie.

Miss Mildred began to tell the story.

"After the burial, everyone came back to the house to visit and eat. Near the end of that time, while Olivia was enjoying being the center of attention, David left the house and went to the barn to pasture the horses. When he entered the barn, Emma was there with her horse. David sneaked up behind her intending to frighten her as a joke, but as he stood behind her, he realized he really didn't want to scare her. It might hurt her feelings and he never wanted to do that. David stood there frozen for a short while without Emma knowing he was there. However, the scent of her hair and the nearness of her flooded his mind with loving memories of the good times and the love they shared together.

"Suddenly Emma turned around with the realization that someone was close to her. As soon as she saw that it was David, she smiled at him and breathed a sigh of relief. They looked intently at one another and David kissed her. His kiss was not like a friend's

266

kiss. It was more like one from someone who had missed seeing them for a long time.

"At first, Emma welcomed his kiss but quickly realized this was not right and she told David. 'No, no David, this is wrong. We can't do this!'

"As Emma pushed him away, David quickly replied to her, 'It can't be wrong, because I still love you as much as I did before I joined the Marines.'

"David told Emma, 'Loving you is not wrong. I will tell you what is wrong. It is wrong for me to be married to a woman I don't love. It's wrong to feel trapped in a marriage because of the lies she made up. You know what Olivia did to us Emma. It was no ordinary lie, and she is no ordinary person.'

"Emma backed away to put more distance between her and David in case someone came into the barn, and she told David, 'Yes I know, ordinarily people live and learn, but even though Olivia is my sister, she just lives to make other people's lives be as miserable as hers.'

"David lovingly told Emma, 'I knew you understood what she did to us. Olivia took advantage of what kind of person you were and knew you would accept the fact that I was married to her, even though she lied. She didn't care. She lied about you to everybody. She used the fact I felt obligated to marry her because of what Mr. Tom did for me. She is so vain. How could I ever have been so dumb to marry her? I should have known she was lying the whole time. She always lies.'

"Emma saw in David's eyes his heart ache and wanted to go to David to console him, but she knew it would be wrong. She also knew that if she did, she might not allow him to go back to Olivia.

Emma being greatly disenchanted, told David, 'The fact remains she is your wife, and no one can change that.'

"David stopped Emma from saying anything else and said, 'All I want to know Emma is . . . No, no, no. All I need to know is how you feel toward me. I'm going to leave Olivia. Our marriage is no good, I can't live this lie anymore. Olivia doesn't love me. She never did. All she wanted was to take me away from you, and you know that is true, don't you?'

"Emma began to cry because in her heart she knew David was telling the truth, and she told David, 'Most of the time the truth is very hard to take, but you have to live with the truth. It can't be changed into something else. David, you gave a vow to God to be her wife . . . it's forever. You can't go back . . . on a promise to God.'

"David again interrupted Emma. 'Emma, I still love you with all my heart. Don't you know that? Oh how I want it to be different from the way it is now. Just tell me you still love me. Just tell me, so we can leave here and go somewhere else and be together right now, today. That is the way it is supposed to be. That is the way we planned it.'

"As Emma listened to David's plea, she said, 'I can't listen to this. I can't do this. This is wrong, and you are making me want to do wrong. You are married to my sister. I can't have you. I can't want you. I can't love you . . . no, it is all wrong.'

"David said to Emma with tears streaming down his cheeks, 'It can't be wrong. The way I feel toward you. It seems so right to me. Just tell me and we will leave here today and go somewhere no one knows who we are.'

"Emma told him, 'David, you belong to Olivia. She needs you. She is your wife. Honor that. Honor her. Don't divorce her, she can't make it without you. Our time together is over. Do you understand?

It's over, accept that. There can never be an *us*. I am sorry things happened the way they did. But it happened, and we must respect our lot in life and move on.'

"Emma walked past David and went to the house as David stood there. He turned his head away from Emma because he didn't want her to see his tears and the sadness from what Emma had just told him. It was as hard on Emma as it was for David, but she could not go against what she knew was right. Following what you know is right is always more important than following the desires of your heart.

"David remembered after he had graduated from school, some boy asked her to go with him to the prom and David was there when he asked her. Emma politely told the boy no, then he asked her if she would ever go anywhere with him. Emma gave the boy one of her retorts, 'How about never? Is never good for you?'"

Miss Mildred Law said, "Emma told me she saw David's sadness. She said David knew any hope of them ever getting together was gone. When Emma said never, it could be etched in stone. The only hope he had to be with Emma was 'till death do us part.'"

Miss Mildred Law continued to tell us, "The next day Emma decided she needed to get back to Washington as soon as she could but before she could leave, she had to take care of legal matters pertaining to Mr. Tom's estate. After she had completed that, I took her to the train station so she could get a ticket. That was when she told me what happened between her and David in the barn."

Mabel told us, "Madea saw David head to the barn. She came to tell me she knew they were there together. We discussed whether we should tell him Emma was in the barn. Madea came to the conclusion to let things work out naturally, and for us not to interfere. We had no idea what went on because he was only in the barn a few minutes when we saw Emma come walking out. We figured not much could have happened it that short time."

Miss Mildred Law laughed as she said, "I might have known Aunt Sis had kept an eye on Emma. She always did."

Miss Mildred Law looked at me and Jeannie and said, "I know you have noticed how ever time Aunt Sis mentions Emma's name. She referred to her as 'My sweet girl.' That lady deeply loved Emma. Sometimes I thought she loved her more than Howard or Mabel. The sun and the moon rose and sat on Emma to Aunt Sis.

"Just before Emma got on the train, we were sitting together at the station. Emma told me she knew it would be best for everyone if she never came back home again. It was the second time she had said that to me. She listed several reasons why she should never come back, but I knew the real reason was because she still had feelings for David. That was when she dropped the bomb on me and said I will never see her again," said Miss Mildred Law.

Jeannie asked, "Was it the last time you saw her?"

Mabel laughed and said, "No, it didn't work out that way. A lot happened right after Emma left, and it brought her back."

# Chapter 17

## *Olivia's Reign*

"Olivia had inherited half of Mr. Tom's estate, while Emma owned the other half. However, Emma told Olivia to use it as if it was her own. Emma smartly set everything up where Olivia could not lose it from mismanagement, knowing Olivia never had managed anything," said Mabel.

"The household income had been cut in half, and it was the major problem at the DeAngelo household. David's disability check each month and whatever monies Emma sent to Olivia was all that came in. Olivia contributed absolutely nothing to the income, and it never dawned on her that she might not have enough to pay all the bills," declared Mabel.

"The few animals on the farm had brought in very little extra income from the sale of milk and cream or eggs. Mr. Tom and Sis handled the sale of those things, but it was only enough to pay for the feed. Occasionally, Mr. Tom would sell a calf, but usually they were kept for meat and milk. Olivia knew nothing about those kinds of things," exclaimed Mabel.

Mabel continued, "The land hadn't been worked to produce any crops in years. Cotton and corn had been their cash crops, but no one in the household was physically able to work it."

With great disdain, Mabel told us, "Not unexpectedly, Olivia's first act of being in charge was to dismiss the most knowledgeable worker in the household. She let Madea go for the second time. She never took into consideration anything her father told her about what Madea meant to this household. Neither did she remember what Mr. Tom told her about Madea raising both Olivia and Emma since Miss Kate, her mother, had died.

"Even with Mr. Tom telling her Sis was family, it made no difference to Olivia. She was going to get even with Madea, by

273

putting her out of the house. Mr. Tom used to say, Olivia never could see any further than the end of her nose. Emma always added to what he said by saying, she would cut off her nose to spite her face," said Mabel as she smiled at us.

"Olivia wanted me to work and live at the house, but because Olivia had let Madea go, I no longer wanted to work for Olivia. Madea convinced me we owed it to the DeAngelo family. She said Mr. Tom took care of us when things were bad, and we owed him the obligation to take care of his family now that hard times have fallen on them," said Mabel.

"Madea told me if I didn't stay to help Olivia, things would quickly fall apart. I knew that was true. The reason Olivia wanted me to live at the house full time was so that I could run everything for her. That would give her freedom to do what she did best, and that was nothing. I told her I could be there maybe ten or twelve hours a day, but I had a responsibility to care for Madea, and I needed some time for myself, too," said Mabel.

Mabel was not happy with Olivia's demands. "I told her I would need more money, since Madea was gone and I would be doing double the work. My request did not set well with Olivia, but she had to agree to it because there was no one else she could get for the small amount of money she paid me.

"Olivia had no idea what things cost. She never had worried about money before. She was forced to learn things were not free. You had to pay for things like electricity, butane, gas for the truck, food, feed for the animals, clothes for everyone, and incidentals. It was all new to her," said Mabel as she chuckled.

Mabel said, "Olivia knew nothing about credit. David tried to explain to her how Mr. Tom put things on credit down at Aull's Country Store. David told her at the beginning of each month, Mr.

Tom would pay them what he owed whenever his check came in. Handling the household finances confused her. She didn't realize that there was more to running a household than just being in charge. She thought you just barked out orders and things got done. She was completely lost, and it terrified her. Any problem that arose would throw Olivia for a loop. I couldn't help myself, but I actually felt a little sorry for her.

"When her boys started seeing girls as being something good instead of being someone to abuse, she had a very difficult time handling that. Both of her boys were well built and good looking young men, and the girls found them very attractive," said Mabel.

"Bernard, without question was the most handsome, the girls swooned over him. He had wavy hair and dimples, and he was smart. He never said anything negative about people, and the girls loved him. Olivia resented her boys being popular with the young ladies, and she tried to make Bernard and Leonard as unattractive to them as she could. She made Bernard rub Vick's salve on his chest every day to repel the girls, she told Bernard he was to wear it every day so the disease Madam Adrienne healed would not come back. Bernard didn't obey her. Leonard said he wiped it off as soon as he left the house," Mabel said.

"Leonard was also good looking, but he wasn't as handsome as Bernard. His attraction was his athletic ability. It made him very popular with both the boys and the girls. He lacked the social skills Bernard had. He was rude and arrogant. He also was lazy and refused to study or work in school, a habit he developed after Emma was made to stop helping him," Mabel informed us.

"Because Leonard had been held back, he was older and more mature than the kids in his class, and he took advantage of that fact. He had his own thoughts about what girls were for, and he wasn't bashful about showing it. He liked touching them, and it got him into trouble," said Miss Mildred Law unhappily.

Mabel said, "David must have listened to what Emma told him from his short visit with her in the barn."

"What are you referring to, Mabel?" asked Miss Mildred Law.

"Emma's request for David to stay with Olivia because she could not make it without him, and he chose to stay with her after Emma left. Physically, David was getting better. He could walk, but he still had a limp from part of his hip being taken off. That injury caused him not to be able to work very long or to be able hold a regular job."

Mabel stated, "When David found out that Olivia had fired Madea again, he became furious. None of his physical ailments seem to make any difference to him as David jumped up in anger from the breakfast table, almost knocking it over.

"He shouted at Olivia. 'Have you lost your mind again?' David sounded exactly like Mr. Tom. He reminded Olivia of what her father had said to her. 'Your own father told you that Sis is a member of the family, and you don't fire someone in your family.'

"The fact that David knew what Olivia's father had told her in private, shocked her. Olivia mistook David's statement as a challenge to her authority and she told him in an uncaring tone, 'Am I not the owner of this house and this land?' Olivia was not looking for an answer. She was making a statement that she was in charge of the household.

"Olivia told David, 'I am sick and tired of everyone telling me how things need to be done. I have a brain, and I can see what is best for my family.'

"Evidently, Olivia pushed the wrong button with David. In anger, David told Olivia, 'Well, I thought I was part of this family too . . . since I am the only man in this family. I thought my input would be considered valuable. After all, I am the head of our family. You do know that I am your husband . . . don't you? Do I count as anything to you?'"

Mabel said, "As Olivia saw how serious David was becoming and what direction David was taking her announcement, Olivia began to weave her magic, turning David's question back on him. She was good at doing that. She tried it with Mr. Tom, too. But Mr. Tom had learned to leave the room whenever she asked him a question. Olivia's questions always led to making him agree to something he knew he would regret. Both Madea and myself had seen her do this many times to both of them."

Mabel dejectedly said, "Olivia always began with a soft, sweet agreeing statement that would take attention away from the real problem. 'Honey, you know I value your opinion and I always take your advice into consideration in anything that I do. You are the most important person in my life. I can't believe that you think I would consider your advice as unimportant. Your thoughts are always important to me, and I know you give them to help me make the best decision for our family.'"

Mabel said, sadly, "Then tears would come and she would turn his anger into compassion and sympathy for her. She was really good at it. Her display of emotion always caused David to become confused about what their disagreement was about. She turned it around by agreeing with him to a certain point, and then she would use his words to flip it around on him to get him to agree with her.

"Olivia said, 'I didn't really want to let Aunt Sis go. It dearly hurt me, too, but I knew that we have such little money coming in, and I didn't want to use your money for things Mabel and I could do. I figured you would want me to use it in other areas to make sure it lasted the entire month for our family. That is how you want me to use it, isn't it, honey?'"

Mabel continued to tell us about Olivia's strategy to get her way, "She would get him to agree with her in something small, then she would continue to have him agree to other small things, and in the end, he would agree with what she wanted in the first place. She always used the same method to seal the deal. She would cozy up to him, kiss him, and be all lovey-dovey to him. It made Madea and me sick, but what always amazed us was that it always worked. I guess that is why they say, men are such fools."

Mabel began to shake her head back and forth as she laughed and told us, "Madea used to say she was good at working the devil's magic because she learned it from Satan, himself. It was the same way the devil tricked Adam and Eve in the garden."

Jeannie asked, "Did David still go along with it, even after knowing it was against what Mr. Tom wanted?"

Mabel answered Jeannie by nodding and replied, "David never mentioned it again. I think he was too embarrassed to bring it up once he realized she had pushed it by him. That too was all part of her strategy: using a man's pride against himself."

Miss Mildred Law enhanced Mabel's concept of how Olivia got things to go her way and said to Jeannie, "Yes, baby doll, she used her charm and good looks all through her life to get her way. It really turned the men on and made all the women hate her."

"Her little lovey-dovey act didn't last too long with David because right after that argument, Leonard got into a lot of trouble," said Mabel. "And his trouble led to even bigger problems for Olivia."

Miss Mildred Law asked Mabel, "Is that when he got into trouble for cheating in school or when he broke into the Legion Hall?"

Mabel told Miss Mildred Law, "It was when he and two other boys broke into the American Legion Hall and ate up their food and drank all the soft drinks. If that wasn't bad enough, they decided to drink the liquor they found for the spring dance."

Jeannie said, "I bet those two wrongs really upset Olivia."

Mabel said to her, "You would think any wrong would upset a mother. It was no surprise to me that Olivia didn't get upset about Leonard cheating in school, she didn't pay any attention to that. David fussed at him and wanted to whip him, but Olivia took Leonard's side on that, too. She told David he had better not ever think about laying a hand on her child. David knew whipping Leonard was a no-win situation that would cause greater trouble, and he just let it go."

Jeannie asked them, "Did it cause more trouble between David and Olivia?"

Mabel was swift to answer that question. "It was the second of three worse kinds of trouble that could happen in a marriage to break it up."

I did not know what Mabel was talking about with the three worse kinds of troubles that break up marriages. I had never heard of that, and I assumed neither had Jeannie. I didn't want to look stupid because I didn't know what the first two kinds of trouble were, either. I knew Jeannie would ask what they were so they could not trip us up, and she did.

Mabel and Miss Mildred Law laughed out-loud as Miss Mildred Law said, "Hell, I have no idea what they are, either. They must be something Mabel has made up in her own mind."

We all laughed, not because we did not know what Mabel was talking about, but because we knew we were in for a treat. I sensed Mabel had inherited the same uncanny ability to uncover people's motives as her mother. Miss Sis could express why people did things in a way that everyone could easily understand.

Mabel stopped laughing and told us, "I thought everybody knew what the number one worst thing was that could happen in a marriage to break it up, and that is to have your partner cheat on you."

Before I looked around, I already knew these three women would be in agreement with number one. As expected, I saw both Miss Mildred Law and Jeannie were nodding their heads in agreement with Mabel's deduction. I agreed to, but I wasn't as enthusiastic about showing my agreement as they were. However, I did agree it was the worst.

Mabel told us what number two was: "The second worst thing to happen in a marriage was for one parent to take sides with their child against the other parent. It always causes a great division between the partners. It usually is very difficult to heal the division, as it was with David and Olivia."

Mabel concluded by telling us the third worst trouble, "Number three is finances, or a lack of finances to make ends meet. David and Olivia were facing that, too. They had just sneaked passed the first one and were about to meet up with number two and number three at the same time. Nothing good was going to come from the difficulty Leonard had brought to this family."

Mabel began to tell us how Leonard got into trouble. "Leonard had gone to baseball practice with two of his friends. They got there early . . . too early. It gave them an opportunity to go exploring because there was not any adult supervision at the Legion Field. The boys decided to break into the Legion Hall to see what was in there. When they got inside, like most boys do, they checked to see what was in the icebox. It was loaded with meat and soft drinks. They helped themselves to the meat too. Later, they found whiskey in the cabinets and decided to try some of that, too. Either they didn't like how it tasted or it wasn't enough for them, but they threw the bottles across the dance floor breaking them. In fact, they broke several more bottles, scattering the glass and liquor all over the dance floor."

Mabel continued. "If they hadn't already gotten themselves into enough trouble in the Legion Hall, they went outside and wrecked a road grader. The road grader had been left by the parish road crew at the Legion field. Believe it or not, they cranked it up and got it moving, but they couldn't figure out how to stop it. Leonard was driving according to the other boys, and they bailed out of the cab leaving Leonard heading toward a building. Leonard turned it away from the building and steered it toward a metal cattle pen. He rammed it into the chute area in hopes to stop it from hitting the building. The road grader stopped and the engine stalled out. By this time the coach had driven up and seen what the boys had done to the road grader and the pen.

"The coach questioned them and found out about the Legion Hall. He brought the boys down to the sheriff's office to report what they had done. The boys told the sheriff everything they did. Their parents were called in. They were told they will have to pay for the damages to the Legion Hall, the cattle pen, and for the wreckage to the road grader. The Sheriff released the boys to their parents' custody and told them they would have to go to court," said Mabel.

"David and Olivia were devastated by this. They couldn't afford any extra debt. Whatever the amount was going to be, any amount of money would be too much for them to handle. Olivia never spoke about the damage or its cost. She was more worried they would take Leonard away and put him in reform school," said Mabel sadly as she remembered how desperate David and Olivia's financial situation was.

Mabel mumbled, "I believe it would have been better in the long run if they had taken Leonard away from Olivia. If that had happened, he might still be alive today."

Her statement made me think about what Howard had told me earlier that morning: how Leonard was killed in an automobile accident running from the law. I did not ask Mabel or Miss Mildred Law anything about it because I wasn't absolutely sure they knew what Howard knew. I would bet both Mabel and Miss Mildred Law knew, but they probably felt there was no need in telling us.

Mabel told us what happened at court. "The judge was related to one of the three boys, and because of that, the boys received only one year of supervised probation. The parents had to pay equally for the damages to the Legion Hall, the food and drinks, repair of the pen, and the repair of the road-grader."

Mabel told us, "David and Olivia talked about disciplining Leonard. They agreed, if they left him unpunished, it could send a signal to him he could do wrong without facing any consequences. David took Leonard to the side of the house to talk with him about being responsible for his actions and to whip him. Leonard admitted he was wrong and told David he knew he deserved to be punished. When David told Leonard to get a switch. Leonard refused, and ran to Olivia for protection."

Miss Mildred Law interrupted Mabel and said, "Please tell me Olivia stood with David and not with Leonard.

"You don't have to that statement, I think we all know what the answer is," miserably said Miss Mildred Law.

Mabel said, "You are right. She came outside with Leonard, and told David in front of both Leonard and Bernard. She wouldn't let him or anyone else ever put a switch to her children. Olivia said if he ever struck one of her children, she would have him arrested."

Mabel said, sadly, "Olivia might as well have shot and killed David right then and there. She murdered any respect those two boys might have had for David. But worse than that, it killed David's respect for himself. Olivia stole David's pride, and she did it in front of her two boys. Even worse, she had no shame about doing it. Olivia had recently attempted to break the number-one worst thing to break a marriage up, and now with this incident, she had broken the number two. Number three was going to hit them when the first installment came to pay for the damages."

Mabel told us, "David's whole demeanor changed toward Olivia after Olivia stood with Leonard against him. David just gave up. He completely quit trying to make the marriage work. He went along with everything Olivia said after that, even if he knew she was wrong. David didn't stay around the house. He fell into a sinking pattern. Each day, after lunch, he got into his truck and went to O'Neil's Bar to drown his sorrow and shame, and he wouldn't come back until late at night. Then he would sleep late and head out again to repeat the pattern the next day.

"One day before noon, Olivia came to David to tell him they didn't have enough money to pay all the bills for the month. This wasn't the first time the money had run out. It seemed always to

283

happen before the end of each month. Olivia insisted David needed to find a job," said Mabel.

Mabel told us, "Olivia's tenacity with David must have brought out the last ounce of fight in him as he responded negatively to her request. It was very strange to see David react so inadequately. He turned to Olivia and told her in as calm a voice as I ever heard him speak.

"David coolly said, 'Olivia, I have given you everything I have left in my life. I don't think I can give you anything more. I don't have anymore. You deceived me into marrying you. Why you married me is still a mystery, especially since you never loved me. Somehow, I believed that you could someday, but it didn't happen. Then, because of the lie you told about Emma, I have lost the only love I ever wanted. I watched her walk off as broken-hearted as I was. I knew it was because of you and your deceit. I saw your father, my best friend, die sooner than he should have because of your lies. I give you every penny of the money I have each month, knowing you can't manage it. You have taken my pride as a man because you can't handle your children. The only thing I have left is my blood and my life . . . do you want that too?'

"Olivia looked intently at David and said in a loftier, more superior voice to David. 'Aren't you a fine one to complain? Look what all I have given you. You have a wife who took care of you when you couldn't do it for yourself. You have children anybody would be proud to call their own. We gave you a home when you had none. You have a farm you refuse to work. I think you have come out way ahead in this marriage deal we have. In fact, I think you have it a whole lot better than I do.'

"Olivia continued to tell David, 'From where I see things . . . all I got from you is a broken down cripple, who feels sorry for himself, and has turned into a drunk. You never cared for me, all you ever wanted was my sister . . . who you can't have now. You never gave me any real love, so I had to go looking somewhere else for it. The only thing I can really say that you brought to this family, or to me . . . was your truck.'

"David stared at Olivia, a smile came across his face, and he told her in as pleasant a voice as he could manage, 'Olivia, I don't know why, but I feel sorry for you. I really do. You just don't see that you have a problem. Do you know what your problem is? You won't let anyone love you because there is no room for them to love you.'

"Then David boosted his tone and forcefully told her again, 'You want to know why there is no room for anyone to love you . . . well, I'm going to tell you why. I think you need to know why. No one can love you because you love yourself so much, there's no room in your heart for anyone else's love.'

"David continued to speak calmly to Olivia. 'And since you think all I ever brought to you or this family is my truck . . . I tell you what! I might as well give that to you, too, since you have taken everything else from me. You were able to take everything because of your lies . . . I'm leaving you today. I am so tired of living this lie with you. Our marriage has never been anything but a lie. You and your lies are not worth my life.'"

Mabel said, "If that wasn't enough, David continued speaking to Olivia about how life was with her. It surprised me that Olivia didn't away. She just stood there, showing no emotion as she listened.

"David told Olivia, 'All you have ever done is smother out life with your lies. You did it with me, you did it with Emma, you did it with your Papa, you are trying to do it with Sis, and you will eventually do it to Mabel, too. There's one more thing I need to say before I go. You have lied so much that you have even lied to yourself. You have made yourself believe you are the most important person in all the history of life. Well, honey, I got news for you. You ain't nothing but a liar and fake . . . that everyone who knows you, laughs at.'"

Mabel said, "David turned his back to Olivia and walked out of the house. She never saw him again."

Mabel declared, "That day, David packed up what little he had, said his goodbyes to me, and went to Madea's house. He told her goodbye, and he left. He did just what he told Olivia. He left his truck and walked down the lane to parts unknown. He just disappeared and we never heard from him or saw him until years later, at the funeral. The day David left was a sad, sad day for me. Not only had I lost a good friend, but I was left in the house by myself with Olivia and her boys."

# Chapter 18

## *Plans Change*

"The news of David leaving Olivia quickly spread throughout our small community," said Miss Mildred Law. "I recall being in town at Mouton's Department Store with my mother, when Mrs. Mouton asked my mother if she knew where David had gone. My mother was completely taken by what she said. She had no idea what Mrs. Mouton was talking about. I could tell by the look on her face that she was asking herself . . . David is gone . . . where? Then she looked to me for help to understand, but I acted as if I was disinterested in Mrs. Mouton's question.

"Of course, I already knew David had left. He came to tell me goodbye and that he couldn't live with Olivia, anymore. He said he had to get as far away from her as he could before he went crazy or became a complete drunk. He didn't have to tell me about their marriage. I saw what a nightmare it was for him," said Miss Mildred Law.

"I recall the last meeting with David at my house. David told me he felt as if he was being forced to leave the people he loved. What he said next didn't shock me. I knew he still had feelings for Emma," said Miss Mildred Law.

"He told me, 'You'll probably never see me again Mildred. Oh, I might write to you . . . but only to find out how you or Emma is. I'm not even sure I'll do that. I came to thank you for being such a good friend to me and Emma. You treated me like I was someone important. I don't get that kind of treatment from many people. Being an orphan isn't easy, but you treated me like I was someone special.'

"David mumbled as he told me, 'I . . . I want you to tell Emma something for me . . . that I will always love her and I am sorry I brought all this calamity on her. It all happened because I was stupid enough to trust Olivia.'"

Miss Mildred Law said, "After David said that, he quickly turned his head so I couldn't see the disappointment and tears in his eyes. He rushed to hide his tears by pulling me close to him and giving me a hard, quick hug, and then he turned and walked away.

"Mrs. Mouton's voice broke my thoughts, as I heard her say . . . 'If it wasn't bad enough that David had a drinking problem . . . and he couldn't manage his finances, now he leaves Olivia and those boys with nothing.'"

Miss Mildred Law abruptly said to us, "One of the things that amazes me about people is how they can misinterpret other people's situation. As I listened to Mrs. Mouton's version of what she believed happened between Olivia and David, I just shook my head in disbelief of her ignorance.

"Of course, I knew what the real problem was between Olivia and David, and it wasn't only finances and drinking. Mrs. Mouton was wrong. David never handled any of their money. Olivia insisted that she was to do that. Olivia's selfishness and her lack of common sense in managing things is what ran David away and caused their breakup. However, I assumed Mrs. Mouton judged the situation from what she knew. She presumed David's drinking was what caused them to run out of money and why he left Olivia. However, the real cause was her underhanded lies and her wicked character. What the people saw was Olivia's pretty face and those two innocent boys. They never saw the evil that came from her heart.

"The news of David leaving Olivia astonished my mother. She told me on the way home, 'It's really hard to believe we could live only a few hundred yards away from Olivia's house, and never know anything happened.'"

Mabel made an insightful statement about Miss Mildred Law's assessment of Olivia's deception: "Yeah, Olivia had everybody fooled. If the people in our community only knew how little Olivia was concerned about David leaving her, they would be appalled. Even worse, she never cared about not having enough money to pay the bills.

"Paying off her debt was never her main concern. It wasn't that a husband left his wife . . . but that *Emma's* David left her. Olivia thought she was more important than anyone else. That's what upset her. To think anyone could walk away from being with her was unimaginable to her!

"Any normal person in the same situation would be concerned about taking care of their children and paying their bills, but that never crossed Olivia's mind. She was overcome by the fact that her *'nobody husband,'* David would even consider leaving her, *Miss High and Mighty.*"

Mabel dejectedly told us, "She really believed she was too good to be left by any man. In her mind, no man would ever consider leaving somebody as beautiful and important as she was. She told me several times after David left her that she had never done anything to deserve being left. How anyone could be that blind was beyond me. I actually began to feel sorry for her because she didn't have a clue to the real problem. And now, even worse, she had no one to blame and to lie about. Everyone had left her but me, and I wanted to leave her too."

Mabel dispassionately said, "The pressure of not having any money, caring for the farm and the house, and having children starting middle school weighed heavy on Olivia. Then, added to that situation, her Papa died, Emma left, she'd run Madea off, Leonard had troubles, and now David had left her. It was too much for Olivia to cope with."

Mabel's voice softened as she told us, "Olivia's behavior became unpredictable, and she began hearing voices. She would talk to the voices and act on what they told her to do. I told Madea about her behavior. She told me to stay close to Olivia so the boys would have someone there if things turned into something worse.

"At first, Olivia's behavior was comical. I thought Olivia was playing a game with me, making me believe she was kidding me, so she could deal with her stressful situation. I played along with her, thinking it all was a sham. Olivia seemed normal to me, except for her talking to some imaginary person or persons.

"That changed when one night around 2:00 a.m., a neighbor's son came to the house beating on the front door and yelling for us to open it. My first thought was the house must be on fire, so I went to wake Olivia to help me get the boys to go outside. Olivia was not in her bed. I thought it strange and assumed she was already outside. When I got outside with the boys, I was relieved to discover there was no fire, but there was no Olivia, either.

"However, I soon forgot about Olivia as the neighbor's boy was in such a panic crying and yelling at me. I continued to look around to see if there was a fire somewhere that I couldn't see. He was trying to tell me something, but he was talking so fast I couldn't understand him," declared Mabel.

"The boy was Leona Jackson's son, he was eleven or twelve. He was crying and not speaking clearly enough for me to understand why he was there. Finally, I understood that he was telling me Olivia was in the truck at their house, in her nightgown, and she had run the truck into the side of their house, trying to knock it down. He said she had a shotgun and was ordering them to get off her land. He said his daddy sent him to get me before she hurt someone," professed Mabel.

Mabel said, "I felt helpless and didn't know what to do. I had her two boys. I couldn't leave them or take them with me. I didn't want them to see their mother in that condition. I was dumbfounded. I had no one to send to get her. I was in a bad predicament, and didn't know which way to turn.

"I immediately told the Jackson boy to go to my house and get Madea to tend to the boys until I could come back. I sent the boys back into the house with strict instructions to wait inside for Madea and not to leave the house for any reason. I left to go to the Jackson's house to get Olivia," said Mabel.

"When I got there, I couldn't believe what I saw. It was just like the boy said: Olivia had run the truck into the corner of their front porch, and the porch roof was hanging down about two feet lower than it should be. Olivia was outside of the truck, in her nightgown, pointing a shotgun at the entire Jackson family. Mr. Jackson was standing between Olivia and his family, trying to protect them by reasoning with Olivia to calm down before she shot someone. All of the Jackson family were lined up against the wall with their hands up as if they were being robbed. They were standing underneath the porch roof crying and screaming, trying to hide behind Mr. Jackson," exclaimed Mabel.

Mabel laughed out-loud. "As I think about it today, it must have looked mighty funny. But that night, it was no joke. Olivia had gone slap-dab crazy."

As Mabel said this, I couldn't picture in my mind Aunt Olivia doing what she said. She was always quiet when I was there. I never once saw her get mad or excited. For me to hear what Mabel was saying was unbelievable. I thought to myself, she must be wrong.

Mabel said, "As soon as I got there, Mr. Jackson muttered to me that I had to do something quick.

"I calmly asked Olivia in a normal voice, 'What seems to be the problem, Olivia?'

"At first, Olivia wouldn't answer me. So I asked her using a louder, more controlling tone, 'What did they do, Olivia?'

"Olivia shocked me when she quickly answered me back, 'Papa woke me up and told me to run these niggers off our land.'"

Mabel quietly said, "When Olivia said that, I immediately knew she had gone off the deep end. I didn't want to upset her any more, so I decided to play along with her. To make her think I was part of her mission, I told her, 'Papa sent me down here to help you.'

"I didn't know how Olivia would respond to that statement. I was scared to death, for me and for the Jacksons, too. But when she turned to look at me, I knew she was listening to me and she might cooperate. I decided to take it a step further by directing her, 'Olivia, hand me the gun and I will hold them here while you get the law. We will run them off your land. Give me the gun Olivia, I will guard them.' Amazingly, she agreed and handed me the shotgun.

"Mr. Jackson must have understood what I was doing because as soon as Olivia started walking toward the truck, he grabbed her to keep her from pulling the truck out from under the porch. Backing the truck up would have caused the rest of the roof to fall on his family. I won't even attempt to tell you what Olivia called Mr. Jackson when he grabbed her, but it wasn't anything nice," exclaimed Mabel.

"I didn't know it at the time, but as I was disarming Olivia, Madea and the boys had arrived and were standing outside in the darkness listening and watching everything that happened. Madea walked over to where Mr. Jackson was holding Olivia. She started speaking softly to her. Olivia broke down and began to cry, calling Madea her mother. They continued to carry on a conversation as if

Madea was her mother, which was another indication to me that Olivia was suffering from a complete mental breakdown. Her boys saw what was happening, and I know they didn't understand what was going on. It upset both of them very much, as it did me.

"We took Olivia home and put her and the boys back to bed. The next morning when Olivia woke up, she acted as if nothing had happened. At first, she seemed normal, until Leonard asked her a question. The boys didn't understand what was happening to their mother and wanted to help her, but as they came closer to her, she would slap at them to keep them away. They cried, and their crying upset Olivia even more. So we moved the boys back into their room. Olivia had completely withdrawn. She began to rock herself back and forth, and went into a panic state," said Mabel, glumly.

"The only person she responded to was Madea. She still thought Madea was her mother. We left her with Madea and did not pressure her in anyway. It was obvious Olivia needed more help than we could give her. We also knew it was not our decision as to what to do. That difficult decision belonged to Emma," said Mabel.

"Madea sent Howard over to the Jackson's place to repair the damage Olivia had done to their house. Mr. Jackson helped Howard and told him to tell Miss Emma not to worry about him going to the law. Mr. Jackson said he understood Miss Olivia had been under a lot of stress with losing her Papa and her husband, that it was just too much for her to deal with."

Miss Mildred Law humbly said, "My mother came to college for me to contact Emma to let her know that Olivia had a nervous breakdown. I was the only one Emma had given her contact information to. Before Emma left, she stressed only to call her in an extreme emergency. We felt this was an extreme situation, so we called her.

"My mother did all the talking because she had firsthand knowledge of what had happened, and she explained to Emma what Olivia had done. Emma told her she would come, but it would take a week or so for her to make all the necessary arrangements to leave Washington. She told my mother to ask Madea and Mabel to take care of Olivia and her boys until she could come. Emma had to quit her job, pack her stuff, clear her apartment, close all accounts, and of course, say goodbye to Charles before she could leave," stated Miss Mildred Law.

"Charles came through for Emma once more by making her return home as quick as possible. Compliments of the US Navy, they delivered her to the Baton Rouge Airport where I picked her up," said Miss Mildred Law, happily.

Miss Mildred Law's manner changed from sad to happy as she told us, "I was always glad to see Emma. She made you feel you were someone special, that you were really loved. I can't exactly explain it. But the way she treated you made you feel thankful that she was your friend. She was genuine. She loved you for who you were and not for what you appeared to be. She unintentionally brought out the best in you. It was refreshing to be around her, I wish I had that ability to make people feel that way."

Mabel quickly replied, "Miss Mildred Law, you have it, too, Just like Emma did. In fact, Emma said she learned it from you."

Miss Mildred Laws said, "Thank you, Mabel, for that lie. But I am no Emma."

The conversation turned back toward Emma and Olivia as Miss Mildred Laws told us, "It was so sad when Emma first saw Olivia, it crushed her. To see her once proud, beautiful sister in such a pitiful condition caused her to grieve for Olivia to be her old self. Emma told me Olivia looked like a dethroned queen who was put in a dungeon. Her cowering in a corner, made her look like a beaten animal. I never cared for Olivia and her attitude, but it was depressing to see her as she was, even for me.

"Emma took Olivia to several specialists in New Orleans. They all agreed she'd had a mental breakdown, but they disagreed on how to treat her. One doctor wanted to treat her with shock therapy. Another wanted to use experimental drugs to see if they could bring her out of this condition.

"Emma had spoken to several specialists in Washington, DC before coming home, and they told her that Olivia might respond positively to some treatments. No matter what was done to her, she would probably regress back to where she was then. They felt the best treatment was to use mild drugs to control her violent tendencies, and give her the support of a loving family. They had seen other cases like this and ensured that with time, she would resume to a somewhat normal lifestyle."

Mabel earnestly said, "Emma valued our opinion. She discussed Olivia's situation with us daily, and we deliberated on what each doctor recommended. It was a tough decision for her to make alone, I was glad it wasn't mine to make. You could tell Olivia understood she had a problem, but I believe she knew she couldn't do anything to help herself. She was fine until she felt stressed. Then she would regress back to talking to voices, rocking, and withdrawing within herself."

Miss Mildred Law said, "Emma took input from everyone, she felt the advice of the doctors in Washington seemed to be best for Olivia. Emma didn't want any doctor to use Olivia as a guinea pig to experiment on. She felt it would be wrong, and we all agreed.

"Another major problem Emma had was what to do about Olivia's debt. It was beyond belief to see how much debt Olivia had accrued in the short time she was in charge. Olivia had enough money available not to be in any debt. She had David's check and the money Emma sent to her each month. It was more than enough to pay the bills, but not enough for Olivia and her desires," stated Miss Mildred Law.

"Emma had Olivia declared mentally unstable by a judge. She needed to do that so she could make the financial moves to bring the DeAngelo family out of debt. Judge Parker, a good friend of the family, was more than glad to help Emma place all of Olivia's holdings in Emma's care, and he offered his services to her if she needed him further," continued Miss Mildred Law.

Mabel happily said, "The first move Emma made was to bring Madea back into the house. That not only helped me, but it was good for Olivia, Emma, and the boys, too. To say Madea never had any education, Madea was a very wise person. She saw things how they were and seemed to always make good decisions. And we really needed that."

Miss Mildred Law said gratefully, "Emma still had some of her back-pay from the war, plus she had saved every penny she could while working in Washington, DC. It wasn't nearly enough for her to be completely out of debt, but Emma had other options. Emma had a talent for making and saving money. My dad said Emma's making and saving money wasn't any talent. 'She was just tight.'

"Emma decided to cut timber from one hundred of the one hundred forty acres they owned. She got a good price for the timber, enough to pay off all the debts. Then she decided to sell the hundred acres and use the money for another purpose she had in mind," said Miss Mildred Law.

"In Washington DC, she had seen what an education can do to help a person have a better life. She made her mind up to do

298

something she always wanted to do, and that was to get a college education. However, she couldn't pursue her desire because of her past and present circumstances, so she decided to help others have that opportunity. I believe that involved you, Mabel, your brother Howard, and Bernard, too," said Miss Mildred Law.

"Emma always wanted to go to college and get a degree, but she didn't because her greatest desire was to marry David and have children. However, the war came and dealt its unusual circumstances. After she left home and went to Washington, she pursued the dream of earning a degree, but life's circumstances had dealt her a different hand, crushing her personal dreams.

"It seemed life for her kept was going from bad to worse, and it continued to look like Emma was intended never to have any joy. Most people in her circumstance would have given up and accepted the low position given to her, but not Emma. She remained hopeful. Emma told me she may not be able to get a degree, but she sure could help others get one. Emma adapted to whatever situation came her way, and she made something positive come from it," said Miss Mildred Law, proudly.

Mabel nodded in agreement with Miss Mildred Law. "She could turn something bad into something good, as she did with me and my brother, Howard. If Emma hadn't helped us, we would have been locked into a life of poverty and hard work with no way out. However, thanks to Emma, she gave me and Howard an opportunity to make our lives better for us and for Madea. There was not another person, black or white, who would do for a black what she did. It was unheard of for a white person, especially a white woman, to pay for a black person to go to college. She did it not for one black, but for two blacks."

Miss Mildred Law told Mabel, "She wanted you two to have an education more than anything else in the world. She felt she

299

owed it to you two. Emma realized she would probably have to care for Olivia for the rest of her life, and she would never have the opportunity to earn a degree. Seeing you two get a degree and get good jobs gave her the motivation she needed to know she had made someone's life better. When she saw you two walk across the stage to receive your diplomas, it was like she had received one, too. It was one of the greatest joys she ever had.

"Emma worked hard to get things going in the right direction for her and the family," said Miss Mildred Law.

"Emma was pretty enterprising. She found many ways to bring money in for the household. She couldn't work a regular job because she had to care for Olivia. I suppose she could have allowed Aunt Sis to care for her, but she was afraid Olivia might get off-track and be too physical for Aunt Sis to handle," said Miss Mildred Law.

"Emma made her money by selling eggs, cream and butter, and honey. She made jellies, took on sewing jobs, and on Saturdays, she sold cakes, pies, and cookies in town. Aunt Sis was right there with Emma to help her through her tragic call in life," said Miss Mildred Law.

Mable reminded Miss Mildred Law about another special thing she did, "Don't forget about what else Emma did for us. She got the preacher to come to the house each week to counsel her and you, too, Miss Mildred Law."

Jeannie, puzzled by what Mabel said, asked—not knowing who to direct the question to—"If you don't mind me asking this, what kind of counseling did the preacher provide?"

Mabel told us, "Miss Mildred and Emma were still having problems clearing the events of the war from their minds. The preacher was helping them to deal with the pain. Their sessions helped me as much as they did Emma and Miss Mildred. I saw with my own eyes how counseling helped them let go of some of their hurt. The preacher's counseling had such an impact on me that I studied the field of counseling in college."

"It took a while, but life for the DeAngelo's was as close to normal as it ever had been since the years that Olivia and Emma were in high school. Everything and everyone in the house prospered for several years under Emma's care," said Miss Mildred Law.

She felt at ease in what she had said, but Mabel was not in total agreement with her. "There is only one thing I believe Emma could have done better."

Miss Mildred Law swiftly responded to her statement, "What was that Mabel? I wasn't aware of anything out of order, unless it is that thing you always bring up in our discussions of Olivia and Emma."

Mabel directed her comment more to Jeannie and myself as to avoid causing any ill-feelings. "The only thing I thought was questionable was that she would allow her lazy, no good relatives to stay at the house for extended times. I know Emma said we sometimes needed a man around the house to do some of the more difficult chores. But all I ever saw them do is eat too much, and they never did any work. They were nothing but bums looking for a free meal, a place to sleep, and something to steal."

Mabel continued her rant: "Madea felt the same way I did. At times, Emma believed the same thing, but she was too tender-hearted to say no to them. Only once did Emma get upset with them. She got fed-up with their mooching and ran them off. I remember what she told us afterward. It was some old Greek saying about houseguests. I have never forgotten it, because it is true: 'A guest is like a fish, in three days they begin to stink.'"

We laughed at the saying, but there is a lot of truth in it. I was there when Uncle Wilson would come to stay. He always called Aunt Emma, 'baby doll.' I could tell it irritated her, but she endured it until he left. Aunt Emma would let him sleep on the back porch. If I was there the same time he was, I had to sleep in the room with Bernard and Leonard on a pallet on the floor, and I was forced to listen to that aggravating, ticking clock.

I recall all Uncle Wilson ever did was eat and complain about his back hurting him. He would corner you and tell you about how important he used to be and how he was the best at doing anything. Each week, he would pay me a nickel to run to the store two miles away to get him some coffee with chicory, a plug of Brown Mule, and little pint of gin. He would always say to me, "Now boy, don't you drop that bottle, 'cause that's my medicine."

There was another uncle or cousin, Herman. He would come to stay, but he usually came in the fall when I was at school. Sometimes he would bring his son, Clyde, with him. I can remember my Mom telling me to stay away from Cousin Clyde because he had been in the prison and couldn't be trusted. He looked like he was evil, so I stayed away from both of them. They both were bad about overstaying their welcome, but Emma felt sorry for them and let them stay.

I could easily appreciate what Mabel was saying was true, now that I am older. However, Emma didn't think like everyone else. She saw good in everyone. She did all she could to bring the best out in them, even when they took advantage of her.

Miss Mildred Law responded to Mabel appraisal, "I have the same opinion you do Mabel about Emma's uninvited guests. But you know how Emma was. If she felt a certain way was right, there was no altering her decision. More times than not, it got her into some strange predicaments."

Mabel laughed and told Miss Mildred Law, "Yeah, like the time we had a run-in with the local Klan."

Miss Mildred Law answered, "Yes! That's exactly what I am talking about. What a daunting time that was!"

Jeannie and I were both stunned to hear of a run-in with the Ku Klux Klan. We cautiously asked, "Y'all had an encounter with the Klan?"

They both looked at each other and broke out in laughter. Mabel said, "One day Gladiola Jefferson came by Emma's house. She was crying and upset, and she asked Emma for help. Gladiola told her the Klan was planning to make a visit to their house on Saturday night. They were planning to burn a cross and beat both Jessie, her husband and their son, Pierre. Pierre was mildly retarded and he made a cultural mistake, and the Klan planned to make an example of them for not following the unwritten code of where a black person's place was in Southern society. Pierre entered the front door at the local café in town to pick up some food for a white man, Mr. Lewis, the man his daddy worked for. Pierre would occasionally help his dad, but one day because Jessie was too busy to go pick up Mr. Lewis' lunch at the café. Mr. Lewis sent Pierre in his place. Pierre didn't know blacks were not allowed to come in the front door and instead were to go to the back door like all the other blacks did. Pierre came in the front door, thinking that was what everyone did."

Miss Mildred Law gave us additional information. "The regretful thing about the Klan's evil intentions is that they knew the boy was retarded and never took that fact into consideration."

Mabel said, "Emma quizzed Gladiola to see if she was accurate about what she was saying. Gladiola told Emma her sister was a waitress at the café, and she had overheard them planning the raid.

They said it would be best on Saturday, that way they would see each other Sunday at church where they could discuss it."

Mabel continued telling us, "Gladiola said also one of the Klansman's wife let it slip to her maid that her husband was going to be on a 'coon hunting party' Saturday night. Gladiola said both of them came and told her what they had heard. She said she was sure it would happen Saturday night and not that night, which was a Friday.

"Emma explained to me what was happening and asked for my help. We brain stormed as to how we thought the Klan might carry it out. We made plans to counter each of their moves, but to be sure our plan would work, we went to a former Klansman for advice. He'd left their hateful organization because he felt that it had nothing to do with what they claimed, Christianity. I'm not going to tell you this man's name even though he is dead now, but his family is still living in this community. The former Klansman got religion, and God turned him away from that group. He felt the Klan was the complete opposite of what they were professing to be. We went to him to find out how the Klan usually carried out their raids," said Miss Mildred Law.

"When he found out we were planning to disrupt their raid, he told us to be careful because they were more dangerous than they appeared to be on the outside. He also said their leader was a vindictive man who would make every effort to get even if they were successful.

"From him, we learned how the Klan would meet near their target, bring their horses in trailers, and ride to the victim's house. They didn't use their trucks at the site because they would be too easily identified. They also used horses to intimidate their victims. They would ride their horses on the edge of the tree-line to the house, dig a hole to set the cross in front of the house, align in a semi-circle behind the cross, set the cross on fire, and call out the family. When the family came out they would grab the man they wanted, bind then beat him, and threaten to kill him and his family if he didn't do what they thought was right. If he had done something they believed to be over the line, they would take him into the woods and lynch him. The ex-Klansman located for them what he believed to be the spot where he thought they would park to begin their ride to the Jefferson's house.

"Emma told him her plan and asked for his help. He took a deep breath and sighed, before he answered her. As he hesitated, Emma and I didn't think he would help, but then unexpectedly he told us he thought her plan would work, and he would be pleased to help. In fact, he told her, he could get four other white men to help in her plan.

"I remember my mother saying one day after she had learned the Klan had made a raid on some poor innocent black family that everybody in the parish knew who was in the Klan . . . even the blacks knew. The Klan members were not too protective of not being known as a member, some even wore it as a badge of honor. The members knew the sheriff would not do anything to stop them. Even though he was not a member of the Klan, he considered them votes, and contributors to his reelection fund. My mother was always disappointed no one would do anything to stop them from doing wrong. She said it was a shame the good people would not stand up against them.

"My father said they had approached him to join the Klan, but he'd gracefully declined. I don't know whether or not he told them why he refused to join them, but I remember hearing him say to me, "God would never endorse a group like that." He told us never to say anything bad about them because anytime you say something bad about a person or a group, it always comes back to bite you or your family. At the time, I didn't understand what he meant, but as I grew older, I understood."

Miss Mildred Law told us what she and Emma did to coordinate her plan. "Emma got everybody together at her house and laid it out. The plan was simple, but timing was crucial. The ten men, five white and five black, would be alternately positioned, hidden in the woods in front of the Jefferson's house. But they would be behind the Klansmen. The lighting of the cross would be their signal to move up into position but keep out of the Klansmen's sight, behind and to the side of the Klansmen, surrounding them.

"As the Klan would be traveling on horseback to the Jefferson's house, Emma would merge in with them, carrying her shotgun. She would be hiding on her horse under a hood and sheet to join them sometime during the ride there. In the dark, she could just kind of blend into the ride as they traveled around a bend without them knowing she was not part of their original group.

"Part of her plan was that there was to be five members of the Jefferson family inside the house, plus me, our white pastor, the black pastor, Mabel, and ten black men with shotguns from the Jefferson's church as back-up in case of trouble. We were also to have a special guest, our deputy sheriff friend in uniform. When the Klansmen called out the family, we would come out of the house in that order and line up across the front porch, with the exception of ten black men who would stay inside with shotguns.

"Emma instructed ten more men with shotguns, which included the former Klansman who volunteered to help them, to be hidden out of sight in the woods and to get into position behind the Klansmen when they set the cross on fire. Then at her signal they were to speak out in a particular order to the Klansmen. She told everyone not to say a word, as she and I were to do all the talking—that was with the exception of the ten men behind the Klansmen.

306

She told everyone the reason they were not to speak was that she didn't want any evil consequences coming to them later. She then explained what order the plan was to follow."

Jeannie, in great eagerness, asked, "What happened? Did it work?"

Miss Mildred Law spoke as if her answer was inconsequential. "Yes, it kind of worked."

"That's it, that's all you are going to tell us," said Jeannie, disappointed.

Again, Miss Mildred Law and Mabel looked at each other and burst into laughter. Mabel delightfully took the lead of telling the rest of the story said, "Miss Mildred Law won't tell you because she is just too modest, so I will tell you what materialized. Their plan was beautiful, the timing of it was perfect, and the psychological impact it had on those men was hilarious."

Miss Mildred Law blurted into Mabel's sentence: "I will have to say it worked better than we even thought. It is always amazing to me how predictable people are. They did everything exactly like Emma said they would. Go ahead Mabel and tell them what happened, I'm sorry I interrupted you."

"Those of us in the house could tell when the Klan had arrived. We heard them digging the hole and the cranking of the metal cans as they poured kerosene on the cross. They must have learned to whisper in a saw-mill, they were so noisy. They set the cross on fire and called the family out, exactly as we had figured. All but the ten black men in the house came out immediately, and I'm sure it surprised them to see they were outnumbered," said Mabel.

Miss Mildred added, "Emma figured the larger number of those who came out surprised them, but she also figured it would not scare them away. She said their pride wouldn't let common sense override it and they would continue. She was right, but she wanted me to add a little fuel to the fire by insulting them. I didn't really know what she meant or what to say, but she said I would know what to say to them when the time came."

Mabel said, "I think you said the perfect thing to them. You asked them if they brought the cross to praise Jesus at our little prayer meeting that we're having. After you said that, I didn't know whether to laugh or duck for cover. Even though they all had hoods on, you started calling out their names. And when you told them, 'Everyone here knows who you are, so you might as well pull those hoods off. I know you must be getting hot under them,' I couldn't believe you said that. What you said really angered their leader, we all could tell he was mad by what he said to you."

Miss Mildred Law interrupted again: "I guess that was what Emma meant by saying I would know what to say. Hell, I couldn't believe they were that stupid. I recognized them by their horses and their saddles. Emma figured it would interrupt their plan enough so the leader would have to speak out and challenge me. That would give her time to see where the leader was and to position herself behind him, and he did speak up, helping to identify himself."

"The leader told Miss Mildred Law they were here for Jessie and his boy. He wanted those two to come off the porch onto the grass. He told her she needed to get everyone else on the porch back into the house because they had some business to take care of," said Mabel.

"Miss Mildred Law responded to his demand, but not like the leader wanted, and she told him, 'That's not going to happen tonight, or any other night. The people of this parish are fed up with this rotten, despicable group forcing their ideology on us. You all are a bunch of hypocrites. I can call out the names of children that you have fathered from this black community. I guess your wives aren't taking care of their business like you want. Isn't that right Wayne Reynolds, how about that, David Quinn, and even you, their leader, Warren Wade? You have had two kids with two different maids, one of them was only fifteen when she had your child. Her child looks just like you. I bet your wife would love to know that. And you are going to come here to these good folks and try to make yourself feel superior by putting them down. You ought to be ashamed of yourselves. If you are not, then I am ashamed for you.'"

Miss Mildred Law said in astonishment, shaking her head, "I said all of that? I guess Emma was right when she said I would know what to say. She knew they would enrage me and I would go off on them. When we were planning, Emma said the leader might react to what I said in a negative way and that would be her signal to show him we had the drop on him."

Mabel said, "The leader first replied by asking, 'how do you know all of this?' Then you stopped him. You didn't give him any more time to respond before you told him, 'I'm not by myself! There are even others in your own group who don't believe what you believe. You better take a look around.'

"The next thing the leader hears is a shotgun cocking right behind him. He turned to see who made the noise and he discovered a shotgun pointing directly at the middle of his back. Then he saw Emma as she was taking off her hood. Emma knew this part of the confrontation would not make them back off either, but there were things that needed to be said before she signaled for the final part," said Miss Mildred Law.

Mabel said, "Having a gun pointed at him made the leader mad, and he told Miss Mildred Law and Emma, 'No two little bitches and a bunch of holy-rollers and their flock is going to stop us from doing what needs to be done.'"

Mabel paused a second to see if Miss Mildred Law would continue with the story, but she did not, so Mabel carried on. "Emma disrespectfully interrupted the leader and cut him off from saying anything else. She told him, 'Well, well Mr. Wade, are you always this stupid or is today a special occasion? If you are saying what I think you are saying . . . then I got two things to say to you . . . First is, I don't know what makes you so dumb . . . but it sure works . . . and second . . . you and these other hooded creatures better have a good life insurance policy for your families, because us two little bitches ain't by ourselves, we are tired of your hollow intimidation.'" Then Emma yelled out into the darkness: 'Tell 'um boys, so they will understand. If they choose so, their days here on earth . . . will be over tonight.'

"The ten men who had surrounded the Klan, two men at the same time cocked their guns as loud as they could and turned on their head-lamps. You know, the nine-volt spot-lights they wear on their heads with the elastic straps, when they go real coon hunting. Immediately after they cocked their guns and the two lights came on, each white man called out the name of one of those in the group. The plan was for them to hear the sound of two cocked shotguns, then the two head lights would shine on him, and then the voice of a white man calling out to them 'You understand, Clarke Williams?' Again a second time they would hear two shotguns cocked, then two spot lights would come on him, and the voice of a white man saying, 'You understand, Bill McNeely?' Then a third time again the sound of two cocked shotguns, then two head lamps would shine on him, and a white man's voice saying, 'You understand, Fred Thompson?' Then a fourth time the sound of two cocked shotguns, two lights would be shined on him, then a white voice saying, 'You understand, Charles Stratham?' Then a fifth time the sound of two cocked shotguns, two spot lights came on him, then a white voice saying, 'You understand, Herman Menson?'"

310

Miss Mildred Law revealed to us this bit of information from their plan as to why no black man's voice was used in the final stage, "Emma felt if they allowed a black man to speak against one of them it might have caused one of them to start shooting. All the Klansmen needed was to think that there were two guns on him. He didn't need to know that one of them was that of a black man. No one wanted any shooting, and when Emma was planning this, she tried to consider every angle they might react to avoid any gun-play. That is why I say that people are so predictable. Emma had them pegged to a tee. But just to be sure we had the advantage, after the last man called out to the Klansman, the ten other men in the house came out handing guns to everyone one the porch."

Mabel said, "It didn't take the Klansmen long to realize they were outnumbered, out-gunned, and out maneuvered. They lowered their guns as if they were about to surrender. That was when Emma rode around to the front and told them. 'All everybody in this world wants is peace. I want peace, you want peace, and these people want peace, too. We all want peace with ourselves, with others, and with God. We need each other in this life. All colors need each other. That is why it is stupid for all of us not to get along with one another. We don't want control and we don't want to be controlled. We just want peace."

Mabel said, "I knew some of them were already planning to get revenge. I didn't want that to happen and I knew Emma would never use any type of intimidation or threaten them in anyway. However, I knew Miss Mildred Law wouldn't let them go without some warning, and she told them this, 'If any of you are planning to get even or planning to hold any grudges, let me tell you what will happen. I have placed in my bank box, letters written to the paper telling them who you are and what all of you have done to these people, from beating them to raping them and having babies with them. If you hurt any more black people in this parish again or take any retribution toward any white people who were here tonight, I will ruin you, your family, and your lives. You know I am not making an empty promise. I will tell everything, so you better watch your step. If that won't keep you from doing right, there is always an alternative. You can't get us all at the same time, so if one of us is hurt in any way, then we all are going to come for you. You put that in your pipe and smoke it, and think long about it.' Miss Mildred Law made everyone acknowledge their agreement. 'And all of God's people said Amen.'"

Mabel said, "Now I don't know where all those voices came from that night, but it sounded as if the whole parish was in those woods, and they responded back to her extremely loud, saying, "*Aaaa-men!*"

Mabel said, "The Klan turned their horses away from the Jefferson's house and rode into the dark. After they left, we had ourselves a fine prayer meeting. We sang and celebrated, we hugged one another and danced. We asked the pastors to pray to bless what had taken place, hoping it would last for all eternity. We were very happy it went as well as it did without anyone getting hurt."

# Chapter 19

## *The Unthinkable*

Mabel began again talking about how motivated Emma's was in stressing the importance of getting a good education to help one to be successful in life. Emma tried to inspire the twins to do the best they could in school. Hearing her reminded me how much our teachers in high school preached you cannot succeed in life unless you have a college degree, especially Miss Mildred Law. I don't know who put that into our teachers' minds, but they sure knew how to deliver the message and make us believe it.

Mabel sincerely said, "Just before the twins started back to school after Olivia's breakdown, Emma told the twins their days of doing poorly in school were over. She used their mother's disorder to help motivate them to do better in school. She told the twins to look at Dr. Taylor and the house and car he has or Mr. Graham, the bank president. He owns a lot of land and has people work for him on his farm. They both have a college educations and it was the reason why they are successful and have money.

"She assured the boys they were smart enough to make high grades in school, but they must apply themselves to accomplish that. She guaranteed them that with a good education they could have a great job, own a beautiful home, and be able to help their mother in her old age," said Mabel, convincingly.

Miss Mildred Law said, "That worked well with Bernard, but Leonard was a different story. He didn't care anything about getting an education. All he thought about was football and girls. When he came into my class, I must have kept him from recess a hundred times because he wouldn't make any effort to try and learn. I whipped him at school and I know Emma got him when he came home, too. He wasn't a dumb kid. He was just lazy and obsessed with sports."

Mabel said, enthusiastically, "Madea was there when Emma had that first serious talk with the twins. Emma told them she expected them to mind her and every adult they came into contact with. Emma told the boys that she was going to be their 'acting mother' until their mother got well. She demanded they were to do as she told them, and if they didn't obey her. She would put the switch on them. She warned them, their mother was not able to save them now from a whipping if they did wrong. Emma made each one tell her they understood.

"Madea said after the talk, Leonard went around the side of the house and started cussing Emma, saying she ain't his mama, and he will do what he wants. Madea told Emma what Leonard said, Emma cut a switch and whipped Leonard for cussing. Madea said after the whipping, Leonard understood Aunt Emma wasn't bluffing," said Mabel.

Miss Mildred Law firmly stated, "Bernard didn't have much problem adjusting. When he went into the tenth grade, he found a steady girlfriend who was actually a good influence on him. She helped him maintain his interest in doing well in school. It was a slight struggle for him at first, but she encouraged him, even though all he wanted to do was play football."

Miss Mildred Law said sadly, "Bernard and his girlfriend were always together, but something happened at the junior prom and they broke up. That breakup might have been for the best, because they were getting too serious about one another."

Miss Mildred Law hesitated as she recalled something else about Bernard: "Just before the end of school, during his junior year, Bernard was given a job tending feeder calves on his uncle's farm. He ran the job like he owned them, and his uncle made money under his care. It taught Bernard responsibility and how to handle money. It gave him the confidence he needed to know that if he worked, he could be successful.

"Bernard was always a very responsible young man; so much so, that he was given the job as a part-time bus driver. He was paid to drive his uncle's car in the mornings to bring our area children to the pick-up point to catch the yellow bus to school. Then in the afternoon, his uncle drove them home. The roads in our ward were too narrow for a bus to travel down, and if it rained it was almost impossible for anyone to travel. Bernard worked hard. He was able to work the calf farm, drive for his uncle, play football, and still maintain high grades in school. I was very proud of him for being so enterprising and dependable," said Miss Mildred Law.

Mabel said with a chuckle, "But there was the other brother, wasn't there, Miss Mildred Law? Bernard did well under Emma's guidance, but it was very different with Leonard. Leonard struggled every year to make passing grades. If it hadn't have been for sports, he would have never made it through high school. The only enterprising thing Leonard did was to work for Professor Westmoreland, the town druggist, after school and on Saturdays. Everybody called the druggist, 'Professor' because he taught science in a college, somewhere. Leonard worked for him both his junior and senior years. I never could understand why the old man kept treating Leonard so nice. From what I was told, Leonard stole him blind by selling candy and funny books out the front door."

"Yes, everyone thought it was strange that Leonard would work for him, especially when they found out what he was," said Miss Mildred Law.

"What was that, Miss Mildred," questioned Jeannie.

"Just let me say it another way, everyone in town said Professor and the black guy who worked for him, you know Mabel, the one they called Sunbeam, was queer. Emma would never believe they were strange, but those two liked having Leonard around because he was a muscular athlete, and they liked looking at him," said Miss Mildred Law jokingly.

They both laughed and Mabel said, pondering, "You know what, I never thought about it, but what you are saying now makes sense about what Leonard kept telling me and Emma about Professor Westmoreland."

"What was that Mabel," questioned Miss Mildred Law.

"Leonard always came home each payday with more money than he should have. When Emma questioned him as to how that could be, Leonard would always tell her that the Professor had given him a bonus for the week. Leonard told us Professor Westmoreland promised to give him a car one day, but to get it, he would have to keep working for him," said Mabel.

"Is that how Leonard got that old car. I always wondered how he managed to swing that deal. I knew Professor Westmoreland liked Leonard, but I didn't know he liked him enough to give him his old car," said Miss Mildred Law.

"Yes, it is hard to believe. I remember the day Leonard drove the car home. He came in on two flat tires. When Emma asked him about the car, Leonard told her the Professor said if he fixed it up, he could have it. Emma didn't trust Leonard's answer, so she drove to town to ask the Professor about it. Professor Westmoreland told her he thought they could use an extra vehicle in the family, so he gave it to Leonard on the condition he fixed it up. Professor said he had a new Impala SS, and he really didn't have any use for his old car," said Mabel.

I remembered when Leonard got the car, it was during one of those summers I spent at Aunt Emma's house. Leonard loved that old car. He would take us down to the creek in it to go swimming, and on the way, he would try to make that car jump over the humped bridges in our parish. He would stomp the gas pedal about fifty yards away from the bridge to try to get it to leave the ground. It gave all of us a thrill. We believed we were flying. We had a great time riding in Leonard's car, but Leonard would get mad if someone dirtied up his car. If you did, he wouldn't let you ride in it again.

Leonard spent a lot of time fixing up the car. After Leonard gave it a tune-up, it ran pretty good. The interior of the car was in bad shape. The seats were torn in a couple of places. He got Madea to sew a patch on the holes and Leonard brought seat covers to go over the front seats. After he dressed it up, it looked real nice on the inside.

Leonard had seen a steering knob in an auto magazine, and he set his heart on getting it. The one he wanted cost a bunch of money, so he started saving for it. Leonard didn't realize if he saved for the knob, he wouldn't have enough to pay for the essentials things such as, oil, gas, and tires. He was forced to give up on the idea of buying it, but somehow, Aunt Emma found out he wanted it, and she got him one like it from Sears. Leonard was thrilled that Aunt Emma had done that for him.

The only thing Leonard didn't like about the car, other than it being old, was the color. He hated it because it was a dreary gray. Leonard decided to try his hand at painting the car. At first, to give him practice, he painted all the metal in the interior. It looked pretty good so he decided to paint the outside. He stripped it down, taped it up and began painting it bright red with a brush. It was hand painted, but he did a good job. There were only a few spots on the hood where you could see brush marks.

Miss Mildred Law delightedly said, "I remember how excited Emma was when Leonard went on his first date in that old car. She was very happy for him. She said it was great to see a little real joy in his life, it did her good to see him happy."

Mabel sorrowfully said, "Dating didn't happen too often with Leonard because he developed such a bad reputation with the girls. He was too fresh with them, and the girls complained to their parents, so their parents would not let him take their daughters out. They wouldn't even let their daughter go with him on a double date. Emma tried to talk to Leonard about it, but he refused to discuss it with anyone."

"Thank God Leonard had football to fall back on, it became his girlfriend. He spent his time throwing that football through the tire swing on the pecan tree and dodging the thorn bushes beside the house. He didn't have any problem getting the college recruiters to take him out on a date. He ate plenty meals with them as they tried to get him to sign a scholarship. Even as a sophomore, they sent letters. That boy could really throw the football, and he was tough enough to run through a brick wall," said Miss Mildred Law, proudly.

Hearing them talk about Leonard being a great football player brought back many memories I had as a kid. When my brother and I played football in the front yard, we would argue about who would be Number 12, Leonard's number. Everybody wanted to be like Leonard on the football field: to run and throw for touchdowns, to score the winning touchdown, and be the hero. He was really a good athlete, and he threw and ran more yards than anybody else in the state his junior year. Colleges everywhere wanted him to come to their school.

Mabel happily said, "Leonard was such a good football player, several schools told Emma if Leonard signed with them, Bernard would get a scholarship, too. Yeah . . . the twins were really excited about playing together in college and looked forward to it happening."

Miss Mildred Law told us, "Bernard had just started college, but he was a little apprehensive about being there. It was an immense change for him because he had never spent one night away from home. He decided to try out for football, but he didn't make the team. The coaches told him they didn't have any more scholarships available that year. They wanted him to come back out in the spring. They were using him as bait to get Leonard to sign with them.

"Back home things were going very smoothly for the DeAngelo's. It had been that way for the past five years. Thanks to a new drug, Thorazine. It made Olivia more manageable and allowed Emma to better care for Olivia. Olivia had progressed, but she had one drawback: she became extremely curious about everything. She would investigate anyone who came to the house, usually by getting directly in their face. No one understood why she did that. We assumed she was trying to recognize who they were. Her maturity level was now that of an eight year old. She wouldn't speak words or sentences, she made hand gestures to communicate to those she trusted. Still, if you asked her a question, she felt threatened or pressured. She would run away and regress to her withdrawn form," Miss Mildred Law mournfully said.

"That new drug, Thorazine also allowed Emma enough freedom to do some jobs to make some money to help pay some of the bills. The drug stopped Olivia from talking to the voices, but another side effect of the drug was that it stopped her from talking, altogether. Emma needed extra money, as she was sending three people to college. Amazingly, she always seemed to have enough money to give them extra money for the incidentals they needed. It was quite an accomplishment for a woman with no regular job," said Miss Mildred Law.

"When Bernard went to college, I went with Emma and Bernard to move him into his dorm. Bernard was really excited, but it broke Emma's heart to leave him there. She cried all the way back home. She loved that boy like he was her own, and I believed he realized she was more of a mother to him than Olivia," said Miss Mildred Law, proudly.

Mabel said, "Madea felt the same way Emma did about Bernard being gone, she missed him, too. You would have thought by the way they acted that Bernard had died. They were depressed. However, with the excitement of Leonard in his senior season, it drowned out the sadness. The high school football team of the last season was state runner-up, and they had almost everyone coming back this season. The team was ranked number-one in the state, and they were undefeated going into the ninth game of the season. Leonard was on a record setting pace with his passing. He was near a thousand yards passing the ball and over a thousand yards rushing the ball. Everything was going great for him. He had a car, he had offers of scholarships from everywhere. He was doing well with his grades, having success on the field, and he was popular at school. He was on top of the world."

Mabel continued, "Madea told me he was becoming too popular at school, getting too big for his britches, as she said. She said this young, pretty little sophomore girl, Jamie McKenzie was coming at him hot and heavy. It had gotten so bad that Leonard couldn't handle it. Her daddy came to the house to complain about Leonard and her. Emma assured him she would handle her end. She also reminded him it takes two to tango. Madea said Emma talked to Leonard, and he told her this girl was chasing him and he couldn't get away from her. He had tried. He said his coach told him to stay away from her, too, but he couldn't control her advances toward him.

"Emma was pleased with the direction the twins were going, and Olivia also kept improving as she began to better relate to the things around her. She understood that Leonard was doing great in sports and was proud of him," said Mabel.

Mabel continued, "Years after she'd had her breakdown, she would never let anyone get close to her. She would push them away in fear. But now, Leonard seemed to have a calming effect on her. Whenever Leonard was near, she would reach out for him to lay his head in her lap, and she would stroke his hair. It's funny because Leonard never had much hair, he had a flat-top haircut. Both she and Leonard seemed to enjoy the closeness they had never shared when he was a child. Poor Leonard. I always felt sorry for him because he was as cold and unloving as Olivia was. This new found love between him and his mother seemed to soften him."

Miss Mildred Law purposely said, "Mabel is deliberately telling you several different circumstances which led up to a specific time and events, because a lot happened at the end of that football season in November, and it changed everything for the DeAngelo family. Mabel and I have debated these events many times, and we still have many unanswered questions."

Mabel said firmly, "I honestly believe the kindness and generosity of Emma is what allowed the unfortunate set of events to start. I am not saying it was Emma's fault in any way, only that someone took advantage of Emma's hospitality."

"I don't agree with that," argued Miss Mildred Law.

"What happened, happened because of the evilness in that pervert's heart, not because Emma was too kind hearted," said Miss Mildred Law plainly.

Jeannie and I had no idea what Miss Mildred Law and Mabel were arguing about. We could tell they had debated this before, and it was obvious they had never come to a firm conclusion as to what happened. Whatever it was, we hoped they would give us some indication as to what was being discussed.

After listening to them discuss this back and forth, Jeannie asked, "What are you two talking about? It sounds as if you need an independent party to make a decision as to who is right and who is wrong. Do you want either me or Blake to help?"

Miss Mildred Law appreciatively answered Jeannie's request, "We would love for someone to be able to give us the answer as to what happened, but only God really knows. Neither one of us know if anything happened to Olivia at all. We are only assuming something evil happened. I'm sorry about this, but we argue about this every time we discuss it."

Mabel affirmed, "I believe Emma's kin came into the house when no one was there and took advantage of Olivia."

"Mabel, tell them frankly what you think happened and what set those events into motion. It was like a chain reaction. The tragedies started with Olivia that November day. All we have to go on is what Madea told us and how Emma reacted after the first incident," said Miss Mildred Law, sadly.

Mabel told us, "That particular November was unusually cold, which is why Emma allowed her Uncle Herman and his son Clyde to stay with them. She felt sorry for them because it was cold. Consequently, she opened up her home to them as she had done for them and others many times before."

Mabel said, "Emma went to Mrs. Babin's home to tailor a dress for her. Emma asked Uncle Herman to go with Madea, to her house to fix a leak in her roof. Madea needed to show him where the leak was and planned to return quickly. Emma asked Clyde to stack fifty bales of hay in the barn loft she had just brought. She needed it done that morning because they were expecting rain later that night. Madea, thinking she would be gone only a few minutes, left Olivia in the house by herself. Uncle Herman needed Madea to hand him the cypress shingles because the roof was very steep, which prevented her from coming back."

Mabel continued, "Each morning, as a part of Olivia's regular routine, Madea would lay out Olivia's prettiest dresses for her to try on. Olivia would spend hours trying on those dresses and looking at herself in the full-length mirror in the big hall. It kept her occupied where Madea and Emma could do their morning chores."

Mabel sadly said, "Madea felt assured she would have extra time to help Uncle Herman with the roof because she had left Olivia before without any problems. However, when she returned to the house, she discovered Olivia cowering in the corner of her bedroom. Olivia was whimpering and talking to the voices again, rocking back and forth in a stooped position with a white garment clutched in her hands. She hadn't done that in years. Madea knew something evil had happened, but she had no idea what it could have been. She tried to get Olivia to come out of the corner, but she refused to leave. Madea asked her what had happened, but Olivia would not respond. She was locked inside of her mind and continued to whimper while rocking and clutching a white garment Madea decided to wait for Emma to come home, and she sat in the room with Olivia until Emma arrived."

Jeannie was stunned to hear something happened to Olivia and hastily asked, "Did you ever find out what caused Olivia to relapse into that withdrawn state?"

"Not really," said Mabel with disgust. "When Emma got there, she couldn't get Olivia to come out of the corner, either. Each time she or Madea pleaded for her to come out or reached to bring her out. She would scream and fight them to leave her alone. However, each Friday, Leonard would come home early to eat his pre-game meal

325

and leave to get dressed for the game. When Olivia saw Leonard, she reached for him. Leonard sat down beside her, and she pulled his head into her lap and caressed him. It calmed her down enough for Leonard to talk Olivia into coming out of the corner and sitting on the bed."

Mabel said, "While taking Olivia's clothes off, Emma discovered that she had bruises on her arms, her shoulders, and her shins. Emma also saw Olivia had no panties on, which was unusual. Emma thought she might have taken them off herself after she got into the corner. That was when Emma realized it was what she was holding in her hands, her panties. We assumed the cause of the relapse was that she had fallen and hurt herself."

"Leonard was excited," said Miss Mildred Law. "This game was the ninth game of the season and their opponent was with the number-one ranked team in the class above our division. Two number-one teams meeting was a big event in our town. Everyone in the parish would be there."

"Emma told me when Leonard went to leave for the game, he came into Olivia's room to kiss her goodbye for luck. Olivia smiled at Leonard as she released his hand for him to leave, everything seemed normal," said Mabel.

"However, that evening, when Uncle Herman and Clyde came into the house to eat supper, as soon as Olivia saw them she became violent toward them. She threw her plate at them, then threw her fork and spoon at them, and when they walked near her, she tried to throw a bowl of food on them, too. She was completely out of control. Madea and I had to hold her down. She wanted to hit them with anything she could get her hands on. Emma couldn't understand what had come over Olivia, it was completely out of character for her to act this way. To protect Uncle Herman and Clyde, Emma asked them to wait on the back porch, and Madea would bring them supper there."

Mabel said, "As Madea took them supper, Emma and I took Olivia into her bedroom. She still was in a panic. Emma wanting to question her more, she knew there was something very strange going on for her to be that upset when Uncle Herman and Clyde walked into the hall. Emma called to mind where everyone was before Olivia was hurt. Everyone was accounted for with the exception of Clyde. Emma presumed the only one with opportunity to come into contact with Olivia was Clyde. She felt something had happened between Olivia and Clyde. It became obvious that Clyde was the target of her projectiles."

Mabel said, "Emma was able to calm Olivia down by talking about Leonard and how good he was doing in football. She knew Olivia would not be able to verbally tell her what had happened to her. Consequently, Emma decided to look Olivia over again to see if her injuries would provide her the answers she wanted. Emma told Olivia they were going to play "dress up" that night. which momentarily excited Olivia, as she was eager to play. Emma and I helped undress Olivia. Emma took everything off of Olivia."

Mabel paused and grieved over what she was about to say, "I didn't see Olivia that afternoon after they re-dressed her, but what I saw that evening was unbelievable. Not only did Olivia have the bruises on her wrists, shoulders and shins, she had large bruises around her breasts, like someone had grabbed them real hard. She had more bruises on her stomach and side, which could have only come from someone punching her. Around her groin area was the beginnings of bruising and on her inner thighs too. No fall could have done all that damage. She had to have been attacked.

"After Emma looked Olivia over very carefully, tears rolled down her cheeks. I never heard Emma cuss before, but she said, 'That sorry son of a bitch, I ought to kill him right now,'" said Mabel.

"Emma had tied all the loose ends together, but she hypothetically said out-loud how she thought the attack happened," said Mabel.

"Emma said, 'Clyde must have come into the house while Olivia was playing dress-up. He probably saw her look at herself in the long mirror in the hall and thought, this is my opportunity, since no one is around. He probably followed her into her room because the room had signs of a struggle. I imagine when Olivia saw him in the room she became curious and walked up to him. Clyde, seeing how beautiful Olivia was and, thinking how easy it would be to take advantage of her and how she can't tell anyone, attacked her. Olivia must have fought him. He hit her to make her submit. That is how she got all those bruises on her stomach and side.'

"Emma paused again as she looked at the bruises on Olivia. Emma moaned in agony and fought to hold back her tears. She told me, 'He doesn't deserve to live. Anybody who would do this to a helpless, innocent person doesn't deserve the air they breathe.'

"Immediately, Emma called out real loud, 'Madea, come here. We need you in here.'

"When Madea walked in and saw those bruises on Olivia, she knew immediately what had happened to Olivia, and she mumbled under her breath, 'Oh, baby. I's so sorry. It be's all my fault. I's never should have's left you's f'ur that's long's.'

"Madea must have put all the pieces together, too. She moved to the mantel to get the shotgun. Emma stopped her and told her in tears, 'Aunt Sis, we can't do anything like that. They will put you in jail. I don't think we can't even have him arrested. It will be his word against hers, and no one would ever believe her because of her condition. All he has to do is deny it, and he will go free.'

"I told Emma, 'We can't let him get away with this . . . and nothing happen to him, it wouldn't be right,'" said Mabel to us.

Mabel said to Jeannie and me, "I can still see and hear the conversation Emma had with those two like it was yesterday."

"Emma immediately wiped her eyes, turned, and walked out the room to where Uncle Herman and Clyde was on the back porch. I followed her, not knowing what was about to happen. I went because I wanted to get my hands on his worthless neck," agonized Mabel.

"When Emma came to them, they could see we had been crying.

"Being concerned, Uncle Herman asked, 'Emma, is everything okay?'"

Mabel said, "Emma didn't say anything to Uncle Herman. However, she turned to Clyde and stared straight into his evil eyes.

"Clyde, looking confused, asked her sympathetically, 'What are you looking at Miss Emma?'

"Emma was angry and told Clyde coldly, 'When I look into your eyes, I see straight through to the back of your head.'

"Emma paused before she coldly said to Clyde, 'Olivia tells me you had a good time with her today?'

"Clyde didn't respond. You could tell he wasn't absolutely sure Olivia could not talk. He was thinking, *They must know*!" said Mabel.

"Clyde said to Emma insincerely, 'What do you mean Miss Emma?'

"Emma told him insightfully, 'Olivia wants to tell you something. She told us what happened today.'

"You could see Clyde's anxiety, as if he was asking himself, *Can she talk?* It took him ten seconds. Then he looked around and raced out the back door," said Mabel.

Mabel said, "Uncle Herman had no idea what had just happened or why Clyde ran. He asked Emma, 'What is going on Miss Emma? Why is Clyde running away?'

"Emma angrily told him, 'Your son raped my sister today and beat the hell out of her. I want you and him out of here right now, and I want you to tell your low-down, good-for-nothing son, that I am going to send the law after him. But if they don't catch him, you tell him this for me, If I ever see him or hear of him in this parish again . . . I will find him and blow his damn head off.'"

Mabel told Jeannie, "We three discussed the situation. We felt that in the best interest of Olivia, Bernard, and Leonard, we would tell no one. Bernard doesn't know today what happened to his mother. We were miserable because we couldn't have Clyde prosecuted. There wasn't enough evidence to prove him guilty. We felt the shame and embarrassment a rape brings on a family, and we wrestled with the unknown of what Leonard or Bernard would do to Clyde if they knew. Not telling them far outweighed taking the chance he would be found guilty or the twins would kill him."

# Chapter 20

## *The Chase*

"That same day I brought Leonard home, near midnight, long after the game was over. I explained to Emma the reason why we were so late. Leonard had dislocated his throwing shoulder at the end of the first quarter. The head coach for LSU was there to watch Leonard play, but when Leonard was hurt, he came down to the sideline to see if he could help. The LSU coach had the police patch a call to LSU's team doctor, a bone-and-joint specialist. He told us to meet with him at the main hospital in Baton Rouge with Leonard," said Miss Mildred Law.

Miss Mildred Law told us, "I went with Leonard to the hospital, the doctor x-rayed Leonard's shoulder and discovered he not only had a dislocated shoulder, but he had a serious break on the collarbone joint that controlled his throwing motion. The doctor gave Leonard a shot to relax his shoulder so he could slip it back into place and then put his arm in a sling to isolate it. Both Leonard and I overheard the doctor tell the LSU coach that Leonard would never be able to throw the ball as he had before.

"It was a very gloomy ride back home as Leonard kept asking if the doctor meant he could never play football again or just this year," said Miss Mildred Law, sadly.

"We both knew exactly what the doctor had told the LSU coach, but Leonard refused to believe it. I can't blame him for thinking he could play again, he had worked so hard to be successful, and hearing the possibility of never playing football again was a very scary thought to him."

Miss Mildred Law said, "I was glad to get him home because he had talked himself into believing he could overcome the injury. He even took his throwing arm out of the sling to prove he was alright. I knew by morning his shoulder would be sore and very difficult to move. After we got Leonard to bed, Emma told me what had happened to Olivia. I was baffled even to imagine Olivia being raped. Emma assured me that she was 100 percent positive she had been."

Mabel said, "Miss Mildred Law, you were absolutely right about Leonard's shoulder being sore. He could barely get out of bed the next morning. When he tried to pick his arm up, he chagrined with pain. He managed to dress himself and came to the table for breakfast, but he didn't eat much. Emma asked if he felt okay. Leonard never answered her. He said he was going to the locker room to watch a film. Leonard said in a couple of weeks he would be ready for the play-offs.

"Leonard looked for his mother. Usually, she came to the table on Saturday mornings. Emma told him his mother was 'sleeping-in' this morning because she was not feeling well. Immediately, he went to investigate. Madea and I followed Leonard into her bedroom to make sure he didn't upset her. Olivia was awake and Leonard jokingly told his mother to look at the sling he had his right arm in. Olivia turned her head away from Leonard in an attempt to discourage conversation. As Leonard moved toward her to place his head in her lap, Olivia got out of the bed and went into the corner cowering and began rocking back and forth," said Mabel.

"Leonard, not realizing what had happened to her, made the statement, 'I can't even get any sympathy from my own mother.' It upset Leonard, his mother not paying him any attention, and he left to go to school as he did every Saturday morning during the football season," said Mabel.

"After the film session, Leonard offered the McKenzie girl a ride home. She had finished prep squad practice. Jamie accepted the ride and Leonard made a stop at their favorite parking spot. Jamie told us later she teased Leonard about wanting to see his injury. She knew there was no injury to see. It was just a ploy to get Leonard to take his shirt off, but Leonard refused. Jamie seductively told him it was easy to take off a shirt, just unbutton your shirt and let it slip off your shoulders. She demonstrated as she unbuttoned her blouse and let it slip down her shoulders all the way to her waist," said Miss Mildred Law.

Miss Mildred Law said, "That damn girl. She should have known Leonard couldn't handle her provocations. Leonard didn't need that temptation at that time. He was too weak to resist his sexual attraction for her."

"Jamie's blouse was at her waist," Mable said, "but she still had a bra on. She said it stimulated Leonard and he went wild. With one hand, he tore at her shorts trying to get them down. When he was unsuccessful with that, he pulled her bra completely off. His reaction scared her, and she told Leonard to stop. But he didn't. He went back to work on her shorts and got them off one leg. He tried to undo his pants and she started crying and asked Leonard to take her home. However, Leonard wasn't through, he laid on top of her trying to convince her she needed to have sex with him. Leonard was unable to carry the escapade any further because of his shoulder. The girl said she continued to cry and plead for him to stop and take her home. Leonard stopped and started cussing. He told her she was always leading him on and when the time came for action, she cut him off. He told her she was wrong to do that to him."

Miss Mildred Law said, "Leonard brought her home. He made a quick drop-off to avoid her father, who had been expecting her to be home for an hour. When he saw that it was Leonard bringing her home, he became very upset. Jamie's father called her to where he was and noticed her clothes were in disarray, and she looked as if she had been crying. Her father immediately questioned her as to what had happened. Jamie began crying, and it triggered her father to be even more suspicious."

Miss Mildred Law continued, "Her father asked her point blank did Leonard do something to you? The girl cried louder as she nodded her head affirmatively. Her father automatically assumed Leonard had sexually accosted his daughter, or raped her. Jamie was fearful of her father and she allowed him to believe the worst. She made no effort to make him believe otherwise. Mr. McKenzie is furious at Leonard, he got in his truck and came to Leonard's house to confront him."

Mabel said, "Mr. McKenzie didn't come to the door and ask to see Leonard. He got out of his truck with a club and started hollering for Leonard to come out of the house. When Leonard arrived at his home, he came into the house, we saw that he was upset and assumed it was because he couldn't play football anymore. But when Mr. McKenzie arrived, he made it very clear that it was something else. Leonard heard him call for him, but he didn't go out. He watched Mr. McKenzie from the window."

Mabel continued: "Emma came out of the house and told Mr. McKenzie Leonard would not come out, especially not to someone with a club. She asked him what seemed to be the problem. Mr. McKenzie told Emma that Leonard had attacked his daughter and he wanted him to tell him what he did. Emma was silent, she knew that defending Leonard would only escalate into a bigger problem. She listened to him. Mr. McKenzie kept demanding to talk to Leonard to find out what he did to make his daughter cry. Mr. McKenzie threatened Emma that if Leonard did what he thought, he wasn't sure what he was going to do to him."

Mabel said, "Emma was astounded by what Mr. McKenzie was telling her and she told him, 'Those are pretty strong accusations, Mr. McKenzie. I think I need to talk to Leonard to get his side of the story, and I suggest you do the same with your daughter. I think after we talk to them we will find it is not what you think. Then we will be able to come together and discuss the situation.'

"Mr. McKenzie would not accept Emma's suggestion. He wanted Leonard and he wanted him that moment," said Mabel.

"Emma told him as nicely as she could, trying not to upset him anymore, 'It's not going to happen today, Mr. McKenzie.'"

Mabel said, "By that time, Madea had walked out onto the porch with the shotgun and Mr. McKenzie got the message. Before he left, he told Emma he was going to the law and have Leonard charged with rape. That he would let the law come out and take him to jail."

Mabel continued, "As soon as Mr. McKenzie drove away, Leonard ran to his car and drove off, too. We had no idea where he went. The police came to the house. They did not fully accept Mr. McKenzie's story of Leonard raping his daughter. They did, however, want to talk to Leonard. They told Emma that they were still in the process of gathering information and needed his version before anything could be done. We told the deputy when Leonard came home, we would bring him to the Sheriff's office."

"Leonard never came home. Early Sunday morning, the deputies located him," said Miss Mildred Law.

"We were told a patrol car spotted him parked next to an abandoned grocery store. The police made an effort to apprehend him. However, hearing Mr. McKenzie say he was going to prison for rape, Leonard made a bad decision to try to elude the police by outrunning them. In the process of the chase, Leonard lost control of his car, went off the road, struck a tree. He was ejected and instantly killed," said Miss Mildred Law, sadly.

"A deputy was at the McKenzie's house at the time of the accident, and a transmission came across his radio saying, 'While in pursuit of the accused suspect, the suspect lost control and hit a tree," said Miss Mildred Law.

"Meanwhile, Jamie and her father had heard the call come over the radio. The deputy at the McKenzie's residence radioed back and asked what condition the suspect was in. There was an interval of several minutes before he received an answer to his request. The deputy involved in the chase radioed back that the suspect had been ejected and is was deceased,'" said Miss Mildred Law.

"The deputy said Jamie McKenzie became hysterical. She began sobbing as she told her father, Leonard never raped her. He had only gone too far, but he stopped when she asked him too. The deputy said Jamie cried, insisting it was her fault that Leonard was dead because she'd led Leonard to believe she wanted to make love to him. She told her father she was just teasing him and things got out of hand.

"The sheriff heard the broadcast about the fatality. He radioed the deputy at the scene asking who the victim was. The call came back as being Leonard DeAngelo. He told the deputies he would go to the DeAngelo residence to bring Emma to the scene. Mr. McKenzie heard the sheriff make that statement and decided to travel to the scene with Jamie," said Miss Mildred Law.

Mabel told us, "When the sheriff came to Emma's house, we thought they were still searching for Leonard. However, the heartbreaking news the sheriff delivered to Emma overwhelmed her. She was in shock. None of us could believe Leonard was dead. Emma was completely dumbstruck. We tried to hold ourselves together as not to let Olivia know what had happened. Olivia had had enough adversity with yesterday's calamity. We knew she couldn't handle that news, too. Emma was worried about Bernard and the impact it would have on him. She asked Madea to watch Olivia as she and I left to go to the scene of the accident."

Mabel said, "The coroner was already there, Leonard was lying in the ditch with a sheet over him. The coroner asked Emma to positively identify him. I went with her, but I turned my head and closed my eyes because I didn't want to see him like that. The two deputies in pursuit of Leonard said the front tire had run off the payment, and when he went to steer it back onto the highway, his car darted across the road and hit a tree. Leonard was thrown out of the car and the coroner said the impact broke his neck.

"As the deputy was telling us how the accident happened, Jamie and her father arrived," said Mabel. "Mr. McKenzie and Jamie walked to where Emma and I were. When Jamie saw the sheet over the top of Leonard she began bawling. Emma moved to console her and Jamie began blaming herself for Leonard's death. Through her tears she told Emma, Leonard did not rape her. She had allowed her father to assume it was what happened because she was afraid of what her father would do to her."

Mabel said, "You could see the surprise in Mr. McKenzie's face when Jamie said that. He immediately apologized to Emma, telling her he should have listened to what she told him. He should have settled down and let Jamie tell him what really happened, instead of assuming the worse. He told Emma he felt responsible for what happened and he was genuinely sorry. As Mr. McKenzie apologized, tears came down his face and Jamie came to comfort him.

"What happened next was incredible. I still can't believe what Emma did after they apologized for being partially responsible for this accident," said Mabel. "Emma asked Jamie to settle down and tell them exactly what Leonard did and not to leave anything out. Jamie told them she was teasing Leonard, trying to get him to take his shirt off. She knew he couldn't because of his injury. She teased him by unbuttoning her blouse and pulling it off her shoulders. She said Leonard went crazy. 'He pulled my bra off, pulled my shorts off of one leg, but he couldn't get my panties down. He tried, but he couldn't. Then he laid on me, trying to convince me we needed to make love. I cried and told him to stop and take me home, he stopped and brought me home.'"

Mabel said, "I didn't detect where Emma was going with her questions, but I knew she had something in mind. Emma stated, 'What you are telling us is that Leonard did not rape you but he did sexually accost you, is that right?' Jamie told Emma she was right, but she redirected Emma's conclusion saying it was she who had steered him on.

"Emma turned to the Sheriff and told him she needed him to do something for her. 'I need the McKenzie's and the coroner to stay here until you get the District Attorney to come,'" said Mabel.

Mabel said, "The Sheriff balked at what Emma had asked him to do and told her, 'Emma, you do know it is Sunday, don't you?'

"I guess Emma couldn't pass up the opportunity to come back with one of her retorts. She told the sheriff, 'Pardon me Sheriff, but you're obviously mistaking me for someone who gives a damn.' I don't know why she told him that, but he recognized she was serious, and he left to tell one of his deputies to get the DA," said Mabel.

"While we waited for the DA, word had gotten out Leonard had been killed. His friends had gathered to see what was happening. Emma moved to where Leonard was lying, Jamie pulled some wildflowers and placed them near Leonard's head," said Mabel.

"Mr. McKenzie and I walked over to where Leonard was," said Mabel. "Mr. McKenzie again apologized to her and told her it was his fault for making Leonard run. He said if he had kept his cool, Leonard would still be alive. Emma turned to face both Mr.

McKenzie and Jamie. 'Let me say this to you two before the DA gets here. This tragedy is not either one of your fault,' she said. 'It's a lesson to all of us. If you do wrong, that wrong will come back at you larger than it was in the beginning.'

"Emma said, 'Mr. McKenzie you did wrong by jumping to the wrong conclusion, and now your regret will be with you for the rest of your life. Jamie did wrong by teasing Leonard, and it came back at her by Leonard's attack. Leonard did wrong by following his wrong desires and running away from doing wrong, and he is gone forever. And me, I did wrong by not making him understand he has a moral responsibility to do right to others. Looking at how this has come together with this sad incident, it has hurt everybody. The sad thing is yet to come, I still have to tell his mother and brother what has happened to him.'

"By the time Emma finished talking to the McKenzie's, the DA arrived around the time I did," said Miss Mildred Law. "The sheriff, his deputies, the McKenzie's, the DA, the coroner, Mabel, Emma, and I were standing by Leonard's body in the ditch.

"Emma became very serious and said, 'There has been a great tragedy today, and we don't need to make it any worse. I believe the thing we need to do that is best for everybody is to head off any more unnecessary grief. Leonard was wrong, he attacked Jamie, and he has been punished for it. There is no use of dragging him through the dirt because he was guilty. I don't want you thinking I'm saying this for Leonard's benefit or for my family's benefit, for we can't correct Leonard now. Nothing anybody says can change what has happened, but what can come out of this can ruin Jamie's reputation and bring undeserved humiliation to her family. This can happen because of the evil that Leonard tried to do to her, and not from anything she did. Bringing shame to them would be a greater tragedy than Leonard's death. I say let us do what is best for everyone and

341

make it official. Mr. DA, Mr. Coroner, Mr. Sheriff, and everyone here, this is what happened: Leonard lost control of his car and was killed . . . period. Nothing other happened today or yesterday. Can we all agree to that and promise God not to say anything different?' Everyone promised to say it was a tragic accident and nothing else."

"Jamie and Mr. McKenzie hugged Emma and thanked her for her thoughtfulness. As I escorted Emma from the ditch, Leonard's schoolmates offered their condolences to Emma. I know Emma appreciated them, but she was far more concerned about telling Olivia and Bernard. That undertaking would be a monumental one But for now, Emma had the daunting task of making arrangements for Leonard's funeral," said Mabel.

"Emma, Aunt Sis, and I went to the funeral home to make the arrangements, while Mabel stayed to keep Olivia at her home. Bernard didn't know about Leonard's death because he and a friend went back to his college Friday night to watch his college play a game on Saturday. Before that game was played, Emma and I drove to see Bernard at his dorm to deliver the sad news. As soon as Bernard saw us there, he knew something bad had happened. Emma told him Leonard had been killed in an accident. Emma hugged Bernard to comfort him. He tried to hold back his tears, but he couldn't as his tears turned into sobs. He tried to drown out his wailing by holding Emma closer, but he couldn't. Seeing Bernard's grief caused all three of us to cry. Even his dorm mother, there at his door, began crying. Bernard was deeply saddened by his twin brother's death."

Miss Mildred Law gloomily told us, "If you have never been to a young person's funeral, where their death was completely unexpected, you will never understand how horrific it is. Seeing so many youngsters cry when they usually are joking and laughing is unnatural. Children their age never think death could come their way. They don't understand that it could only be a breath away. The

342

people who admired and knew Leonard and his family, lined up a hundred yards outside the door of the funeral home to pay their last respects. The funeral home remained open two hours after it was to close because of the large outpouring of people."

Mabel said, "School closed Tuesday for Leonard's funeral. Emma asked Jamie McKenzie to sit with the family. It was a kind gesture on Emma's part. She felt that it would allow Jamie to have closure and eliminate any suspicion of wrongdoing by Leonard or Jamie."

Mabel said, "We wondered if we needed to tell Olivia about Leonard's death and bring her to the funeral. Bernard reasoned that if Olivia understood, she would be out of control. If she didn't understand, it would make little difference whether or not she was there. Bernard felt it would be best to tell her later. We all agreed."

Mabel continued, "They let the coach eulogize Leonard. He said some mighty fine things about Leonard at first I thought he may be talking about someone other than Leonard. Now, don't get me wrong, Leonard had his good side, but he never showed it until he became popular. Which goes to show you how success can transform people into someone else. Usually, success changes people from good to bad, but in Leonard's case, it actually made him a better person. Before his success, he was as much like his mother as a child could be, and I think Miss Mildred and I have told you enough to know how that was.

"Madea told me she had never seen that many people at the cemetery before. She said the black folks came to show their respect to Emma and the family. I agreed with Madea, there were a lot of people there. After the final prayer, Leonard's schoolmates did not want to leave. They hung around like they were waiting for Leonard to come and join them. As kids always do, they have a difficult time letting go," said Mabel.

# Chapter 21

## *Not Again*

"The day after Leonard's funeral, Emma was still troubled about telling Olivia about the tragedy. Emma was emotionally drained, as were we all. We needed some time to catch our breath from the recent events in the DeAngelo family. These calamities had come so swiftly," said Mabel.

"Emma was concerned about everyone," said Miss Mildred Law. "She asked you and Bernard to take the rest of the week off from college. Emma thought having familiar faces around would help Olivia not notice that Leonard was gone. And it would give her time to gradually adjust to losing Leonard. It was Emma who needed her love ones around her more so than Olivia."

"Yes, you're right," said Mable. "We did take off from school, but having us around did not keep Olivia's mind away from Leonard. She was fine during the day, but when evening came and he didn't show up, she started searching for him. It was a sad to see the confusion in her face. She knew he was missing and we could tell she was looking for him. It got worse by supper time. Olivia went outside to where Leonard usually parked his car, only to find it was not there. She came inside, picked up his football, went to the front porch, and sat in the swing. She sat out there most of the night waiting for Leonard to drive up. We peeked out the window to check on her. While waiting on Leonard, Olivia would hug Leonard's football," said Mabel.

"We allowed Olivia to stay up later than normal that Wednesday night. I think she would have stayed outside all night if we'd let her. We brought her inside and dressed her for bed. She went and got into Leonard's bed instead of her own. Olivia did not want to leave Leonard's bed. Only Madea could persuade Olivia to come to her room to sleep. Olivia had never done that before. We thought it unusual. It showed that she missed her son," said Mabel, sadly.

Jeannie said unexpectedly, "Mabel, you're making it sound like she knew Leonard was dead. Is that what you are telling us?"

Mabel replied, "We finally came to the conclusion that somehow, someway, Olivia knew Leonard was gone and never coming back. After putting her to bed, we discussed it and convinced ourselves . . . Olivia must understand. However, what she did the next morning confirmed our belief and made it clear to us that she did know."

Jeannie, in great eagerness promptly asked, "What did Olivia do to convince y'all she knew?"

Mabel discussed Olivia's instinctive grasp of the situation. "Early the next morning, Olivia awoke us with loud moaning and uncontrollable crying. We rushed to see what was going on, and we found Olivia had laid all of Leonard's clothes on her bed, and she was hugging and caressing them. You know, the same way a wife does when her husband dies. She was trying to capture his lost scent. It was more than we could handle. We tried to hide our emotion from her, but it was obvious she was heartbroken. No matter how badly Olivia had treated us before her break down or what we thought about her. No one wanted to see Olivia in that state of mind. We allowed her to continue lying on Leonard's clothes in hopes it would help her through this difficult time."

Jeannie asked, "Did Emma ever directly tell Olivia about Leonard's death and that he was never coming home?"

"No!" said Mabel. "She never got the chance too. Emma did everything she could to hold her family together. All the suffering she went through from her childhood until that point, it was all for her family. She went from one tragedy to the next, as if that was how life was. Her first real tragedy came when she thought her one true love was killed. She becomes a POW and comes home to find

348

her fiancé is alive and married to her sister. She is forced to leave the home she loved, then loses her father. Her sister has a mental breakdown, and she's forced to care for her and raise her kids. She struggles to get out of debt that she didn't create. Her sister is raped, and now, Leonard is killed in a car wreck. Emma had no real stretch of happiness. It seemed as if her life was lived for nothing but sorrow. And then that girl goes and dies."

When Mabel summarized Emma's life, so many memories came flooding into my mind about the wonderful summers I'd spent with the DeAngelo's. My life would have never been the same if I had never known them. They filled the empty, boring blanks of a child's life. That beautiful woman, who was loved by so many, who sacrificed her life for others. To hear Mabel say or even think Aunt Emma's life was for nothing, no way would I ever believe that.

I didn't know what Jeannie was thinking, but I am sure after listening to these two magnificent women that she would never believe Emma's life was for nothing. Listening to all the good she did for others, always helping them have a better life. She stood for fairness and doing right. Her life would make anybody proud to have lived it.

I thought back to how many bad situations she helped others through, many times without being asked. She could take an awful situation and make something good come from it. Any person who had that gift . . . there was no way her life was lived for nothing.

If I had to choose one quality that stood out about Aunt Emma, it would be that she was completely unselfish. We live in a world where so many people don't take time or have any interest in others. They are only concerned about themselves. Those kind of people are easy to pick out in a crowd, but then along comes a person like Aunt Emma. She always had the time and patience to listen to your problems, your ideas, your dreams, and even your reasons why you did things a certain way. If she felt you were pursuing the wrong goals in life, she would gently guide you away from them and replace them with godly goals that would enhance your life. She could actually make you believe you can accomplish them with perseverance. Aunt Emma didn't stand head-and-shoulders above anybody. She just knew how to make you feel appreciated and loved . . . and that made you feel special, and it motivated you into believing you could do anything.

Miss Mildred Law used to tell us that every person is a leader. We are all born leaders of someone. But to be a leader, you must believe you are one and be that person every day. By being genuine and real. We are to use the strengths of others to make them stronger, then praise and reward others for doing what is right. That will motivate them to work harder for you and others.

Miss Mildred Law insisted that we were to fear nothing, meet trouble head-on, and depend on God for everything. He will take you through any trouble. She would always end her mini-sermons by saying, "If you want walking, talking, living proof of what I am saying, then watch my friend, Miss Emma DeAngelo. She lives it every day."

It always made me proud to hear Miss Mildred Law end her sermonettes that way. I would stick my chest out and say, "She is my aunt."

When Uncle Tom died—I was really close to him—his was the first funeral I had ever attended. Seeing someone I knew being dead was traumatic for me. Aunt Emma saw how it affected me, and she came and comforted me. Even though Uncle Tom was Aunt Emma's father, she took the time to show me compassion, when in reality, it should have been me giving her comfort.

After Uncle Tom's funeral, Emma suggested that we build a tree house in honor of Uncle Tom, and it would be our sanctuary. It would be a place we two could come whenever we were sad to remember the fun things we did in life. It would make us happy again. I thought it was a great idea, so we built it.

She insisted we put only things in our tree house that made us happy. She put a favorite plate in the tree house that belonged to her mother. She said the plate always made her think of how happy her Papa said she made him. I brought a rubber airplane Uncle Tom had bought for me at the variety store. I told her when I saw it that I would remember Uncle Tom and how he always made me laugh.

As I held those fond memories in my mind of my Aunt Emma, Jeannie broke into my train of thought with a puzzling question, "Mabel. I don't want to sound stupid, but did you just say Emma died then? Or did I make a wrong assumption?"

Miss Mildred Law realized that Mabel was not clear in what she said, so she told Jeannie before Mabel could answer , "No, Honey. I think Mabel either miss-spoke or she was thinking too far ahead of herself of what the final impact of Leonard's death was. Emma didn't die, it was Olivia."

Jeannie apologetically asked, "Did Olivia die of a broken heart? What happened?"

Miss Mildred Law exclaimed, "The next day, Thursday, the day after Olivia woke up the whole house with her loud crying, she went into the barn. No one knew when or why she went to the barn. All we know was she was in the barn when she died. The coroner said her death was the result of an accident. She fell from the barn loft and died from a broken neck."

Miss Mildred Law continued telling us about the unusual facts surrounding Olivia's death. "The Sheriff investigated her death

351

and told us it looked to him like she jumped to her death. In fact, it looked as if she dove head-first. He based his opinion on how far away from the edge of the loft floor Olivia was found. He said if she accidently fell, her body would have been much closer to the edge of the loft, two to five feet, at the most. Olivia's body was nine feet from the edge of the loft, and it looked like she ran and dove because the first impact was the top front of her head."

Jeannie made the statement, "Poor Emma, poor DeAngelo family. At least what was left of it. They just finished burying one and now only days later they are going to have to bury another family member. How dreadful it must have been to have your heart broken again that soon. How in the world could they afford another funeral? It must have been very difficult on Emma both financially and emotionally."

Mabel quietly told us, "Yes, it was difficult on her. However, you could never tell how much it troubled Emma. She just moved forward. I am not saying she was emotionally detached from Olivia's death or Leonard's death or didn't care. Those two events happening so close together numbed Emma. Emma said calmly, 'God will provide.' We knew the money was short, but thank God for the Fontenot's. They were the brothers who ran the funeral home and they told Emma not to worry about the cost. She could take as much time as she needed to pay them for the funeral."

Miss Mildred Law said, "Emma had the Fontenot brothers to take care of the body, and she purchased the casket from them. However, to save money, she held Olivia's funeral at her house. She borrowed the Sheriff's tent to cover the grave site in case of inclement weather. She got her friends and family members to dig the grave at the family cemetery, and Mr. Jefferson offered to carry the casket to the cemetery in his carriage with his mules pulling it, all for free.

Emma decided to wait to have the service on Sunday, which allowed her enough time to get everything together."

Mabel said, "Every detail of Olivia's funeral was well planned by Emma. Emma left nothing to chance. Emma said she felt Bernard deserved nothing less than to have his mother go out in dignity. However, what happened at that funeral was unimaginable."

Miss Mildred Law exclaimed, "Mabel, I'm not sure you used the right word to describe what happened. It was more along the lines of being absurd or inconceivable. Some might even say it was comical. It would have been funny, but it upset the family too much to say that. Let us just say, what happened was in bad taste."

I remembered the funeral, even though I was just a young child. I was mad because Olivia died. That was why I went to the tree house, I was unhappy and wanted to go to the happy place Aunt Emma and I had built.

It was time for the funeral to start, and they sent Howard to get me, but I wouldn't come. He went back and told my dad, and he came to get me.

He didn't whip me or force me to come inside to the service. He knew I was upset. Instead he told me a story about how life was. I listened closely as he talked about our old dog Chief. I loved that dog. He said God had sent us Chief to teach us how to love, when God let Chief die, God did that to teach us how to let go of those we loved. He asked me if I remembered how happy I was when God sent us a new puppy that we named Dixie. God sent Dixie into our lives to teach us that there is room enough in our hearts to love others. In life, we are to love and we are to let go of that love. And then we are to love again. My dad said that today is a time for us to let go, and that is why I was needed to be at Olivia's funeral.

It was difficult for us to enter the house, it was full. People were standing everywhere, the front and back porches were even full of people. Every room had people in it except the mystery room. There were even people outside under the pecan trees in the backyard.

Everyone in the house had been waiting on us to start the ceremony. There was a small aisle for us to walk down to get to where the family was seated in the kitchen. They moved the dining table outside and placed Aunt Olivia's casket where it was, in the wide hall. The casket was sitting on the Fontenot's rolling gurney, which was designed to roll and fold up underneath the hearse when it struck the back bumper, allowing the casket to slide inside.

Mabel broke my train of thought as she said, "The preacher just started his eulogy, then David came into the house and brought some woman with him. The preacher was speaking about who God's children were, and how Olivia was one of His children. The preacher said, 'Happy are God's children because they are sorry for their sins, that God will comfort them. Happy are the pure in heart. God will call them His children.' When the preacher said, happy are those who are persecuted in His name, for the Kingdom of heaven is theirs. I guess David couldn't take any more of the preacher's sermon telling everyone Olivia was one of God's children, and that she was sorry for her sins, that she was pure in heart, and that she was persecuted. When the preacher said she was persecuted, that was when David stopped the funeral by hollering out, 'Wait a minute preacher, that's not completely true about Olivia.' His actions may have been off-key, but his timing was perfect.'"

"Yes, David stopped the eulogy, I never saw anyone ever stop a funeral. It was unheard of, but David did," said Miss Mildred Law.

"After he hollered that out, he limped from the back of the hall to where the casket was and he told the preacher 'I never saw Olivia being persecuted before, either. Preacher, Olivia was never persecuted . . . because that was her job, to persecute others. Olivia was never the child of God, she was the child of the devil.'"

I can remember that incident from my childhood. The main thing I remember was that you could actually hear the people groan when David said that. He turned to look at Olivia in her casket, then he reached down and took hold of the front of her jacket and he shook her so hard that the gurney collapsed with the coffin falling to the floor. He never let go of her until he loudly told Olivia's body, "I'm glad you're dead. The only thing you did when you were alive was to lie to people and ruin their lives."

David held Olivia's body above the casket with two hands and yelled, "You are where you belong." He let Olivia drop back down into her casket, and the people groaned again.

I didn't know what the proper etiquette was for a funeral, but I knew David wasn't following it. I remembered how quiet it got in the house when David dropped Olivia back into her casket. What I remembered the most was hearing both of those clocks on the two mantels ticking. Even with all those people in the house, it was that quiet. You could hear those two clocks ticking. After releasing Olivia's body, David turned to the family and dropped down on both knees.

Miss Mildred Law said, "Everyone was astounded, in shock. David turned toward the family and apologized to them for his behavior. He told them he was sorry he'd interrupted the service, but he had to tell everyone exactly how Olivia was."

Miss Mildred Law continued to tell us about what happened at that funeral, "David, still on his knees, paused as tears rolled down his cheeks. He looked at Bernard and told him personally how sorry he was that he had to hear that was how Olivia, his mother, had treated people. He also said to Bernard what he was the sorriest about was . . . that his mother was evil and mean."

Mabel gloomily said, "What David said was the truth, but he chose the wrong time to let everyone know. I thought to myself, *not now David, you should have done this years earlier, but not now.* I actually felt sorry for David. My sorrow for him didn't last long because he did another outrageous deed. He grabbed Emma's hands and proposed marriage to her, right there in front of Olivia's casket, at her funeral. Can you believe he asked Emma to marry him at his former wife's funeral, and she hadn't even been buried yet?"

Mabel said, "Everybody in the house heard him, including the woman he'd brought to the funeral. She screamed at him and began pushing everyone out of the way to get to David. When she got to him, she attacked him while he was on his knees. She beat him to the floor, and the Sheriff had to pull her off of him."

Miss Mildred Law reluctantly spoke up, "If that wasn't ugly enough, then my crazy brother, Frank, believing Emma might still have feelings for David showed his ignorance. Frank was concerned she might say yes to David's proposal. So, not to be outdone, Frank pushed his way through the crowd to make his proposal to Emma for the third time. Evidently, this scene upset Bernard as he attempted to beat Frank up, but Emma and Mabel stopped his efforts. What a mess all of this had become. It had to be a great embarrassment to Emma, I know I was embarrassed for her."

All of a sudden, to my amazement Jeannie asked, "Could anything worse happened?"

Mabel and Miss Mildred Law looked at one another to see which one would answer her question. At first, neither one spoke up. Then, Miss Mildred Law said, "As usual, in any crisis Emma took charge the way she did in most situations. She had the Sheriff take David and the woman outside to the 'trouble tree' on the side of the house. She told me to bring Frank and Bernard and follow the Sheriff outside.

"Emma called for everyone's attention in the house to herself and announced in an incredible, calm voice: 'Please don't leave, the funeral will resume in just a few minutes. I need to go outside to comfort some misguided mourners.' Emma walked out to talk with them," said Miss Mildred Law.

"If that had been me, I would have had David, that woman, and Frank arrested and put in jail. What they did was too bizarre. However, this was a DeAngelo funeral with Emma in charge. She didn't operate like the rest of us. She was too tolerant of other people's stupidity."

Miss Mildred Law caught her breath and said, "When we arrived at the pecan tree, Emma surprised me when she thanked them for coming to the funeral to pay their respects to her sister. I couldn't believe she thanked them after that scene. It must have shocked them, too, because everyone immediately settled down.

"First, she tells the woman she was sorry David upset her. Emma told her he was usually not like that. She looked at David and said, 'David, you and I were once very close. In fact, so close we were to marry, but God didn't allow that to happen. I have accepted that and you need to do the same. Evidently, we were not meant to be married, and I will never marry you. You need to move on with your life. This lady you brought must think a lot of you. Maybe she is the right one for you. But it is not me,' Emma said.

"She continued: 'Frank, I have always known how you felt about me, and I love you for feeling that way toward me. I don't love you in the way that would ever cause me to marry you. You can do better than me. Go find yourself a wife. She is out there somewhere.

357

We are here to show our sympathy to those who have lost a loved one. We are not here to complain how hard a life we have had or to find a wife. This is a funeral. Let us act like it is a funeral. Do we all understand each other now?'

"Emma waited as she looked at each person individually and said, 'Now let's go back inside where they are waiting on us to mourn the loss of my sister, your mother Bernard, your wife David, and a friend to you, Frank. I would appreciate your compassion in this matter.'"

Mabel respectfully said, "Emma turned and walked back to go into the house and everyone followed her. We had no more problems that day. After the service, we walked to the cemetery behind Mr. Jefferson's mules pulling the carriage to lay Olivia to rest at the cemetery."

Miss Mildred Law said, "A couple of days after the two funerals passed, I went to visit Emma to see how she was doing. She still was having problems adjusting to the fact that Leonard and Olivia were no longer alive. Olivia and Emma were never close as sisters. In fact, Olivia was always very jealous toward Emma. Olivia always felt Emma had received the best while she received what was left over. I guess if I was her, I would have felt the same way, too. However, Olivia brought all of it on herself. She lived her life for herself and didn't care about anyone else's desires or needs. Emma knew she felt hostile toward her, but she tolerated her because she was her sister. It was only after her mental collapse that Emma's feelings toward Olivia changed. After the breakdown, Emma loved her as if she was her own child more so than as a sister. Olivia had never allowed Emma or anyone to get close to her, she was always independent and never relied on anyone. What had happened in that short stretch of time was a very strange twist of events.

"Emma was still grieving, she grieved more for Leonard because he never had a real chance at life. Emma had been tough on Leonard, and she had grown to love him as if he was her own," said Miss Mildred Law.

"She spent a lot of time teaching him how to cope with failure and to realize others don't always live up to our expectations. Leonard was stubborn. He thought he knew what was best for him and everybody else, too. Whenever someone didn't do as he thought they should, he would become impatient and angry toward them. Emma tried to teach him to respect and to be responsible to others. She spent a great amount of time preaching to him on how other people depended on him and looked to him to lead them in the right direction. Leonard grew to learn how to relate to others and show some compassion and to have some patience with them. He understood she was guiding him right, and he grew to love Emma for the special attention she gave him. The only problem was that he'd never had the time to show others all he had learned from his Aunt Emma," said Miss Mildred Law.

"Madea noticed after Leonard and Olivia were killed, all Emma did was take care of the animals, sit on the porch, and stare out into the pasture. Madea said Emma didn't talk much to anyone or eat very much. She just sort of sulked around, and Madea became very concerned about her," said Mabel.

Jeannie spoke up, "I guess you can't blame Emma for being desponded. She had been carrying the weight of everybody's world on her. And when their world fell, hers fell too. She must have really been hurting inside because she probably felt she had let them down."

Miss Mildred Law listened closely to what Jeannie said and told us, "I came over to her house about a week later to check on Emma again. She told me how empty the house felt without Olivia and Leonard, that she felt like she didn't belong there anymore. I didn't know what to say to her, I knew she was hurting. Mabel, you know how she was. She was always calculating every possibility for her situation. She was usually so positive but this time I could tell she had doubts."

Miss Mildred Law said, "I remember Emma said that when God is getting ready to do something in someone's life, He always begins with a shake-up. She said God had without a doubt really shook up her life to get her moving in the direction He wanted her to go. I knew when Emma started talking about God, something was about to happen. When she told me she had been thinking about leaving and going back to Washington, I didn't say a word because I recognized it wouldn't be long, and she would be gone again."

Miss Mildred Law's demeanor became even more serious. "Emma said she'd come to the realization that her life in Louisiana had been nothing but a series of catastrophes. She felt like someone had put the "gri-gri" on her. That's a Cajun jinx, a curse on your life. She felt if she could get from under everything here in Louisiana, she could make a new start. It shocked me. It actually hurt me to hear her say those words. It really made me sad, I didn't want to lose her again. I knew I was being selfish by wanting her to stay, but I didn't care. If she left, it would be like another death in her family to me.

"I knew she had decided to leave when she said, 'No one knows what God has in store for us in life. God wants us to remember life is a jigsaw puzzle, and we don't have all the pieces. He sends those pieces to us a little at a time. But one day, as we begin to see the picture coming together, things will make more sense than they do now. But for now, we are supposed to trust that God knows best. You know Mildred, I'm really having a hard time accepting those pieces He has given me, and believing He really does know what is best,'" said Miss Mildred Law.

Miss Mildred Law continued. "Emma said she needed to go somewhere to find peace and happiness, and at twenty-nine years, all she had ever had in life was heartbreak. She asked me, 'is that how life is to be lived?' She told me she hoped not, because if it is, it's not worth living. We hugged and cried together. Without saying it, we both knew she had made up her mind to leave Louisiana."

Mabel said, "That same weekend Emma and Miss Mildred Law met with Bernard, Madea, Howard, and myself at her house. It had been a while since we had been together, but Emma and Miss Mildred Law arranged it. We were sitting at the table and Emma made the announcement that she was leaving Louisiana. It was a shock to us. She never told us where she was going and we didn't ask. I assume the reason we didn't ask was that we felt she would tell us later, but she never did."

Mabel said, "Emma laid out her plan of what she was going to do with the place. She told us she was going to sell the tenant house to Madea and fifteen acres of land for ten dollars. She handed a ten-dollar bill to Madea and told her to use it when they went to the lawyer's office to pay for the land and house. She told Bernard that the rest of the land and the house was his. It was a gift to him. She told Howard, Bernard, and myself that she was going to leave enough money for us to finish college. Howard and I had only a year left and Bernard had two-and-a-half years left before he graduated. She told us when we graduate, she would sent us five hundred dollars apiece to help us get started in life. She said Miss Mildred Law would oversee the money and be sure it was used accordingly. They were to go to her whenever they needed it."

"Later that same week, all six of us met in the lawyer's office to sign the papers. Emma had everything ready for us, it was a bitter-sweet moment in that they were getting something nice, but at the same time they were losing something of greater value: Emma. One would have thought it would be an emotional time, but it wasn't. No one was joyous or unhappy about the deal, at least not until Emma announced that she would be leaving the next morning. Emma requested we not be there when she left. She told us, we all knew how we felt toward one another, so it would be best if we didn't make it any more difficult than it had to be to say goodbye," said Miss Mildred Law.

Miss Mildred Law said, "Of course the next morning we all were sitting on the front porch waiting for her to come out. She said she knew we would be out there, and the reason she knew was that we had always been there for her all her life. She told us we were the joy of her life and without us, she would have never made it. I didn't offer her any goodbyes, yet, because I was driving her to the train station. I saw how difficult it was for her to sever those bonds between her and the ones she loved. It was like she was letting go of a lifeline from a boat in the middle of the ocean, never to see us again."

Miss Mildred Law said with tears in her eyes, "Neither Emma nor I said a word to each other as I drove her to the bus station. The emotion in the car was too heavy. Neither one of us could talk without bawling. It wasn't until I turned the key off to stop the engine that Emma told me, 'God couldn't have sent me a better friend in all the world than you, Mildred. I couldn't have picked one any better, if I had done it myself.' I couldn't say a word."

Miss Mildred talked about their parting scene through her tears, "Emma told me something extraordinary, 'Everybody in life has basic needs. You know, like food, water, shelter, clothes and to be loved. But I really believe God wants us to have another more important need.'

"Emma paused. I listened as she continued speaking. 'I think God wants everyone to have contentment in their life. I feel I can't have that contentment He wants me to have until I find someone to love and someone to love me. I really want to find that someone, and for us to grow old together loving one another. I really believe it is how God wants it to be,' she said.

"Emma told me she was not going to give me a contact number or address this time and she would not write, either. She said she was making a clean break from Louisiana. It would be as if she'd never lived here. She said some words next that I wished I had never heard her say because I knew she meant them, this time," Miss Mildred Law said.

"Emma stated, 'Mildred, I will not come back again.'"

Miss Mildred Law sadly said, "We hugged and kissed each other goodbye and I barely squeezed the words from my mouth: 'I love you, Emma.'

"Emma stepped out of the car. She got her bag from the back seat and shut the door. She smiled at me, turned, and walked into the train station."

# Chapter 22

## The Reunion

Miss Mildred Law grabbed Jeannie's hands and said, "Sweetheart, after she left, I found myself each day, filled with thoughts of Emma. I wondered where she was and what she was doing. I felt certain she would search out Charles Winston to help her get a job and a good place to stay. However, it was just an assumption on my part. I never really knew. I wasn't absolutely sure she would carry through with her choice to never to return home this time. However, I felt she would never return, since she believed she didn't have anything or anyone to draw her back. In my heart, I wanted her to come home. I didn't say anything right away because I knew it would upset Aunt Sis even more than she already was. She was devastated over Emma's leaving. We all were, but Aunt Sis, more so."

Mabel said, "Yes, Madea did take it very hard. She went through the same stages of sadness as if Emma had died. At first, she was sad that she left, then she became hurt because she received no word from her. Finally, she became disillusioned with Emma. When Emma had not contacted anyone to let us know she was okay, Madea became angry at Olivia. Madea has stayed angry at Olivia ever since Emma left. She believed Olivia was the one who made Emma's life here so miserable, and it was why she left."

"It wasn't until both Bernard and Mabel kept insisting that I contact her to find out how she was that I divulged what she had told me," said Miss Mildred Law.

"When I told them that Emma did not give me a contact number or address, they demanded we go to the law to find out if she was still alive. Madea was very upset at me, and she was looking for someone to blame. She was leaning heavily toward me, and I didn't want that burden. I finally gave in and told them that Emma said she was never going to call, write, or come back. What Emma said was a total surprise to them, and they had difficulty understanding why. I told them that Emma wanted to make a clean break from all the tragedy she had encountered here in Louisiana," said Miss Mildred Law.

With no emotion, Mabel said to Jeannie and me, "She meant it, too, because one day, out of the blue, Emma did come home."

Unexpectedly, Mabel stopped talking. Jeannie and I were confused at that statement; we looked to Miss Mildred Law to add to Mabel's account, thinking they would express great joy and excitement that they did get to see their dear friend once more. Oddly, neither one said anything. Instead they both fought off showing their sentiments. Tears rolled down their cheeks. Finally, Mabel gathered herself. She revealed what brought on their sudden change in emotion and said, "Emma came home all right, but in a coffin, seventeen years later."

Immediately after Mabel told us Emma had died, she said, "It is still unknown to us today as to why her body was shipped home . . . or what she died of . . . or why her husband did not escort the body home. There wasn't anything told to us about her life or death. Nothing. We were left in the dark not knowing why or what had happened. All we knew was that her body was shipped home by Charles Winston, her husband, to be buried in the family cemetery," said Mabel.

Mabel's declaration stunned both Jeannie and myself as to why there was so much unknown about Aunt Emma's death. I didn't know the circumstances surrounding her death because I was working out of state. I knew Aunt Emma had moved away from Louisiana, but hearing her body was shipped back to Louisiana from Washington, DC, for burial was strange news for me to hear. The mystery surrounding her death raised even more questions in my mind. My mother had called with the sad news that Aunt Emma had passed away and they buried her while I was gone. I knew Jeannie had to be surprised hearing that she died and was sent home in unusual circumstances.

Immediately, Jeannie said, "She was too young to die, and then you are telling us she was married and her own husband did not bring her body home. How strange that is. I wonder why?"

Miss Mildred Law said, "No one came with the body! It was shipped to the funeral home with instructions not to hold a wake and to bury her in the family cemetery at the foot of her father and mother's grave, with no public ceremony."

Jeannie again asked the probing question, "You mean there was no regular service or visitation for Aunt Emma either? That is even stranger."

"No honey child, there was not any planned service for her, we were told it was at Emma's bequest. Charles Winston sent her body here to be buried next to her family, and Rev. Herman Cook was to handle the arrangements. It was intended to be a quiet ceremony at the family cemetery, with no one in attendance," said Miss Mildred Law.

I hesitated before I spoke up because I thought Miss Mildred Law was wrong, but I asked, "Are you sure Miss Mildred Law? I distinctly remember my mother telling me a lot of people were at her service."

Mabel abruptly answered me to clarify what had taken place. "You are absolutely right, Blake, but the original plan was to have no wake or no service. However, Mr. Fontenot, the funeral home director had a major problem. He did not know who the lady in the coffin was. He was confused as to who Emma Estelle Winston was. He had never heard of anyone who lived in our area with the last name Winston. He needed Reverend Cook there to clarify who was in the casket, so he could open the grave."

"I know you two are having difficulty understanding exactly what happened, so allow me to clear up some confusion," said Miss Mildred Law.

Miss Mildred Law continued. "There was a mix up in the communication between her husband, the preacher, and the funeral home director. Charles Winston either forgot to tell the funeral home director who his wife was related to or he assumed the preacher would tell him. We don't really know why there was a mix up. But I believe God did it as an act of providence to allow word to get out as to Emma's sudden death and that she was about to be buried without any service."

Jeannie interrupted Miss Mildred Law. "Why would Aunt Emma ask to be buried without any ceremony? I don't understand. What was she trying to do? Was she trying to sneak her death by everyone or was she afraid no one would remember who she was? She hadn't been away that long."

"She had been gone seventeen years. We don't think she was concerned that she would have been forgotten. No, we believe it was nothing like that. You must understand how Emma operated, she had to control everything, including her own funeral, and us too when it happened. By making her own arrangements, she wasn't trying to sneak her death by us. No, not at all! She was trying to prevent us from going through another grief-filled event of the DeAngelo family. It was her way of protecting us from another DeAngelo tragedy," said Mabel.

Miss Mildred Law resumed telling us about what had taken place when her body came home. "When the funeral home director realized he didn't know who the Winston lady in the coffin was, he tried contacting the preacher. However, the preacher was unavailable for him to talk with because he was at a retreat. So he opened the casket to see if he could identify the body. He immediately recognized it as Emma DeAngelo.

"It was shocking news that Emma DeAngelo had died and she was going to be buried with no ceremony. We decided, there was no way we would let that happen, knowing it would be a great travesty. The funeral home director was deluged with complaints, and he insisted it was out of his hands. He stated his job was to hold the body to be delivered to the cemetery for burial, that the preacher was designated to handle the funeral arrangements, but his duty was to follow her request."

"We searched for the preacher to get him to change the arrangements. We found him at a retreat in the woods at some Baptist campground," said Mabel.

Miss Mildred Law added, "When we found him and explained that Emma's body had been shipped home to him, he immediately stopped us from saying anything else. When Pastor Cook heard about Emma's request, it was a shock to him. He became emotionally distraught, which was a surprise to us. We never knew he was close to Emma. His honest reaction of not knowing Emma had passed away changed the approach of our complaint. It humbled us as we explained that he was designated to handle the arrangements. We explained our complaint was that there was to be no wake, and it was to be a closed ceremony at the cemetery. We expressed to him that we wanted a service."

Mabel said, "The pastor was very much closed-mouth about what we asked of him. He told us he would leave immediately and check into what was asked of him. We followed him to the funeral home. He read the instructions and asked the funeral home director a couple of questions. The preacher paused to think and gave us his response.

"Pastor Cook wisely said, 'I know how much you all loved Emma, I loved her too. She was a wonderful person who enriched all of our lives. Emma requested no wake and a quiet ceremony at the gravesite. I have to honor her request, as I would for you, or anyone else. However, I don't think it would be out of order for us to have a quiet private graveside service with a few friends in attendance as long as it is quiet and private. Let us meet in my office, and we will plan the graveside service for Emma.'"

Miss Mildred Law said, "Honey, did we hold a quiet, private, beautiful ceremony to honor Emma? Word of a graveside service with Emma's friends went out into the community. The plan was that just a few friends would attend, but it looked like everyone in the parish came. I never knew Emma had so many friends. People met at the funeral home and followed the hearse to the cemetery. Her procession was at least two miles long. When we got to the cemetery, many more people were waiting for Emma's body to arrive. People came from everywhere. It was heartwarming to see so many people paying their respects to her.

"Mabel's church came and they sung, *Beulah Land*, and Emma's church sang the song, *Precious Memories*. It was magnificent," said Miss Mildred Law.

"We picked a burial site away from the family, but still it was at the foot of her parents. The gravesite was surrounded with many wreaths of flowers of all sorts. They lined the fence and all around the gravesite. The pastor's words were uplifting as he spoke of Emma. He used some funny antidotes from Emma's life to keep the mood light, but his words made us all glad we had known Emma. It truly was a happy celebration of her life. We couldn't help crying because we loved that girl. But our tears were tears of joy. We all felt she deserved nothing less than the best, and that was what we tried to give her," gladly said Miss Mildred Law.

As I listened to Miss Mildred Law weave her words together to tell us of her love for Emma, I knew I was truly blessed to have her as an aunt. I looked at Jeannie, and I could see that she'd actually fallen in love with my Aunt Emma. I felt she had been given a good look at my Aunt Emma and her love for others. As I looked around, I saw a strange sight. Mabel was sitting with a smile on her face and tears rolling down her cheeks. I knew how much she loved Emma and her family. Life hadn't been easy for her and her family during those times, and yet she was not ashamed to show her love for this white woman.

We were all sitting in the cemetery with tears in our eyes, basking in the sunshine of memories of our times with Aunt Emma. It felt great to me to learn as much as I had that day about Aunt Emma's life. But just as her life ended, so had our time together, and our conversation about my Aunt Emma. We were about to say our goodbyes to each other when we saw Bernard walking toward us with his wife, Mary Lou. They seemed to be in a hurry to reach us, so we waited for them to come to us.

Even though there was an eight-year age difference between Bernard and Mary Lou, they seemed to be the perfect couple. Bernard married Mary Lou about a year after he got a job as a science teacher and coach in a nearby parish. Bernard and Mary Lou never had any children, and they lived in the old DeAngelo house.

When Bernard and Mary Lou arrived, they spoke to Miss Mildred Law and Mabel, but when he looked at me, Bernard grabbed me and hugged me tightly. It reminded me of the times we wrestled, and he bear-hugged me to make me say, "Captain Boss." He let me go and told me how good it was to see me. He really made me feel good. I introduced Jeannie to both him and Mary Lou and showed them our kids, who were now helping Mr. Stevenson pull bushes to the burn pile.

Bernard told us excitedly, "I am so glad to catch all of you together before you left. I already told Howard and Aunt Sis the news the preacher told me. He wants us and a few others to meet him here with Aunt Emma's husband, Charles Winston. He is coming here today. Charles Winston gave the preacher a list of names to meet with him at Emma's gravesite around three o'clock. He wants to meet all the people Emma talked about during their marriage."

Miss Mildred Law looked at Mabel and said elatedly, "I have been wanting to talk to him for years. I have a lot of unanswered questions for him. Maybe he can shed light on some of the mysteries we have about Emma when he arrives."

After Miss Mildred Law said the word mystery, Bernard eagerly said to me, "You know Blake, how you always wanted to know what was in the locked room at Papa's house? The one you called the Mystery Room?"

At first I didn't realize what Bernard was speaking about, and then it dawned on me and I said to Bernard, "Oh yes Bernard, I remember now. The room was always locked and no one knew what was in there, did they?"

Both Mabel and Miss Mildred Law chimed in; they wanted to know what was in that room, too. It was a mystery to everyone, not even Emma or Olivia knew what their papa had kept in that room. Uncle Tom protected that room, and did not tell anyone what was in there.

Bernard answered, "Not only did I find out what was in there, I also found out why Papa named us twins, Leonard and Bernard."

Miss Mildred Law was losing her patience and said to Bernard, "Boy, are you going to tell us or am I going to have to get your wife to step on your toe to make you tell us what was there?"

We laughed at what Miss Mildred Law said, knowing she meant it only as a joke. However, we all were bursting with anticipation of what Bernard had found in the room.

Bernard explained. "I needed a bathroom in the house and decided the Mystery Room would be the logical choice to place one. At first I was hesitant to break the lock off, but Mary Lou reminded me that I had always wanted to know what was in there. She told me to go ahead and open it."

Bernard paused before he told us what he saw, "I found that the room was a memorial to the children that Papa Tom and Grandma Kate had lost. Papa must have built a small rocking crib for each child they lost, evidently they lost four children before Mother and Aunt Emma were born because in each crib was a certificate from the church with their names and birth and death date in it. Two of them were still-born, and the other two lived less than two months. Their bodies are buried over in those four unnamed graves that only have crosses with initials on them."

Bernard pointed to that area of the cemetery. Bernard said, "The two children who lived two months were named Bernard and Leonard. I presume it was who we were named after."

Mabel added, "I vaguely remember Madea telling me after Leonard died, something about Mr. Tom and Miss Kate losing children before he died. I didn't understand it then because it was a distant memory, but it makes sense to me now. Madea said when Leonard was killed, that he wasn't the first Leonard who had died in the family. Madea said Olivia didn't want to name her boys when they were first born because she didn't want them. Mr. Tom named them at the hospital so they could have names placed on their birth certificates."

Bernard said sadly, "Don't misunderstand me, I loved my mother, but Aunt Emma was more of a mother to me than she was. Aunt Emma was the one who put the fear of God in me and made me do what was right. She always encouraged me to do my best, even when it was easier to do otherwise. She gave her time, her efforts, and her money to help me through college. I would have never have gone to college if it were not for her. She even sent me money after I graduated to help me get started."

Bernard continued telling us about Aunt Emma. "It wasn't until after she left that I really appreciated all she did for me, I never got the opportunity to thank her. The main thing she taught me was how important it was to help others, and because of what she did for me, paying my way through college, I have been able to help others go to college, too. Her giving me the gift of a college education made my life easier, and I learned to pass that gift onto others."

It was near 3:00 p.m., and the people Charles Winston requested to come to the cemetery came walking up toward Emma's gravesite. First, was Miss Sis and Howard, then came Frank, Miss Mildred Law's brother, and Sophie's father. He had lost his wife a few years back to pneumonia. Just as they approached us, the preacher and Charles Winston drove up. None of us except Miss Mildred had ever seen Charles Winston before. He was a tall man, strikingly good looking, and he was in a Navy uniform, a two star Admiral. From my understanding, he had been appointed by the President as the new Secretary of the Navy.

The preacher wanted to introduce us, but the Admiral stopped him, saying he believed he could name us from the way Emma described each one of us. To my amazement, Charles Winston placed every one of us correctly. He even knew who Jeannie was. He thanked everyone he invited for taking time out of their day to come. He told us he understood we had many questions to ask, but he believed if we allowed him to speak to us as a group, it would answer most of our questions.

Charles Winston smiled as he scanned the group. "Emma had not forgotten about you, no way. She kept up with each one of you, and I know you are wondering how she could have done that if she never talked to any of you. I will tell you how. When she first came back to Washington, she was a broken woman. She was nothing like the woman I knew as a POW or when she first came to Washington. She was always positive and full of life, believing life was always good and anything could be overcome. Her circumstances had changed her. It was as if she had lost her determination to live. She had even lost interest how things were back home because of all the tragedy she had undergone here."

The Admiral continued, "I'm not saying she didn't love the people here or even her home, but she had lost her zeal to enjoy life. As I talked to her each day, I realized just how unhappy she was with all that had transpired. But I know she was not unhappy with the people who had shared their lives with her. She truly loved you."

Charles Winston continued, "Her gloom made me want to do everything I could to bring her out of her depression. After I discovered what had happened at home, I realized she never had the opportunity to do the things in life most young people usually get to do. And I thought that maybe that was why she was so unhappy. Her life had been difficult enough to have broken any person's spirit. I don't know how she lasted as long as she did.

"I decided to try to bring some happiness back into her life, and to help her relive parts of her life she had missed out on. I romanced her like we were teenagers. I tried to sweep her off her feet. I brought her flowers and candy. We went on dates and picnics. I tried to do everything I could to make her fall in love with me, again. I don't know if you knew it or not, but we' fallen in love after she saved my life when I was a POW in her hospital in the Philippines. I was fortunate enough to help her get a good job in Washington where she felt she was making a difference in people's lives. And she was, and that was important to her," said Charles Winston.

"It took me months to get her to come out of her depression and make her realize I loved her and wanted to marry her. Finally, I began to see that little twinkle in her eye that she once had. Even her keen sense of humor came back. I was so happy to see her come back alive. As we began to make plans for marriage, I could tell she was once again happy with her life, and I was happy for her," said Charles Winston.

Charles Winston looked at each one of us. "I knew she was at the point of wanting to learn how her loved ones were back home when she began talking about the people and things she'd done as a child, and how she loved those times. I convinced her how important it was for her to stay in touch with the people and the place she loved so much. I made her understand how it was what made her so special.

"I encouraged her to contact someone, even if it was in secret to keep her up on what was happening back home. She wrote to Reverend Cook to be that secret someone, and he agreed to do it. At first, they communicated by letter, but when Reverend Cook got a telephone, she would call him each month to ask about each one of you. She began to look forward to making her call home at the end of the month to get all the news. I think Emma even said, the Reverend looked forward to her calls, too," said Admiral Winston.

Charles Winston said, "Before we married, Emma stayed in a little duplex apartment. Believe me, it was little, and it was cheap. She didn't believe in wasting money. She saved all the money she could and sent it home, to whom I didn't know. She had an elderly neighbor who had adopted her as her mother. They took care of each other. In fact, she was Emma's maid of honor at our wedding. We were married in my father's rose garden in Virginia. I don't want to sound like I am bragging, but she and I were very happy together.

"Later we were blessed to buy a little thirty-two acre horse ranch. It was in the county, just outside of Washington. The house and barn were run down, but Emma thought it was a mansion in heaven. She planted a rose garden and a vegetable garden. It had woods and a little open pasture. Sometimes, when I came in and couldn't find her in her favorite room, the kitchen, I knew exactly where she was. She was in the barn, or should I say, laying on the roof of the barn looking up at the clouds or the stars. I never understood her attraction for doing that, but she called it her little retreat. She loved our place, but her heart was here in this parish and with the ones she knew and loved. It was her real home."

Charles Winston said, "Emma told me one day, out of the blue, that she always wanted someone to do things with her who cared about the things she liked. She said she thanked God each day that I loved doing things with her, and I was what made her happy. I want you to know this. It was easy making her happy, and we had a very happy life together.

"Right before she died, we talked about her coming home to visit with you. At first she wasn't sure she wanted to come, but the more we discussed it, the more she became eager to come," said Charles Winston.

"She even sat down and wrote notes of what she wanted to say to each one of you whenever she saw you. She told me that she learned something from each of you. I asked you to come here today, so that I might share with you what she wanted to tell you," Admiral Winston, said.

Charles Winston pulled out a tattered, folded-up sheet of paper he had in his inside coat pocket and began by saying, "I have been holding on to this paper for over two years. Emma finished writing this to you just before she died. I'm not sure of the order she was going to deliver her comments to you, but I will just go down the list in the order she wrote them. She worked on this for weeks, and I know it was important to her.

"Reverend Cook, you were first person on her list. She wanted to thank you for being her rock in her times of need. Your counseling of her and Mildred helped put them back on the right path to following God. You filled the hole in her life by keeping her close to the ones she loved back home. She writes that she learned to love herself from you, and gives God thanks for you," said Admiral Winston.

"Frank you are next, and she has three question marks next to your name. I'm not sure why the three question marks are there, but I guess it is associated with what she wrote. She tells you to get married, that there is hope for you to be as happy as she is. I don't know the history behind this, but I am sure you do. She says she learned perseverance from you," said Charles Winston.

"To Sophie's father. I don't know why she didn't write your name down, but I know she knew it. She wanted to tell you a day doesn't go by where she doesn't think about what Sophie did for her. She wanted to tell you she appreciated how gracious you were to her when you found out why Sophie died, that she learned forgiveness from you and wanted to thank you for it. She writes that she has honored Sophie's memory and you will understand how later.

"Mildred, you're next. She put stars all around your name. Emma wrote there wasn't another person on this planet as loyal a friend as you. She says you were closer to her than a sister, or anyone. She wrote that you two were twins, Siamese twins joined together at the heart. She says she missed the closeness and the funny times you two had shared. She learned love from you, and she writes thanks for loving her and putting up with her," said Charles Winston.

"Mabel," said Admiral Winston. "Emma writes that you were her real sister. You two had shared many great and terrible times together. She writes that she could never have made it through them without you. She writes that she learned dependability from you. She knew you would help keep Mildred straight and take care of your mother, too. She wants to thank you for understanding her family and that she could never repay the debt she owes you and how much she loves you.

"Howard: You are the big brother that took care of her and her family. You were the strength of the family. She writes that she learned toughness from you, and she knows you are good for the kids that you teach because you know what is right. That one characteristic was what she admires about you the most. You do what is fair and best. She wants to thank you and tell you she loves you, too," said Charles Winston.

Charles Winston called my name. "Blake. Reverend Cook has kept her up on your life, too. She writes that she learned from you to give of herself graciously. She says you have done well in your choice of a wife. She says that she has heard she is a fine mother, and she takes care of you just as Emma used to. You were the younger son she never had, and that she learned how to be a mother from you. She writes, she loves you and gives her thanks to Jeannie for taking care of you.

"Bernard and Mary Lou," said Charles Winston. "She puts you two together because she writes that she started the work in making Bernard respected and now she is passing her work onto you to complete. She writes that she is proud of you two. She hopes you two are as happy as she and I are. You were the older son she never had, and from you she learned joy, because you brought her so much joy. She loves you and is proud of you.

"Last of all, but surely not the least is you, Miss Sis. Emma puts kisses around your name and writes that you were the mother she never had, a mother even to those who had mothers. You couldn't have been any better for her unless you were an angel. Then she notes that you are an angel. She writes that she learned humility and wisdom from you. You were the wisest person she ever knew. She writes she loves you and could never repay the goodness and love you showed to her and her family."

Admiral Winston folded the paper up, put it back in his pocket, and stated: "Emma was content with the life we shared, and I know she was happy with me, too. But there was still something missing in her life, something she felt would make everything perfect for us. She wanted children, and near the end of her life, it became her passion. We tried to have children but we couldn't seem to get pregnant. Emma wanted to be able to come home to show everyone how proud she was of me and her children. We tried for years to have children, but we had no success. Finally, four years ago, God blessed us with a child. Emma had a very difficult time carrying the baby to term. We thought we had lost the baby on three different occasions. Her delivery was very difficult, and we almost lost Emma, too. The doctor told us if she were to have another child, it could kill her. However, Emma disregarded the doctor's opinion and said if God wanted her to have another child, she would. She and I were so proud and happy to have our baby."

Charles Winston said, "I can't tell you how proud I was to watch Emma take care of our child. I loved to watch her be a mother. Whoever she learned it from, did a good job teaching her to be a good mother. She was a great mother, a mother who took care of every little detail of loving and caring for our child.

"Emma teasingly would tell me, she was the modern day version of Joseph in the Bible, for God had intended her to go through all kinds of tragedies to bring me into her life. She told me each day that God brought me into her life to bring her happiness and contentment in life.

"But you all know Emma . . . to her good, was just good. She wanted the best for her family," said Charles Winston as tears welled up in his eyes.

"If she made up her mind to do something, you better get out of her way, it was going to happen. She decided it was best for us to have another child, no matter what any doctor told her," said Admiral Winston.

"Well, two years after the birth of our first girl, Emma became pregnant again. The pregnancy was difficult from the beginning. Emma must have realized something was not right with her pregnancy. Her troubled pregnancy was the reason she began writing these notes for you, she knew her situation was serious. She made me promise, if for some reason, she couldn't see all of you and deliver them to you, that I would read them to you," said Charles Winston.

Charles Winston lamented as he told us, "After the baby was delivered, the doctor came out of the delivery room and told me things were not going well for Emma and not much better for the baby. The doctor was honest with me, as he said it looked to him that Emma would not make it. He took me back to her, and when she saw me, she smiled and asked how our baby was. I kissed her, and told her the baby is doing great. She asked how she was doing, and I told her not too well. Emma looked at me, smiled, and said, *'You don't say!'* Then only moments later she slipped out of our lives."

I don't know how Charles Winston managed to tell us about Aunt Emma without breaking down, because we did. I could never have delivered that talk if it was Jeannie. I sensed the Admiral was not through with all of his story and I was right. He continued telling us more after he composed himself.

"The reason I shipped Emma's body home instead of burying her in Virginia was that she told me it was where she wanted to be. She gave me those instructions of how to lay her to rest if she didn't make it through the delivery. I tried to reason with her, but she insisted. As bad as I wanted to come with her, I couldn't come because of complications with the new baby, but I knew she would be in good hands with the people who loved her. During our marriage, she told me everything she could about each one of you. I feel like I have known you all of my life because Emma made you seem so real to me," said Charles Winston.

As soon as the Admiral made that statement, a small girl came running toward the Admiral, yelling, "Daddy, Daddy. You promised to show us where Mommy is. Where is she? I want to see her!"

The Admiral scooped up the little girl and gave her a big kiss. He turned her to face us as she was smiling and laughing. He told us all, "I would like to present to you our first child, Sophie. She is four and full of life! Also I want you to look at who's coming through the arched gate. Our nanny is carrying our second child . . . and her name is Emma."

MULLEN   You Don't Say A
        Story About My Aun
        Emma
        Mullens, Moon.
        18.00

6/16

CPSIA information can be obtained at www.ICGtesting.com
Printed in the USA
LVOW10s1907080616

491762LV00019B/782/P

9 781944 680527